AF348515

Barbra Streisand
ON THE COUCH

By Alma H. Bond, Ph.D.,

author of the *On the Couch* Series

bancroft
press

Although factual information forms the core of *Barbra Streisand:
On the Couch*, the book is a work of fiction, and is not necessarily a
complete or historically accurate rendering of her life. The work draws
upon some of the well-known details of Ms. Streisand's history as well
as speculations about her that have appeared in print. It is also based
upon the author's impressions and analysis of Ms. Streisand, whom Dr.
Bond has admired from afar for half of her life. It is this great admiration
that led to the writing of this book. It is emphasized that the author did
not serve as Ms. Streisand's psychoanalyst at any time.

Cover and interior illustrations: Mary Grace Corpus
Interior Design: Tracy Copes

Published by Bancroft Press
"Books that Enlighten"
P.O. Box 65360, Baltimore, MD 21209
410-358-0658 | 410-764-1967 (fax)
www.bancroftpress.com

Library of Congress Control Number:
ISBN (cloth) 978-1-61088-211-8
ISBN (paper) 978-1-61088-212-5
Printed in the United States of America

To Barbra Streisand,
The funniest person I've never known

February 6, 2015

I had just finished with my last patient of the day. It happened to be my birthday, my 92nd, and I was in a hurry to get home to dress for a party given for the occasion by my friend, Pat LaMarche. My secretary, Rivka Ruben, had already left the office and I was about to close up shop when there was a loud thumping at the door.

Curious as to who might be calling at this late hour in the mugger-glutted city of New York, I looked out through the peephole on the door. There, I saw a frumpy-looking woman, a scarf wound around her head, and a face that seemed somewhat familiar. Who could that be, I wondered, and why was she bothering me on my birthday?

She knocked again, even louder this time, shouting, "Open up, Doc! You're supposed to be a doctor, aren'tcha? Well, I wanna see ya!" A bit intimidated by her bluntness, but curious, I opened the door.

She put out her hand brusquely. Her hand and arm were graceful and lovely, with half-inch long fingernails manicured with blood-red polish.

"Yes?" I said. "What can I do for you?"

She answered in a heavy Brooklyn accent with a slight, open-mouthed pucker. "I was drivin' around the city and thought of ya. Until the day she died, Marilyn Monroe told everybody in Hollywood that you were a wonderful analyst. The scuttlebutt around town was that if she had continued her treatment with ya, she would still be alive. I might have just been a little kid starting to make the rounds back then, but I remembered your name and thought I'd check to see if you're still kicking."

"Thank you," I said. "I'm flattered. But who are you?"

She continued as if she hadn't heard me, the words shooting out of her mouth as if fired by a machine gun. "I was driving by your office and got this sudden urge to see if ya were here. So I parked my car by a fireplug. I wanna see ya. Knowing me, if I don't act on impulse, I probably wouldn't be here."

I hesitated. "Well, it's a bit unusual, but since you are here, let's talk briefly. But first tell me who you are."

She looked surprised that I didn't know. She pulled herself up to her full five feet five inches and said proudly, "I am Barbra Streisand. Ya must be the only person in the world who doesn't recognize me. Can I sit down now?"

Though accustomed to seeing celebrities, this one almost knocked me off my feet. I took a deep breath and said, "Excuse me, Ms. Streisand. I wasn't expecting you. By all means, have a seat."

She took off her raggedy coat and scarf, which I now understood to be a disguise, and plopped herself down on Rivka's swivel chair. The next thing I knew, she was shouting, "Whee," and rolling across the office floor. "I feel like Miss Marmelstein again! Ya know, the part I played in *I Can Get it for you Wholesale.*"

After shaking my head to recover from the shock, the likes of which I had never seen from an analytic patient or even a guest, I decided I was being tested. Back in the early '60s, I had actually seen the play, and I'll never forget Yetta Tessye Marmelstein, the bizarre, beehived, unloved child of nineteen, who swooped down and swiveled her chair around to ask why all the other girls got called by their first names right away. 'Oh, why is it always Miss Marmelstein?' I remember thinking how talented this quirky, unknown actress who played the hilarious character was, and that we would be seeing more of her in the future. Little did I know how accurate my prediction would be!

Thus began the psychiatric interview to end all psychiatric interviews. Without her disguise, Barbra looked quite different. Her hair was straight, shoulder-length blonde, flecked with gray, and hung loosely down the sides of her face. She had a way of stroking her naturally shining hair with her long, pale, spiky fingers, as if she were soothing a crying child. She had azure-blue eyes that appeared to sparkle with amusement, a mouth with slow-curving rises and sudden soft valleys, and a startling promontory of a nose—all in all, a dramatically distinctive face, with sculptured features that would attract any viewer like a magnet.

She wasn't pretty, I thought, but I had never seen anyone who looked so alive. When she talked, everything seemed to move together, her slightly crossed eyes, her sensitive, humorously curved mouth, her lengthy nose, her graceful hands. I felt exposed. Why did I feel the woman could see through my professional reserve, and knew everything about me? *She must have extrasensory perception*, I thought. I would bet no one ever got away with lying to her.

"Well, Doctor Dale," she said, bringing her joyride to a stop, "whatcha think? What about it?"

"What about what?" I answered.

"Will ya see me for analysis or not? Or are ya turned off by my impulsivity?"

I hesitated. It was true that I was used to potential patients treating me with deference, and thus found her "spontaneity" in the present situation preposterous. And besides that, I wasn't sure I liked her. There was a grandiose, narcissistic, hostile quality about her that I found off-putting. But I know my job isn't to like people; it's to help them, so I decided to give her a chance. And besides, her celebrity status did intrigue me. So I decided to briefly interview her, even if it was my birthday, and I really did need to get home.

"Let's talk," I said, opening up my office door and beckoning her to enter.

Unlike most patients, she went through the door first.

February 7, 2015

"Are ya one of those analysts who never open their mouths except to say 'Hmmmm?' If so, I can leave right now."

I smiled and said, "No, I say a few words now and then."

She smiled, too. "Oh. A funny one. That's something new. I guess I'll stay a while. Ya want me to tell ya why I'm here?"

I nodded.

"Well, the thing is, Doc, I've been in analysis for thirty years now..."

"*Thirty years*?" I said, in shock.

"Yes. I'm a slow learner."

I smiled.

"Thirty years, with a million different analysts," she continued. "And I still don't understand myself any better than the day I walked into the door of the first one. After thirty years of so-called treatment, I still don't understand why I do some things. I wish my life was more peaceful. I wish I got less angry. I wish I could rise above certain feelings."

She shook her head, and said, "Psychoanalysts! I think they're all psychos themselves. Same-old, same-old, all the time. They're all quacks. I've paid them enough to buy Yankee Stadium. I'm thinking about suing for my money back. Can ya do any better?"

"That remains to be seen."

"If you're not sure, then why should I come here?"

"Maybe you shouldn't."

"Yeah? Well, I wanna. When can we start in earnest? But first I have an important question to ask ya."

"Yes?"

"Are ya Jewish?"

I hesitated. It was best that patients know as little as possible about the analyst's life, so they would be free to fantasize about the doctor in any way necessary, in order to develop a workable transference.

"Why do you want to know?" I asked.

"Because I use a lotta Jewish words, and I gotta have a doctor who understands me."

"Let's just say I understand Yiddish."

She grinned and said, "Mazel tov!" She hesitated for a moment and then asked, "But what kind of goyish name is Darcy?"

I could see that this was one patient I wouldn't be able to follow the rules with, so I answered her question. "My mother loved *Pride and*

Prejudice," I said.

"Smart lady," she answered. "Mothers! Oy vey. I guess ya wanna know about mine."

I nodded.

"Is it necessary? I've kvetched about my mother to shrinks for thirty years, and where has it gotten me? Here!"

This time I laughed.

"Okay. We're in business. I guess I have to follow the doctor's orders, though you'll learn soon enough that I practically never do. But I'll make an exception just this once, because I like ya..."

She likes me? She *likes* me? From her brash demeanor, I never would have guessed. "Why don't you like to follow orders?" I asked, after recovering my equilibrium.

"Because I learned very early in life that the people giving the orders were almost always wrong, and the only way to get what I wanted in life was to follow my own nose." She laughed. "Its size gave me a head start."

"Didn't that get you into trouble?" I asked.

"Ya can bet your britches it did. I was in the high school principal's office more often than in the bathroom, which is saying a lot. I even ate my lunch in a toilet stall, because my classmates didn't like me. They laughed at the weird *schmattas* and called me 'Schnoz,' and I wanted to escape them. I dressed the way I wanted to, and it was like no one else. I wore a black skirt and sweater, black shoes and stockings, and a black leather bag, to show everybody I didn't give a damn what they thought about me. Of course, I really did care, but I did everything I could to hide it. But I was a good student. So I guess the principal thought it was worthwhile putting up with my *meshugas.*

"I had one girlfriend at Erasmus High, Susan Dworkowitz. She was probably the only person in the school weirder than me. She wore pasty white makeup, spaghetti shoes, black stockings, and had a black pixie haircut. I liked how we dressed and thought everybody else looked middle class. Susan couldn't afford to be choosey, and sought me out. Since I couldn't afford to be choosey either, I accepted her friendship.

"My choice of a boyfriend was equally strange for the times. I set the school abuzz with talk of him. His name was Teddy and he was a black guy. We used to walk around hand in hand. That was pretty revolutionary in those days. Although I've always been color blind when it came to race, I didn't go out with him because I especially liked him; I just liked to shock everybody.

"My mother had a fit. 'What!?' she said. '*My* daughter going out with a *shvartza*!? Your father would turn over in his grave!' I didn't think so. I believe my father would have looked beyond Teddy's color and seen the kind of person he was. My father was like me: He never judged a person by the color of his or her skin, but by personality and talent. I already knew this when I was a child, and am ashamed for my country that I have to make a point of it even now.

"Nobody else liked me in those days. I'm never sure anybody does, to the present day. Even my mother didn't like me. She loved my little sister Roslyn much more, because she was beautiful. My mother thought I was a skinny stick of wood, and called me '*mieskeit.*' In case ya ain't a real Jew," she said to me, giving me a dirty look, "that means ugly.

"Her idea of being a good mother was to drown me in chicken soup. Hmmmm. I wish I had some now. Ya don't cook, do ya, Doc? What I really wanted from her was love, which I didn't get. She never thought I had any talent and always tried to discourage me from being an actress. She would say, 'Forget it, Maidele. Get a good job like mine as a secretary in a public school and be assured of a decent living. You'll never make it as an actress because you're too ugly.'"

At this point, I was starting to think Barbra was pausing too long, but she eventually continued without encouragement.

"Can ya imagine a mother saying that to her daughter? Well, at least I knew where I stood with her and didn't have to pretend to love her. But on thinking it over, I should be grateful to her. I have a funny quirk—if someone says I can't do something, I have to do it no matter how hard it is, just to prove 'em wrong. If my mother had believed in me, I'd probably be—God forbid—a little Brooklyn housewife like her.

"I knew then that I had to be a somebody, that I had to grow up and be great. I couldn't just be good; my nose was too big." She put her hand on her nose in what I later learned was a characteristic gesture.

"My family and friends made me feel I was too ugly to live. When I was nine years old, I read a pamphlet about cancer, which listed nine symptoms of the disease. I was convinced that I had every one of them, with only six months to live. 'I'll show them,' I thought, with one hand held dramatically across my forehead. 'I'll die a tragic death. Then they'll be sorry they treated me so badly!' Unfortunately, I lived, and forgot about my tragic early demise.

"You'd think I'd have been jealous of Roslyn, but I wasn't. I used to love my little sister and pretend I was her mother. I played with her, rubbed her back, and bribed her with coffee ice cream so she'd stop crying. She adored me, and probably still does. When I sang, *she* sang. When I danced, *she* danced. I taught her how to harmonize on 'Row, Row, Row Your Boat.' I used to love her beautiful, fat face, because she was so much prettier than me. I guess I treated her the way I wanted my mother to treat me. She was my first child. God, what happened to us? We hardly ever talk to each other anymore."

Barbra with sister Roslyn Kind in 1969, a time when the two were close.

February 1, 2015

To my surprise, Barbra sat quietly for a few moments at the start of our next session. Then I said, "Tell me more about your mother, Barbra."

"Okay, Darcy. My mother, Diana Kind, believed in spanking kids. She thought it saved psychiatrist's fees. Well, it certainly didn't save me any! My mother believed in the old Jewish saying that when a child gets spanked on the tush, it finds its way to her head, so the head clears up. I don't seem to recall that *On a Clear Day You Can See Forever* was about spanking children. But wait'll you hear her best advice; 'Never give your kids too much praise.'

"In fact, she always tried to tone me down because she thought I had an exaggerated opinion of myself. Who, ME?" She crossed her eyes and looked to the ceiling. "She said later she just made that kind of remark to calm me down. And how did my mother 'calm me down?' She said, 'Don't forget, ya got everything good from me.' Boy, did I not get calmed down! I haven't stopped running since I was two. Did you ever hear such terrible advice about raisin' children? I think you should write a book about it."

She laughed. I did, too.

"By the way, Doctor, how much do you charge?"

I told her.

"What! You gotta be kidding! That's twice what my last doctor cost. Can't you come down a little?'

"Sorry," I answered. "That's my fee."

"Even for movie stars?" she asked wistfully.

February 11, 2015

Barbra came in more subdued this session, and seemed to have lost a good deal of her Brooklyn accent. I wasn't surprised. After all, I had seen her in *The Prince of Tides*, in which she played a highly educated psychiatrist. I silently wondered if she expected me to perform as she had in that movie.

As an old hand at psychoanalysis, she slid right onto the couch and said, "Well, whadya want me to talk about, Doc? More about my mother, my father, my sex life, my dreams?"

"Tell me who is important to you."

Without missing a beat, she said, "Only one person has ever really mattered to me my whole life, and that is my father."

"Your father?" I said with surprise. "I thought you said he passed away."

"Alive or dead, my father is the only person I ever really loved." She tried not to cry.

I waited.

After a few moments, she continued, "You know, there isn't even a picture of us together. His books were down in the cellar, tied up with string. When I found them, I gobbled them up, and I still read them when I miss him. When I was little, I resented him for making me the only kid on the block who didn't have a father. When a person grows up missing a parent, there is a huge hole in her that screams out to be filled. In my case, it made me more sensitive. It made me feel more and sense more than other people.

"I've spent my whole life trying to find my father. My mother never talked about him. When I asked why not, she said she didn't want to upset me. What a dumb woman! I wonder what he ever saw in her. Even though he died when I was only fifteen months old, I've convinced myself I remember him picking me up and carrying me down the street sitting on top of his shoulders. In my memory, real or imagined, I truly felt on top of the world. 'Hey, everybody, look at me! I'm the tallest person in the world!' My father was a wonderful man. No guy I've ever met has lived up to the person my father was.

"His name was Emanuel Streisand, but everybody called him Manny. Sometimes I wake up at night and hear soft voices calling, 'Manny, Manny, Manny...' When I try to find him, the voices disappear. It always makes me cry. My father was a leader from the time he was a young child. He was adored by his brothers and sister and all the neighborhood kids. He was a handsome boy, and he later became a handsome man, with wavy brown hair." She was silent for a few moments, and then said, "No wonder I like to stroke men's hair." Her eyes filled.

"Manny was so smart he was able to skip two grades. Is it surprising that I graduated high school at sixteen like my father? Anyway, he was also a good brother. He read to his siblings every day, and helped them with their homework. At his brother Phil's Bar Mitzvah, he read passages from the Torah. He was an athlete, too. He played handball and tennis at a time when no other Jewish boys did. He did it all! No wonder I've had so much trouble finding a good man in my life. None of them lived up to him. Nobody even came close.

"In his last year of high school, he decided he wanted to be a teacher. He began attending college when he was only sixteen, with a double major in English and Education. Manny was the first Streisand to attend college. His father kvelled over him. He said, 'He's so smart he could be president! I'm so proud of him I could bust!'

"My grandparents also told me he worked in their fish store in Brooklyn while he was going to New York University. Brilliant as he was, he wasn't above cleaning and chopping the fish, wrapping them in newspapers for the customers, and sweeping the floor. From the delivery truck, he lifted the heavy boxes filled with fish until his back gave out on him. He went on to Columbia University for his Ph.D.

"Too bad he never finished. He met and fell in love with my mother, and she made him stop school and work full time so they could get married. Stupid woman! Why did he listen to her? But I know from experience that when you're in love, you do what your beloved wants you to. Too bad he had such poor taste in women! His dream was to move to California and become a writer. He never achieved that dream, either. I had to do it for him.

"When he grew up, he made a good living teaching truants and delinquents at the Brooklyn High School for Specialty Trades. He also tutored after school at a yeshiva and every summer at educational camps. In the words of Thoreau—he underlined them in a book I still treasure— he loved turning the 'free meandering brook' of a wayward adolescent's life into a 'straight cut ditch' of education, discipline, and prospects for a future.'"

She paused, and turned to look me squarely in the eyes. "A good man, yes. But where was he, Doctor, when his own 'wayward adolescent' needed him so badly?"

I had no answer, other than to say, "I'm sure he didn't plan to die so young."

"He was twenty when he met my mother," she continued. "She was born Ida Rosen, but changed her name to Diana. Wasn't Ida good enough for her? Anyway, that was the end of my father's college career, as they fell in love and got married a year later. Needless to say, if I were my mother, I would have made him continue his schooling.

"Of course they couldn't afford a honeymoon, so they drove into Manhattan in his rickety Tin Lizzy for a Broadway show and a night at a nice hotel. I wish I could've been a fly on the wall and watched them in bed, though I can't imagine anyone wanting to fuck my mother. I couldn't stand it when she even came near me.

"On their way home to Brooklyn, the driver in front of them braked sharply, and my father was unable to stop his car in time. He banged into the car, and his head was thrown against the windshield so hard it cracked the glass. Within a few days, he began to suffer dizzy spells and horrendous headaches. He took a lot of aspirin, but because he was not a complainer, nobody knew how much he was suffering. He and my mother apparently had a happy marriage for a few years. My brother Sheldon was born, and Manny was promoted to assistant superintendent.

"Everything seemed to be going fine until one terrible day he twitched and convulsed uncontrollably. He fell to the floor unconscious. The doctor said he'd had an epileptic fit brought on by the accident five years before, could have another episode at any moment, and nothing could be done. I hate doctors! (No offense to you, Doc.) Why didn't he try harder? He was supposed to be an expert. Some expert! If I were that doctor, I would have tried to cure Manny to my last breath.

"On April 24, 1942, I was born, and completed my father's happiness. I was said to be a bright-eyed baby with a ready smile, who was so fascinated with everything around me that I rarely cried. I guess I haven't changed that much. My head was a little too big for the rest of me and I was completely bald until I was two. Some people even recommended at some point that I be the next Gerber food baby. How blind can you be?

"Everybody said my father was crazy about me. Everything was wonderful, except that his ghastly headaches continued. I like to think that when he held me, he felt a little better. But on August 4, he awoke with an even worse headache than usual. But never one to complain, he went to work and coached the swimming team. By midmorning, the pain had gotten so severe he felt sick in the stomach. He thought he would go back home and lie down for a while, and asked Diana to wake him up in an hour.

"She followed his instructions, but no matter how much or how long she shook, he wouldn't wake up. Terrified by his shallow breathing, she called for an ambulance. 'He is going to be all right. He is going to be all right. He has to be,' she kept reassuring herself while she waited. But he wasn't all right. He died in the hospital before his parents could get there to say goodbye. He had suffered another seizure, and was pronounced dead of respiratory failure. My poor father! Cheated out of a rich lifetime he had worked so hard for.

"All because of a bad driver! Damn him! I hope he banged against the wall until his *kishkes* fell out. Such an asshole shouldn't be allowed to drive. Because of that bastard, I lost my wonderful father." She sobbed until the end of the hour.

As she was leaving, she came up to me and said timidly, "Can I touch you?"

I said, "Of course."

She hesitantly put out a finger and lightly touched my cheek.

I felt bad that I had to end the session, but the next patient was waiting. Sometimes it's hard to be a psychoanalyst.

February 13, 2015

"How do you feel today?" I asked. "That was quite a session we had the other day."

"Nah," she answered. "I like to be worried. It keeps me calm. Anyway, I think about my father all the time and like to talk about him. It brings me closer to him."

"I'm glad to hear it," I said. "This means you're a good candidate for analysis."

"After thirty years, I should be."

"So tell me what happened after your father died."

"It was a terrible time. My mother spent most of her time crying in her bed. She didn't go out or do the shopping; she fell completely apart. My grandmother and aunt made sure my brother Sheldon and I were fed, but otherwise nobody paid much attention to us. It's a miracle we survived.

"My aunt said she came into the apartment once and saw a dirty little baby screaming in her crib. When she went to pick me up, I turned up my nose at her. It must have been a good size, even then, so there was plenty to turn up. 'Who is that *mieskeit*?' she asked. 'She can't be a Streisand. We have only beautiful children in this family.' If I know me, I was thinking, 'Who needs you to pick me up? I want my papa.'

"My mother was never very affectionate, but after my father died, she left me completely alone. She was lost in her own despair. When I read of Jacqueline Kennedy crying in bed all day after Jack was killed, I always think of my mother. Both women had good reason to cry. It's a miracle they ever stopped.

"When my mother got well enough to work again, she dragged herself off to a bookkeeping job every day, and I lost her physically as well as emotionally. Every morning when she was leaving, I clung to her leg and screamed, 'Please, Mama, don't leave me. Please stay home... Please... Please... . Please. You might never come back, like Papa, and I'll have nobody left at all.' She would push me away and say, 'Don't be ridiculous, *bubbala*. I'm only going to work. You wanna eat, don't you? Then let go of my leg.'

"I was shuttled so often from one caretaker to another I may as well have been an orphan. My Uncle Murray said I was left so often with friends and relatives that I always felt deserted. I didn't just *feel* deserted, Uncle Murray. I *was* deserted. But maybe I should be happy about that. As one of my favorite authors, C. S. Lewis, said, 'Hardship often prepares an ordinary person for an extraordinary destiny.' Instead of being an ordinary dowdy typist, no one can deny that my career and life have been extraordinary. I wouldn't have had it otherwise."

When, somewhat later, I told her we had to call a halt to the session, she got up and threw me a look that could melt icebergs.

February 16, 2015

"To pick up where I left off last session when you threw me out," she said, tossing me another killer look, "life wasn't all that bad, despite the terrible shortcomings of my childhood. I was too excited about investigating the miraculous world around me to live entirely in despair. As soon as I learned to crawl, I got into everything. I spent all day checking out and tasting everything around me. I loved the world so much I refused to go to sleep until I dropped over from sheer exhaustion."

"Psychoanalytic researcher Dr. Margaret Mahler spoke of babies as having 'a love affair with the world.' It sounds like that was particularly true of you."

"I agree," Barbra said. "A pencil, a cup, my mother's lipstick—experiencing them all had me bubbling over with joy. One time I climbed on top of my mother's bureau and, finding her makeup, rubbed bright red lipstick all over my face. Just as I stepped backward to admire my first makeup job ever, my mother came into the room and rescued me from disaster. I've liked to do my own makeup ever since. Unlike most actors, my makeup artists simply sit and hold my containers of makeup. Needless to say, they aren't too happy about it. Nor was my mother, who gave me a *potch* on the *tush* for ruining her lipstick.

"We moved in with my grandfather, Louis Rosen. He was my mother's father, and he wasn't much of a substitute for my father. He was a grouchy old man who only wanted peace and quiet, and had no patience with a prepubescent boy and a mischievous toddler. We were squeezed into his tiny apartment like sardines in a crushed can. Grandfather and Grandmother slept in one bedroom, and Mom and us children in the living room, which had been converted into a bedroom.

"My mother and I slept in one bed and Sheldon in a cot at our feet. Our bed took the place of the usual living room sofa, and I grew up thinking that couches were just for rich people. I still get pleasure when I walk through my living room and see all of the couches arranged there.

"Although World War II was over and America had begun its economic recovery from the Great Depression, the Rosens and the Streisands didn't share in America's economic recovery. My mother spent most of her time away from work worrying about herself and her fatherless children, and wondering if we had any future at all.

"My grandmother did the best she could to care for us, but she was seventy years old, overweight, and asthmatic, so *I* had to take care of *her*.

I'm not kidding. I had to walk her up and down the stairs and take the dishes off the table when I was three years old. I told my mother, 'I've been doing all the work around here ever since I was three years old.'

"She thought that was hilarious, and for years told the story to anyone who would listen. I didn't think it was funny. When I was four, my mother sent me to nursery school, and to her sister's farm in Colchester, Connecticut for the next two summers. Things were a little better there. I had the chickens to play with.

"The only good thing about life with my grandparents on Polaski Street was the music. Grandfather Rosen sang traditional Jewish songs every Sabbath and on holidays. He had a beautiful voice, which my mother also inherited. I guess you can say I take after them in that respect. I sang along with him before I could talk. Those are the first songs I remember singing. I still can't hear 'My Yiddishe Momma' or 'Hatikvah' without my eyes filling up.

"We had a neighbor, Tobey Borokow, who for some reason took a liking to me. She called me *bubbela*—her little sweetheart. She often took me in her arms and held me, which is more than my mother ever did. I probably have Tobey to thank for helping me become an affectionate person. I didn't have any toys, so I played with a hot water bottle and pretended it was a doll. The good woman knitted me a sweater for it."

"How sad that was the only toy you had," I commented.

"Oh, I wouldn't say that," Barbra answered. "Every night before I went to sleep, I would fill it up with hot water, hold it against me, and pretend it was a warm human being. It was much warmer than a real doll, and put me right to sleep."

"You were a creative little girl, Barbra, and even created a mother for yourself."

"Yes, probably my creativity saved my sanity, and may have even kept me alive. When I was five years old, I started elementary school at the yeshiva on Willoughby Street where my father had once taught. It felt good going to his school. As I passed each room or hallway, I would think, 'My father was once here! I wonder if his spirit is still around?' That was the first time I remember thinking, 'Papa, can you see me? Papa, can you hear me?' That thought later developed into the famous song in *Yentl*.

"I was a great student—had a 94 average—but I always got bad marks for behavior. For some reason, the teacher didn't like me. I would sit there wildly waving my hand every time she asked a question, but she would always ignore me. But nobody was going to tell me when I could talk, so I shouted out the answers anyway. That didn't go over very big with her. I always had lots of questions, like when we studied the Bible. It didn't make any sense to me. The world was made in seven days? Come on, you gotta be kidding! I can't even make a latke in seven days.'

"Today," I said to Barbra, "we would call it 'oppositional defiant disorder,' but back then you were simply called a 'bad kid.'"

"Even worse than the teachers," Barbra continued, "the children were cruel to me. I was not a pretty girl. It didn't help that my own mother constantly told me so. I was as skinny as an eel and so uncoordinated I often tripped over my own feet. I still do, but now people think it's cute. My head was too large for my body, and my nose stuck out so far I could follow it down the street. Even worse, I was a little cross-eyed, and became the favorite butt of jokes in the school. I was called 'big beak,' and 'cross-eyes' and '*mieskeit*'—the last one the kids must have picked up from their parents.

"I was very lonely in school. I had no one to talk to. The smart girls I wanted to pal around with weren't interested in talking to me, and I wouldn't be seen talking with the stupid ones. You know Groucho Marx's remark, 'I wouldn't join any country club that would have me as a member?' That's me. I wouldn't talk to any girl dumb enough to talk to me, so I just had to learn to live with my loneliness.

"A gang of girls gathered around me one time calling me names. I started to cry. They yelled, '*Pishmeshame* on Barbra. *Pishmeshame*! She's a cry baby!'

"I said, 'I'm *not* crying. I just have something in my eye.' But they really did get to me," she said, putting a finger on her famous nose. "Even now, when the reviewers and columnists say I'm beautiful, I think, "Come off it! Don'tcha know I'm a '*mieskeit*'? I guess you never get over being called that as a child."

February 18, 2015

During the prior session, Barbra must have gotten upset talking about being made to feel she was a "mieskeit." Rather than starting off this session as usual, by talking about herself, she opened with a "joke." "A friend and I were playing a game of make-believe psychoanalysis. In a rich Viennese accent, my friend said, 'Zis iss Dr. Kronkheit. Loosen up and say de first ting that comes into your mind. I quickly replied, 'How much does it cost?'"

I think she is trying to tell me something, and it isn't good, I said to myself, but decided it was too soon to deal with her hostility.

Since our last session had ended with Barbra not feeling too great about herself, I decided to start this session out in a way that I knew would make Barbra feel good. I said, "Barbra, you are 73 years old, but you look as radiant as a starlet. With your shining hair, soft skin, and gorgeous figure, you look at least three decades younger. How do you do it? Do you exercise?"

"What! Are you kidding? I am adamantly opposed to exercising."

When I looked surprised, she said, "Don't think I haven't tried it. In the sixties, I worked out with Lotte Berk, better known as 'The Ogre of Yoga,' who dreamed up a regime of ballet, yoga, and orthopedic exercises that must have been invented by the Spanish Inquisition. I congratulated myself for staying with her for two weeks.

"Then," she went on, "I attended Body Design, the famous Beverly Hills studio, for a while. Fellow sufferer Cher noted that I reluctantly did a few leg lifts and then walked around and talked to the other exercisers until I was kindly asked not to return to the class.

"I also signed up for Pilates seventeen years ago, but I couldn't even pronounce the word let alone do the exercises.

"I thought maybe if I installed exercise equipment in my Malibu mansion, I could keep to the routine better. I tried it for a week and then threw it out. Placed in the middle of my living room floor, it looked to be in poor taste. Aesthetics are more important than exercise any day," she added.

"Somebody said I was the worst tennis player he had ever seen. He had a point there. I tried playing tennis for a while with Jon Peters, my old boyfriend, until he hit one of my breasts with a tennis ball. 'Don't worry,' I said. 'I have another one.' Unfortunately, my sense of humor is better than my athletic ability. That was the end of my tennis career.

"I even hate doing vocal exercises," she continued. "And I'm dead set against warming up. It's just too boring. And besides, I'm too old for all that stuff. If people don't like the way I sing, they don't have to listen."

I said, "It seems you sound perfectly fine without them."

"You're darn right," she answered. "I've managed to stay at the top of the heap for six decades without any of that exercise crap. When I first started out in Hollywood, fortunately for me, it was no crime to have curves, so I've never denied myself goodies the way my young colleagues do these days. Interviewers have made a point of commenting over the years that I continually nibble at cheese while talking to them.

"They should see me every night stuffing myself with coffee ice cream. At one time, I installed a small refrigerator by my bedside to hold bricks of Breyers coffee ice cream. It's still my favorite food. But you can't buy Breyers bricks in Los Angeles for love or money. All you can get around here is Haagen-Dazs," she says. "I don't like expensive ice cream, despite my friendship with Richard Baskin. The richer it is, the more I hate it. Breyers is a thin, icy ice cream with air bubbles. It reminds me of Brooklyn."

"I wish I had your metabolism," I said. "I have to limit myself to one treat a day."

She looked surprised. "Well, whatever you do, keep doing it. You look great to me."

I must admit the compliment felt great, coming from one of America's most glittering stars.

"Lately, when even I thought I was getting fat," she continued, "I tried a few diets that were all the rage at the time. Carrie Wiatt, a big-name nutritionist, put me on a low-carbohydrate, high-protein diet, which is full of fruits and vegetables and allows no processed foods, which I love. Do you think that worked? Not on your life! It failed mostly because I love pancakes, and eat them for breakfast every single day. Next I fooled around with the Jenny Craig diet. But," she admitted forlornly, "I kept right on eating like a pig, and ate the Craig stuff for dessert."

"You have such beautiful skin color, Barbra," I said. "Do you sit in the sun?"

"Nah," she responded. "I avoided the sun long before it was popular to do so, and I always wear sunscreen. So I guess you can say I take care of myself when it makes sense and isn't too difficult to do.

"I'm also very careful about makeup and refuse to allow any foundation on my face except for a cream hand-blended for me.

"Laura Mercier, the famous French makeup artist, said something I absolutely adore about my skin. She attributed the famous 'Streisand glow' to something intangible: my character. She said, 'When you fall under the spell of Barbra's beautiful voice, you don't think of her nose or her make-up—just that she has a magnificent character.' Isn't that lovely?"

"Indeed it is, Barbra." We sat there, quietly pleased with each other.

Then I said, "How about plastic surgery? How do you feel about that?"

"Well," she answered somewhat reluctantly, "one reason for my smooth, wrinkle-free look is the surgeon's art, although I resisted the temptation for many years. When I finally had the surgery done, I was embarrassed, hoping no one would find out about it. But after I was photographed coming out of a private clinic with my face and neck covered with a straw hat and scarf, the cat was out of the bag. Despite all my denials, it was evident to everyone that Barbra Streisand had had a facelift. Now I couldn't care less. What I see when I look into a mirror is what is important to me.

"Are you wondering why I never had my nose fixed?" she suddenly said.

I was, but hadn't wanted to ask.

"At eighteen, I absolutely rejected a nose job," she went on. "While all my Jewish girlfriends had their noses shortened in their late teens, I refused to, because I was afraid it would ruin my voice. Now I wouldn't have it done because of my identity. My nose is me. Besides, back then I didn't have the money to have my nose fixed."

"Did you ever seriously consider having it fixed?"

"In my early days, when I would have liked to look like Catherine Deneuve, I considered having my nose done. But I didn't trust anyone enough to do the job. If I could do it myself with a mirror, I would straighten my nose and take off that little knob of cartilage from the tip.

"When I was young, everyone would say, 'When are you gonna get your nose fixed?' It was a fad, with at least one of the Jewish girls at Erasmus Hall High School having their noses done every week, taking perfectly good schnozzes and whittling them down to nothing. The first thing someone would have done would be to cut off the bump on my nose. But I happen to love that bump, and I never would have it removed.

That's my idea of beautiful. I certainly don't like tiny little noses or pugs. Can you picture me with a pug nose? It just wouldn't fit my personality, to say nothing of my face.

"I have a strange face. It changes very much from angle to angle. Sometimes I think I really look beautiful, and a lot of times I believe I look terrible. It's a shame. But on the other hand, I'm not going to cry over it. I'm trying to be in the moment, and I'm enjoying my life."

"Good for you, Barbra. You don't need a nose job, although you were probably the only woman in Hollywood to say so. It's that kind of thinking that makes you who you are."

I was becoming impressed by the integrity of this woman. In a world not overly saturated with seeds of morality, she seemed to stand out as a unique flower.

February 20, 2015

At just about the time I was expecting Barbra to arrive for her session, I heard a lot of cussing in the waiting room.

"Fuck, shit, piss, damn it to hell!" someone hollered. I opened the door and saw it was Barbra.

"What's the matter, Barbra?" I asked.

"Something terrible. I just broke one of my Mandarin fingernails. It will take me at least a year to grow it back."

I breathed a sigh of relief. "Is that all? One would think from all the commotion that you had broken your back."

She followed me into the office, looking as if the world was coming to an end.

"Tell me, Barbra, why are your nails so important to you?"

"You'd think a so-called analyst would know the answer to that question. I need the nails because I'm not beautiful."

"What has beauty got to do with it?"

"You know I was always called a '*mieskeit*' when I was little. When I got to high school, I decided that if I couldn't have a beautiful face like all the other girls, the least I could do was to have something about me that was beautiful, so I chose to grow long nails." (She held out the hand without the broken nail.) "Here, see? Aren't they gorgeous?"

"Yes, Barbra, they are. I've never seen nails that long and immaculately groomed. But you yourself are a beautiful woman now. Why do you still need the long nails?"

"What kind of analyst would ask a question like that? You may think I'm beautiful, and I'm happy you do, but that is purely a matter of opinion. *Yours*, not mine."

"What do you mean?"

She paused a moment, and said with a sad expression on her face, "When I look in the mirror, I do not see a sophisticated movie star or an Academy Award winner. I see the ugly face of little Barbara Streisand. No expensive hairdo or stunning gown can change that. So yes, I still need the long nails!"

She abruptly stood up and said, "I can't stay here now. You are no help to me today. You may not agree, but sometimes there are more important things in the world than psychoanalysis. I've kept the broken part of my nail and have to hurry to my manicurist to see if maybe she can find a way to fix it."

She slammed the door on her way out. I shook my head. She was right. There are some things more important than psychoanalysis, though I don't think nails are one of them. I consoled myself with the thought that when she felt more secure, she wouldn't be so in need of her Mandarin fingernails.

February 23, 2015

I began the following session with, "Last time we talked about your nails. What about fashion? Do you follow the current trends?"

"Hell no!" she answered. "I wear an old hat that is a work of art. My favorite evening gown is fifty years old and makes me look real sexy. I do what is right for me. When I was singing in night clubs, I felt it was a waste of money to spend hundreds of dollars–which I didn't have–on clothes, so l came up with the idea of a gingham gown. I thought, why wear beads in a night club? People should be coming to hear me sing, not to look at my clothes.

"In my opinion, a gingham dress is just as pretty as a beaded gown. I've always done what I want to do, and how I look follows who I am. I wear sweaters and slacks as often as I can. They are far from glamorous. And I've always felt gawky. I mean, I was never able to get a modeling job. I'm probably the least attractive woman in show business. Every time I look in the mirror, I get a bit of a shock. That's *me* in the mirror? That old lady? You've got to be kidding! I still feel so young inside."

I disagreed. I thought Barbra to be rather lovely. But I didn't say so. She already knew what I thought about her appearance.

"My hair has always been…well, my hair," she continued. "In a little shop in London, l had it cut by a barber, and told him the way I wanted it. He came before Jon, of course. I figured out how to make up my eyes by studying light and shadows in paintings.

"I hate buying clothes. My best friend, Donna, is a fashion designer, and she sends me outfits. And Renata Buser, my loyal assistant for decades, does the shopping for me.'

"Tell me about this best friend, Barbra. You hadn't mentioned her before."

"Donna Karan is very important to me, as I never really had a best friend as a kid. She says that when she was a freshman at Hewlett High School on Long Island, New York, she was so crazy about me that she had daydreams that she *was* me. If someone asked her her name, she had to bite her tongue not to say 'Barbra.'" She laughs. "She cut her hair to look like me, and listened to my music night and day. She even mimicked one of my mannerisms, her hand on her jaw.

"Strangely enough, it was a sweater that brought us together in 1977. Specifically, it was a chenille burgundy pullover that caught my eye while glancing through a copy of *Harper's Bazaar.* Donna had designed the sweater for Anne Klein's fall collection, and I knew I had to have it.

"My friend Ilene Weston, an interior designer, called Donna and arranged for us to meet. Donna was so looking forward to it that she cleared her schedule completely and got her hair, makeup, and nails done on the day we were to meet. When I first laid eyes on her, I couldn't believe what I saw. I thought, 'What's with this woman? She's shaking like she has the palsy.' I looked at her like she was some weirdo, so I told her to sit down and compose herself.

"Well, we soon got over that. I zeroed right in on the sweater and its matching hat, and said, 'Donna, you've got to get me a set.' But nothing in this life seems to go easily, at least for me. The month before, both pieces had to be removed from stores after Donna accidentally set one of them on fire with a cigarette, in her shrink's office, no less. I'd love to know what her session had been about that day! She refuses to tell me, but I'll bet it was terrific! Since they were obviously flammable, the garments were labeled too dangerous to sell, and taken off the market.

"Donna said I absolutely couldn't have the set, because she could just see the headline, *Barbra Streisand goes up in flames in Anne Klein sweater.* Wouldn't that do a lot for Anne's business, to say nothing of Donna's reputation! I even offered to sign a legal waiver, but Donna stood her ground. That's one of the things I like most about her. She's no patsy.

Barbra with designer Donna Karan in 2011.
Barbra and Donna have remained friends throughout the years,
and Barbra supports Donna as much as Donna supports her.

"In the end, I managed to get my hands on the sweater and hat behind her back. There's not much you can't get if you're willing to pay the price. The two pieces are soft, cuddly, and not itchy. I can't wear wool, so the outfit was among my favorites for years. I'm not sure what happened to the sweater, but I still wear the hat. I love it. You might have seen photos of me in it—I wear it a lot. Donna nearly fell over when she found a picture of me wearing them. She said, 'It was my first but far from my last indication that Barbra Streisand never takes no for an answer.'

"I forgave her for not letting me get the sweater and hat, and our relationship progressed from hero worship to a real friendship, so that today we consider each other family. Donna even keeps a special Barbra room in her house, where I stay when I visit.

"The better Donna and I got to know each other, the more we realized how much we had in common. We have the same insecurities. Inside, I'm still the girl from Brooklyn, and she the girl from Queens. We even sound alike, with the same accent. I needn't add that Donna is a very generous, loving, and sweet person to whom I can confide almost everything. If I said to her, 'Donna, I just killed my mother,' I'm sure she would reply, 'You must have had a good reason.'

"We also have had similar struggles balancing work and our personal lives. I feel guilty for not being there enough for her daughter, Gabby. Donna regrets not being around enough for my son, Jason. We're both very Jewish, and full of Jewish guilt. Our families travel and spend holidays together, and I was very close to Donna's late husband, Stephan Weiss. Donna says he adored me, and that every time she wanted something, she'd ask me to call him. He could never say no to me. I like to feel I helped her get through the terrible year after he died.

"That very special sweater also marked the start of my love affair with Donna's designs, leading to decades of our working together. She says that I taught her to understand the body on a different level, that I understand every angle of how I look because my attention to detail is beyond anything she's ever seen. Thanks, Donna, but I think it's your talent you're describing.

"When Jim and I got married, I of course asked Donna to make my wedding gown. I sent her sketches of what I wanted, but she didn't like them. My drawings were cut on the bias and flowing, and she wanted me to wear something more revealing. She made both my dress and hers, and she let me decide. Of course, I chose hers." Barbra sat silently, with a smile that seemed to light up her entire body.

"You really love Donna, don't you, Barbra?"

She nodded.

"It's wonderful you have such a close, dear friend."

February 25, 2015

Returning the next session to the topic of clothing, I asked, "What do you *like* to wear?"

She replied: "Simple things with elasticized waists so I can eat. Mostly I wear blue jeans and tee shirts around the house. I'm not much of a fashionista. At work, I'm more likely to wear comfortable but frumpy schmattas. The cleaning lady dresses better, or so I've been told."

We chatted some more about clothing, but nothing of significance was said.

Oh well, you can't win them all, I said to myself.

"This was a nice session," she said on leaving the office. "We should do this more often."

Barbra performing. Her own personal style rejected the norms of the time.

February 27, 2015

The next session, Barbra returned to the discussion of her behavior at school and her oppositional defiant disorder.

I said, "These patterns of behavior often result in impairment at school and/or other social venues. Did they for you?"

"I'll say," she answered. "When my mother said, 'You wanna eat, don't you?' Even if I did, my answer was always 'No!' My mother was always bothering me about eating. Jewish children were supposed to be fat, and I was skinny as a toothpick. If I stood next to Twiggy, I would make even her look fat. I guess it made Diana look bad as a mother. I was always too busy reading and singing to take time to eat. My mother made me some god-awful hazuri called a guggle muggle. It was a shake with a raw egg in it.

"It was supposed to fatten me up, but it was so disgusting I would hold it in my mouth, and when she wasn't looking, spit it down the toilet. She would sit me up in my bed and force-feed me. To tell you the truth, I didn't mind because I enjoyed the attention. It was the only time I got any from her. No wonder I didn't eat! I wanted love but she gave me food.

"I first decided to be an actress when I was five years old. My neighbors, the Borokows, had the first television I ever saw. I watched TV there whenever they let me, and I fell in love with the flickering images behind the glass. I adored the laughing and the singing, which were so different from the drab atmosphere of my house. 'That's how I'm going to live when I grow up,' I thought.

"My mother said, 'Once Barbra saw television, that was the end of it! She was determined to become one of those happy people on TV. No more typist for her! She loved to sing, and sang before she could talk.' I sang wherever I was, in the hallways of Pulaski Street, on the steps outside the building, and on the fire escapes. Some of the neighbors loved it, and yelled, 'Hey, Barbra, sing some more for us,' while others just slammed their windows shut.

"When people wanted me to go on singing, I was only too happy to oblige. But showgirl that I am, the entertainment didn't stop there. I'm double-jointed. For an encore, I lay down on the pavement, wrapped my legs around my neck, and rolled back and forth like a ball. They clapped louder for the rolling than for the singing.

"When I was seven years old," Barbra continued, "I got my first taste of a real audience's approval, when I sang in the assembly program of the yeshiva's PTA. If I hadn't been convinced before, their thunderous applause hooked me for life. I stood there shaking and thinking, 'Who, *me*? Could they really be clapping for *me*?'

"I ran offstage and asked my mother, 'Well, Mom, what did you think?'

"She replied, 'Your arms are too thin.'"

March 2, 2015

"Wouldn't you like to hear about my sex life, Doctor? It's much more interesting than my childhood."

Actually, I would, but I smiled and said, "Whatever you want to tell me, Barbra."

"Well, I guess I *should* tell you about the worst few years of my life, before I get into the exciting stuff," she said sadly. She was quiet for a long moment. Her face contorted. I waited.

"In 1949, when I was seven," she began, "I already knew what I wanted to be and where I wanted to go. It didn't include going to camp. But my mother didn't ask me, and sent me away to a Hebrew health camp to 'fatten me up.' It didn't. I loathed both the camp and the food, which was so bad I kicked it under the table. I always hated camp, but this one was the worst of all, because it was there I first met my future stepfather, Louis Kind. Yeah, Kind. You heard me right. Would you believe it? Nobody has ever been less aptly named. He should have been called Louis Louse.

"My mother was forty years old at the time and out to get a man before she was too old. She was still pretty, if a bit plump, but she had no trouble finding dates after her period of mourning was over. I hated them all, especially the fat butcher I caught kissing her. His arms were around her neck and I thought he was strangling her until she started to laugh. I used to yell and holler every time she went out with a guy, because I was scared she would never come back, but I screamed the loudest when she went out with Kind. He was good-looking, tall, and a sharp dresser. Though I hate to admit it, he also had nice Old World manners. That is, until you got to know him. He was sixteen years older than my mother. He got along well with my grandfather, and told my mother he loved children. Yeah! Sure! Like I love Hitler. What a lie that turned out to be!

"When my mother said she was planning to visit me at camp, he asked if he could come along. She was delighted. I wasn't. I suspected right then that if he was coming to visit me, things were getting pretty hot between them and she might even marry him. I was horrified at the thought of anyone, especially Kind, replacing my dear father. I barely looked at him when my mother introduced us, and remained sullen the whole time they were there.

"When they stood up to leave, I packed my little bag and crawled into the back of the car, screaming 'You can't leave here without me!

I won't stay here another minute!' My mother did her best to talk me out of it, but to no avail. She had no choice but to take me with them. I remember the trip home very well. The three of us sat in glum silence the whole time. He hated me ever after. I can't say I blame him. I was obnoxious. Whenever he came to take my mother out, I would pull her by the skirts, screaming, 'Please don't go away, Mommy. Stay here with me!' He tried to win me over by bringing me a doll. I banged her head against the wall until it broke off.

"Soon, my mother got pregnant, but Kind, having failed in one marriage, refused to marry her. When it was no longer possible for my mother to hide her condition, her compassionate father, who considered himself deeply religious, threw her out of the house. She rented a one-bedroom apartment made of cinderblock and steel for herself, my brother, and me. It looked like somebody's cellar, but it was all she could do to raise the $105 a month it cost. I hated it. Finally, she persuaded Kind to do the decent thing, and he reluctantly agreed to marry her. I was eight years old at the time.

"On their wedding night, Kind started to go to sleep in my mother's bed. I kicked and hollered so loud that I was allowed to sleep in my usual spot next to my mother. I'm sure that endeared me to him even further.

"Less than a month later, their daughter, Roslyn, was born. Of course she was a beautiful, plump, happy child— just the opposite of me.

"If I thought I had had it bad before, I didn't know from nothin.' My mother paid all her attention to the baby, and forgot I even existed. Kind fell in love with Roslyn, and lavished all his affection on her. According to him, she was the most gorgeous, smartest, and gifted baby in the whole world. In contrast, he loathed me. He saw me as a whimpering, whining, infuriating brat, who was unpleasant to look at.

"In the seven years we lived together, I can't remember one nice word he ever said to me. On the contrary, he was nasty as could be. When I saw him being nice to everyone else, I tried really hard to please him, but without success. He was verbally abusive, saying unbelievably mean things about me and criticizing my looks and my clothes in front of my friends. When he compared Roslyn and me, which he did all the time, he called us 'Beauty and the Beast.' When I asked him a question, he ignored me and pretended I wasn't there.

"One time he took all my friends out to the Good Humor truck in front of the house and bought a bunch of ice-cream cones. He carefully handed them out to my friends but didn't give me one. 'Where's mine?'

I asked. 'You don't get any,' he said. 'You're too ugly. No ice cream for the *mieskeit*!' I threw my head in the air and said, 'I don't like ice cream anyway!' And then I ran home crying. Perhaps that is why I love coffee ice cream so much, and keep refrigerators of it in practically every room of my houses. I can have coffee ice cream now whenever I like, so there, Louis Kind!"

I gasped at the story. She looked up at me in surprise. "Are those tears in your eyes?" she asked me in disbelief.

I nodded.

"Why?"

"That is the cruelest thing I've ever heard anyone say to a child."

"Really?" she answered. "I thought I deserved it. I had another problem, a physical one, which drove me nuts," she said. "I had a constant unpleasant ringing in my ears, called tinnitus, which I have to the present day. Can you imagine what it is like never to hear a silence? I could be in the middle of the Sahara Desert, and be overcome with the roaring in my ears. I wrapped a bandana around my head, but it only intensified the sound."

"A fan once came up to me and said she wished she had my money. I said, 'I'd gladly give you my money if you'll take my tinnitus along with it.'"

"Did you go to an audiologist for treatment?"

"Yes, lots of them. They said it was psychosomatic, a symptom of the childhood mistreatment I went through. But if thirty years on the couch haven't cured it, that can't be true."

I promised myself I'd see if we could do anything about it.

March 6, 2015

"I was very jealous of the rich Jewish girls at school," she began. "You know, the ones who wore beautiful clothes and could buy anything they wanted. I had fantasies that I could live in their shoes. Sometimes when I've won another award, I wonder what happened to those girls, and am so happy that my fantasies didn't come true. I wouldn't be one of them now for anything in the world! I love being Barbra Streisand, although at the time, if you'd told me I would feel that way someday, I wouldn't have believed you.

"I used to lie awake at night, wondering why my father had to die. 'Why did you have to leave me, Papa?' I kept asking. 'Didn't you like me? Did I do anything wrong? We were two of a kind, and we could have been so happy together.'

"Every other girl I knew had a father. When a kid grows up missing one parent, there's always a huge gap that has to be filled in one way or another. It's like someone who is blind; they hear better. Helen Keller developed her innermost self to a point hitherto unknown in such individuals. As for me, I, like Keller, felt more, and I sensed more. I also wanted more than anyone else, and it left me open to life. I think I owe a lot of my talent to the fact that my father's death left a big hole in me that only acting could fill.

"An alien from Mars couldn't feel more different from the rest of the world than I did. And yet, somewhere inside, I always knew I was as special as my father. We were both brilliant in school, unlike my dumb mother, and like him, I could read people's minds and know if they were telling the truth."

"You seem to be very good at that."

"Even with *you*?"

"Even with me."

She said, "Aw!" and her face lit up with delight.

"Anyway, back to Kind. My mother's marriage to him didn't last very long," she continued. "They separated when I was in my early teens. He often stayed away from home for days at a time—I suspect he had a mistress—and when he did come home, he and Diana fought violently. He verbally tormented all three of us, calling Diana a dumb ox, ugly, a leech, and a nag, and then began to abuse her physically as well. He punched her so badly, she was often covered with bruises. She told the neighbors she had fallen down the steps. Do you think they believed her?

Come on! How many times can you fall down the same steps?"

"Do you think his vicious treatment of your mother influenced your relationships with men?" I asked.

"What kind of dumb question is that? Of course it influenced my relationships with men! I thought that's the way men are supposed to treat women. I probably wouldn't have stayed so long with Jon Peters otherwise. That's the main reason my present relationship with Jim is so good—he always treats me with kindness and respect, and would never raise a hand to me. It's a good thing, or he'd be out the door before he knew what was happening to him!

"There was only one good thing about Louis Kind—he had a television set. I used to sit in front of it for hours at a time, and fell in love with Milton Berle, Sophie Tucker, Bob Hope, Jackie Gleason, Lucille Ball and, most of all, Ed Sullivan, who presented the best singers and comedians of the era.

"I was sure I could be as good as they were and looked forward to the day I would join their ranks. I never had a moment's doubt that time would come. I'd stand in front of the bathroom mirror and imitate them perfectly. I tried smiling seductively while brushing my teeth, or I'd pretend to be smoking, with great sophistication, a cigarette in a long holder.

"I pictured myself in a gorgeous gown dancing under a dazzling chandelier, serenaded by Clark Gable and Marlon Brando. Sometimes my daydreams would even make me forget my miserable existence. I fell hard for Marlon, and thought he was the most gorgeous guy in the world. 'Life is beautiful in the movies,' I mused. That's how I was gonna live when I grew up. The clothes were stunning, the hairstyles exquisite (unlike mine, which my mother called 'three pieces of string'), and even the streets were beautiful—no clotheslines hanging from windows.

"Stunning men falling in love with beautiful women, like I would be some day. And oh, the kisses! For a girl who was never shown any affection, getting kissed like that was the height of my ambition. I used to dream I was Jean Simmons kissing Marlon Brando. 'I'll show 'em!' I thought. 'I'll get to be the biggest, greatest star in the world.' I had to be great. I couldn't just be a medium success. My nose was too big." She again put her finger on her famous nose. I wondered why she did that, and determined to ask her some time when it was appropriate.

March 1, 2015

"I spent a lot of time at the movies during my teenage years," she began. "I spent so much time in those dark theatres because I didn't want to go out in the light, where the world was cold and lonely and strange. Nobody could see me in the movies. They helped me to be hopeful."

"Hopeful about what, Barbra?"

"Hopeful that someday, in some way, I would be the one living the happy life, in a place where I truly belonged and could find love. I thought of myself as a misfit. I couldn't picture me ever having children or a husband or a home. I couldn't picture myself with any kind of normal life. So you can see how important the movies were to me. When I was a girl, I didn't even know I was going to an art house. But I came out of Erasmus Hall High School knowing I wanted to be an actress, so I wrote book reports on Stanislavsky." She laughed. I didn't.

"Next door to the high school was an art house," she continued, "and I would go there whenever I could escape my mother and school and watch art films. I remember being fascinated by Kurosawa's *Seven Samurai,* and the Greek movie, *Phaedra,* with Melina Mercouri. I was upset when she quit acting to go into politics. I remember thinking, 'How could she prefer being a senator to being a great actress?' Later, when I was asked to run for senator, I was flattered, but I stuck to my guns, and remained an actress.

"I always loved seeing good films. The images stuck in my head and comforted me when I was lonely. I hate seeing lousy films. They also remain indelibly in my head, and I don't need to have those images there. I have no compunctions about walking out on a film I don't like.

"I loved to go to the movies above all else. But even if I could scrape up enough money to go to a film on a Saturday afternoon, I rarely had enough money to ride the bus home. That didn't stop me, however. I would come up to a cop wearing my most forlorn face, and say, 'Sir, could you please tell me how far it is to walk from here to Nostrand and Newkirk Streets?' The policeman inevitably would be horrified that such a little girl needed to take such a long walk and asked me to wait until the next bus arrived. Then he would ask the driver to let me on the bus for free. It was great! I saved the ten-cent fare for the next movie.

"Mother charged in court that Kind abandoned us for weeks at a time, leaving his family with no income. When he did return, my mother told the judge, he flaunted his affairs with other women. He called my mother obscene names, threatened and battered her, and treated her cruelly and inhumanly. He alternately persecuted her, beat her up, and neglected her in his mean, harsh, freakish, inconsiderate, stingy, and vicious manner.

"Kind denied all of his wife's accusations and testified in return that Diana nagged him all the time, threw things at him, and hit him. He said she yelled so loud the neighbors complained. He didn't mention the shouting *he* did which terrified me so much that I hid my head under the blanket, sometimes for hours at a time.

"The judge granted my mother a decree of separation and ordered Kind to pay her alimony of thirty-seven dollars a week. It was a rare week that he paid it. My mother tried to sell undergarments and girdles in the laundry room to supplement what little income she had, but I don't remember her ever selling any.

"We had practically no money at all. In fact, we often didn't have enough to eat. I was hungry so often that it felt normal to me. When we got to the starvation point, my mother would make me sneak down the stairs to steal the bottles of milk left by the milkman outside the neighbors' doors.

"I can't talk about this anymore today," Barbra said, getting up to leave. "It makes me too sad."

I was relieved. I couldn't stand another minute of it, either.

March 11, 2015

"We've about run my stepfather through the wringer," she began. "But there is something about my mom that I don't understand. I think you probably won't either."

"Try me."

"Must I? God, I've kvetched about her so much I can rattle it off by rote. But I guess one more thing won't hurt. By the way, Doctor, you should know that thirty years is enough. This is my last stand. If it doesn't work with you, Dr. Freud and I are through!"

"Sounds fair to me."

"Okay. On to Mom... again. When Jason was a baby, I used to pick him up and nuzzle and kiss him for as long as he would let me. I liked nothing more than to have time off from work and to play with him. He has been the love of my life since the first moment he curled his little fingers around my thumb in the delivery room. I really love my son, and can't imagine abusing him psychologically or neglecting him. What I can't understand is how my mother could have been so disinterested in me from my babyhood on. I've never seen a baby I didn't want to cuddle."

"I don't believe she was always disinterested."

"What? Are you calling me a liar?" she said, standing up as if to leave.

"No, of course not. But I do have some new research that may interest you." Barbra sat down. "People tend to treat their babies the way they themselves were treated as children. I believe there was a time you do not remember, the time before your father died when they were both happy that you were born. It was probably when she was nursing you."

"Yeah, well I'm a bit old to go back to her breast."

I said, "It's tragic that your mother was so unavailable and abusive to you when you were growing up and really needed her, and I know that her neglect has caused you great misery all your life."

"You're not kiddin,' Bub."

"But perhaps we're being too hard on her. In my opinion, your love of your son is evidence that there was a time in your life when you did have a good, available mother, or you wouldn't be able to be so loving a mother yourself. Do you realize that the loss of your father devastated your mother to the point where she could think of nothing but her own pain? I am not excusing her, but she had nothing to give. Your mother is not alone in this. Traumatically bereaved parents are preoccupied with loss and frequently have trouble making themselves emotionally available to their infants. It is only in recent years, after the tragedy of 9/11, that researchers began investigating how to help the bereaved parent and child."

"You may have something there. But you couldn't expect a little baby to think of that, or to forgive her."

"Right. But you aren't an infant now. You are a grown woman, and knowing that meanness wasn't behind your mother's mistreatment of you and that she couldn't help herself may allow you to understand, if not forgive her. It can help put everything in its place."

"Yeah, well don't hold your breath," she said.

March 13, 2015

Barbra rushed in in a state of great excitement.

"You may be right about my mother, Doc," she all but shouted.

I restrained my impatience and waited.

"I had the greatest dream last night," she went on. "In the dream, I'm a baby. I'm sitting in a high chair next to a pretty young lady who looks how my mother might have looked when I was an infant. She has red hair and blue eyes like mine, and is wearing some kind of green apron embroidered with a teddy bear I don't remember ever having seen. Oh... Maybe Jason had one like that when he was little. In this dream, I reach out and take her hand. It is warm to the touch. I could really feel the warmth. She picks me up and holds me close. Usually I am freezing no matter how warm the room is, but when she holds me close, I feel warm all over. It feels very real," she says practically in tears.

"It *is* real," I say, feeling moved. "When something *feels* real in a dream, it's because it *is*. Your dream is a memory of your mother before your father died."

Barbra's eyes filled up as she said, "I guess I really did have an okay mother." She got up from the couch, came over to my chair, put her head on my lap, and cried.

March 18, 2015

Barbra came in the next session with a dazzling look on her face and said, "Doctor Dale, a miracle has occurred."

"What is that?"

"You know I told you how I always hear noises in my head. Well, in the days since having the dream about my mother, I've noticed the ringing in my head getting dimmer and dimmer. And today when I woke up, it was silent! I can actually hear myself think! What do you think made the racket disappear after so many years?"

"You said the quiet frightened you. In your mind, what is scary about silence?"

"When I think of quiet, I think of being alone. As long as it is noisy in my head, I don't have to feel abandoned. I can always believe I am surrounded by loving people. In my head, it's been like it was before my father died, when my mother and father loved each other and were happy. The noise sounds like a roomful of happy people all talking at once."

"Very good. The tinnitus is a psychosomatic memory about your mother. There was a time when you were a baby that you didn't feel alone at all, because you always had a loving mother with you. You didn't need any noise to feel together with her. Your dream brought back that warm, affectionate mother, and you no longer need to drown out the sounds of loneliness."

"Psychoanalysis is wonderful," she said, the tears running down her face. "And so are you."

"Thank you, Barbra. But you had the dream, and the courage to welcome the image back into your life of the warm, wonderful mother you once had. You don't need the racket anymore."

March 20, 2015

"Barbra," I began the next session, "your fabulous career is a very important part of your life, but you haven't talked about it much. I love hearing about your past, but I'm interested in your daily life too! Tell me something about it."

"Well, where to begin? I always had an extraordinary work ethic, and have supported myself since I was ten years old, when I worked as a cashier in a local Chinese restaurant. My grandmother used to call me *farbrent*, which means 'on fire.'"

"Barbra, all your childhood ambitions have come true. Does the reality of success measure up to your youthful dreams of glory?"

"Nah," she answered. "It doesn't even come close. You never really achieve your dreams, even if other people think you have, and that's depressing. To me, the excitement of life lies in striving for success rather than attaining it. For example, I used to think a mark of success would be when I could afford to have my own chauffeur, and I thought I would love it. But it turns out I can't stand the idea of someone waiting around for me in case I decide to go out somewhere. So I fired him and drive myself.

"I have a beautiful library at home that is full of wonderful books. But do I make time to read them? Nah! Instead of enjoying my success, I instantly set out to obtain more. And it's not hard to find things to do when you're a person like me who insists on doing everything herself. I have to design my own album covers, because nobody else does them right. On my TV shows, I oversee the lighting, the sound, and everything else, as well as being the producer. And who do you think writes my shows? Do you believe I could just recite someone else's words? Of course not. Being me, I have to write the shows, too.

"Nothing I do can be ordinary. Everything has to be a success. I'm taking Italian lessons and hope soon to start piano and ballet lessons."

"Barbra, you sound a little negative today. Is anything wrong?"

"Yeah. What's wrong is that I'm hungry. I don't do hunger very well. It makes my stomach ache. I was hungry too much as a kid. Now I can't even find time to eat. How about feeding me some food instead of words?"

"I wish I had something to give you... Why do you think you are so unhappy, Barbra?"

"How the fuck should I know? You're the doctor. You tell me!"

"All right, Barbra. I will. You've told me many times how negative your mother always was with you. If you performed well, and you asked her how you did, she would answer something like 'your arms are too skinny.'

"You have done what we in analysis call introjection; when you were little, you pasted into your own mind a little image of the bad mother who says derogatory things to you. This little figure in you takes over where your mother left off and continues her nasty abuse of you. Instead of recognizing the wonderful work you do and glorying in your incredible success, you listen to the introjected voice of your mother telling you how inadequate you are.

"Never mind the reality. Little children believe that mother knows best. And in your own mind today, you still believe that. If she said you are incompetent, that's what you accept as the truth, although there isn't another person in the world who would agree with her."

"So how do I get rid of her?"

"We will examine each comment she made and decide with your grown-up mind how correct she was. For example, are your arms really too thin?"

"Of course not. I'm known to have a beautiful figure."

"Good. We can cross that one off your mother's list of malicious cracks. As your analysis proceeds, you will remember nicer things about her, and these memories will reassert themselves and gradually replace the bad introjection. Also, I hope your experience with me will give you a more favorable introjection to tell you the truth about yourself."

"I only wish. When is all this going to happen?"

"It has started already. Somewhere deep inside your, you know how much I think of you, and you have told me many times that it has comforted you. If it didn't, you wouldn't continue to come here."

"You may have something there. But couldn't you please rush it up a little, so I can stop hurting?" she asked.

"How do you feel this minute?"

She thought for a moment and then said with surprise, "Funny, I feel a little better!" She paused. "Can I bring your magic wand with me and take it out whenever I feel depressed?"

"Exactly! That's the way it works. The good analyst/mother will always be available inside of you if you listen for her voice."

I smiled. She smiled back, and she went on with the story of her adolescent yearnings.

"I wanted to be a star as long as I can remember. I was never contented, always unhappy, always trying to be something I wasn't. One big reason I wanted to be a star was that being a movie actress makes you a little bit immortal. As much as anything, it ensures that you will be remembered. Life is so short. It hangs by a thread. Maybe I won't be around after today. Like my father, I may be here today, gone tomorrow."

March 23, 2015

"I hate to admit it," she began, "but you were right about my mother. Every once in a while, she did something really nice. For my fourteenth birthday, she bought tickets for the last row of the balcony for me and my friend, Anita Sussman, for $1.89 apiece to see a Broadway matinee of *The Diary of Anne Frank*. The leading role was played by Susan Strasberg, the seventeen-year-old daughter of Lee Strasberg, the famous head of the Actors Studio. Although she wasn't bad, I knew in my heart that I could have played the part better.

"Although the dreary setting of the play depressed me (it was too much like where I lived), Anita and I both loved the show, and cried when it was over.

"Come to think of it, why couldn't I have had a father like Lee Strasberg?" Barbra demanded to know. "Then it might have been me up there on Broadway instead of Susan Strasberg."

Unfortunately, my telephone picked this moment to ring. I usually don't answer during sessions, but I was expecting an important phone call from my son about the birth of my grandchild, and I made an exception, excused myself, and listened to the good news.

"Sorry, Barbra," I said. "But it was a call I had to take. I hope it's okay with you."

"No!" she shouted. "It is *not* okay with me! You insult me when, during a session I'm paying blood money for, you indicate that someone else is more important to you." She paused and then said, "In fact I am going on strike. Next session I'm going to paint a sign that says. 'We won't take this lying down,' and march with it all day in front of your office."

I hoped she was kidding.

March 25, 2015

She began her next session without mentioning my so-called insult of her a few days before, but continued with the story of her career.

"People always think I was a big success as a singer right away," she continued. "But that's not the way life is. I have to tell you about my first tryout, which broke my teenaged heart. I was a freshman at Erasmus High auditioning for the Erasmus Glee Club, a talented group of singers who put on Christmas and Easter concerts every year. I didn't tell anyone, but I had a special reason for wanting to become a member. The director was a dark, handsome Italian man named Cosimo DePietto. I had a fantasy that he would be so carried away by my magnificent voice that he would fall madly in love with me, make me his special protégée, and help me become a world famous singer."

"He would replace your missing father."

"Right, though I never thought of that then. But it wasn't to be. I am very good at reading people's emotions. When I finished singing *I Wish You a Merry Christmas*, I looked at him and saw that he was completely unimpressed. A few days later, he confirmed what I had known instinctively and told me I had flunked the audition. The official reason he gave was that I couldn't read music. Years later, I found out he had told a teacher that he didn't think I had any talent. Nobody is going to turn me down without a fight, so a few months later, I tried out again. And again I was rejected.

"Furious by this time, I came up with a terrific idea. I made my mother take me to a studio where they cut a record of my singing. I sang *One Kiss*, a song made famous by Jeanette MacDonald, whom I adored. Then I auditioned a third time for DePietto by giving him the record. This time I made the Glee Club.

"Whether he decided I had talent after all, or just was sick and tired of auditioning me, I'll never know. But I had made it and became a proud member of the Erasmus Glee Club. But I still don't think he was all that impressed with me, because he had me stand at the end of the back row of singers, where I was almost hidden by the curtain.

"I got even with him, though. After a few months, I quit. No talent Barbra! Me, who later was called the most talented person in Hollywood! I hope to God DePietto was aware of how famous I became and what an asshole he was! It would have served him right.

"But do you know, at night sometimes when I can't fall asleep, it still hurts when I think of his rejection. The summer I was fifteen, I badgered my mother to give me money to pay for an apprenticeship at the Malden Bridge Playhouse, near Albany, New York. I didn't know it, but I actually had a hundred and fifty dollars my grandfather had left me. My mother wanted to use the money to pay for a dentist. I'd had to have two baby teeth pulled when they became infected, which left two gaping holes in the sides of my mouth. I said, 'I don't need the teeth fixed, Mom. I can fill the holes with Aspergum, which is the same color.'

"I nagged the poor woman so much that, to get me off her neck, she finally let me apply for the apprenticeship. I lied about my age—you had to be seventeen to get in. It was a turning point in my life.

"I played a Japanese girl in *Teahouse of the August Moon*, a teenaged tomboy in *Picnic*, and a sexy secretary in *The Desk Set*. Guess which part I liked best? It was the sexy secretary. At last, I had found a place where I belonged. I was in heaven the whole summer.

"I must say that my feelings of belonging were not reciprocated by a few of my colleagues. Once, when I was in the toilet stall, I overheard two of them talking about me. 'Did you see that?' one of them asked her friend. 'That Barbra shoved right past me in line to get into the stall! Nobody likes her. She's overbearing to the point of rudeness!' I laughed. I was sure the girl was jealous of me because I was a much better actress and had received a great notice from the local newspaper, which said, 'The girl playing the office vamp is very sexy.'"

"What? Me sexy? Were they crazy? I was only fifteen years old! At the time, I was much less interested in sex than in becoming a star. I was someone who skipped adolescence altogether."

"That's very insightful of you, Barbra. Most people with that kind of development would not be aware of it."

Looking pleased, she continued, "I thought about what the girls had said, and thought maybe they had a point. Nobody had ever taught me good manners. We never ate meals together at my house or had conversations like normal people. The extent of our mealtime talk was 'Pass the salt.' I don't think I ever heard anyone in my family say 'please' or 'thank you.' I ate standing up, right from the pot on the stove. Sometimes, I gobbled my food with my feet up on the table."

March 26, 2015

"When I got home from summer stock, I talked my mother into letting me take the subway into Manhattan several nights a week and on weekends so I could work as an (unpaid) apprentice at the Cherry Lane Theatre in Greenwich Village. When I wasn't sweeping the stage or helping actors learn their lines, I was a gofer who brought in food for the cast from the local stores. I didn't care how menial the tasks assigned me were. After all, wasn't I working in the theatre?

"Then something happened that changed my life forever. Anita Miller, the actress who played the part of Avril in Sean O'Casey's play, *Purple Dust*, took a liking to me. Her husband just happened to be Allan Miller, the famous acting teacher. Anita raved to Allan about me, saying, 'You've just got to see this girl, Allan! She's a little weird, but there is something about her I've never seen in anybody. She is—I don't know how to explain it—unique. When she's on the stage, you can't take your eyes off her. I think you should give her a scholarship to your school.'

"He answered, 'Are you nuts, Anita? I'm not going to encourage a fifteen-year-old high school junior to go into the theatre. It's tough enough for older actors!'

"Because Allan wouldn't take me into his classes, Anita encouraged me to try out for the Actors Studio. I had to lie again, since the Studio accepted no one under eighteen. Since I'm a pretty good liar, nobody questioned my age. It was my acting skills they questioned. Although I gave what I thought was a terrific performance in a scene from N. Richard Nash's *The Young and Fair*, I was rejected. I bawled my eyes out. I thought, 'Here I am at the advanced age of fifteen and getting nowhere.'

"Determined to help me get somewhere in the theatre, Anita now wouldn't take no for an answer from her husband, and brought me home to dinner. We had prepared another scene to show poor Allan, who was a prisoner in his own house, and had no recourse but to watch me perform. I guess I wasn't so hot.

"Allan said later it was the most embarrassingly bad acting he had ever seen. 'That creature couldn't act her way out of a paper bag.' he said. 'Her arms and legs are all over the place, and she looks absolutely disjointed. She looks like a wasp.' But, like his wife, he was impressed with my vitality, my rawness, my ferocity, and my determination, and offered me a place in his acting school. I grinned. I knew it all the time.

I was on my way to becoming a great actress!

"His acceptance encouraged me to change my reading habits from *Nancy Drew* mysteries to biographies of Sarah Berrnhardt, Eleanore Duse, and all the important actresses I could find in the Public Library at 42nd Street, and the great plays by Shakespeare, Chekhov, and Sophocles. And because I secretly believed that singing would be my route to the Broadway stage, I also listened for hours to recordings of the great singers of the day, like Ella Fitzgerald, Sarah Vaughn, and Billie Holiday. I wanted to learn all I could about phrasing and vocal techniques."

"Did you ever take singing lessons?" I asked.

"God, no! I sing the way I talk. It just comes out. I hold a note as long as I want to. I hear it in my head. When I imagine it, I do it. If you have no imagination, how can you do anything worthwhile? I became famous because I trust my instincts. I also read about the physiology of singing. And I have a lot of self-doubt. I think it's necessary to feel some self-doubt in order to become a successful entertainer. You have to have some, because it motivates you to do better all the time.

"As a teenager, I was very ambitious and dreamed of acting the roles of Medea, Juliet, and Hamlet someday. After all, I thought, if Sarah Bernhardt could play Hamlet, so could I. I guess my self-confidence balanced out my self-doubt, huh? I guess I'm still a little bit in love with Sarah.

"One of my most treasured possessions is a bust of Sarah Bernhardt, sculpted by the great lady herself. And on the wall of my study across from a work of Klimt and a small portrait by Tamara de Lempicka are three huge Mucha theatre posters of Parisian productions starring Bernhardt. They are the only posters I ever bought, because those three roles are the ones I've always yearned the most to play," she said. "Camille, Hamlet and, especially, Medea.

"I did Medea when I was fifteen in acting class in New York, and I still think it was my best work. I'll always remember one of her lines: 'I have this hole in the middle of myself,' just like me," she mused. "But it seems the older and more successful I am, the lazier I become, and I've never returned to the theatre.

"That's why I love being in the movies," she said. "I can be seen performing all over the world while I'm actually at home taking a bath. Sometimes I still daydream about playing the great classics. But I'm just too unwilling to exert myself. It will have to wait until my next lifetime.

March 21, 2015

"After weeks of scut work, Allan finally offered me a part in his class. It was a scene from Tennessee Williams' play, *The Rose Tattoo.* I read it and thought, 'I can't possibly play this role.' It was a hot sexy scene in which a teenager tries to seduce her boyfriend, who has promised his mother he wouldn't take advantage of her. I thought, 'I am a virgin. What do I know about sex?' So I called Allan and told him I couldn't play the part.

"He said, 'Don't be silly. Of course you can play the part. Just try to find a way to do it by acting like it has nothing to do with sex.'

"'That's interesting,' I told him. I remember thinking, 'I believe I can do that.' I rehearsed it all week, and at the performance in front of the class, I shocked the boy I was playing the scene with by jumping on his feet, tickling him, poking him, and even climbing on his back. I aimed to touch every part of his body with one of mine. I guess it was good. The class cheered us when it was over. Allan told Anita, 'It was awkward and sad, but also a touching portrait of pent-up adolescent sexuality.'

"I don't know whether the scene in 'The Rose Tattoo' awakened my sexuality or if it was just a coincidence," she began, "but my first sexual experience was not far behind. Roy Scott, another of Allan's students, was entranced with me. I was thrilled, for no other boy had ever shown an interest except to laugh at me. Not only that, but he was an 'old man' of twenty-three who was devilishly handsome, and all the girls in the class were in love with him. He said he was fascinated with my quirkiness, my blue, blue eyes, and my flaming red fingernails.

"Used to the blond cheerleader type of girl, he whispered in my ear while we were doing the scene, 'In your own way, you are quite wondrous.' I thought it was part of the play. But when he continued to say such exciting things to me, I began to believe it. What girl would want any more? It didn't take much for me to lose my virginity to him.

"But to my surprise, the experience turned out to be a big flop. When we finished, or I should say when he finished, I thought, 'Is that all there is? Why do people make so much fuss about sex? I'd rather eat coffee ice cream.' Nevertheless, I enjoyed his company and began to sleep over in his room in a nearby residential actors' home, telling my mother I was babysitting.

"Now that I think about it, I have a different opinion about having had sex with him. Because of my indifference to it, and him, it took me years to get over my lack of interest in sex. It wasn't until I fell in love with Elliot Gould that I began to enjoy it because we had so much fun. Girls of today want to lose their virginity as soon as possible. I think that is a big mistake. I think they should wait until they fall in love, and not have sex because everybody else is doing it.

"My mother regularly called the Millers and screamed at them for 'corrupting my sixteen-year old daughter.' When she learned that I was sleeping with Scott, she blew her stack and threatened to call the police if I didn't come home. I knew she meant it, so I thought I'd better go back to Brooklyn…for a while, anyway."

"Did you ever go back to Scott?"

"No. I found somebody I liked better."

"Tell me about him next session."

"Are you kidding? You're making me leave just when things are starting to get juicy."

"Sorry about that, Barbra. I have another patient waiting."

"Some friend you are!" she said, getting up and pretending to stomp out of the room.

April 1, 2015

Barbra came into the office and, as if she were directing a movie, instinctively picked up where she had left off.

"I have to describe a scene I played which I still think was great. In one of my acting classes, we were asked to portray an inanimate object. Most people chose a children's toy like a doll, but since when am I like most people? I picked a chocolate chip cookie. I was kneaded into a sticky batter and stuck into an oven, where I got all swollen and began to burn. When someone took me out of the oven, the air melted my outer layer but left my insides mushy. When a person began to eat me, my head dropped lower and lower, until I disappeared into the ground.

"When I finished, the whole class clapped loudly, which they never did for any other student. My roommate and classmate, Marilyn Fried, saw the improvisation and said, 'Barbra, you are going to be a great actress.' I answered, 'Don't I know it!'"

I was impressed. "That sounds highly original, Barbra. I imagine most actors wouldn't have the nerve to think that, let alone to say it. "

She grinned and said, "*Chutzpah* is not a trait I lack! I said it then and I'll say it again, 'Don't I know it!'"

We both burst out laughing. She may have suffered at one point from poor self-esteem, but by this point she certainly didn't lack for confidence in her abilities. I guess that's the way it is with all great talents. It reminds me of a story I heard about Ethel Merman. Somebody once asked her if she ever got nervous before a performance. "No," she answered. "If I didn't know I could do it better than anyone else, I wouldn't be up there making a fool out of myself."

"I'm getting the impression that you have trouble trusting anyone other than yourself."

"It's true, and I include even you. I am the only person I know who always has the right answers about myself."

"Why don't you trust me?" I asked.

"My mother always gave me rotten advice, so I guess everybody is like her. I can't remember a single instance where I didn't know something better than my mom. Everything she told me about myself turned out to be bullshit. For instance, she wanted me to learn to be a typist. She said that was the only way I would ever be able to support myself.

"If I had listened to her, I'd have spent my life sitting behind a desk somewhere banging away on a typewriter... or a computer keyboard these days. Nobody ever would have heard of Barbra Streisand, the actress, producer, director, writer, singer, and editor. There'd be no awards, no works of art from me, and no millions in the bank. "

"Do you think I'm like your mother, Barbra?"

She thought for a moment and then shook her head and said, "No, not at all."

"Then perhaps you can check me out and see that I'm not your mother and that maybe I do know a thing or two."

She laughed and said, "You may be right, but don't count on it. If you are right and I am wrong, it will be the first time in my life." She laughed again and said, "Well, I'll see what I can do. There's always a first time."

April 3, 2015

"I want to start today by telling you about my next lover." She swallowed and hesitated.

"Yes?" I said.

"It's still hard to talk about him. First of all, he was such a tremendous influence in my life, I may owe my career to him as much as to anyone else. And secondly, he rejected me. And you know I don't get over rejection easily. But I'll get to that later.

"I first met Barry Dennen face to face on stage at the Jan Hus Theatre on East Seventy-fourth Street, where a group of us raggedy youngsters put together our first and last show, Karel and Josef Capek's *The Insect Comedy*, billed as 'a parable of the human condition.' I think it would have been better named 'a nightmare of the theatrical condition.' I was cast in three roles–in my first big play, keep in mind–one of two main butterflies in Act One, a messenger in the third act, and the second moth in the epilogue. I also swept the stage between acts.

"Barry was a handsome twenty-two-year old from a very wealthy Los Angeles family. I was as impressed by his background as any kid brought up on the lower east side would be. Like me, he was obsessed with the theatre, but unlike me he had plenty of money to indulge his obsession. Every shelf in his Ninth Street Greenwich Village apartment sagged under the weight of thousands of vintage records he had collected. They consisted of all the great singers of the day: Al Jolson, Edith Piaf, Ethel Waters, Fanny Brice, and Ruth Etting. My hungry sixteen-year-old eyes nearly popped out of their sockets when he showed me all the old Bette Davis and Mae West movies he had recorded.

"To my great surprise, he was as captivated with me as I was with him. He thought *The Insect Comedy* was a dreadful production, tacky and amateurish. But he found my acting 'unspeakably funny,' as I clumsily chased after a boy butterfly, improvising, 'Oh, you great big strong handsome thing!' while fluttering my transparent wings with wire antennae flopping over my eyes.

"The play, if you can call it that, closed in three nights. But the critic Frank Ashton gave me my first review when he mentioned that I was one of the inhabitants of 'Butterflyland,' where the girls try to attract men, but don't get anywhere because they all are killed off too soon. Although it was no rave review, I was thrilled to be mentioned. 'Me, the mieskeit, in a Manhattan newspaper!' I raved. 'Wait until the girls at Erasmus High read that!'

"After the show shut down, my friendship with Barry blossomed. We started to date, talking late into the night at a nearby coffee shop, then watching late shows in his eleventh-floor apartment, which was cluttered with unique objects like peacock feathers, antiques, Tiffany lamps, and exotic candles.

"Soon, we were together practically all the time. I loved that I had found a man from whom I could learn, and asked him countless questions about the theatre, literature, and art. He loved that I hung on to his every word. He knew something about everything, and I felt that talking with him made up for the college education I lacked."

April 13, 2015

"Well, back to my so-called career. I trudged around Broadway on a series of humiliating visits to producers' offices, all of whom rejected me. I shook my fist at the snotty secretaries and threatened them with, 'Someday you'll be sorry. You'll plead with me to work for you and I'll say, 'Fugoff! Where were you when *I* needed *you*?'

"I found one way of meeting my needs: I took to shoplifting. But not like other adolescents steal. I never do anything like anybody else. I walked around a department store and checked all the floors and wastebaskets until I found a discarded receipt. I would look around the store for the items listed on the receipt, take them to the register, and ask to return them for a refund. It was an easy few bucks.

"Often I would sneak books into my backpack. I rationalized that books should be free; you shouldn't have to steal them. I especially loved stealing salt shakers. I love them, and have quite a collection. I have to add that these days I pay for them.

"I stole candy, gum, jujubes, Babe Ruths, and cookies—whatever I could slide into my pockets. It was great fun to steal. Things seemed of much greater value than if I paid for them. It was not just the package of gum that I stole, but also the wrapper, the joke inside, the colors, and the printing, to say nothing of the joy of pulling the wool over the eyes of the managers. Boy, oh boy! Those were the days! But unfortunately, I decided I had to quit. Success is nice in lots of ways, but there's something I dislike about it. People recognize me all the time. It makes it hard to steal. Can you imagine the uproar it would cause if the headlines shrieked, 'Multi-millionaire Barbra Streisand caught shop lifting!'

"Why do you think you stole?" I asked. "Surely there was a reason other than that it was fun."

"I can't think of any. What do you think?"

"I think you were a deprived child who felt you deserved better in life. If you couldn't get what you felt entitled to, you would get it any way you could, even if it meant stealing. And remember, your mother told you to steal milk from the neighbors, when there wasn't money to buy any. If your mother said it was OK to steal, then your conscience didn't have to bother you about it."

"You're right about that. It still doesn't bother me that I stole. I was hungry, and not about to live with my hunger.

"But just when I was eating a dinner of crackers and soup made from ketchup and hot water in Horn and Hardardts, a miracle of miracles happened. My new agent Marty Erlichman managed to get me a club date at the Blue Angel. Opening night went great, and I got a standing ovation. I thought, 'Oh boy! I can eat real food for a while.' On the second night, my mother came to see the show. I was wearing a white lace bed jacket from 1890, with pink satin shoes I had found at the bottom of a barrel at the Salvation Army thrift shop. I thought I looked terrific and said to my mother, 'Don't you think I looked beautiful?'"

"She answered, 'You looked like you were singing in your nightgown.' Oh, my mama!"

April 15, 2015

"But more significant than the club date was something that happened earlier in the day that changed the course of my life forever. I tried out for a role in a new musical called *I Can Get It For You Wholesale*. The play was about a crooked character named Harry Bogen, who battles his way up the Garment District ladder.

"Jerome Weidman, who wrote the play and the book the play it was based on, was sitting in the audience when I was auditioning. I hate auditions, by the way. They should *know* I'm good without my having to try out! Anyway, also sitting there was the composer, Harold Rome, and the director, Arthur Laurents, who was directing his first play. I stumbled onto the stage in my Persian lamb coat, which I had bought at a thrift shop for ten dollars.

"Someone said it looked like the hide of a neglected horse. I also wore dirty white sneakers, and my hair was dirty. (I never expected to get the part, so I didn't bother washing.) I took my red plastic briefcase I had just bought at Woolworth's and hurled it at the startled pianist. Because I had stapled the pages to each other beforehand, they unfurled like a fan. The people in the audience guffawed, as I had known they would.

"They said to come back that afternoon and audition again for David Merrick, the producer. I did, but he wasn't as impressed as the others, and decided he didn't want me in his show. According to a note I saw years later, he wrote, 'Very talented! But who needs another Jewish broad?' He said I was too ugly and he liked only beautiful girls. Sounded just like my stepfather," she added, "and Merrick didn't buy me any popsicles either." She placed her finger upon her nose.

"How upset were you when the important producer called you ugly?"

"Not at all. Why do you ask?"

"I've noticed that you frequently put your finger or your hand on your nose when you talk about being beautiful. Why do you do that?"

"I do it because if I call attention to my deficiencies first, so people won't bother to mention them."

"Do you think I am going to call you ugly?"

"No, I don't think so," she said with surprise. "I guess I can drop that gesture around here!"

"Good for you," I said. And that was the end of her characteristic movement, at least in my office.

"Notwithstanding Merrick's decision, Laurents and Rome insisted that I play the role of Miss Marmelstein, the frustrated spinster of a secretary—the role you said you saw me in—and eventually they talked Merrick into hiring me."

"A real rite of passage."

"Huh? Yeah. So I ran around the stage yelling, 'Will someone please call me? I just got my first telephone installed and nobody has ever called me on it. *Please* phone or I'll have to have my mother call me.'"

This woman is hilarious, I thought. *I can see why she got the part.*

"That night, to my amazement," Barbra continued, "the phone did ring. It was Elliot Gould, the play's goofy looking star. He said, 'You said you wanted somebody to call you, so I'm calling,' and hung up before I could catch my breath.

"The big shots must have liked me a lot, because they went right to work expanding my role. They gave me the lead in three songs, along with my solo, 'Miss Marmelstein.'

"At the first rehearsal, while all the other actors were ostentatiously listening to the director and taking notes, I was writing my bio for the show's Playbill. I thought I knew what they would say, so why should I waste time? I began with 'I was born in Madagascar and raised in Rangoon.' When the producers objected to my taking license with the truth, I said, 'Look, nobody is gonna be interested in a person born in Brooklyn. Everybody's so sick and tired of Brooklyn they could plotz. Not that I don't love it, but I've spent nineteen years living there. Enough is enough, don't you think?' They left it in.

"I don't mind telling you that I gave them trouble from the beginning. They wanted me to sing my solo standing up, but I wanted to sing it sitting in Miss Marmelstein's chair on wheels, in which I could careen around on casters from one end of the stage to the other. I never listened to my mother, and I always turned out to be right. Otherwise, I'd be a real Miss Marmelstein behind a typewriter. So why *should* I listen to them?

"The director and I locked horns and neither of us would give in. 'I *wanna* do it my way,' I insisted. '*Why* can't I sit in the chair? Isn't that what secretaries do all day long? Sit in a chair?' I thought I'd show him, so I gave a standing-up performance of the song. It was rotten. 'You did that on purpose!' he scolded me. 'You were lousy on purpose!'" She smiled. "'Now, would I do a thing like that?'"

"So, even though our affair was long over by then, I turned to the one person whose opinion I trusted—Barry Dennen. I told him about the situation. He said, 'Stick to your guns, Barbra. You know better than anyone else how you should play the role.' He also advised me to have a stagehand shove me from the wings onto the stage so that I entered the play sliding across the floor. In the Philadelphia tryout, I risked losing the role. I disobeyed Laurents' instructions and slid across the stage in the chair. The audience went wild. They stomped and applauded for five minutes. The director grudgingly admitted I was right. 'Keep your goddamned chair,' he said."

"You were very courageous, Barbra," I said.

"Or foolhardy," she countered.

April 20, 2015

"During our tryouts in Philadelphia, Merrick wanted to fire Elliot, who he said was a lousy actor and as odd- looking as I was. Also, Elliot sweated so much that he had to be toweled off by the crew every chance they got. He shook off so much sweat that the people in the front row needed umbrellas. Merrick even auditioned other actors for the part, but, as with me, Laurents, Weidman, and Rome insisted that Elliot stay in the show.

"He and I had a lot else in common. We both were Jewish and came from working class people in Brooklyn. His whole family was shoveled into a two-room apartment, and he slept in his parents' bedroom until he was twelve. He told me some great stories about their bedroom activities. He said, 'I would pretend to be asleep while actually enjoying listening to their shenanigans. I learned all I needed to know about sex by the time I was five years old.' At least I slept with my mother and was spared Elliot's sexual education."

"You may have been lucky," I said. "A lot of harm can be caused by kids seeing their parents having sex. It is called 'The Primal Scene.'"

"Primal shmimal," she answered. "It would have been more interesting than listening to my mother snore."

In spite of myself, I had to laugh.

"Elliot and I met face to face for the first time the day rehearsals began for *I Can Get It for You Wholesale*. He was a strange-looking guy of six-foot-three who weighed 206 pounds—he looked like a huge teddy bear. And inch for inch, his nose was a good match for mine.

"Elliot told me later that I looked like a complete weirdo when I walked on stage, in my thirty-five cent shoes dug out from the bottom of a Salvation Army barrel, my torn black hose, a weird *tchotchke* shaped like a snake around my neck, and my hair plastered into an oversized bun molded like a cheese Danish. He nonchalantly handed me a cigar, and we shared the smoke.

"Elliot soon was walking me to the subway every night, stopping along the way to indulge our mutual love for horror movies, playing Pokerino, checkers, chess, and Monopoly in the arcades, and gobbling up coffee ice cream cones. After I finished mine, I ate his, too. He didn't object. He really was a kook, stopping total strangers on the street to tell them a joke, or suddenly breaking out into a ribald song. One time, when he was singing 'Climb upon my knee, Sonny boy,' I put out a hat and collected money from passersby. I liked him because he wasn't normal. Like me.

"One winter around two A.M., we were wandering around the Rockefeller Center skating rink when he started chasing me with a snowball. He grabbed me and we began a spirited snowball fight. Being bigger and stronger than me, he won, and grabbed me and washed my face with snow. Then he very tenderly kissed me on the lips.

"He had never before held me or anything like that, but when he rubbed my face with snow and kissed me very lightly, I found myself feeling something I hadn't felt for anyone since Barry Dennen.

"It seems that despite his having dated several chorus girls in the show, Elliot was a virgin. He thought I was one, too. I wasn't about to enlighten him. One night shortly after our snowball fight, we went to the Bellevue Stratford Hotel to consummate our relationship. His virginity didn't hold him back much.

"We made so much noise in our love-making that fellow cast members complained that the sound of our headboard banging against the wall kept them awake for hours. Once, when I was completely nude, Elliot, as a joke, pushed me out of the room, locked the door, and wouldn't let me back inside. I banged on our door until every other door in the hallway opened with people yelling 'Quiet out there. Don't you guys ever sleep?'"

"You stood out there *naked*?" I asked with widened eyes.

"Sure. What else could I do? Go down to the lobby?"

"You have a point there," I answered.

"Speaking of nudity, I've changed a lot in how I think about it. In my early days, I was, if you can believe it, a bit of a prude. Although I was a Brooklynite and sometimes had a dirty mouth, underneath I was really very straight-laced and conventional, like a good Jewish girl should be. I didn't smoke, drink, or use drugs. I even found it immoral for a woman to dance with a man who wasn't her husband. I almost died from embarrassment when somebody told me that the actors take off all their clothes in *Hair*. I said, 'You mean they *actually* show their *you-know-whats* to the audience?'"

We both laughed.

"Elliot and I were like two crazy kids together," she continued. "He assuaged the pain of Barry's rejection. We were very natural with each other, and did not have to put on airs. I never had to try to impress him, as I did Barry. We were both from Brooklyn and Jewish, and had the same oddball sense of humor. With him, I had the fun I never was able to have as a kid. We would throw food at each other in restaurants and chase each other around hotel hallways.

"He was the best friend I always wanted and never had. He protected me and made me feel small and feminine. It was the two of us against the world. I even felt pretty when he stared at me with those huge, velvety-brown eyes. I loved to watch him pull his big mitts through his thick curly brown hair. One day I woke up with the thought, 'I'm in love. We are Romeo and Juliet.' He gave me something I'd never had before—a normal, natural love."

Barbra and her first husband, actor Elliott Gould, when they were still happy together.

April 24, 2015

"Also for the first time in my life, I had my own apartment. It was in a building on Third Avenue over Oscar's, a fish restaurant. I didn't mind the smell, because my father had lived over a fish store and I enjoyed being like him. Also, it was the only apartment I could afford. The rent was pretty cheap—sixty-two dollars a month—probably because of its location. You gotta make choices in this life, don'tcha?"

I nodded.

"I lived with the smell of fish," she continued, "so I could afford to buy clothes, and furniture, and have a telephone. I tried to cover up the smell with scented candles and Chinese incense, but Elliot gagged on it and ran up the stairs holding his nose. He soon got over that, and for the duration of the play, we holed up together in that tiny flat, which was cluttered with thrift shop bargains I'd piled up, like tarnished old shoe buckles and discolored pharmacy jars.

"I still love bargains, and search them out all the time. If it's cheap, I'll buy it, whether I need it or not."

I smiled, remembering how she had tried to bring down the cost of her analytic sessions.

"The bathtub was in the kitchen," she continued, "and we kept a sheet of plywood over it to serve as a kitchen table. When we wanted to take a bath, we had to take off the dirty dishes piled on it and fill the tub from kettles of boiling water. If it limited the number of baths we took, nobody complained.

"Our meals usually consisted of frozen TV dinners—my favorite was fried chicken. Sometimes my mother brought us chicken soup, which kept us going for a week. Like twins, we made up a special language called 'Hangi,' so nobody could listen in on our intimate conversations.

"In a ceremony in which we exchanged drops of blood, we solemnly promised never to be apart on our birthdays. Our only window looked out onto a black wall. I didn't mind; I prefer night to day, and in our apartment, it was night at all hours. The floor sloped so badly that we had fun rolling a marble from one side of the apartment to the opposite wall. I hung up empty picture frames and told people it was because I couldn't afford to buy anything to put in them. A toilet seat hung next to the empty frames.

"We didn't have a bed, but slept curled up around each other on a cot. Oh, to be young again! We thought up special presents for each other. He gave me a blue marble egg I still cherish, and I bought him a gold cup that I had inscribed, 'First Annual Alexander the Great Award.' He was a lover of the great Greek conqueror.

"Unfortunately, we were often awakened at night by scratching and squealing. I remember one night when I jumped up on top of my second-hand Singer sewing machine and shrieked, 'A yard-long tail is sticking out from under the tub!' It was a rat. He was a very smart rat, too. He always managed to eat the cheese we put out for him without springing the trap.

"We were unable to get rid of him, even though we called in firemen, so we decided to just live with him. After all, he didn't take up much room. We named him Oscar in honor of the restaurant of the same name beneath us. He was there as long as we were. He's probably still there.

"We lived together through the run of the show. I can't say I was happy, but it was the closest I'd ever come to it."

April 27, 2015

"*I Can Get It for You Wholesale* opened on the blustery night of March 22, 1962 at the Schubert Theatre. The songs used traditional Jewish harmonies that are right up my alley. Although I have never been a fully practicing Jew, I've always felt very Jewish. With a nose like mine, how could I feel otherwise?

"I'm a Jewess to my core, although I'm irreligious. I'm a good person, which feels very Jewish to me. I don't think there is enough support for Jewish artists and Jewish culture, so I try to support them. But I don't go to shul on the Sabbath. I'm not a born-again Jew."

"You feel loyal to Judaism?"

"Yeah. I'm proud to be a Jew. I always feel holy when I light the Shabbos candles, even if I forget to do it some Friday nights.

"Anyway, back to the show. Except for me, the reviews were not so hot. In fact, the *Times* said that except for my scenes, the show was as quiet as Seventh Avenue on Yom Kippur.

"Poor Elliot was especially criticized for being unappealing and uninteresting. I felt very bad for him, because I got incredible reviews. They said I was nothing less than a triumph. The great Leonard Bernstein, who was sitting in the first row at one performance, stood up and applauded loudly.

"Following his lead, the entire audience rose to its feet for a prolonged ovation. Every review said I was the show's saving grace. The one that pleased me the most said that Erasmus High School should call a half-day holiday to celebrate my success. Ha, Erasmus High! I always said they'd be sorry someday for the way they treated me! I'm only happy I never believed them."

"I have to say that you're right, Barbra. Most people would have been so thoroughly discouraged by that kind of treatment that they would have given up."

"Most people didn't have my mother to toughen them up. I think I'll thank her for trying to strangle my career. Would you believe she left the show still saying, 'I think you'd be better off being a real typist. Then you would be sure to make a living.' *Oy vey*!"

"One of the nicest incidents concerning *I Can Get It for You Wholesale* happened fifty years after it opened. A tall, handsome young man named Mark Flicker waited backstage for me. 'I'm delighted to meet you, Ms. Streisand,' he said. 'I have something I've been wanting to tell you for years. When I was a little boy of seven, my parents took me to my first Broadway show, *I Can Get It for You Wholesale*. I was absolutely fascinated by you. I thought you were hilarious as Miss Marmelstein and the most wonderful person I had ever seen. Nobody existed on the stage but you. In fact, you changed my life. I have been a devoted theatregoer ever since. And I wouldn't miss anything you're in for all the tea in China.'

"I took his hand, folded it into mine, looked directly into his honest brown eyes, and thanked him warmly. I even considered having an affair with him, but decided against it. And poor Mark is gone and lost forever.

"Of course Elliot and I had our bad moments. I would always tell him if I thought his performance wasn't up to par. He is very sensitive and I hurt his feelings. But you know me and I always tell the truth. We made love a lot, but we fought all the time, too. We argued in restaurants, screaming at each other so loudly in taxi cabs that one driver threw us out. 'I don't have to listen to this crap,' he said. I locked Elliot out of the apartment at least five times, and once I stormed out in a rainstorm, only to come back dripping wet and fall into Elliot's waiting arms.

"Elliot thought I didn't know how to feel love. He told me, 'You're just like your mother. She thinks affection is something people use to get something they want.' At the time, I had to agree. What else could love be?"

May 1, 2015

"My agent, Marty Erlichman, spent over a year trying to get record companies to sign me, but that wasn't as easy as everybody thinks. Record executives kept making rude remarks about the size of my nose, my unattractiveness, that I was too quirky, too flamboyant, and 'too Jewish.' Worst of all was the guy who roared, 'We can't hire her! She looks like a woodpecker in a captain's cap!' It took me a long time to get over that one. I was not the sweet, squeaky-clean, all-American girl type who was then all the rage, and apparently I was too sophisticated for *American Bandstand*.

"Columbia was then at the top of the recording company list, the Cadillac of record labels. But Columbia's president, Goddard Lieberson, who was called "God" for good reasons, always said, 'No way! I don't like her looks, I don't like her, and I won't have her on my records.' But when I showed up with the rest of the cast to record the sound track of *I Can Get it for You Wholesale*, he bit his tongue and had no choice but to allow me into the studio.

"I was not surprised that Goddard objected to having me in the cast when Columbia was preparing an album to mark the twenty-fifth anniversary of the garment industry musical, *Pins and Needles*. But fortunately for me, *Wholesale*'s composer, Harold Rome, threatened to cancel the entire recording if I were not hired, because he felt I possessed a unique and eerie understanding of music dating back to the 1930s. Even 'God' can change his mind sometimes, and Goddard finally did.

"*Pins and Needles* and *Wholesale* were selling very well, but 'God' still refused to sign me to an exclusive contract.

"My career took a giant leap up the ladder during the summer of 1962. I was stopping the show eight times a week at the Shubert, then sprinting for a cab every night after the show to perform at the Blue Angel, where the audiences cheered me for ten minutes at a time. And I was even welcomed onto a show guest-hosted by Groucho Marx. Would you believe I got more laughs than Groucho? When he complimented me on my success, I said, 'If I'm so great, how come your announcer is still calling me Barbra Streesand?'

"Groucho said, 'Barbra, you are only twenty years old—Lord, was I ever that young?—and I keep hearing about you from people all over the country.'

"I answered, 'Nothing they can prove, I hope!'

"'Well,' he continued, 'they are talking about you for the Fanny Brice story, and that's pretty big pickings.'

"'I guess that's good,' I answered. 'But how come the salesgirls still don't wait on me in Bergdorf's?' The audience howled.

"A few days later, I scored another hit. I was invited to appear on *The Tonight Show*, with host Johnny Carson. The show was so successful that Carson invited me to return as a guest every month for the next five months.

"*I Can Get it for You Wholesale* closed late in the year, after three hundred performances. By that point, though, I didn't mind, because the play had started to make me feel claustrophobic, and I didn't want to be on the stage anymore. I crossed off each performance on my calendar. I wanted to quit, but couldn't.

"I hated doing the same old things the same old ways, and got sick to my stomach every night before the show opened. That's how I knew I had to be in the movies, where you do a scene once and never have to do it again. I couldn't stand doing the same damn performance every night. I always have to be in the moment, and everything must be fresh and real.

"For instance, I couldn't bear it when the plastic flowers on stage were dusty. If everything isn't fresh and real, I am unhappy. And when I am unhappy, everybody is unhappy! You know, been there, done that. I spent the last few months sleepwalking through the part of Miss Marmelstein. So when the closing notice for *I Can Get it for You Wholesale* was posted on the bulletin board, I went whooping down the halls, ignoring the weeping cast members, and shouting, 'I'm free! I'm free!'"

May 4, 2015

"The next week I appeared on the great Ed Sullivan Show, singing 'My Coloring Book' and 'Lover, Come Back to Me.' As with *The Tonight Show*, my appearance on the Sullivan program proved to be yet another upward step in my career. I was signed to do an album, which I was sure would make me a star. I recorded eleven songs in three days—all the studio time that Columbia's eighteen-thousand-dollar budget would allow. The album began with 'Cry Me a River,' and added my favorite nightclub songs, 'Who's Afraid of the Big Bad Wolf?' and 'Soon It's Gonna Rain.'

This 1962 appearance on "The Ed Sullivan Show" was one of her first big TV appearances and what helped launch her music career; she finally got signed after this.

"When I listen to that first record now, I shudder. God, how did they ever like me? It embarrasses me. The ending was awful. It was *Happy Days*, but sounded like the end of the world. I whined 'Oooo, aaay' until my voice actually cracked. It sounded nuts, but in a sense, it was me at my purest. I yearned so much it came through in my voice. It's like a little bird's—very thin, very high, and very young. My voice has gotten much better as I've matured. It is warmer and more mellow, though I can't sing as far up the scale. You win some, you lose some. Anyway, it got me my start in the recording business, which has made me an incredible amount of money."

"Why do you sing, Barbra?" I asked. "I'm sure it's not all for the money. Does singing answer your need to be great?"

"I'll say what Maya Angelou said when she was asked that question, 'A bird doesn't sing because it has an answer. It sings because it has a song.' Or Martha Graham who, when asked what her dance meant, replied that if she could put it into words, she wouldn't have the need to dance. If I could explain why I sing, I wouldn't have to sing at all."

I smiled. "I believe that, Barbra. I think you would sing if it didn't pay you a penny. Incidentally, which do you like better, singing or acting?"

"The way I do it, there isn't any difference. I see myself as an actress, and all the songs I sing are just little plays."

"I understand," I said. "That's why you are so good at both."

"People like you think I sing great," she said disdainfully, "but you don't know how I feel inside. I know how Mozart felt when he said, 'If you could only hear how it sounds in my head!'"

"Maybe," I said, "but you sound pretty great to me!"

She nodded and continued, "I was so young then—only twenty years old, but going on forty, according to my mother. Elliot saw me differently. He said, 'Barbra is twenty-two, going on eight.' Who is correct? Perhaps both, at one time or another. Even as a child, I seemed to have the kind of self-confidence I had only seen before in Ethel Merman. I *knew* I could sing. I *knew* I was good. As Kate Smith sang long ago, 'Nobody had to tell me. I knew it all the time.' You have to dream, and then you'll be able to fulfill it, but first you've got to have the dream.

"I take good care of my voice. I don't smoke or drink, or eat highly seasoned foods, although I love them, and I don't drink any extremely hot or cold beverages. To be as good as I need to be, I have to have absolute control of every detail, in both films and records. A lot of technicians hate me for this, and only want to get home to their families. But I won't let anyone leave no matter how late it is if I'm not satisfied that every detail is perfect.

"The editors tried once to 'clean up' my album by removing my breaths between phrases. 'Oh no you don't!' I yelled. 'Put them right back in immediately! Don't clean so good! You took out what is natural, and natural is good.' I rejected all their attempts to give the album a clever name like *Sweet and Saucy Streisand*, and insisted it simply be called *The Barbra Streisand Album*.

"The great composer, Harold Arlen, who wrote 'Somewhere Over the Rainbow,' was crazy about my work. 'Did you ever hear Helen Morgan sing? Or laugh at Fanny Brice's or Beatrice Lillie's jokes?' he asked. 'These were the great performers of all time, and I fully expect Barbra Streisand to join their ranks.'

"'What?' I teasingly said to him. 'Why are you comparing me to all those dead people?'"

May 6, 2015

"Three weeks later, I was on my way to Las Vegas, where I was to be the opening act for Liberace at the Riviera Hotel. Mid-June temperatures were at their highest when I arrived, schlepping my suitcase, exhausted and sweaty from the terrible heat. My luggage was filled with the gray and light-brown gowns I had chosen for the event.

"I had decided to dress down for the occasion, to stand out against all the six-foot, practically bare-assed hoofers. It was a big mistake. The audience reacted very tepidly to my act. They preferred the naked ladies, and the hotel threatened to fire me. But Liberace, who admired me greatly, had other ideas. He would open the show in a red sequin tuxedo, and introduce me, this time wearing a gold lamé gown and some showy, borrowed earrings. I did not receive a standing ovation, but the crowd was much more receptive, and the reviews were superb.

"The best part of the gig was the tremendous amount of money I was paid. It was the most I had ever made for an engagement, and raised my compensation level ever after. My contract even included such things as a flower-filled suite and gardenias in the toilet bowl. At one point, I complained to the maid that there was no soap dish in the bathroom.

"'You'd think with all the money they're paying you, you could afford to buy your own soap dish,' the maid snorted. When I told my dear mother how much I was making, she said, 'Why are they paying you so much money just to sing?'

"Elliot, who was appearing in a play in England, cheered me on from afar, soothing my nerves and telling me how much he loved and missed me. He kept hoping each night that a closing notice would be tacked up on his backstage door, and was constantly disappointed that none appeared. He wanted only to come home and see me, and make sure we had a future together.

"It was Liberace's birthday, and I had to help him celebrate. I decided to make him a cake, and brought it to his party. After he blew out the candles and served the guests, Liberace sat down and downed a huge chunk of chocolate cake. Then he got the most peculiar look on his face. 'The frosting on this cake is too rough,' he said. 'It tastes like marbles.'

"'Well, I had a little problem,' I answered. 'I ran out of confectioners' sugar and used flour instead.

"'Don't worry about it,' he said. 'Your cake will make a great doorstop.'

"I planned next to appear with Liberace in Lake Tahoe. Then I would fly to New York and begin work on my third Columbia album. But Elliot couldn't wait that long. He flew directly from London to Las Vegas, where I was still appearing. Liberace's birthday wasn't the only one I had to attend to—it was Elliot's too, which he wanted very badly to spend with me. We were having dinner in a small coffee shop, when, at my instructions, the waitress brought in a cake with a candle on it for Elliot to blow out.

"'Make a wish,' I said.

"'I hope the Dodgers win the pennant,' he said, as he blew out the flame. Don't you love the man? One evening over dinner, Elliot leaned across the table and said, 'Let's get married.'

"'Sorry,' I said, 'but I'm not ready yet.' Although Elliot was very disappointed, he kept after me, sure that eventually I would change my mind. A few days later, we left in a rented car for Lake Tahoe. There, I received a standing ovation at every performance, with a smiling Liberace always giving some nice acknowledgment of my performance. I guess he forgave me the birthday cake.

"Elliot never left my side. Nor did he gamble anymore–he had a terrible problem with it before–which I took as a good sign. I counted on his being there when I came off the stage, to give me a big bear hug and tell me how great I was. He never gave up entreating me to marry him. Eventually, he wore me down, and I accepted his proposal.

"On September 13, 1963, we drove to Carson City. With Marty Erlichman as best man and no maid of honor (I didn't have a woman friend that close to me), we were married by a justice of the peace who had never heard of me, but seemed shocked at the passionate kiss Elliot and I exchanged at the end of the ceremony. Didn't any of the couples he married love each other? Nobody seemed to notice that the bride wore blue jeans and a tee shirt. At the end of the no-frills ceremony, Elliot let out a whoop, picked me up, and carried me to the car. 'Hooray!' he shouted. 'You are finally Barbra Streisand Gould!'"

May 11, 2015

When Barbra came in for the next session, she began to talk about her next album. I reminded her that she had been talking about her singing career, before telling me about her marriage with Elliot. Didn't she want to continue with that?

But nobody can tell Barbra Streisand anything, least of all what she should talk about.

"Since I'm paying for these sessions, I have the right to pick my own subject!" she loudly declared.

"You certainly do," I answered.

"Well, I've had enough of Elliot for a while anyway," she said. "I want to talk more about my career."

"Sorry about that, Barbra," I said. I felt bad about the blooper I had made, and resolved to talk less in the future.

I wished all my patients had Barbra's ability to speak up about what was on her mind. Then maybe there wouldn't be so many ten-year-long analyses.

"The first film I made was *Hello, Dolly,* the film adaptation of the beloved Broadway musical of the same name," she said. "Did you see it?"

I shook my head no. "Sorry, I missed that one."

"Then I'll tell you a little about it. Only a little, though, because I'm not going to waste my session educating you." I smiled.

"The movie is about Dolly Levi," she continued, completely oblivious to my amusement. "She is a *shadkhn* who likes to arrange furniture, flowers... and lives. Sound like anyone you know? Dolly, a widow, falls in love with an almost millionaire and Yonkers merchant, Horace Vandergelder, who has designs on another lady—one who owns a hat boutique. With some fictitious scheme, Dolly convinces the two of them to go to New York. There the *shadkhn* fixes up the hat boutique owner with Vandergelder's head clerk, so Vandergelder becomes available for Dolly herself."

She looked at me with her perceptive eyes and asked, "Does that sound interesting to you?"

"Indeed it does," I answered, relieved that it really did. There would be no point in lying to Barbra Streisand. She would see right through it.

"I just might order it from Netflix," I added.

Satisfied that I was telling the truth, she continued with her saga.

"Gene Kelly was the director, and I co-starred with that *farbisener* Walter Matthau. What I needed was a Rhett Butler. What I got was Walter Matthau. You know how grouchy he comes across on the screen? Well, that doesn't hold a candle to how nasty he is in person.

"He must be related to Louis Kind. You won't believe how rotten Matthau was to me. When we were standing outside of Vandergelder's feed store, I told everyone of my great idea for how the scene should be shot. Matthau snarled, 'Who the hell do you think you are, Barbra? Since when are you the director of this film? Why don't you shut up and let Gene do the directing?'

"Trying hard not to cry, I gave it back at him, 'Look who's talkin'! Why don't you ever learn your lines like a decent actor? You're just jealous of me because you know in your heart that I'm a better actor than you'll ever be!'

"He countered with, 'Listen, you little *pisher*, you might be the singer in this movie, but *I* am the actor. You can't act worth a butterfly's fart!'

"'I'm the star of this God damn movie! I shouted. 'It's not called *Hello, Walter*. So shut the fuck up and get out of my face!'

"I was so humiliated I couldn't bear him a moment longer, so with tears running down my face, I ran away. He yelled after me, 'Go on, tootsie pie, run. Everybody hates you in this show and can't stand to have you around. Betty Hutton acted like a big shot too, and now she's filing for bankruptcy.'"

"It took a long time before I could stop crying and was able to return to the set. But the payoff came later when he was asked by a reporter if he ever would act with me again. 'Sure,' Matthau said, 'in something suitable, like *Macbeth*.'"

May 12, 2015

"The war between us raged on for as long as the filming lasted. I had known from the start that there would be trouble. I didn't like Gene Kelly and he didn't like me. And besides the fact that the stinker Matthau was co-starring, I really was much too young for the role. Ruth Gordon had originated it on Broadway in *The Matchmaker* when she was in her fifties. In the first screen version, Shirley Booth was sixty when she played Dolly. Ginger Rogers, Ethel Merman, and Pearl Bailey, all older actresses, had also played the role. I was only twenty-six years old.

"But Gene convinced me that I could play Dolly as a young woman whose much older husband had passed away. I reluctantly agreed, saying, 'Okay, I guess that happens sometimes.' When the producer Ernest Lehman said, 'You are such a vivid personality, your voice is one of the all-time greatest, and I know you are going to be an extraordinarily successful movie star,' I couldn't resist. I also liked the idea that Dolly the person was a laugher. It was a nice change. I'm not a laugher. I learn something from every movie I'm in. Playing in this film taught me how to laugh at life, which was announced in a big headline in *National Inquirer*, 'Barbra Laughs!' I didn't think it was funny.

"Ernest Lehman, the film's writer-producer, took my side in every dispute with Walter. But then, he really liked me. In fact, he couldn't take his eyes off me. It made me self-conscious, and I said, 'Stop looking at me so much, Ernest!' He even thought some habits of mine were cute. Not everybody would agree with him.

"If I happen to want it, I have a little habit of taking a bite of food from anyone's plate. He told a friend, 'Barbra used to take the food right off my plate. Even if I was hungry, she'd take the food out from under my mouth. She has all kinds of little quirks like that. She does whatever she wants to. She doesn't say, 'I can't do that because it isn't proper.' There is no proper or improper to Barbra Streisand; there is only what she wants to do. To tell you the truth, I find it kind of friendly.'

"He loved how much I talked, too. He'd say, 'She used to call me any hour of the night she wanted to, and complain, 'That lousy Walter did such and such to me,' or 'Would you please call Gene and tell him such and such?' I didn't mind because I stay up real late anyway. When she didn't call, I would think, 'Call and bother me some more, Barbra. Please!'"

"The only time I challenged Ernest was during the recording of one of the show's tunes. He said, 'Barbra, you didn't sing the melody on the final word in the second chorus.'

"I glared at him and answered, 'Do you realize, Mr. Lehman, how much I get paid *not* to sing the melody?' That quieted him down, and there were no more comments about my singing or not singing the melody!

"Anyhow, much as I didn't like the movie, I had to take the role. I really needed the money. Elliot wasn't working and was gambling away all my savings. As Herbert Hoover once said, 'About the time we can make the ends meet, somebody moves the ends.' I'm glad he said something good.

"Gene Kelly had as many doubts about me as I had about him. 'Barbra,' he said the first time we met, 'is there any truth to the rumors that you are difficult to work with?'

"'Who, me?' I asked in surprise. 'I may be a *bissel meshuga*, but difficult to work with I'm not.' I then proceeded to advise him on everything from photography to wardrobe to the music. He resented most of my ideas and usually ignored them. Even worse, what I wanted *from* him I never got. I badly needed help on how to interpret Dolly's personality, a topic which didn't interest him at all. I got great support from Herb Ross and Will Wyler that had gotten me through the trials and tribulations of *Funny Girl*, but none at all from Gene Kelly in *Dolly*.

"Whether he didn't know any better or was just being mean, I'll never know. But as a result, my character wavered from Mae West grandiosity to Fanny Brice's baby-faced humor and back again to little ole Barbra Streisand. *Oy gevalt*! I'm embarrassed when I even think about it. Not my best movie, as you can imagine. Whenever I don't listen to my heart, I get into trouble."

"That's great advice you're giving yourself, Barbra," I said. "It reminds me of the remark of Pascal you quoted to me, 'The heart knows things the mind will never know.'"

"Hmmmmm," she said smilingly, "it looks like you really listen to me. I can't say that about all my other shrinks. A lot of them used my hour to catch up on their sleep."

I tried hard not to beam at the compliment.

"With all the arguments and disagreements," she went on, "the film cost twenty-four million dollars by the time it wrapped up, the most expensive musical ever made. I was delighted to be finished with the whole miserable business—the backbiting, bitterness, and humiliation.

"Not surprisingly, *Hello Dolly* fizzled. The filmgoers must have known Pascal, too. Or read the lousy reviews. I returned to New York to await the opening of the movie of *Funny Girl,* which I believed would determine my true future as a Hollywood star."

Barbra as Fanny Brice.

May 13, 2015

"In the meantime, even though three albums of mine had been recorded, it wasn't until February 1, 1963 that my first album was released, and I set out on a nationwide tour to promote it," she said. "I sang in Boston and Cleveland, and most important, appeared on *The Mike Douglas Show*. The show was important to my career because it introduced me to a host of national daytime television viewers for a whole week.

"Strangely enough, this was the very audience the Columbia executives were convinced I could never attract. Why? Because I am Jewish? Didn't they ever hear of *The Goldbergs*? You couldn't go past a home in Brooklyn, including my mother's, while Mollie Goldberg's radio shows were being broadcast and not hear her voice shouting out the window, 'Yoo hoo, Mrs. Bloom!'

"The Douglas show did a lot for my album, which sold out in twenty-four hours. For five days in a row, I played in skits, interviewed guests, sang all the songs in my album, and clowned and kidded around with Douglas. I liked him a lot. Too bad he was happily married!"

"Not everything went as well as I had hoped. Of all places to fail, I conked out before the 'rocks and lox' set of affluent Jewish retirees at the Eden Rock in Miami Beach! They were so busy telling Jewish jokes to one another that they hardly even applauded me. I've never had a more dismal audience. Go figure!"

"You're right, Barbra. I've always found that while I can accurately predict the actions of individuals, it is almost impossible to tell in advance how crowds will behave. Anybody who has tried to leave New York for the Hamptons on a weekend can bear me out. Sometimes the roads are empty, and sometimes the traffic is bumper to bumper. I left one time at 5 am, hoping to beat the mob. But of course on that day everybody else had the same idea, and it took me five and a half hours to make a trip that usually takes two and a half. As you say, 'Go figure!'"

She laughed and said, "Regardless, I wouldn't play the Eden Rock again if the Lord Himself flew down on a golden bicycle to escort me!

"My hurt feelings were hugely assuaged when I played San Francisco's the 'hungry I' the next week, where I created a sensation among gay men, who thronged the nightclub to see me. Thank God for gays and lesbians. They are the backbone of my fans. So many came that they created a fire hazard, which was reported in newspapers all over the world the next day.

"It didn't hurt my self-esteem any that my salary had jumped from three hundred and fifty dollars a week to two thousand, five hundred. During my record-breaking run at the 'hungry I,' Columbia rereleased my recording of 'Happy Days' to secure more radio airtime for the album. To my surprise, *The Barbra Streisand Album* climbed up to the top ten on the *Billboard* charts, and remained there for an astonishing one hundred and one weeks. I'll say it again: 'Go figure!'"

"That one is no surprise to me, Barbra. But how many people in this world get what they deserve? I'm happy that you're one of them."

"You'd think I'd be happy, too. But the whole experience left me confused and drained. What does it mean when the audience applauds? Does it really mean I was good or just that they think they *should* clap? I don't know how to respond. Should I give them money? Should I lift my dress? Should I just say thanks? I respond much better to the lack of applause. I don't react to good reviews, but only remember the bad. Then I know I'm still little Barbra from the lower east side.

"You don't know the half of it," she continued. "I am heartsick at all the 'crazies' who wait with autograph books for me outside the stage door. I once had to scream at them, 'Get out of my way! Don't you have anything better to do than stand around and wait for me? Jesus! Go home and get a life!'

"And then a secretary from Columbia came up to me and said, 'I love you.'

"'What are you talking about?' I answered. 'You don't love me. You don't even know me!'

"But worst of all was when a taxi was waiting for me in a terrible downpour, and a young man threw his coat down so I wouldn't have to step in a puddle to get in.

"'Stop that!' I yelled. 'Pick up your coat right away. Don't you know you're as good as me? You shouldn't behave like that for anyone.'

"And then there was the time in a restaurant when I was enjoying a good meal. A woman came up to me and said, 'I hate to bother you, but—' I put down my utensils, looked her straight in the eye, and said, 'You hate to bother me? You *hate* to bother me? Then why do you do it? Why don't you just admit that you're bothering me and don't give a damn if you do or not?' The woman slunk away and I doubt if she'll ever bother any star again."

"Barbra," I said, "why do you treat your fans so badly? After all, it is their love of you that makes you so successful."

"Good question," she answered. "I guess I treat them the way my mother treated me. That's the only example I ever had on how to treat people."

"Do *I* treat you badly?"

"No, not at all. You are always very nice to me."

"Then how about taking a page from my book and treating your fans the way I do you? After all, you are my livelihood, just as they are yours."

"Hmmm. I'll think about it."

"Don't think my comment means that I don't admire your ability to be honest at all costs, Barbra. I couldn't say such a thing as you did to your fan if my life depended on it."

"Why not? Does the whole world have to like ya?"

"I'm afraid so. Perhaps that's why the whole world loves you and I'm lucky if a few happy analysts think well of me."

To my surprise, she said, "Nobody's perfect, Darcy, but I love ya. I'm just lucky that I'm not a person who needs people."

I couldn't decide whether to smile at the irony or groan.

May 15, 2015

"After my great success at the 'hungry I,' I appeared on Dinah Shore's NBC talk show," she began. "Guess who happened to be watching the show? None other than John F. Kennedy, the President of the United States! You quote Jung as saying that there are no coincidences. So maybe it was just meant to be.

"Anyway, the President invited *me*, the little *mieskeit* from Brooklyn, to the White House to entertain at the White House correspondents' dinner. Wearing a cleavage-baring white satin gown and never taking my eyes off the most gorgeous president the U.S. ever had, I sang 'Happy Days Are Here Again.' I must say that the entire power structure of Washington sat there mesmerized, and then broke out into stupendous applause that made me forget the experience at Eden Rock.

"When it was time to stand in the receiving line to meet the President, I was warned that JFK didn't give any autographs, as it would take up too much of his time.

Barbra speaking with President John F. Kennedy, 1963.

"When it was my turn to meet him, he asked, 'How long have you been singing?'

"'Oh, for about as long as you've been president.' He laughed. Then I said, 'Mr. President, my mother who lives in Brooklyn loves you and has your photo hanging in her kitchen alongside my father's. She'll kill me if I don't get your autograph.'

"'Certainly. Lean over,' he said to my friend Peter Daniels, 'so I can write my autograph on top of your back.'

"'Thanks, Mr. President,' I said. 'You're a doll.' Needless to say, the autograph has remained one of the great treasures of my mother's life. It may even have led to her forgiving me for not becoming a school secretary.

"The next day, Merv Griffin asked me if the president had written an inscription along with the autograph. 'Yes,' I answered with a straight face. 'He wrote, 'Fuck you—The President.' I wish!

"Six months later, Kennedy was assassinated and Lyndon Johnson became president. I was heartbroken, along with the rest of the country. I was invited to come to the White House on the evening of LBJ's inauguration in 1965 to be part of the celebration, along with many other stars. But this time I sang as badly as I felt, and Carol Burnett stole the show with her breathless rendition of 'Hello, Lyndon.'

"For the first time in my life, I didn't care. I sang for Kennedy because I loved him, but singing on the evening of Johnson's inauguration was the most dreadful experience I ever had. Here stood this coarse, rude man who was there because JFK was dead, and it was just awful. He didn't deserve any better. I still cry when I see JFK's photo on TV."

May 16, 2015

"My fourth movie was *The Owl and the Pussycat*. One of the reasons I accepted the role was that I wanted to be in a film where I didn't sing. 'I'm an ecktress, not a singer,' I used to say. I still needed to prove it.

"It began as a two-character Broadway play by Bill Manhoff about a stodgy author and his neighbor, Doris, a foulmouthed, freewheeling prostitute: me. Manhoff wrote the part of the hopeless, hapless hooker for a black actress, but that changed when I was cast in the role. I set about studying the role by spending a lot of time talking with real prostitutes in a high-price bordello. As I waited for a limo to pick me up, some business men came in. One asked the madam, 'How much for the Barbra Streisand look alike?'

"'Hmmmm,' I thought. 'Maybe I should try it. It would top my Actors Studio training.' The madam didn't think it was a very good idea.

"In the movie, George Segal played Felix, the male lead. The heart and soul of the story is the relationship between his character and mine. He was utterly appalled by my lifestyle, and I was turned off by his prudishness, but we were made for one other. Each of us supplied what the other character lacked. We played two self-deluded opposites, who, after many verbal and physical fights, sexual incidents, and role reversals, discarded our pretensions and happily formed an unlikely romantic duo.

"The film represented the last work of my beloved cinematographer Harry Stradling, who'd previously photographed me so beautifully. Stradling, unfortunately, died during production. I was broken-hearted and thought he was irreplaceable.

"One thing I really like about this movie is that you can actually watch our relationship develop. In all too many romantic comedies, the leading characters meet and immediately fall in love for no obvious reason. In this film, we started off disliking each other, but as we interacted, the sparks began to fly and our underlying chemistry came through.

"We were definitely an odd couple, but demonstrated very well that opposites do attract. It was fun making the film because it was a different kind of part than I was used to playing, a rougher character than in any other movie, although I suppose it is obvious that underneath it all, I'm still a Jewish girl from Brooklyn. Some of my young fans think Doris is who I really am."

"Barbra, is it ever hard for you to know who you really are, because you take on so many different roles?"

She smiled, and said, "Not really. But I don't think an actor can play any role without finding something of the character inside himself or herself. When I take on a new part, I always look for the seeds of it inside myself. As the great Russian teacher Constantine Stanislovsky once said, 'If you're playing a murderer, you don't have to kill a person. You can just remember what it feels like to kill a fly.' While the script of *The Owl and the Pussycat* was fantastic, it wouldn't have worked if George Segal and I hadn't actually shared a chemistry. In my opinion, we were great together. I like him personally, and loved it when he said, 'There's Brando, and then there's Barbra!'"

I smiled and said, "Freud would agree with you. He said everybody is capable of doing anything, including all the perversions."

"Smart man! So you see, I always know who I am because every role I play is a different part of myself. Put them all together and you get... me."

"So your acting actually helps you to know yourself better, not worse!"

"From your mouth to God's ear," she said with a wry smile.

"One of my favorite scenes is when I describe to Felix some of the many bizarre sexual requests I had fulfilled. Felix exclaims, 'Doris, you're a sexual Disneyland.' I must say that, from this movie, I learned a lot that no nice Jewish girl from Brooklyn should ever get to know.

"One thing that makes me furious about the DVD version of the movie is that my 'Fuck off!' line was cut, which leaves the scene without a punch line and completely ruins it. What's with Hollywood, anyway? They leave in completely disgusting scenes and cut out a good, funny joke! That's supposed to make people moral? Come on! No wonder I wanted to be a producer!

"One of Doris's lines that makes me laugh every time I think of it is when she hisses to the would-be writer about the opening line of his novel, in which he has the sun spitting out the morning, 'You'll never be a writer, because the sun doesn't spit!' It is a very funny romantic comedy, and I really loved doing it."

"It sounds great," I said. "I'll have to buy it."

"Don't bother," she said. "I'll bring you a copy. But on one condition..."

"What's that?"

"That you promise to tell me if you don't like it."

"Don't I always?" I said.

That night a package was delivered to my apartment. It was the DVD of *The Owl and the Pussycat.*

Barbra and George Segal in The Owl and the Pussycat, Barbra's fourth film and first film in which she did not sing.

May 18, 2015

"I liked it! I liked it!" I shouted, as she came into the room.

"Of course you liked it. It's a great film!" she countered. "Well, let's skip the movies for a while and go back to my men. I know we left off when I was married to Elliot, but I feel like jumping around a bit today. You lean forward with such interest whenever I talk about any of the men—more than with any other topic I bring up."

"Am I as transparent as all that?" I said.

"You'll like this," she continued. "I had a little list. It consisted of world-famous men I'd wanted to sleep with. Some, like Marlon Brando, Warren Beatty, and the Prince of Wales were checked off early. At the top of the list of remaining names was that of Pierre Trudeau, the head of the Liberal party and Canada's head of state."

*Barbra and
Pierre Trudeau.*

My ears perked up. *She's right*, I thought. *I do like this!*

"Pierre Trudeau was tall, attractive, and unmarried at the time, a tasteful balance of opposites, an elegant, private, and dignified man who was also charmingly bohemian. And it all flowed through him so naturally you'd hardly notice it. He was always ahead of his time.

"Both personally and professionally, Pierre was a complicated and exciting man, with a sense of humor and a keenness that charmed everybody. I admired him greatly for ignoring conventions, such as the day he famously wore open-toe sandals into the staid House of Commons. Sound like anyone you know?

"There was an odd serendipity about our meeting. During a rare period when there was no man in my life, my friend, Cis Corman, and I were looking through *Life* magazine, laughingly checking to see if there might be a suitable candidate for me. There was a picture of Pierre that I stared at, and then told Cis, 'He can park his shoes under my bed any time.'"

"She said, 'Are you joking?'

"'I mean it,' I said. 'I never joke about men I want to fuck.'

"'Well,' she said, 'I wouldn't be surprised if he ends up in your bed. You're pretty good at getting what you want.'

"'Yeah,' I murmured. 'That's my greatest skill. I'm even better at that than at acting.'

"Before the London premiere of *Funny Girl*, I flew to London, where I was to be presented to the Queen. In England, you're not supposed to speak to the monarch before being addressed by her. But since when do I follow the rules?

"'Your Majesty,' I said, thinking maybe I could make a feminist out of the Queen, 'can you tell me why English women have to wear gloves and men don't?' The Queen was taken by surprise, and said, 'I'll have to think about that for a moment.' Then she said, 'I suppose it is simply a tradition.'

"'Well,' I muttered within earshot of the Queen, 'I think men's sweaty hands should be covered, not ours.' Do you think that's why I was never invited to the palace again?"

I smiled.

"Then I was invited to a party by Princess Margaret and seated at her table. When she told me how much she had liked my performance, I said, 'You should come back some night when your sister is not here!' Apparently neither the Queen nor her younger sister have much of a sense of humor. Margaret told the newspapers she had been confused by what sounded to her like a hostile remark. Unfortunately, neither of them are feminists.

"I've been studying mysticism and reading ancient history. Do you know that before Cleopatra's reign, many civilizations were run by women? When the men took over, the world went to pot. Now we're seeing the rebirth of woman power.

"I did something for women's lib that pleases me," Barbra continued. "While I was filming *The Way We Were,* I requested that my driver be a woman. She was a nice-looking young lady named Beverley Robilotte, who lives in Amsterdam, New York. She drove me to work every day. Some of the shoots lasted all night, and Beverley had to work night shifts. Her husband wasn't too happy about it, but since it was a once-in-a-lifetime thing, he tried to be understanding. I enjoyed having a woman driver. First of all, I think women drive more carefully. And secondly, if you feel like talking, you have more in common with a woman. Also, they know when to keep their mouths shut."

May 19, 2015

"Well, back to Princess Margaret's party. Trudeau was also there. I made out better with him than I had with the princess. I looked at him and he looked at me, and we were both hooked for the next two years. When a reporter asked him how long he had known me, he answered, 'Not long enough.' A few weeks later, I flew to Ottawa. There, the prime minister escorted me to the ballet, where we held hands all evening. I also attended a session of Parliament, during which Pierre and I kept looking at each other and exchanged a series of hand waves. George Hees, a member of the Tory opposition, remarked, 'I would like to ask the prime minister a question, if he can take his mind and eyes off the gallery long enough to answer it.' Pierre blushed. I banged the metal railing in front of me with my umbrella.

"As my friendship with Pierre evolved, he invited me to Ottawa to attend the opening-night performance of the National Ballet of Canada. I knew I'd have a good time, since my lucky number is 14, and he lived at 14 Sussex Drive. Pierre, like me, held himself and others to strict disciplines. Very little took precedence over his strict regime, and guests all knew they had to be out of the mansion by 10 pm…except me. I was invited to stay. I woke up happily the next morning thinking, 'Pierre is the First Man of Canada in ways that would surprise his countrymen!'

"I said, 'Pierre, if the people of Canada knew I'd spent the night with you, what would they think?' He laughed long and loud, and said, 'There's no place for the state in the bedrooms of the nation.'

"He came to power in 1968 when he was almost fifty. But to the crowd of groupies who followed him everywhere, he was a rock star who represented the spirit of the age. He was tall, attractive, youthful, irreverent, and adventurous. He had a silky charm about him, and was not at all stodgy. He was the first–and maybe last–PM who looked good in blue jeans. He also looked good without them. He was lucky to be able to conduct his love life in an era when the personal lives of politicians were off-limits to the media. His affairs would draw a lot more attention today.

"But during his time as head of the government, he was a model of dignity and humanity, qualities the international community noted by nominating him for the Nobel Peace Prize, and awarding him the Einstein Foundation International Peace Prize. What impressed me most was that he always did everything with his own flair and sense of justice. That was the key to all he was and did.

"During an interview in *Playboy,* a reporter asked me if Pierre had proposed to me. I said, 'I won't answer that question, but I will say that I seriously considered becoming the First Lady of Canada.' It's one thing to play a great lady on the screen and quite another to be one in real life, like Grace Kelly in Monaco. I had it all figured out. I'd learn to speak French, which would be fun because I like to learn, and I planned to make films only in Canada. I would campaign for Pierre—I really am an activist at heart—and to become involved in causes I believed in, like abortion, even if he didn't.

"But he was a practicing Catholic, and a Jewish girl from Brooklyn just wouldn't sit well with the Pope. So that was the end of my marrying a head of government. I'll bet I would have done a good job. At least I wouldn't have driven off a mountain top like Grace did.

"I'm very proud to have been a part of his life. Too bad it couldn't have lasted."

She looked at me with a funny expression, and said, "Didn't I say that before about Elliot? What *was* there about me that kept me from having a lasting relationship then? Well, don't answer that, Doctor. Sometimes it's better not to know."

May 20, 2015

The next session, after giving the matter a considerable amount of thought, I said, "Barbra, tell me about your readiness to have affairs. Why do you think you need so many?"

"Are you criticizing me?" she demanded.

"Of course not. I'm not your mother. But I think the answer to my question will reveal something very important about you."

"Alright," she said a bit skeptically. "Let's see: Among the most notable men I've slept with are Bill Clinton, Pierre Trudeau, Prince Charles–don't tell the Queen, Marlon Brando, and Warren Beatty. Wow! The list impresses even me."

"So you have picked the most famous men in the world to have sex with."

"I guess you could say that," she answered laughingly. "I'll bet no other woman since Helen of Troy has slept with so many great men."

"What do you think you got out of it? Was the sex with them so much better than with ordinary men?"

"Not at all. Not mentioning any names, but sometimes it amounted to nothing at all. I have much better sex with Jim. I guess I didn't do it with famous guys for pleasure," she added thoughtfully.

"Then why?"

She paused for a moment. "My mother again, of course. If all these great men find me desirable, then she must have been wrong in what she thought of me. There goes another bad introjection!" she said, sounding like the intelligent student she is.

"Good. But there is another reason you had sex with so many men that is unconnected to your mother. These great men were all men of power—father figures. If you slept with them, it was as close to having your father as you will ever get."

"Do you mean I want to sleeped with my own father? What a dirty mind you have, Doctor! May I suggest a good analyst?"

I laughed. "Every little girl wants to, to some extent. As you must know, it is called the Electra complex, which is the equivalent of the Oedipus complex in males. Your father died before you could grow out of the wish, as little girls ordinarily do."

"The only picture I have of him and me is me with my arm around his tombstone."

"Oh, Barbra," I said, coming over to the couch and taking her in my arms. The American Psychoanalytic Association wouldn't approve of it, but I couldn't help myself.

The little orphan girl in the body of a woman sobbed in my arms for the rest of the session.

May 21, 2015

"Well, enough of my love life and my father for a while, and back to the drawing board," she started. "One of the many people who admired my performance in *I Can Get It for You Wholesale* was Jule Styne, the author of *Gentlemen Prefer Blondes* and co-author of *Gypsy,* which in my opinion is the greatest Broadway musical ever. Maybe I'll play in it someday. Anyway, he had been asked to write *Funny Girl,* a comedy about Fanny Brice, a homely radio personality, film and stage actress, singer, comedienne, and TV star. She was known mostly for her character, Baby Snooks.

"Fanny Borach, Fanny Brice's real name, was born on the Lower East Side of Manhattan in the late 19th century and, like me, was Yiddish through and through. To my surprise, I discovered that she had neither a Brooklyn nor a Jewish accent. When asked how she came to sing in a Jewish accent, she replied, 'I needed a song to try out for *College Girls.* I asked Irving Berlin to write one for me, and he wrote me 'Sadie Salome, Go Home.' He sang it with a Jewish accent. I didn't even understand Yiddish. If he had sung in an Irish brogue, I probably would have become an Irish comedienne.' Funny, huh? She was as natural a comic as I am.

"After hearing her sing in dialect, Ziegfeld hired her for seventy-five dollars a week to appear in his *Follies of 1910.* Berlin wrote the music and lyrics for 'Goodbye, Becky Cohen,' also to be sung in dialect. It was a big hit, and thereafter she used the dialect in her comedy skits.

"Incredibly, considering her looks and obvious ethnicity, she, like me, achieved great success in her various careers. I think I was preordained to play her. We were both relentlessly ambitious and funny, and nothing was big enough to hold either of us down. Do you know any other actress better suited for the role? I don't. From the beginning, I knew that *Funny Girl* would be my ticket to fame. Everything in me was now geared to becoming a star. If I succeeded—and I refused to believe I wouldn't—I would have arrived. As usual, my premonition turned out to be correct.

"Fanny was not your usual simple-minded, light-headed musical comedy actress. A woman after my own heart, she was strong-minded, outrageously funny, and a wise woman with whom audiences could identify. She once said, 'People like to feel miserable. Make them laugh and they'll forget about you in two minutes. But make them cry, and they will remember you forever.' Like me, Fanny Brice could do both. She thought she was fortunate to have been born ugly, because it gave her the ambition to become a great star. That sounds like what I always say about my mother, that her being so critical is what led to my success. You know, every cloud has a silver lining. Mine is lined with gold.

"We were so alike in a deep spiritual way that it was spooky. I knew I could do her justice by being true to myself. Things like copying her walk didn't interest me. I cared only about capturing the essence of Fanny, which was so similar to the essence of Barbra.

"Fanny went on to marry Nick Arnstein. They had two children. Nick was a compulsive gambler, and Fanny spent much of her life and income trying to keep him out of jail. She did not succeed. When he left her to marry another woman, her heart was broken in two. She never recovered.

"Fanny died of a stroke at sixty. That seems so young to me. I think she died of a broken heart. If she was like me, she never got over rejections. After her death, Norman Ratkov wrote a biography of Fanny that upset her daughter, Fran, so much that she had her husband, the agent Ray Stark, pay $50,000 to purchase the rights to the book and have the manuscript destroyed. Stark later decided to turn Brice's life story into a film.

"Many producers had turned down the project, saying it was not commercially viable, in part because Fanny was too ugly and Jewish looking (sound familiar?). But Stark finally got David Merrick to turn his idea into a musical comedy. Merrick then signed up Jule Styne to write the book for the show. The producer also hired Jerome Robbins to direct it.

"Mary Martin wanted to play the part, but Jule said, 'What? Are you crazy? That *shiksa*? Fanny has to be played by a Jewish girl, and she's got to have a schnoz!' Then Stark suggested Anne Bancroft, but Styne argued, 'I told you, there is no way Fanny Brice can be played by a *shiksa*!'

"Styne came to see *I Can Get It For You Wholesale*. Impressed by me, schnoz and all, he invited me to dinner with him at Sardi's. I said, 'Can you please get us a front table so everybody can see me?' He laughed and obliged. I was very comfortable with Jule from the word go. I knew he came from a lower-class family who ran a mom and pop grocery store. We talked about everything under the sun—movies, music, actors—everything, that is, except Fanny Brice.

"Isabel Lennart had written the book of the musical as a juicy love story. She couldn't see the weird, unglamorous Barbra Streisand playing this world-famous entertainer. Marty Erlichman disagreed. After the performances of *Wholesale,* I was still doing the late show at the Bon Soir when Marty brought Styne and Merrick to see my act.

"Do you happen to know about Anne Mary Lawler's poem, which appeared in the *Philadelphia Public Ledger* a long time ago? It goes, 'Yes, dreams do come true, if you dream them long and hard and earnestly, and never, never give them up.' I carried it around in my wallet until it crumbled to little pieces. Well, miracles can happen. I've proved that. The men agreed that they had found their Fanny Brice.

May 22, 2015

"And best of all, Styne came to see my act every night for the next month. He closely studied my personality, my acting, and my vocal technique, and wrote the score of *Funny Girl* specifically for me. So *Funny Girl* really could have been called *Funny Barbra*. Styne also dragged Stark down to see the woman he believed had to play Fanny Brice. Stark was greatly impressed and brought his wife to see my act. Unfortunately, she disagreed with her husband and said, 'Are you kidding? I will never allow that ugly woman to play my mother!'

"Probably because of Mrs. Stark's disapproval, many other actresses were considered for the part in the months that followed, including Kay Ballard, Mitzi Gaynor, and Carol Burnett, but no one was chosen. I held my breath.

"Two weeks after Carol Burnett turned down the part, saying that it called for a Jewish woman, Ray Stark made a decision. 'We gotta go with the kid,' he told Styne and Robbins, the director. On July 25, 1963, the press announced that I'd been selected to play the role of Fanny Brice. I slept with the *Times* story under my pillow for a whole week.

"The reporters gathered around me for the first time, and I told them, 'Fanny and I really are very much alike. How she talks is like I talk. When she sings, it's like me singin'. Neither of us could ever take advice from anybody. Like me, Fanny would never listen to her mother, or even to Florenz Ziegfeld, for that matter. I should be perfect in the part!

"*Funny Girl* takes place in Manhattan around the time of World War I, before I was born. It opens as the Ziegfeld Follies star Fanny Brice is waiting for her husband Nicky Arnstein to be let out of prison, where he had served an eighteen-month sentence for embezzlement. The story then moves into flashbacks on their first meeting and their subsequent marriage.

"Fanny's life story was so much like mine that I felt like a reincarnation of her. She is first shown as a stage-struck teenager, just as I was, but she got her first job in vaudeville If I had been born earlier, I may well have gotten my start that way, too, as so many great comedians did. She met the charming, debonair Arnstein after her debut performance, which reminds me of first meeting Elliot at the rehearsals of *I Can Get it for You Wholesale.*

"Again, like me and Elliot, Fanny became a great star, while Arnstein's career went down the drain. The charming Arnstein didn't have much trouble seducing Fanny, who loved him so much she quit the Follies to be with him. Here's where my path and Fanny's diverge. No way would I give up my career for any man. Although I wouldn't like it, I can live without a man. But without my career, I would surely die.

"For a while, Nicky was a successful gambler—I guess Elliot was too. At least he didn't tell me about the thousands of dollars of *my* money he lost. Nicky agreed to marry Fanny only after he won a fortune playing poker aboard the RMS Berengaria. The couple moved into an expensive house and had two children. She did me one better; I have only the one child.

"Fanny eventually returned to Ziegfeld and the Follies. Meanwhile, Nicky's failing business ventures forced them to sell their beautiful house and downsize into an apartment. Unlike Elliot, Arnstein refused to allow his wife to support him. I respect him for that, although I always told Elliot, fool that I was, that it wasn't *my* money in the bank, it was *our* money. Desperate to have an income in order not to feel inferior to Fanny, Nick was swept up in a bonds scam and imprisoned in Leavenworth and Sing Sing for embezzlement. Fanny was heartbroken, and counted the days and hours until his release.

"After Arnstein was released from prison, Fanny realized that their marriage could never work, and reluctantly agreed to a separation. Again like me and Elliot. He and I loved each other so much it took a long time before I could accept that we never could have a happy marriage. Under the best of circumstances, show business marriages are very hard to maintain.

"In our case, the discrepancy in our careers was too much for any normal man to live with, let alone a sensitive actor like Elliot. I believe that if Elliot had been as successful as I was, we would still be married. Likewise, if we hadn't been in show business. Lots of couples stay together who don't love each other nearly as much as Elliot and I did. And still do.

"Sometimes, regardless of his lack of professional success, I am sorry I divorced Elliot." She stopped speaking and a lone tear rolled down her cheek. I waited a moment and then asked what she was thinking.

She answered, "Except for my current husband, nobody has ever loved me as much as Elliot did, and probably still does. Maybe I would be better off if we had stayed together…But then think of all the fun I would have missed! Marlon Brando, Prince Charles, Pierre Trudeau. No, it was right to leave Elliot. Being me, he never would have been enough…"

May 23, 2015

"Well, back to *Funny Girl*. Despite my success at the try-outs, I almost didn't make it. In fact, on the first day of rehearsals, I nearly got fired. The wise Ruth Gordon said, 'Barbra is great, but she is not yet good.' When I tried out and sang so beautifully, the director said I had broken everyone's heart. But as I struggled with breathing, blocking, and phrasing, Kanin said, 'What's with that gal? She can't even walk across the stage without falling all over her feet. She sounds like a kid trying out for the senior high school play.'

"I was supposed to end the song with an 'Eeech!' But I guess I didn't get it right, because Kanin called out, 'You are overdoing it!'

"'Tell me what you want,' I said.

"'Just make it more natural,' he answered.

"'Miss Streizund... '

"'My name is not Streizund. It is Streisand!' I barked. I became terrified when I saw Ray Stark standing up and coming towards me.

"I yelled out, 'You're making me lose my confidence. I'm doing my best to do whatever you tell me, but I can't sing when I try to do what you say. I need to sing the way I *feel*.'

"'You are doing all right,' Stark said. 'You are good.'

"'No,' I shouted. 'It ain't good enough for me to be *good*. If I'm not going to be *great,* I won't play the part.'"

"Stark called off the rehearsal, and we all said our good-byes. I knew they had someone else lined up if I didn't work out, and I was up all night worrying that I was going to be fired.

"When I came to the next rehearsal, everybody was so still it felt like a morgue. *They all know I am going to be fired*, I thought, *and are feeling sorry for me*. I began to sing, and didn't think I was any better than the day before. At one point, Stark started to come up to the stage and I thought, *Uh oh, this is it! Bye bye to Broadway, Barbra!* He really *was* going to fire me. But thank God for Jule Styne. He raced after Stark and practically wrestled him to the floor. He said, 'Damn it, Stark, leave her alone! Can't you see that is how she works on a part? She'll be terrific! Just you wait and see.'

"At the end of the song, I had to take a deep breath so I would be able to hold the final note on 'Nobody, no, nobody is gonna rain on my parade!' I forgot to take the breath, and when I got to the end of the song, I just couldn't make it. I ran off the stage sobbing.

"To my surprise, they came after me yelling, 'No, no! Don't go away. That was great! Not being able to sing the final note added to the intensity you were feeling in the song.' Everybody broke into cheers and applauded wildly. From that moment on, I was in."

"You were very courageous, Barbra," I said. "You could very well have been fired."

"Thank you, but that was only the beginning of the ups and downs I went through. Over the next three months, I stayed on that roller coaster—being brilliant, then almost being fired for incompetence. Which was I, superb or inadequate? Sometimes I didn't know myself.

"I wasn't the only problem the show had. The reviews we got out of town were so bad that Stark seriously considered closing the play. The musical he had struggled to produce for over a decade made it to Broadway by only a fraction of an inch. I really lead a charmed life, at least sometimes. If he had really closed the show, there would be no Barbra Streisand as the fans know her today.

"Perfectionist that I am, I paid attention to every little detail, which annoyed the rest of the cast, who had to stay overtime because of me. But if I were going to let people's perceptions stop me, I'd be sitting behind a typewriter today as somebody's school secretary. I wouldn't accept a costume that didn't feel exactly right to me, however loud the wardrobe mistress yelled. If I didn't like a song, I refused to sing it, even if the songwriters stood on their heads. I insisted that every lyric say exactly what it meant and mean exactly what it said. None of this sticking in words to make a rhyme!

"Carol Haney, the choreographer, and I were always fighting. She didn't think I was a very good dancer. She was right, but since when has being wrong stopped me from doing what I want to do? People said behind my back that I had a lot of nerve acting like a star, but thank goodness I did. I *know* what is right for me, and I refuse to compromise. I'd rather be fired.

"So everybody was always mad at me. Even though I was the star, I always felt like an outsider. I knew I was up there alone, having only myself to rely on. I was well aware that I had to carry the show on my youthful shoulders and that if I failed, the show would fail, too. That's a pretty heavy load for a twenty-one year old."

"Or for anyone else, for that matter," I said. Barbra's smile indicated her understanding.

"It was particularly hard for me to cry on cue," she continued. "Or to do anything that didn't come from my gut. I had forgotten what I'd learned in acting school, when Miller, my teacher, had solved the problem. Knowing how much I like to eat, he said, 'Imagine someone made you a beautiful chocolate birthday cake. And just when you are about to take the first delicious bite dripping with chocolate, the director throws the cake on the floor.' I began to sob like a baby. After I remembered Miller's brilliant image, I no longer had any trouble crying on cue in *Funny Girl*.

"Elliot was in New York and, while we were out of town, tinkering with the show, I felt very lonely, with no one to confide in. The record executives were now ganging up to cash in on the *Funny Girl* casting. Only five days after the announcement was made, they released *The Second Barbra Streisand Album*. It was an immediate hit and remained high on the charts for seventy-four weeks. I guess I was getting up in the world, wouldn't you say, Doc?"

"No doubt about it."

Her crooked smile told me that she was pleased with this comment, too, but didn't want to show it.

May 24, 2015

"Now that I was making so much money," she said, "Elliot and I could afford to move out of the apartment over Oscar's Salt of the Sea. We reluctantly said good-bye to Oscar the rat. We considered taking him with us, but didn't because we thought he would miss his friends.

"We moved to a twentieth-floor duplex on Central Park West. The apartment had ten-foot ceilings, six glass chandeliers, wrap-around terraces where I could have a garden, and a winding staircase that led to our bedroom with a hand-carved wooden French canopy bed in it. I felt like I lived in Versailles. The little girl from Brooklyn was living in a palace! I could really make an entrance gliding down those stairs, if you know what I mean.

"I didn't have much time to enjoy our new quarters, however. The next week I headed out to Los Angeles for a two-week engagement at the Cocoanut Grove. If you think I was a success at the Bon Soir, you should've seen me at the Cocoanut Grove. The applause was so thunderous I thought it would bring down the stars in the heavens. The club was so mobbed you practically had to know somebody big like Daryl Zanuck to get in. The doorman wouldn't even let *me* in once. I screamed out, 'Hey, I'm Barbra Streisand! I'm the star of the show!' Fortunately, I yelled so loud the stage manager heard and came to rescue me."

I could tell Barbra was in her "funny" mood. *She acts that way when she wants to avoid painful feelings,* I thought. *I'll try and see if I can get under it this time, without hurting her feelings.*

"When I next appeared at the Coconut Grove," she said, "I was flabbergasted to enter the room and find it filled with famous people like Henry Fonda. I was the only one in the room I didn't recognize. I was also surprised to see the room was so wide. I said, to a big laugh, 'If I had known I would be surrounded by people on both sides, I would have had my nose done.'"

"Barbra," I said hesitatingly, "you are very funny, and I do enjoy your jokes. But much of your humor is what we in analysis call resistance. That means you are funny to keep down feelings of grief or sadness. Are you trying to stay away from something that pains you today?"

She looked at me in surprise, and said, "How did you know? I've been telling you about the fun Elliot and I had early in our relationship, but I don't want to continue with the saga. You're so right: It is too painful. Can't I just skip that part?"

"Maybe if you face it, it will begin to hurt less."

Her face saddened. "I was a tremendous success in three short years, and it looked like Elliot wasn't going anywhere. For a long time, he couldn't get any work at all. I guess you could say unemployment was an affront to his masculine identity. I'm sure it would be hard for any man to take, as in *A Star is Born*. I know it would be impossible for me to live with.

"We began to fight all the time—at home, on the streets, in restaurants, in taxis, and even at parties. We fought everywhere, no matter how public the place. We even had a loud fight in the main public library, and they kindly asked us to leave. Elliot made me so mad I couldn't control myself. Like when I bought a piano, painted with beautiful rose-colored scenes. He was furious.

"'How the fuck can you buy a piano without consulting me?' he screamed. I was even madder than he was. 'I bought it because I love it,' I said.

"'Well, I hate it,' he responded. 'I've never seen a more hideous piano.'

"'It's an original,' I said.

"'Yeah,' he answered. 'So is a hippopotamus. Who needs a red piano with naked women painted all over it? It belongs in a bordello.'"

She giggled. "I wasn't about to tell him, but he had hit the nail exactly on the head. I had bought the piano, inexpensively, from the estate of Edna Milton Chadwell, the madam of the infamous Texas brothel that inspired the movie and Broadway show *The Best Little Whorehouse in Texas*."

Barbra became serious again. "Our fight continued. When I'm mad, I'm afraid I'm not very nice. 'I make the money,' I told him, twisting the knife into his weakest spot. 'Nobody can tell me how to spend it.' He began to cry. I felt awful, and wanted to drop dead on the spot.

"The only piece of furniture we didn't argue about was our platform bed. We both wanted it to look like a stage setting. 'It should look like the place Desdemona got strangled in,' he said, in one of our lighter moments. On the table beside the bed was a photo of me licking a huge lollipop. On it, it said, 'I wuv you, Ellie.' I must have written it during our better days.

"To make himself feel better, Elliot began to gamble. Soon, he was losing hundreds of thousands of dollars of *my* money. He bet on every game on the boards, and once lost $50,000 on one football game. I said, as kindly as I could, 'Elliot, you'll have to stop gambling, or we won't have any money left, no matter how much I make.'"

"'Yeah?' he sneered, 'Try and stop me.' I knew my success threatened his manhood. Foolish woman that I was, I hoped he would get a job soon and it would make him feel better, and he wouldn't need to gamble. After all, I told myself, it is only money. I can always make more.

"Of course his gambling affected our sex life, too. Gambling *becomes* the sex life of the gambler, and we often went many weeks without having sex, which for a passionate woman like me is no picnic.

"Gambling wasn't Elliot's only problem. He also was into drugs, and developed a heavy pot and upper habit. I wasn't interested in drugs, because I was afraid it would affect my performances, so both his habits separated us even further.

"'Aren't you worried that taking drugs will affect your work?' I asked him. He said he sometimes smoked while he worked, but that he turned off when he felt he needed all his wits about him. Apparently, that wasn't very often. Being married to Elliot at this time was not easy, to put it mildly.

"A few days before *Funny Girl* left for try-outs in Boston, Elliot got a part in the TV movie *Once Upon a Mattress*. Although it was only two weeks' worth of work, it was his first job since *On the Town*. Glad he was working at last, I left for Boston without him. I was given a suite at the Ritz Carlton. My leading man was Sydney Chaplin. His room was right down the hall from mine."

May 27, 2015

Barbra's next session continued with comments about "Funny Girl" during its out-of-town tryouts. "Sydney and I disliked each other at first, and were constantly checking to see who had the better lines and songs. As a result, our chemistry on stage wasn't so hot. I don't know what happened to change things—maybe I was just lonely for Elliot or settling into a part in which Fanny is deeply in love with Arnstein, but Sydney suddenly started looking very good to me. I sensed that he felt the same way about me.

"I had a lot to gain by encouraging our mutual attraction. I was very flattered to have the attention of my striking, distinguished-looking leading man, who just happened to be the son of the great Charlie Chaplin and the silent screen leading lady, Lita Grey. I liked having a confidante in the middle of the otherwise unfriendly company, and I knew our scenes together needed to improve. He arranged quiet dinners for the two of us. It was nice to be with a man who could pay the bill for a change. Soon, we practically wore out the carpet between our rooms.

"Naturally enough, our new relationship changed what went on between us on stage. It generated a new excitement between us and changed *You Are Woman* into a sexy, sensual song. The intimacy also made our final parting in the play much more poignant. Before that, nobody, including me, cared if Fanny left Arnstein or not.

"Unfortunately, Broadway columnists picked up on our romance. Earl Wilson wrote, 'What Broadway star and her leading man are an item offstage as well as on, and is infuriating his lovely wife?' Nobody mentioned my husband, but whatever his shortcomings, Elliot is no fool. He began to call and harangue me all the time about Sydney. He was very jealous, and I was furious with him for upsetting me at a time when I needed all my wits about me.

"By the time the show returned to New York from Philadelphia, I had ended my affair with Chaplin. You won't believe what he did about it. Apparently, he is a little boy at heart who can't stand rejection. He responded with a year of disagreeable, terribly unpleasant behavior that ended with my bringing him up before Actors' Equity. Unfortunately, he can be so seductive he could charm the wallpaper off the walls, and was there. I didn't stand a chance."

"What did he do that was so unpleasant?" I asked. When she told me, I could hardly believe that this famous, handsome popular star could behave like a kindergartener kicking a fellow student in the shins.

"It will take a year to tell you how bad it was," she answered. "During our most intimate love scenes, he would murmur obscenities in my ear worse than those of a drunken sailor. I'm as good a cusser as anyone, but I won't lower myself by repeating his vile remarks. He changed his lines and stage business whenever he could so I would forget my next lines. When we passed each other on the stage, he would purposefully bump into me.

"One time he pushed me so hard he knocked me over. He acted like he was helping me to get up off the floor, but he yanked my shoulder so hard I had to go see a doctor. It still hurts. He would mutter and say awful things to the rest of the cast about me, making sure they were loud enough for me to hear."

"That's incredible!" I said. "Whatever was the matter with the man? Who would believe a man who looks and acts like such a gentleman could be so vile?"

"Don't worry about it. I gave as good as I received and cussed at him a blue streak. On the stage, when we were taking a bow and smiling happily, we were saying 'Fuck you!' to each other.

"He gave an interview to the New York *Daily News* which revealed his problem: He was insanely jealous of me.

"'I'm a nobody in this play,' he said. 'I'm supposed to be a co-star, but it turns out I'm just a straight man for that Streisand woman. I'm just that guy in white tails that nobody, including the audience, roots for. By the end of the play, I'm slapping the baby, kicking the dog, and then leaving Fanny. When we leave the theatre, the whole audience is waiting for her to autograph their programs and nobody gives me a second look.'

"He no longer would accept notes or suggestions from the director, saying, 'Forget it! They're *her* ideas. I'm sick and tired of doing the show *her* way. From now on, I'll do it *my* way or not at all!' Worst of all, during our most intimate love scenes, he took to whispering 'Schnoz!' in my ear. Once, during an intermission, he really got to me and I was so upset I ran to my dressing room in tears. The stage manager had to push me back on stage for the second act. I've taken a lot of B.S. in my time, like when I was a little girl in school, but it was never in front of an audience. I'm a pretty tough lady, but that was one insult too many.

"Well, I have my ways of getting revenge. At one performance, in the most intimate scene in the play, he was pretending to nuzzle me and kiss my neck. When he muttered 'nose' in my ear, I bit him on the neck—so hard he bumped against a pipe and got dizzy. It turned out he had suffered a concussion."

We both couldn't help laughing. "Poor guy!" I said.

"Yeah," she answered. "I'm cryin' my eyes out for him. He left the play in June 1965. Nobody—least of all me—was sorry to see him go."

Sydney Chaplin was not only the leading man in Funny Girl opposite Barbra, but also (briefly) her lover and confidante.

May 29, 2015

Barbra opened her next session by returning to stories about Elliot. "Next to Sydney, Elliot began to look pretty good, and I began spending most of my free time with him. Although we fought all the time, we still had a lot of fun together. We touched each other a lot, which I love, because nobody ever touched me as a child. Elliot's arm was always around my waist, and my hand on his chest or arm, and I loved to run my hands through his beautiful curly hair.

"We always shared our food, me taking huge bites of his sandwiches and him slurping my chicken soup. We were constantly whispering secret jokes to each other in our made-up 'Hangi' language, like two little kids. I have a quick temper. In fact, much of Hollywood regards me as a 'power-crazed castrator,' but Elliot knew exactly how to handle me. He always stood up to me. I admire him for this, for I detest people who let me intimidate them.

"I consider them wishy-washy wimps without a backbone. I won't allow one near me. And, whatever the cost, I refuse to be a wimp myself! If I had let my mother intimidate me, where would I be now? In the shithouse, that's where. If I had listened to the producer of *I Can Get It For You Wholesale*, I wouldn't have rolled myself across the stage in Miss Marmelstein's chair in the scene that made me famous at the age of twenty."

"How did you know you were right and he was wrong?" I asked. "After all, he was a world famous producer and you were only a little kid in her first Broadway show. Most novices would have been terrified of getting fired if they didn't follow instructions."

"I just knew in my heart what was funny and that he was wrong. I'd rather be fired than go against my instincts. In the same way, if I had let the producer of "Fanny" intimidate me, we would have lost the biggest laugh of the season or maybe ever, when over his repeated objections I stood at the top of the stairs on opening night in a wedding gown with a pillow on my stomach to make me look pregnant."

"That's why you are world famous and most young actors have to give up and go home."

"You're right. One of the best actors I know had to slink back home to Chicago to work at McDonald's in order to support his family. I've been far luckier."

"I wouldn't call it luck, Barbra. You are a highly gifted woman. And you were from the beginning."

"Thank you," she said. "Well, back to Elliot. Whatever his flaws, he never was afraid of me. Intimidation reminds me of the word 'appeasement,' which Roosevelt defined as 'the process of feeding a crocodile one person at a time in the hopes that it will eat you last.' That's what it's like when you yield to intimidation. It's the beginning of the end. That's why I will never yield to intimidation, or stick with anyone who does."

"In any event, my long hours of rehearsals, plus all the time I had to spend relearning lines and songs that were rewritten every day, left Elliot alone a lot. His employment in *Once Upon a Mattress* had not brought him any new jobs, and he worked only twelve weeks that year. It is very hard for a man to be supported by his wife and not have any cash in his pockets. He stood in line for months collecting fifty dollars a week until the unemployment ran out, which didn't help his self-esteem any.

"So of course he went back to gambling, investing my money and hoping to make some for himself, but succeeding only in losing what he had put in the pot. I can see now that I was so busy trying to wow the critics in *Funny Girl* that I was of no help to him at all. If I had been available to him, maybe, just maybe, I could have rescued the marriage. But as some wise person used to say, 'We grow too soon old and too late smart.'

Barbra in her Broadway debut,
I Can Get It For You Wholesale, 1962.

May 31, 2015

"Would you believe that the day before *Funny Girl* opened in New York, both the first and last scenes were still not set?" Barbra continued. "And this in a top Broadway musical! I was supposed to enter leading two Russian wolf hounds on a leash. Russian wolf hounds are classy dogs, I suppose to emphasize the fact that Fanny was one classy lady. Well, the dogs didn't know they were supposed to be aristocrats and stopped mid stage to lower their bottoms and do the unclassiest thing dogs are capable of. The audience howled. Embarrassed, I hurried off stage.

"So shortly before the play opened, the hounds were fired. The revised scene had me sweeping across the stage but sans wolf hounds... and sans carefully thought-out motivation. It was even worse with the last scene. It still was not written three hours before the curtain went up opening night.

"I was in a panic, of course. Would I remember my new lines? Would I be able to sing in tune? On cue? Would the audience accept me as the great Fanny Brice? Elliot was at his best. He stayed by my side all the time, assuring me that I would be great, and giving me back rubs and massages to relax me. I smoked one cigarette after another until my throat was burning up. Not such a great idea for a star singing the hottest numbers of the show.

"After what seemed like an eternity, the stage manager called 'Places,' and walked me across the vast area that led to the door through which I was to enter the stage. Milton Rosenstock conducted the orchestra's last notes of the overture. My knees were wobbling as the curtain began to rise and I was supposed to stride onto the stage like a queen. I must say I felt more like the court jester than a queen, but think I hid it well.

"Then came the shock of my life. Wild applause began the moment I set foot on the stage. I had no idea that so many of my record fans would want to see me in person and attend the show. The applause grew louder and louder after each song. As you know, I, like Fanny, can be very funny, even if *you* want to call it resistance," she said, tossing me a dirty look. "I sensed that my acting and singing were overcoming the weakness of the script. My nervousness completely evaporated and I *became* Fanny Brice.

"One fabulous scene remains the all-time favorite comedy act of my long career," she continued with a straight face. "When the curtain goes up, I am standing regally at the top of a long winding staircase, dressed in my elegant wedding gown. My hands are wrapped around my huge belly. I am pregnant. I say, '*Oy vey*. Am I beautiful!' It brought the audience to its feet."

I couldn't contain myself and a loud *ha ha ha* burst out of me. Barbra ignored me, as though she expected me to laugh like everyone else. Analyst or not, I did.

"It was my idea, of course, which they gave me trouble about. In fact, the director actually ordered me to remove the pillows stuffed under my gown. Being me, I took them out for rehearsals and put them back in on opening night. So not only did I not get fired, but they left the scene in as I played it. There wasn't a single performance in which the sight of the pregnant bride didn't get a standing ovation.

"When I was a little kid of maybe four or five, I would listen to people talking and sense when they were misinterpreting each other. I always felt I knew what was going on underneath their spoken words. I remember how frustrated I was at not being able to tell them, and I've been frustrated ever since by people who interpret wrongly. I'm always aware when people are coming on, or someone does a dishonest thing. When I walk into a room and something isn't right, I am able to sense it.

"When I got to be fifteen years old, I realized that most people, if they pretended to be something they were not, were nothing. But if they just were themselves, if they were just *being* and not acting a part, they were fascinating, because they were just being human. Once they began to act, they were false. They were their insufficiencies. But once they were just nothing, they were something. I am nothing false, which makes me a something."

"I ought to have you come and talk to my less honest patients," I said.

"Sure, Doc" she said. "How much will you pay?"

June 1, 2015

"After his work ended, Elliot became more depressed than ever," Barbra said at her next session. "My growing success made him feel more inferior every day. I suspect he also continued to brood about Sydney. And his depression was contagious—he made me feel lousy, too. He got it into his head that having a baby would bring us closer to each other. I said, 'Elliot, that's one hell of a reason to have a baby!' But there was no talking him out of it. I guess he felt that impregnating me would make him feel like a man again, and give him back his self-respect. Also, getting pregnant was the one thing I couldn't do without him.

"So he pulled a trick on me. He got me drunk and practically raped me. I was so out of it I didn't know the difference. *And he didn't wear a condom.* When Elliot found out from my doctor that I was pregnant, Elliot asked the doctor not to tell me until my show had successfully opened. Would you believe the doctor called Elliot before he called me? How sexist can you be? And the doctor listened! As if Elliot was the one who was pregnant.

"When I did find out, the heavens opened up for me, and I felt bathed for days in a white light like Jesus. I hadn't known I wanted a baby so much. Now I think it is the single greatest thing that ever happened to me. Although I was furious that I'd had nothing to say about it, I'll be grateful to Elliot all my life for making it happen.

"I read all the medical books I could get my hands on. If I know what is going on inside of me, I feel more in control. I've been fascinated all my life by the way our bodies work. I'm not squeamish about it like many women, or upset by a few drops of blood. I find it simply incredible how our organs all function together like a well-coached football team. Each part has a separate job in the process of growing a baby, and each part is set off by complex signals from one to the other. It's the greatest miracle in the world. There must be a God!

"When I was four months pregnant, Elliot and I had a terrible argument. I shouted, 'I hate you! I don't want to bear your child,' and ran into the bathroom and locked the door. When I wouldn't open it, he was so mad he kicked the door down. He later apologized, and said, 'You are a big baby yourself, but I shouldn't have kicked down the door.'

"I wouldn't talk to him for a week, until he went down on bended knee and said he would never do anything like that again. Foolish me. I believed him. Three of our houses have had broken doors to prove what an idiot I was. We both refused to pay for fixing them, and as far as I know, they remain, to the present day, wildly swinging off their hinges.

"As for Elliot's idea that having a child would bring us closer together, he was dead wrong. This makes me overwhelmingly sad, as we had hoped against hope that having a baby would bring us closer to each other and bind us together forever. Unfortunately, that was not to be. Jason simply gave us more to argue about: how to feed him, hold him, change him, and even whether or not he should be punished when 'necessary.' Of course, Elliot thought he should be. I yelled, 'If ya ever lay a finger on that child, I'll kill ya! And I'm not kidding!' I would have, too. But he never did."

"Many couples have told me they believe that having a child will heal their disintegrating marriage," I said. "But they are unrealistic. I have to tell you that in all my years of experience as a psychoanalyst, I have yet to hear of a failing marriage being saved by having children.

"On the contrary, the strain of raising a child, which includes sleepless nights, a tremendous amount of money, jealousy that the other parent prefers the child to himself or herself, and the loss of personal freedom encountered in raising children, tears many fragile marriages to pieces."

Barbra looked relieved. "That makes a lot of sense. You make me feel better that I wasn't to blame for ruining our marriage.

"Of course, it didn't help that Elliot asked me point-blank if it was true that I'd had an affair with Sydney Chaplin. I, who am always honest, said yes. It hurt him to the quick, but to his credit, he never mentioned it again."

June 3, 2015

"Unfortunately, Jason was a breech baby and, after nine hours of difficult labor, the doctors had to knock me out to cut me open and lift him out of me. I'll never get over that I missed the greatest moment of my life. The most wonderful experience anyone could possibly have and I wasn't there!

"But when I woke up and the doctors put my son on my stomach, I cried me a river, and thought, 'He looks just like my father.' Then I thought, 'Something is wrong here. I'm only a little girl myself. How can I possibly be a mother?'

"Jason weighed in at a healthy seven pounds, twelve ounces, and I was delighted to see that he had my brilliant blue eyes, the only thing about my face that I ever liked. We sent out a birth announcement in which a stork, holding a beautiful baby, says, 'Well, here I am!' The announcement described him in only one word, 'Gorgeous!'

"Elliot never stopped bragging about Jason. You'd think he had been the one who gave birth. He went up and down the corridor stopping and grabbing by the collar anyone who was unlucky enough to pass by, saying, 'Listen to this! All the babies in the nursery are crying. Only one baby is quiet: My baby, Jason! The lady standing next to me said, 'Look at that incredible baby! He has his eyes wide open!' Elliot said, 'He looks just like Barbra with her beautiful blue eyes, except he has my dark hair and a cleft in his chin. I like him! I think we'll keep him.'

*Barbra and Elliot
with their son Jason.*

"Having a baby also gave birth to a whole new me. At last, I knew who I was—Jason Gould's mother. For the first time in my life, it gave me roots. 'Hey,' I thought, 'I'm normal at last!' Elliot agreed. He said, 'Barbra is a typical Jewish mother. If the baby sneezes, she falls apart.'

"For two months, I holed up with Jason in our Central Park West apartment and wouldn't let anyone else touch him. I bottle-fed him, burped him, changed his diapers, bathed him, and put him to sleep. Elliot said I woke up at night just *before* the baby cried. Even the interviews I gave the magazines and newspapers at the time had more to do with Jason than with me, although I have to admit they did stress the effect he was having on me. But you know how it is, Doc.

"After three months, hanging around all day got boring and I turned him over to a full-time nanny. But before hiring one, I interviewed thirty-five women to make sure she was the best one. And then, of course, I kept checking her out so much I might as well have been taking care of Jason myself. That was the most creative time of my life, when Jason was an infant," she continued wistfully. "I should've had ten more children."

June 5, 2015

"Things picked up for Elliot in the '70s, thank goodness, when the shaggy Gould with the guilty look emerged as the prototypical counter-culture movie hero. After starring in *Bob & Carol & Ted & Alice*, he was cast in a string of hits. In *M*A*S*H*, he played Trapper John. He played the odd army surgeon in *Getting Straight, Move*, and *I Love My Wife*. How ironic! *Time* nominated Elliot as the 'Star for An Uptight Age.'

"He was even tagged *Star of the Year* by the National Association of Theater Owners. I was delighted for both Elliot and Jason, who badly needed a father he could respect. Then maybe he wouldn't have to call himself Jason Streisand. 'And maybe,' I thought, 'if Elliot is making so much money, he won't feel so inferior to me, and we can really be together again.'

"Needless to say, Elliot began to look better and better to me. 'Good,' I thought, 'now he can gamble away his own money.' So I flew to Stockholm where he was making the film *The Touch* with Ingrid Bergman, and told him I wanted a reconciliation. I expected him to throw his arms around me and shout 'Hooray!' To my shame and utter humiliation, he refused!

"After all his protestations of eternal love, I couldn't believe it. It seems the bastard had fallen in love with Jenny Bogart, the daughter of director Paul Bogart, and wanted to marry her. She was only eighteen years old, but beautiful and vulnerable. A friend said that Jenny was about as different from me as any two people could be. Heartbroken, I returned to New York, where I could curl up by the fireplace and silently mourn our irreparably broken marriage.

"Elliot came back for a little while, but of course it didn't work. After a long series of knock-down, drag-out battles, we finally agreed to a separation in 1969. We had been married for nine years. I told the papers, 'We are separating to save our marriage, not to destroy it.'

"But Elliot contradicted me and told the reporters, 'We are no longer trying to save our marriage. Barbra loves only Barbra. She really bugs me, and I've had all I can take of her. She is a major star, but do you think that makes her happy? Not on your life. She is constantly complaining, and I am sick and tired of listening to it.' I thought that was very ungenerous of him. I would never say such a thing about Jason's father."

"I wobbled home in utter dejection, and two years later we mutually filed for a quickie divorce in the Dominican Republic. It was granted. I think neither of us has ever gotten over it. To me, it felt like my father had died all over again."

June 8, 2015

"Back to Jason. He was a bright, creative, high-spirited child. Do you think his first word was Mama or Daddy? Not Jason. It was 'hat,' because he saw me wearing so many on the set of *Hello, Dolly.*

"He always was a precocious child. When he was three years old, he was watching television when a clip of me in *Funny Girl* came on the screen. In it, I was on a tugboat singing 'Don't Rain on My Parade.' Jason stormed up to me and yelled, 'Mommy, I sawed you on that boat. Why didn't you take me on it with you?'"

That set Barbra off again on the subject of what Jason has to say, i.e. "God, grapefruit is so sour! How do you eat it?" and how he always says okay with a question mark after it. Like "Okay, Mom?" Barbra beamed. She glowed. Then she became serious. "As a mother, you really see how every mistake you make has an effect on your child. It's a terrible responsibility, but very exciting.

"I would *never* lie to him. And if I make a commitment to him, I have to follow through. My mother would be about to take me to the movies and something 'important' would come up and we didn't go. I think that is terribly unfair to a child, and if you do it often, he or she will never believe you about anything. I never forced Jason to eat, so he really enjoys his food. My mother always forced me.

"As I've told you, I was a pathetically skinny child who was sent to health camps and made by my mother to swallow tonics holding my nose. The camps were miserable. When I got there, they'd dump me in the bathtub and then put me into a scrungy uniform. I looked like the cat's pajamas. I hated it. From that time on, any time I went to the country, I got allergies. I don't have to tell you, Doctor, that they were psychological in origin.

"Another thing about Jason," she continued, "is that I've always encouraged him to do what he wants. My mother never encouraged me." She paused. "Jason had a mother who works. Who is to say whether that was bad or good? At least he'll have some respect for me as a human being, and realize his mother is a person. Then it won't be so devastating when he sees my flaws. It won't be so terrible when he finds out that I'm just as human as everybody else.

"I've always taught him to be open about sex, and not to be a prude the way I was when I was young. As a seven-year-old, Jason was standing on a step in a swimming pool in front of two little girls, with his swimming trunks pulled down exposing his little ding-dong. One of the girl's fathers smacked him on the behind and said, 'Don't do that in front of little girls!'" Later that night, my secretary told me what had happened. I said, "Do you happen to know of any seven-year-old hookers?"

I couldn't help laughing. Dr. Freud would not have been happy about how I was conducting this analysis.

"Isn't it funny," she mused, "that I raise my son so differently than the way my mother raised me? I thought people are supposed to bring up their kids as they themselves were raised. I do everything exactly the opposite of how my mother did it, thank God! Where she said mean things, I say only kind words. Where she thought nothing of slapping me in the face, I would die before I raised a hand to Jason. Whereas she discouraged my ambitions, I always tell Jason he can be anything he wants, if only he works hard enough at it. Whereas she told me I was ugly, I always tell him how gorgeous he is."

"It may seem funny to you, Barbra, but you are just as dependent on your mother on how to raise your son as any other mother."

"How can you say that? Everything I do with him is the exact opposite of what she did with—and to—me."

"True. But what you do with him is to think of what your mother did to you. Then you do the opposite. You know what to do with him because of what you learned from her *not* to do."

She laughed, and said, "Thanks, Mom! I guess I did learn something about mothering from you after all."

June 10, 2015

Barbra came into the office with a brooding look on her face, and said, "A strange incident happened with Jason when he was a very little boy that I've been wondering about ever since. I'd like your opinion on it, Doctor."

"Certainly."

"He stood up to his full two feet and announced to me, 'My name is Jason Streisand.' I said, 'No, dear, your name is Jason Gould.' He began to cry and shout, 'No, no, no! It's Jason Streisand!' I couldn't lie, but took him in my arms and told him I'd love him if his name was Moishe Pipic. It made him laugh and we both felt better. What do you think of that story, Doctor?"

"I think he made a lot of sense. You were the highly successful parent and Elliot was depressed and not making it. Under the circumstances, I don't blame Jason for wanting to be a Streisand."

"Thank you for saying that, Doctor. I've always blamed myself for that, like I somehow convinced him that I was the better parent. I feel that way about a lot of parts of his life…I was always encouraging him not to be ashamed of being naked, and think that maybe it contributed to his… sexuality. You *know* that Jason is gay, don't you?"

I nodded. "It's been in all the papers."

"Yeah? Well, lots of things are in the papers that I wouldn't use to wipe my ass with! But this one happens to have been correct. I think I should have known then, since he wanted to be like me, a woman, and not Elliot, the so-called man in the family. I've always been afraid it was my fault."

"It's nobody's fault, but simply the way Jason developed. Psychiatry no longer considers homosexuality an illness or a perversion but simply another way of being."

She smiled.

"Speaking of Jason's being gay, Barbra, how do *you* feel about it?" I asked. "And no jokes, please."

She is a brilliant woman who well understands the concept of resistance. She thought for a moment and answered, "In many ways, I don't want my son to be anything but what he is—an intelligent, sensitive, kind, loving, decent human being. He is a gifted singer, writer, actor, and filmmaker. I get a lot of *naches* from him. What more could any parent ask? I am blessed to have him for a son. Maybe I am prejudiced. All parents believe their child is extra special, and I'm no different.

"Everyone who knows him agrees that I have a wonderful son. He also has excellent judgment, and I always ask his opinion if I don't know what path to follow. For example, I didn't much like the song 'Enough Is Enough' at first. He made me record it with Donna Summer in 1979 when he was only nineteen years old, because she was his favorite singer. It's been bringing in carloads of cash ever since.

"Speaking of Donna, and of asking advice, a surprising exchange happened between us when we were recording 'No More Tears.' We were very close, like two high school friends. I regarded Donna as the top disco singer of the times, and didn't hesitate to ask her for advice about disco. 'What!' she exclaimed. 'You are *Barbra Streisand* and you are asking *me* for advice?'

"Back to Jason. To show you the kind of person he is, he was offered twenty million dollars to write an exposé of me. He turned it down. How many children would have done that for their mothers? Somebody should have asked me to write a book about my mother! Boy, I would have jumped at the chance!

"He told a reporter, 'My mother is a real *mensch*. She's complicated, but there's a lot of heart and soul to her. She's unbelievably sensitive and a generous human being. She is full of love. Keep your offer. There is nothing unfavorable I could say about her that would make an interesting book.'" Barbra smiled. "I guess I can't have done too badly with him if that's what he thinks of me."

"You did very well indeed!" I said.

She continued, "Something strange happened about his being gay. On July 1, 1991, a London tabloid ran a story headlined *Barbra Weeps Because of Gay Son's Wedding*, in which he supposedly married an underwear model named David Knight, whom Jason had never even met. Jason was furious, and started to sue, but then desisted because he thought it would only spread the story.

"He eventually came to terms with it, and even began to think it was funny. I never did. What bothered me most was that the tabloid said I refused to attend the 'wedding.' If my son was getting married to a chimpanzee, I would be there. My only wish for Jason is that he experiences a life of love, joy, happiness, and personal and creative satisfaction."

"That's lovely, Barbra. You are indeed blessed to have so fine a child. I'm also sure that what you say is what you really have in your heart for Jason. But you have told me only what you want for *him*. Isn't there something you would like from him for *you*?"

Her eyes filled with tears. "You're pretty shrewd, Doctor Dale. I'll tell you the truth, although I wouldn't admit this to anyone else. It is hard for me to accept his homosexuality in one respect only: I want a grandchild of my own to continue my father's name, and now I'll never have one."

"I'm sure you know, Barbra, that many gay couples hire a surrogate mother or adopt a child. Jason is still young enough at forty-eight to settle down with a life partner and give you the grandchild you want."

"Yeah?" she answered. "He said he'd rather have a dog." I couldn't help laughing.

"He is also very promiscuous, and known as the lover boy of gay New York City," she went on. "I can understand why. He is handsome, charming, and very, *very* loving. He says he treats his boyfriends the way I treated him. Strangely enough, underneath his charm, he is somewhat shy and nervous–like guess who?–and doesn't like to talk about himself very much. He also has a beautiful voice. I guess being Barbra Streisand's son doesn't hurt. You know he is HIV positive, don't you?"

"That must be very frightening for you," I said. "But the new medications do very well at keeping positive HIV from developing into full-scale AIDS. To the best of my knowledge, there is no reason he couldn't father a baby with a surrogate, or at the very least, adopt one, along with his dog. I know many gay couples who have raised wonderful children. The sex of the parents doesn't matter. What counts is their love for the child."

It was the end of the hour. She stood up and came over and took my hand. "Thanks, Dr. Dale," she said, the tears running down her cheeks. "You make being gay sound so normal."

"It is, as much as being left-handed is normal for some people."

"I feel much better about it now. If I get nothing else from my analysis, I'm glad I came to you. This session made it all worthwhile."

I squeezed her hand and wiped away a tear or two of my own. I knew how she felt. It is moments like this that make my entire career worthwhile.

June 12, 2015

"Hey, Doc," she began, "how about let's talk about food today?"

"Why not?" I answered.

"Well, you geeks have some weird ideas of what us guys should talk about."

"Oh?" I said. "I wasn't aware that I thought you guys should talk about any subject in particular. What did you have in mind?"

"Well, like sex, for one thing," Barbra said. "And sex for two, three, and four things, for that matter."

"I'd rather talk about food," I said.

She laughed. I did, too. "You know I'm only kidding. You can talk about anything you want. Tell me about you and food."

She smiled. "I was always a fussy eater. I told you my mother thought I was built like a burnt twig and was always trying to pour chicken soup down my throat. Being a rebel, I wouldn't eat at all. So now I never like to sit down at a formal dinner. I'd much rather stand up in the kitchen and eat out of two or three pots on the stove. It tastes better to me that way. I have an appetite like a six-year-old child. When he was six, Jason ate healthier.

"I love soda, coffee ice cream, malted milks, banana splits, hot dogs, French fries, and the kind of bacon you get in a greasy spoon restaurant. I also love Jewish deli, like knishes, dill pickles, and latkes. The more calories it has, the better I like it. I also love baked potatoes. But they are no good fresh, and must be old and cooked and reheated a few times to get the real taste.

"But do you know what really fascinates me? Can openers and magnetic potholders. Likewise apple-corers! And grapefruit knives—it took real genius to think that one up. I'm jealous it wasn't me. I love to eat and sometimes eat so much I don't stop until I throw up."

"Are there any foods you don't like?"

"Yeah. I loathe eggs, especially raw egg whites. They taste like snot to me." We both gagged.

"I was eating at a party given by Princess Margaret for me in New York," she went on, "where they served coq au vin. Did I want any? Of course not. What I had a craving for was rice custard—rice custard *without* any raisins. Some people like rice custard with raisins, but I will only eat it without any. I couldn't say, 'Sorry, Princess, but I can't eat this fancy stuff.' So I smeared the gooey chicken around on my plate and left as soon as possible.

"Then Elliot and I searched the town for an open diner where I could get my pudding. Of course at that hour, most were closed, but we scoured New York and finally found a dim little café open down by the waterfront. I was thrilled to find that they had rice custard. Unfortunately, it was rice custard *with* raisins. I nearly cried when I saw them. But Elliot picked them all out for me, one by one, until we had pudding without raisins. I gulped it down like a starved lion who stumbles upon a sleeping lumberjack. No food has ever tasted better in my entire life."

We both burst out laughing. "That sounds just like you, Barbra," I said, and barely refrained from giving her a lecture on nutrition.

"I soothe my frazzled nerves with food. You should've seen me at lunch the other day at the studio. I was supposed to be on a diet. I was in a fish mood, so I ate a shrimp cocktail, Dover sole, poached halibut, and flounder off the bone. Then I finished up with rice pudding (without raisins). I ate like a horse. I have to be careful or I'll begin to look like one.

"During the decades I've been a star, I've improved. But sometimes I've had to eat like a star to keep up my strength."

June 15, 2015

"Barbra," I asked, "you told me about your divorce, but I don't know what happened after that. How did you cope?"

She laughed. "With difficulty. I coped by finding a boyfriend. In fact, as many as I could. The first one turned out to be a fiasco. I was filming *On a Clear Day You Can See Forever* in Brighton, England, and kind of got a crush on George Lazenby, who starred as James Bond in *On Her Majesty's Secret Service*. He came down on his motorcycle to visit me, and took me for a ride on the seat behind him. I held onto him tightly and screamed as he sped down the highway with the wind blowing through my hair.

"When we came back, I invited him up to my room, where I fully intended to have sex with him. He took me in his arms and kissed me, but something stopped him from going any further. I don't know what. Maybe he was scared of me. But I didn't care why. The next time he came up and tried to kiss me, I pushed him away. Nobody, but nobody, turns down Barbra Streisand! I've gone through too much to take rejection from some two-penny British actor. I don't get rejected anymore. I'm the one who walks away.

"In no other profession do people have to take as much rejection as actors do. Yes, even me, and you are talking to someone who has worked more than any other actor I know. How many jobs has the average person been fired from in a lifetime? Maybe five or six?

"An actor goes through the meat grinder fifty times a year, if she is lucky enough to be asked to try out for that many parts. In every one of them, she faces the possibility of rejection, no matter how famous she is. In a lifetime, that can add up to two thousand rejections. Two thousand!

"And it hurts every time as much as it did the first time, like when I got rejected for the Erasmus Glee Club by Mr. DePietto in high school more than fifty years ago. It still pains me. Yeah, in high school, and this from an Academy Award winner! So I make sure I don't get rejected anymore. I'm always the one who walks away."

"I can understand how you feel, Barbra," I said. "But I believe that sometimes one person rejects another for reasons that have nothing to do with the person rejected. Maybe the rejecter has a stomach ache, or had a fight with his wife and is taking it out on the first person he runs into. If you leave the scene before a final judgment is made, you risk losing out on what could possibly be the greatest film ever made. You miss much that is important in life if you throw out the baby with the dishwater.

"Eleanor Roosevelt once said that, to be in politics, you needed the hide of a rhinoceros. That is just as true for an actor. Perhaps you can learn to stay in the picture even though your feelings are hurt. In that case, you will find out that you can survive rejection."

She was quiet for a change. I took her silence to mean that she accepted my words.

"Speaking of *On a Clear Day You Can See Forever*," she said with a change of mood, "I want to tell you a little about it. In the film, I play Daisy Gamble, a chain smoker who's afraid to fly because of regulations that forbid the habit during takeoffs and landings. I agree to be hypnotized by psychiatrist Marc Chabot to cure my smoking habit. I attend a seminar given by Dr. Chabot—Yves Montand—who, although charming, seems strangely unpersuasive to me as the psychiatrist who falls in love with my former incarnation.

"The professor discovers that not only am I a psychic with ESP talents, but I am the reincarnation of an early nineteenth century English courtesan-turned-aristocrat named Melinda Tentrees. The prof falls madly in love with the memory of Melinda, all the while despising the sweet but irritating Daisy. To say that this is confusing is putting it mildly.

"Tad Pringle, played by Jack Nicholson, is a guitar-playing hippie who's seen so little it's hard to know he's in the picture. Chabot is constantly hired and fired again by the vacillating school president, played by Bob Newhart, when the media discovers his activities. I insist that I have lived twelve times before and promise to return to Chabot to marry him in the year 2038.

"For the movie, it was very important to me that Arnold Scaasi create Daisy's gamin look, and that Cecil Beaton, the famous British photographer designer, originate Melinda's elaborate Regency period costumes.

Barbra coped with a confusing time in her life while filming the confusing movie On a Clear Day You Can See Forever in 1969.

"I'm very interested in the subject of this movie, as I myself had a supernatural experience with ESP that led to the making of my film, *Yentl*. In my visit to a medium, my father came to the table and advised me to go ahead with the picture. As you know, it was one of the greatest successes of my lifetime, so how can I not believe in ESP? I'll tell you more about it another time. But I have something else I want to talk about today—men.

"The first guy après-Elliot was the blond, handsome, boyish twenty-nine-year-old actor, Ryan O'Neal. I met him at a Hollywood dinner party, which I had not wanted to go to; I usually hate parties. Thank goodness I let myself be dragged to that one, because sparks immediately flew between us. I fell for his surfer-boy looks and healthy physique, which fit right in with the persona I was trying to develop of a slim, tan, blond-streaked California girl—yeah, me, the Brooklyn girl with the big schnoz.

"Ryan was famous for appearing in over five hundred TV soap opera episodes, and he had won a Best Actor nomination for his role in the movie *Love Story*. An ex-boxer, he made me feel protected when we went out together. With a simple show of his muscular arms, he was able to scare off the obstreperous fans who always surround me.

"He also had a widespread reputation of being a great sexpot. According to Joann Moore, his actress ex-wife, he was a terrific lover who knew how to give a woman the greatest pleasure she had ever experienced. When I heard this, I was naturally curious, and a little voice in my head said, 'Try him out and see if what Joann said is true.' I did. It was.

"He had not yet divorced his second wife, so we tried to keep our relationship secret, but after we showed up together at a James Taylor concert, the media got hold of us like a dog with a bone, and never let go.

"Peter Borsari, a Hollywood photographer, tried to take a photo of us as we were going to a Mama Cass Elliot concert, but we objected. Borsari waited until after the concert and snuck up on us again. A nearby actor grabbed Borsari's camera and broke it. The photographer yelled, 'I can sue you for that!' The actor yelled back, 'Sue me all you please. I don't have two nickels to rub together.'

"The story was splashed across all the tabloids in the United States. They said, 'Barbra has got herself a boy toy, a gorgeous *goyische* guy with not much in the upstairs department.' They added that O'Neill had hooked up with the most popular actress of the times simply to further his career. They should only *ver gehardget* for saying so! I think he really cared about me.

"There were a lot of men I could have dated, but I wanted Ryan. Although there was a wonderful physical attraction between us, what grabbed me the most was his charm, his wit, and his mind. That's right, his mind! He made me laugh a lot, which not many people do, because they are intimidated by me. Unlike most of my dates, he was not in awe of me or my successful career. That's why I like you, Doctor. You treat me like a human being, not an icon."

I was pleased, although little did she know how impressed I really was by her. "Thank you, Barbra," I said. "I am delighted to know you feel that way."

"My pleasure, Doc!" We both smiled.

"I loved that Ryan never called me Barbra," she continued, "but always made up some hi-fallutin' name like Schmendra or Honeyballs. I would yell, 'No! No! That's not my name! My name is Barbra!'

"'OK, Sadie,' he would answer. I felt like Jason when he insisted his name was Jason Streisand, not Jason Gould.

"Ryan had a fine mind, and was a true amateur philosopher. I learned a lot from him. Nothing pleases me more than when a man I am involved with is smarter than me. When I know my mind is superior to a man's, it's the beginning of the end. Ryan knew everything about Hollywood, and how to stay out of trouble, which is something I'm not so great at. I listened carefully with my three ears and soaked up his knowledge like a dry sponge.

"We had a fight on our very first date. He won. I was delighted. That was probably the first thing that drew me to him.

"Our romance continued to grow during the early months of 1971. We no longer worried about being seen together in public, and we went to parties and the beach together whenever we pleased. There was a lot of bantering between us, and we made each other laugh all the time. For someone like me, who is happiest when she is miserable, that is no mean achievement.

"Jason adored Ryan and couldn't wait to see him, which pleased me no end, because I felt he needed a strong man as a role model. Which is more than I can say about Elliot. When Ryan escorted me to the opening of his latest film, *The Wild Rovers*, we sat on the front row holding hands, and allowed photographers to take photos of us. By then, we didn't care who knew about our romance."

June 17, 2015

Barbra picked up and ran with her Ryan O'Neal story right from the beginning of our next session. "Newspapers around the world ran headlines like, 'A new love story?' We were young, in love, and about to make the film, *What's Up, Doc?* together. It was a remake of a hilarious old movie called *Bringing Up Baby*, which had starred Katharine Hepburn and Cary Grant.

"Our director, Peter Bogdanovich, turned the film into an equally delightful romp that was a big hit both with the critics and the box office. I adored Katharine Hepburn as a child. Little did I know that one day I would follow in her elegant footsteps. It is one of the perks of being a star myself.

"The movie is modeled after the screwball comedies of the '30s and, in my opinion, is one of the finest remakes of a great comedy ever made. Usually, remakes of movie classics are idiotic and practically never as good as the originals. This new version was original enough to make it completely delightful.

"The film is set in San Francisco, where Ryan plays an absent-minded musicologist named Howard, who applies for a grant to work on his formula about primitive man's relationship to baked rocks. Howard is accompanied by his fiancée, who is played by Madeline Kahn. She's so funny that I'm jealous. I mean really. I know what Lauren Bacall meant when she told me at the Academy Awards, 'You are so good I want to slap you.'

"In the hotel pharmacy, Howard meets Judy Maxwell, an anarchist and accident-prone academic—a genius who's been thrown out of many universities for such things as accidentally blowing up a chemistry lab. Judy is played by guess who? The three of us get involved in a screwy subplot involving mixed-up suitcases containing Howard's rock formations, Judy's clothes, and the rich Mrs. Van Hoskins's expensive collection of jewelry. I'm not sure to this day that I completely understand the storyline.

"Of course, there is the usual car chase up and down the hills of San Francisco, ending with a procession of cars hurtling into the Bay. Does anyone ever make a movie in San Francisco without a car chase in it?

"The script by Buck Henry is full of little comic jewels. One of my favorites is, 'Has anyone ever told you that you're very sexy?'

"'Actually, no.'

"'Well, they never will.'

"Ryan is excellent as the bewildered musicologist, which didn't surprise me. I most love the moment in the film where I sing *As Time Goes By,* perched on top of a piano and seducing him. It wasn't too hard to do, both in and out of the movie. There are many hilarious scenes in the film—the chase through San Francisco, the courtroom scene at the end–'First there was this trouble between me and Hugh.'... 'You and me?'... 'No, me and Hugh.' It reminds me of 'Who's on first?'–and of course, there's the scene where I am wearing only a towel while hanging out a seventeenth-story window.

"I must admit I was terrified I would fall, even though I knew I really was only hanging out of the second story. I also was worried that my towel would fall off, and there I would be, standing stark naked in front of hundreds of fans watching the scene down below. It reminds me of nightmares where similar things have happened. The
movie has so many twists and turns, and it's perfectly funny and old-fashioned. I'm so glad I made it."

Barbra and Ryan O'Neal joking around on the set of What's up Doc?.

I made no comment.

"You're not saying anything, Doctor. Did you see the film?" she asked.

I nodded.

"Did you like it?

I waved my hand this way and that.

"Oh. Well, what *did* you think of it?"

"I thought it was a little bit funny and a little bit boring."

She laughed and said, "At least you're honest."

"Do you mind?" I asked.

"Not really," she answered. "I'm a tried and true Democrat. What I really believe is 'to each her own.'"

"Ryan had that irresistible little-boy quality about him. In my heart, I'm a typical Brooklyn Jewish mother, which is probably why we got along so well, at least for a while, anyway."

"What ultimately happened, Barbra?" I asked.

"No good thing can last forever," she replied, "and that included my romance with Ryan. During the filming, he proved not to be as bright as I had thought, and I found myself losing interest in him. He also seemed to like the ladies too much, and you know me: I'm not gonna let myself be put on a back burner, even by a gorgeous goyish guy. So I gave him his walking papers."

"You didn't miss him long, I gather," I said.

"Nah," she answered. "There are lots of fish in the sea. Red fish, blue fish, green fish, gold fish. And I wanted to catch every fish I could while I was young and sexy."

June 22, 2015

"My next film, *Up the Sandbox*, was altogether different," she said on coming through the door, as if she couldn't wait to begin her session. "It tells the story of an intelligent young upper Westside housewife and mother of two who feels trapped by an unwanted pregnancy. She punctuates her hum-drum existence in Walter Mitty fashion with a series of fantasies, from blowing up the Statue of Liberty to attacking her bossy mother. When I agreed to play Margaret Reynolds in the film, I was delighted," she continued, "for I thought it would give me the chance to express some of my deepest feelings about women and women's liberation.

"I agree with most of the thinking in the movement," she answered, "like equal job opportunities, equal pay, the fight against traditional role-playing, and even abortion, because I feel very strongly that women should have the right to say whether or not they want babies. Nobody has to agree with my opinions. So you can say that I am *for* women's lib, but with certain reservations."

"Like what?"

"Like I also believe there should be space allowed for mothering. Many women today are in conflict about their role in society. They want to do important work, but they still have the instinctual need to have babies and raise a family. I think a woman should be allowed to do whatever she wants to do, and if she chooses to stay home and be a wife and mother, more power to her. Every woman should strive to do a good job in whatever field she chooses, whether it be as a good mother or as a successful career woman. Do you agree?"

"I couldn't agree more."

"I'm glad to hear it,' she continued. "Otherwise, much as I like you, I'd have to quit."

I was beaming inside but tried not to show it.

"In the film," she continued, "the diatribe by a visiting revolutionary who looks like Fidel Castro is interrupted by a rebuttal by a Manhattan housewife who happens to be me. A confrontation with him is part of the plot in which I, the wife of a brilliant professor and mother of two, seeks my identity in a changing world. Castro argues that women should be liberated so they can become more like the military men of Cuba. In a burst of courage, I stand up and contend that Castro is trying to cast women in male roles. My character believes that the world would be a much better place if men would become more like women and be kinder and gentler. In real life, I really do think that.

"The police start to arrest me, but Castro shouts to let me be. Then in a bit of silly fantasy, he begins to dance. It turns out that Castro's beard was pasted on him, and he has breasts because he's actually a woman."

I said, "That does sound rather silly." We both laughed.

"For me, the best part of the movie was that Jason made his first movie appearance. Do you remember the scene where Margaret is pushing a child on a swing? Well, that child was Jason. Sometimes, I think maybe I did him a disservice casting him. Once acting gets in your blood, you get hooked once and for all!"

"Maybe," I said. "Or it may be that his inherited talent from both parents would have come out sooner or later."

She smiled and said, "You have a nice way of making me feel better, Doctor."

June 24, 2015

I opened the next session by saying, "Barbra, you're such a female activist that I wonder if you've ever been the victim of male chauvinism."

"Certainly. I still am," she answered promptly. "What woman hasn't been? Even women shrinks make less than the men, except for you, Doc, to whom I bow my head, even though I protested the gigantic fee at first. I've had to put up a big fight to get paid as much as men for my starring roles, and sometimes I still don't. For instance, Robert Redford made much more money than I did in *The Way We Were*, even though I had a larger, more important part. That was the only way we could get him to be in the picture.

"It is much harder for me than a man to be hired to direct a film, although I have no doubt I am one of the finest directors in Hollywood. I come by it naturally. A director has to be bossy and opinionated, and I don't have to tell you I am both.

"And I don't get a lot of the Academy Awards due to me because of my sex. I hoped to change some of that, to make it easier for me and all other women to get the equal treatment we deserve. One of the aspects of our sexist society that hurts me the most is that women's ideas are immediately rejected because they originate in a female mind. For the sake of both sexes, that has got to change. Men don't understand that they are cheating themselves as much as they are short-changing women.

"In film, that kind of discrimination has been the bane of my existence. I've had plenty of great ideas, which I've expressed long and loud. But because I am a woman, they were mostly disregarded. That's the main reason that I, Paul Newman, Sydney Poitier, and Steve McQueen started our company, *First Artists*, so I could make the kind of films I wanted to.

"Then, too, there is a terrible prejudice against actresses. We're supposed to look pretty, read our lines, and then shut up and go home. But I'm not the type of

Barbra was aggressive in both her relationships and her career.

woman to merely shut up and go home. With producers Robert Chartoff and Irvin Winkler and director Irvin Kershner, I was active in all matters at the company, including script and budget.

"As you know, my strength is in instinctive matters," she continued. "For instance, I am able to detect falseness in dialogue or a song and can find ways to get around it better than any man I know. Then too, I must admit I also liked the company because it afforded me a chance to earn big money like the men. Everybody thinks I got ten percent of the gross of all my pictures," she added. "Those people don't know their asses from their elbows. The pictures earned about sixty million dollars, so I ought to have earned six million. Right? Wrong. The first picture I got ten percent of was *What's Up, Doc?* I pleaded with producer Ray Stark to give me ten per cent of *Funny Girl*, but the stinker wouldn't do it. So he got three and a half million while I ended up with *bubkes*. Do you think that's right, Doctor?"

"Of course not, Barbra," I agreed. "I think you are doing a lot of good with your films, and admire you for having the courage to change the world for the better for women everywhere, including me."

"Even *you*? With all the money you make?"

"Even me," I said.

June 26, 2015

During the next session, Barbra continued to discuss her films. "The movie version of *Funny Girl* was my next big picture—and I do mean big! In fact, I think it set me on the map as a big-name movie star. Omar Sharif, who had appeared in *Lawrence of Arabia* and *Dr. Zhivago*, was cast as Nicky Arnstein. He was sexy, suave, and debonair, and an excellent card player in real life. He even wrote a couple of books on the subject.

"In the beginning of the discussions with Columbia, he wasn't wild about playing opposite me. He thought I was ugly, and said, 'How is this unattractive girl ever going to play a leading lady?' But the next day he changed his mind, and said, 'I looked carefully at her and didn't think she looked that bad, and began to find her more and more appealing. Soon I was madly in love with her.' From that point on, there was plenty of sexual chemistry between us," Barbra continued, "which boded well for the movie, and maybe, a little voice inside of me hinted, even for a little romance on the side. Despite being Egyptian, he seemed perfect for the part of the Jewish Arnstein.

"He also seemed perfect for me. I even gave an interview to the press in which I said I was crazy about the guy. I couldn't wait to get up in the morning and go to work because I knew I would see Omar there. I was miserable on the days he didn't have to report. Hollywood was ablaze with rumors that we were about to leave our mates and marry each other. Wyler coyly remarked, 'If all Jews and Arabs got along like Streisand and Sharif, the war would soon be over.'

"Would you believe it? Omar even offered to get circumcised for me, if it would make me happy. Now what man would willingly do that? I told him it wasn't necessary.

"Unfortunately, back in June 1967, only seven days after the newspapers had reported on his being cast as the leading man in *Funny Girl*, war broke out in the Middle East between Arab and Israeli forces. Sharif's casting triggered hostility in both warring nations, and a movement began in Egypt to revoke his citizenship. Adding to the highly charged atmosphere, photos taken during rehearsals of me and Sharif in a passionate embrace hit newspapers all over the world. You think that was trouble? My mother was quoted by the media as saying, 'My daughter ain't gonna work with no Egyptian!'

"Trouble was also brewing in Hollywood, where support for Israel was strong. Columbia insisted on throwing Sharif off the picture. But the director, William Wyler, shouted, 'Absolutely not! If you do, I will quit. We are in America, the land of the free, and it is despicable to think we would fire a man because he is an Egyptian.' Admiring his courage and outspokenness, I took the same position.

"Not that I'd had any doubt before about where I stood on the subject of Israel. My heart, of course, was with its survival. Only a few days before, I had given $400,000 to the Emergency Campaign for Israel, and sang at a concert for Israel at the Hollywood Bowl. As a result, all my films were banned for decades in all Arab countries. Too bad for them! Plenty of other countries made *Funny Girl* a box-office success all over the rest of the world.

"Omar was funny about it when he was quoted in the papers. He said, "Before I kiss a girl, I don't ask her nationality, her religion, or her occupation.' I don't remember him asking mine, either. He wouldn't have gotten very far with me if he had.

"At the time, Elliot's gambling problems continued, though, unlike Arnstein, he never went to jail. I guess I should've been grateful I was spared that humiliation. As my mother always says, 'Thank God for small favors.' Can't you just see the headlines? 'Barbra's spouse thrown in clinker!'"

June 29, 2015

"In 1967, I took a rare weekend off from *Funny Girl* to film a TV special," she began. "I appeared at Central Park's Sheep's Meadow to sing before a crowd of 135,000, the largest crowd ever to come to see a single performer. I loved this, of course. You know me, Doc. I love to be first. The free concert paid off handsomely, for it resulted in both a prime-time special success, which was a milestone in free entertainment, and a top-of-the-line record album.

"But unfortunately, something terrible happened during the concert. Only three hours before the show was to begin, some nut phoned in a death threat because of my support of Israel. I was terrified that being in the spotlight would make me a perfect target for the kook in the audience. I stood frozen at the entrance to the stage for what seemed like hours. It took a shove from a technician to get me out there. All the while, I was thinking, 'My God! What am I doing here? This is not stage fright. It is a thing called *death*.' Pro that I am, I walked out with outstretched arms, as if nothing were wrong. The audience broke into wild applause. I said, 'Hold on, there. I ain't done nothin' yet!'

"I walked all over the stage as I sang, hoping my constant movement would make it harder for anyone to take a shot at me. Fortunately, when I saw the show on TV, I looked perfectly natural. But I was so *bachaded* I forgot the lyrics to some of the songs I'd been singing for decades. Nobody seemed to care. Except me.

"A few weeks later, I was back at the Hollywood Palladium, performing another show to benefit Israel. It was all I could do to drag myself onto the stage, but I didn't want to let down either Israel or my fans. This time, there really was a crazy in the audience whom security had discovered. Carrying a .45 caliber pistol, he was captured and hauled away. I didn't learn about it until after the performance was over. It was a good thing too, or I never would have made it through the show.

"But that second trauma produced lasting results. From that moment on, I was flooded with a deep-seated terror of performing in public. It was so paralyzing that I never completely got over it. In the fall of 1984, I again became the victim of a raving lunatic. A former mental patient broke into my house in Beverly Hills. He was apprehended and held for psychiatric observation. No sooner was he released than the intruder began to send me death threats in the mail. Fortunately, he was arrested again and placed under long-term psychiatric evaluation.

"The disturbance at the Palladium certainly did nothing to lower the panic that flooded me about performing in public," she commented.

"I may be able to help you with that, Barbra," I said. "Freud helped soldiers traumatized in the war to get over their panic by having them repeat the incident over and over again until they mastered it. We can do the same."

"You're the doctor! I'm willing to try anything."

So we decided we would go over the incident session after session until we both felt she had gotten a handle on it. I hoped it would help.

Despite the circumstances, Barbra gave a stunning
concert performance that day in Central Park, 1967.

July 3, 2015

"Barbra, you said once that you really are an activist at heart. That is a very important part of you, it seems. Tell me more about it," I said.

"Okay. You're helping me get over my fear of performing in public slowly but surely, and it will help me to sing again. I thank you for that. I'm planning a concert in the fall to raise money for the fight against AIDS. I'll tell you why it is so important these days. I always go against the norm. As you know, after the threat against my life during the Central Park concert in 1967, I froze, and refused to perform in public again. I never thought I would return to singing publicly.

"But then, I never dreamed that with all the advanced technology today there would still be starvation of bodies and minds and the possibility of nuclear catastrophe. I can't remain silent any longer. By being silent, we give consent to the idiocy of countries spending billions of dollars on weapons, instead of educating our children, subsidizing our farms, doing medical research that will save lives, and developing safe sources of energy.

"My voice is vital, just as yours and everyone's is. Sometimes we forget that, and the enormous difference that individuals fighting evil can make in history. I feel that I can do the most good by singing, and will sing again to do what I can to bring about a safer and better world. But no matter what I do, rest assured that I won't lose me."

"You are a good woman, Barbra. Have a happy 4th of July," I said, as she stood up to leave.

Barbra Streisand is not a person who indulges in small talk. She did not respond.

I felt a little embarrassed.

July 6, 2015

The next session, Barbra returned to her discussion of *Funny Girl* and her affair with Omar Sharif. "After the shooting was finished and Omar was packing to go home," she said, "I decided I wasn't happy about the final scene in which I sang 'My Man,' the song Fanny Brice sang most effectively. Sharif was still in love with me, and rushed back to the studio so that his presence could help me sing this sad song more realistically.

"Alone in the studio, we acted out the final poignant moments between Fanny and Nick. Then, full of emotion, I stepped in front of a black curtain and sang 'My Man.' By the time I finished, the script girls and tough crew members were sobbing away. So was Omar. What he didn't know was that not only were we acting out a love scene between two actors, but I was dropping him for real and using the emotion to make the scene more believable on screen. Was that rotten of me? Maybe. But the movie was over, and all I wanted was to go home to my Elliot, who unfortunately, did not feel the same way about me.

"Around this time, I met the Maharishi Mahesh Yogi, the Indian spiritual leader who had become famous as the guru to the Beatles. One night after a party, Marty Erlichman and I went on a pilgrimage to meet the Maharishi in his room at the Plaza Hotel. The room was tiny. When we entered, the Maharishi was sitting in the middle of a bed in the lotus position, holding a rose in his teeth. I wondered if the scene had been staged for our benefit.

"A small man, he was dressed in white ceremonial robes, with long greasy hair falling uncombed around his shoulders. I stood at the foot of the bed, waiting to be enlightened by his words of wisdom. He spoke in a squeaky voice about the power of transcendental meditation, and shouted, 'Rejuvenation has arrived!'

"I wasn't impressed. 'Whaddya mean by that?' I asked.

"He took the flower out of his teeth and said, 'If you let consciousness go where it wants to, it will take you to the greatest happiness.'

"'Well,' I said, 'since I normally go to the point of my greatest unhappiness, it must mean that my greatest happiness comes from being unhappy.'

"The Maharishi looked a bit befuddled, and apparently had no answer to my philosophical inquiry.

"I doubted if I would join him or the Beatles again in a quest for enlightenment."

July 8, 2015

Barbra entered the office for her session, stopped, looked at me, and said, "Well?"

"Well, what?"

"Don't you notice anything different about me today?"

I looked her up and down and said, "Sorry, Barbra, but for the life of me I don't. I give up. What's different?"

"How come you don't notice my hair?"

"What about your hair?"

"Oh you shrinks! If I sneezed, you'd analyze it. But when something important changes, do you notice? No, you are too busy following the books! Check out my hair, DOCTOR! I had it curled. Normally, I wear it straight, because I have naturally straight hair."

I looked carefully at her, and said, "So it is! But why does that matter so much?"

"Don't you shrinks notice anything that Freud didn't dictate? All my life, I've wanted naturally curly hair. When you finally get something you've always wanted, don't you think that's important?"

"Indeed I do," I said musing. "I wasn't thinking. In fact, I empathize with you."

"So how come you didn't notice? Analysts are supposed to notice everything."

"You're right." I debated whether to tell her the truth, and decided with Barbra that truth-telling was always a good idea. "My experience is the exact opposite of yours, Barbra. *I* have curly hair," I confessed. "When I was a child, I used to cry that I wanted straight hair like all my friends had. They could wear it long all the way down their backs, while mine always shot up into little curls. Maybe I just didn't want to remember how painful it was."

"Okay, I'll forgive you this time, Doc," she said, cracking her elfish Streisand grin, which reeked of mischief and charm. "But may I suggest you find yourself a good shrink?"

July 8, 2015

By the next session, it seems, Barbra had completely forgotten about our little comic tussle the day before (or pretended that she had), and returned to her story about her relationship with Elliot. "The world did not know yet that Elliot and I were planning to go our separate ways. So he flew out to California to discuss divorce and to keep up appearances by accompanying me to the forty-first Academy Awards ceremony on April 1, 1969.

"We were very tense on our endless drive down to the Dorothy Chandler Pavilion in the new Los Angeles Center, and tried to refrain from discussing anything personal. Seeing him again with Jason, I realized what a wonderful father he was. Jason idolized him, and I found myself seriously reconsidering whether we should file for divorce.

"We stuck to the discussion of the ceremony to come, in which I had been nominated for best actress, along with the formidable actresses Katherine Hepburn for *The Lion in Winter*, Vanessa Redgrave in *Isadora*, Patricia Neal for *The Subject was Roses*, and Joanne Woodward in *Rachel, Rachel.*

"The outfit I wore was something else again. People who saw me in it have never let me forget. It was a revealing see-through, black chiffon pajama set with white Puritan cuffs and a collar with black-jet traces. When I say it was revealing, I'm not kidding! It had been designed for Daisy in *On a Clear Day You Can See Forever* by Scaasi, but was rejected as too exhibitionistic for Broadway.

"When Scaasi designed it, he hadn't realized that both layers of fabric would become transparent under the glare of television lights. Shocked faces turned to stare at me as we entered the packed auditorium with its gleaming crystal chandeliers. Millions of people all over the world were treated to a clear view of my ample derriere.

"The next day, the newspapers were filled with stories about the tastelessness of my apparel, and my apparent desire to moon the world. I'd had no idea when I wore it to the Academy Awards that the outfit would become transparent under the lights! I was embarrassed, but it sure was an original for the times."

"Would you have worn it had you known?" I asked.

She smiled and said, "No comment!

"Ingrid Bergman was the Mistress of Ceremonies for the Academy Awards that night. Looking luminously beautiful as only Bergman could, she opened the envelope containing the name of the winner for best actress of 1969. Then a strange look crept over her lovely face. 'It's a tie!' she shouted. 'Katherine Hepburn for *The Lion in Winter*,' then waited for what seemed like an eternity until the prolonged applause had abated. 'And Barbra Streisand for *Funny Girl*!'

"I dashed up to the platform, where two gargantuan golden Oscars guarded the rear and stood next to a faintly amused looking Bergman. Hepburn was in New York, and her award was accepted for her by her director, Anthony Harvey, who then stepped off the platform.

"'Congratulations!' Bergman said warmly. I grasped the golden Oscar in my hands and yelled, 'Hello, Gorgeous!' Then, remembering my manners (which do pop up on occasion), I said, 'I'm delighted to be in the company of so illustrious an actress as Katherine Hepburn.'"

"Much as I liked getting the long overdue Oscar, Elliot gave me a present that in a different kind of way meant just as much to me. It was a gold-covered bagel. Only Elliot could have thought of that. It brought back golden memories of our days over the fish store, and made me cry.

"The morning after the Oscar awards, I called my mother and said, 'Hey, Mom, what did you think of the ceremony last night?'

"She answered, 'Why were you wearing your underwear in public?'"

Barbra with her first Oscar.

July 15, 2015

"Today I want to tell you about one of my favorite films and one of the best I ever made. In a nutshell, the plot is 'girl loves goy, girl gets goy, girl loses goy.'"

"*The Way We Were*," I practically shouted.

She looked pleased and quipped, "You win the $50,000 question, Doctor!"

"Barbra," I said, "that is one of my very favorite movies, too. I saw it only once years ago, but was very moved by it. I still think about it often."

"You have good taste, Doctor! I happen to believe it is one of the best films ever made by anybody."

"I'm not going to dispute that," I said. "But what do you want to tell me about it, besides that it is a great movie?"

"Funny that you liked it so much," she mused. "What do you say we analyze why?"

I laughed, and said, "We'd better not go into that one, Dr. Streisand! You might not like what you find out."

"OK," she said. "I'll let you off the hook—this time." We both laughed.

"Refresh my memory," I said. "Tell me about the movie."

"That's something I'm happy to do, because I'm still in love with the film. It is about two Cornell University students who are the quintessential star-crossed lovers. I identified immediately with the very radical Katie Morosky, the passionate, headstrong, outspoken firebrand. Robert Redford starred as the laid-back Hubbell Gardner, who was born with a silver spoon in his mouth and never let this Brooklyn-born *mieskeit* forget it. We are very attracted to each other, me sexually, but him only intellectually.

"Never were two lovers more different. To my character, he is my fairy tale prince brought to life, and as an unambitious man, he is captivated by the force of my energy, my moral principles, and my drive. Knowing him makes me feel like a princess, and not a Jewish *meshugena* from Brooklyn. He hopes, I suspect, to vicariously take on my character traits that he lacks.

"Oh, the way they used to make movies!" she exclaimed. "If only they still were making them that way! Hubbell Gardner is a typical four-letter WASP jock while I, Katie Morosky, am a socialist activist who has to struggle to make the rent because I'm Jewish, poor, and plain. Does that sound familiar? I'm a communist who protested the civil war in Spain and Hitler's rise to power in Europe, and has to work three jobs to pay for my schooling. He is passionate only about sports and couldn't care less about politics. How different can two people be?"

I had to admire her insight and told her so.

"From the beginning, I could see only Robert Redford in the role of the apathetic, politically uninvolved, golden-haired boy," she went on as if I hadn't said anything, "but he turned down the part. He found the script overly sentimental, the character of Hubbell Gardner one-dimensional, and the political message 'bullshit liberalism.' Moreover, he insisted that the politics and romance in the script wouldn't mix. Perhaps most important, he thought his proposed part was much less important than mine, and that the film would be 'my show.'

"For a star of his magnitude, that was no small criticism. Once I get an idea in my head, however, that's it! I *had* to have Redford for the role. And what Barbra wants, Barbra gets. Though I consulted many important producers and directors, neither they nor I had a clue about how to hook him. Then one night I woke up at 3am flooded with the idea that Redford might be persuaded to take on the role if his good friend, Sydney Pollack, was hired to direct the film.

"Pollack agreed that Redford was exactly right for the part, and, moreover, was the only important actor who would not be overshadowed by me. He tried hard to convince Bob to accept the offer.

"'Are you nuts, Pollack?' Redford shouted. 'It's a lousy script, the part is too small, and there is no way the political and love stories can mix!'

"Twelve writers were brought in to try to make the script meet Redford's needs, but none were successful. I became more and more distraught. I thought, *I have to make this film, and I have to have Robert Redford play opposite me!* After several rewrites by Paddy Chayevsky, thank goodness, Hubbell grew into a grimmer, more complex character. But ornery soul that he is, Redford still rejected the role. Just when I was about to give in and offer the part to Ryan O'Neal, Redford relented, and said he would play the part for a percentage of the gross and a salary of one million, two-hundred thousand dollars.

"I was peeved, because I was to be paid only one million dollars, which was less money than my co-star. But Redford was so perfect for the role that I accepted the embarrassment and agreed.

Barbra with Robert Redford, who was less interested in their off-screen relationship than their on-screen one.

"Before rehearsals started, I wanted to have a talk with Redford so we could get to know each other and share our thoughts about the film. But wouldn't you know? The stubborn man refused to see me! He said it would be better if we came to the film as fresh new professional acquaintances.

"I was very upset, and felt he was avoiding me. '*Why* can't we meet? I asked Pollack. 'I'm only asking him to have dinner with me, not to marry me.'

"Pollack talked to Bob, and he finally agreed to meet with the two of us. Bob must have been afraid of me and thought he would be safer from my wiles if Pollack served as a chaperone. The three of us met at my house, and the minute my eyes fell on him, I was smitten. What a beautiful man! He was all the things I was not—gorgeous, a goy, rich, and golden-haired, with a huge trust fund. My infatuation with him must have been apparent, because gossip on the set was rampant that I was trying to steal Bob away from his wife."

"Were you?"

"The answer, I'm afraid, is yes. But, unfortunately, he was not for sale. In fact, nothing at all happened between us off-camera. He was completely faithful to his lucky wife, and remained as distant and inaccessible to me as he had been before our dinner.

"Every night, as was my wont, I would call the director and quiz him about the day's shooting. 'Was I any good?' I would ask. 'How did I photograph? Are you making sure that my nose doesn't look too long? Can you give me a motivation for why I come into the dining room, living room, bedroom, kitchen? I can't think of any.' Pollack, I must say, was amenable to all that, although I overheard some crew members say that he complained to them, 'That Barbra never shuts up!'

"The nerve of the man! I only wanted him to be helpful. The one person I did not dare to bother after hours was Robert Redford. He had made it clear that when he went home, he was going home, and wanted it to stay that way. But, on the set, I did assault him with important questions and comments. The crew members, who get to hear everything, told me they heard him say, 'Barbra talks and talks, until she drives me nuts!' What's with these men, anyhow, that they don't like a little verbal exchange?

"At one point, I asked Pollack what Bob thought of me. He answered, 'I think each of you is in awe of the other. After you see the daily rushes, you both ask me the same thing. 'How does Bob/Barbra do it? I stank next to him/her, didn't I? He/she is so great and I am so lousy!' Sydney Pollack always made us feel better by saying, 'You were great!' Even if we weren't."

July 17, 2015

Barbra returned to talking about the story of the film. "The first scene of the movie takes place at the El Morocco nightclub in Manhattan at the end of World War II, with me catching my first glimpse of Hubbell, who is having a drink at the bar. He is simply stunning in his dress-white Naval Officer's uniform. In fact, I gasp when I see him, because I have never seen such a beautiful man before. I am the frizzy-haired, frumpy campus activist, who is managing to pay my tuition by handling the cloak room at the club, while he was born to more money than he could ever spend in his lifetime. The opening scene sets the tone for the rest of the movie.

"By the time we got to the bathtub scene, Bob had relaxed around me and was able to be warmer. In fact, we got very good at making wisecracks and telling jokes to each other. He used to make me howl when he tried to say Yiddish words, and some of the repartée is reproduced in the film.

"One of our biggest problems was that we each wanted to be shot from the left side of our face, because we both felt we looked better from that angle. Bob has some moles on his right cheek that detract from his perfect beauty, and my nose looks longer when shot from the right side. The technicians overcame the problem by shooting face-to-face close-ups with a soft light behind us to remove any harsh shadows. If only all my problems were solved so easily!

"A reporter, without adding the obvious— she's no beauty—asked Bob how he explained my appeal. Bob answered, 'It is hard to put into words. The way I see it, her femininity brings out a man's masculinity, and her masculinity brings out a man's femininity. Is it clear what I mean?'

'Sure,' the reporter answered. 'Clear as mud.'"

Barbra returned again to the movie's storyline. "Despite our intensive attempts to get our relationship to work under the most difficult of conditions, including World War II, McCarthyism, Hollywood at its best and worst, and the simple fact that we just aren't right for each other, Hubbell and I can't manage to get it together. Katie is a deep and highly original thinker, with an I.Q. that is through the ceiling, while Hubbell is shallow, conventional, lazy, and a snob.

"Who was it that said that in every pair of lovers, there is one who loves and one who is loved? Katie loves Hubbell deeply, while he relates to her in his usual laid-back way. Sometimes life imitates art. That's pretty much the way it was between us in real life. I would have had an affair with Redford in a minute, but he was a faithful devoted family man who wouldn't even give me a second look.

"Wouldn't you know it? When I finally find a man with integrity, he uses it against me! Of course, that made me want him even more. He has a quiet dignity about him and a sharp intelligence. There is always something going on behind his eyes. He is a person of many conflicting layers, some deeply passionate, which he tried to conceal—at least from me—and others highly judgmental. At that point, he had been married to his wife Lola for fifteen years. I was thinking, *Why can't I find a guy like that who isn't happily married?*

"Lola Redford did present a problem to Bob at least once, or so I heard. A rumor was going around that when she heard about how close he and I were getting, she was furious with him and threw a glass of red wine at him, which ruined his white dress shirt. Whether it was true or not, I was delighted by the story. With Robert Redford, you don't ask whether it's true.

"I have to tell you about something that upset Redford, and still makes me laugh whenever I think of it. There is a scene in the movie between the two of us that takes place in a hot tub, and we were supposed to be naked in it. I wore a mesh-colored bra and panties.

"Can you picture lying naked next to a man you love who won't give you a second look? If I look ecstatic in that scene, it's because I was! It was almost as good as the real thing. I would have been delighted to wear nothing at all next to that gorgeous golden-haired goy, but the director wouldn't let me. He said if I did, the film would be censored.

"Being a very modest person, Bob wore not one but *two* jockstraps, which he hoped would hide any erections he might have. But unfortunately, or maybe fortunately, the outline of the jockstraps showed up on the screen, so the director made him take them off. Bob's face turned redder than the sun on a hot August day, but he obeyed Sydney's instruction and silently removed the straps.

"But the minute the scene was over, he slid beneath the water and pulled them back on. I must admit I pretended to drop my ring and took a quick peek at him beneath the water. All I can tell you is that I'm still mourning what I missed.

"'Why? Why? Why doesn't he love me?' my character keeps asking herself. 'I'm not pretty enough for you, am I?' she asks him. 'Isn't that our problem?' He doesn't answer. Katie shakes her head and adds, 'OK, so don't answer! But rest assured that nobody will ever love you like I do.' Redford, distant, icy, and beautiful, has to agree.

"'And I don't have the right style for you, do I?' she continues.

"He solemnly answers, 'No, Katie, you don't have the right style for me.'

"'At least you're honest. OK, so I don't have the right style for you. I'll change.'

"'Un uh, you can't change. You're your own person. That's who you are.'

"'But then I won't have you. Why won't you let me have you?'

"'Because you push too hard, every goddamn instant. You don't ever give me a moment to relax and enjoy life. Every little thing is too damn serious for you. I can't drop my toothbrush without getting a lecture.'

"'If so, it's because I love you. I want you to be better than you are. I want you to be a wonderful person, the great author you have locked up inside of you, instead of the mediocre screenwriter you are now. I want things to be better with *us*. Sure, I make waves. You have to, if you want to improve things. And I'll keep making them until you have become everything you have it in you to be. You should appreciate that I push you, because you'll never find anyone else who believes in your potential like I do.'

"'I know that, Katie.'

"'Then why don't you come back to me?'

"'What makes you think things would be better if I came back? What would be different? Neither of us can change. People don't. We are who we are. If I come back, I'll still be who I am and you'll still be you. We'll both lose.'"

"Then Katie begins to cry and says, 'Wouldn't it be lovely if we got past all this nonsense and grew old together? Then everything would be simple and uncomplicated; the way it was when we were young.'

"'Katie, you're dreaming. It *never* was uncomplicated.'

"I think Hubbell was wrong," Barbra said. "The *We* in the title, *The Way We Were,* refers to everybody in the world, not just Katie and Hubbell. It is the way all of us used to be when everything mattered and we cared, the way Elliot, Oscar the rat, and I were when we lived in that cheap apartment over the fish store. Sometimes I think I was better off then.

"One of the other scenes in the movie that always gets to me is the one after Hubbell and I break up, where I telephone him sobbing and say,

'This is the kind of thing where your best friend comforts you. But you are my best friend, Hubbell. I never had a better friend. So can't my best friend come over and comfort me?'

"When I think of that scene, I always cry.

"But the ending was the most moving scene of all, Dr. Dale, don't you think? Nobody can watch it without cracking up. I know. I was in it, and I can't!'

I said, "Neither can I, Barbra."

July 20, 2015

Barbra sat down, crossed her legs, and enthusiastically announced, "Today I'm going to tell you about a biggie—my love affair with Jon Peters, one of the great loves of my life."

"Jon Peters, the hairdresser?"

"Dr. Dale, don't tell me you are calling him the hairdresser, too! It makes me furious that the media always refers to him that way. But I have a right to expect more from you. True, Jon can cut and style hair with the best of them, but he is so much more than that. For one thing, he was the multi-millionaire owner of a string of beauty salons."

"I'm sorry, Barbra. I didn't know."

"Well, you should have. If you've read about him, you must have picked up a lot more information about him than that."

"You're right. I won't make that mistake again."

"OK. I guess I'll forgive you... this time. But it is a sore spot with me. He has remained one of the great loves of my life, even though we are not together anymore, and I can't bear to see him demeaned as a *grubber yung*. Don't let it happen again, or I'll quit. There are thousands of analysts, but only one Jon Peters."

"True. I promise."

But like the proverbial dog with a bone, she was not ready to drop the subject. "I can't understand how a woman who's supposed to know all about my mind could say such an insensitive thing," she said. She picked up the small statue of Freud on my desk and threw it against the wall. "There! Now we're even!"

Barbra had done what we in psychoanalysis call "acting out," which is greatly discouraged. But in this instance, because I was at fault, I decided to make an exception and tackle her act-out tendency at a future date. Besides, the statue hadn't broken. And even if it had, I could always buy another, and there is only one Barbra Streisand. It was good for her to express her violent feelings and find out that I could accept her in all her moods.

"OK, Barbra," I said. "I guess I deserved that. Now let's get on with it."

Although my colleagues probably would disagree, I had apparently done the right thing in breaking an analytic rule. To my surprise, she grew somber and said, "Thanks, Doctor. Not many people would forgive me for that. My mother would have said, 'You *meshugena*, you! You're breaking up the house,' and smack my face good and hard." She rubbed her cheek as if it still hurt.

I was moved. "You are very welcome, Barbra," I said. "But we have to stop now. Another patient is waiting in the waiting room."

"What? Stop now?" she countered angrily. "Just when I am getting started?"

"I'm afraid so," I answered, realizing how few people say no to the great Barbra Streisand.

She got up from the couch, gave me a dirty look, left without saying good-bye, and closed the door nearly hard enough to break the glass.

Whoever said that therapists are overpaid?

July 22, 2015

"Sorry we had to end your last session in the midst of your story about Jon Peters," I said. "Shall we get on with it today?"

She lit up with an inner glow characteristic of her. "To sum it all up before I go into all the details, I met this wonderful man who swept me off my feet, turned both my professional and personal lives inside out, and made me feel as if Marilyn Monroe didn't hold a candle to me as the greatest sex object of all time. For some reason that I still don't understand, he was able to touch the deepest part of my heart."

"Who knows what draws people together," I said. "I've been a psychoanalyst for more than fifty years, and I'm no closer to the answer today than the day I picked up my first psychology book."

"Yeah? Well, if I ever find out, I'll let you know."

"I wouldn't be surprised," I said with a smile. Her brilliant blue eyes shone in response.

"I met him in the summer of 1973 and, the minute I laid eyes on him, I was attracted to the dark, intense, twenty-eight-year-old with a stallion's mane of thick, black hair. He drove up to my house in his flashy red Ferrari. I was taken with his low-cut shirt, Indian necklace, and skin-tight leather jeans, which left no doubt about his masculine attributes. *Who is this person with a Gucci bag slung over his shoulder?* I wondered. *I've never seen anyone like him.* He greeted me with, 'Babe, you are the most beautiful woman I've ever seen.'

"Imagine how that went over with me! He meant it, too, or my shit detector would have gone off. Then he said, 'Hi there, you sexy little ball of fire!' That also went over big with me, the little girl no boys paid any attention to in high school. From that moment on, he wouldn't leave me alone. Nor did I want him to.

"I knew right away we were meant to have an important relationship. But I guess I was pretty scared of that connection, and kept him waiting for three quarters of an hour while I recovered. He was furious, and said, 'Don't you ever keep me waiting again! Nobody, but nobody, keeps Jon Peters waiting! Clients pay me hundreds of dollars for a styling, but I've dropped them for less reason.' I smiled when I turned my back on him and he murmured, 'You've got a great piece of ass there, kid.'

"That made my spirits soar to the sky. I thought, 'I could really like this guy, but I better go easy with him. He just isn't my kind of person. I've always gone for distinguished men like doctors or lawyers. I had just returned from a visit with Pierre Trudeau, who is more the type of man I've always liked. Jon looked more like a junior member of the Mafiosa. So when he asked me out, I thought I'd be sensible and turn him down.

"Well, nobody turns down Jon Peters," she continued. "He kept calling me day and night, until he wore me down. The day of our eventual first date, he drove up to my house in a green Jaguar. He was wearing designer sunglasses, a velvet smoking jacket over his black leather jeans, a tight tee-shirt, and a huge silver cross. *He's as quirky as I am*, I thought. Unable to resist him any longer, I accepted his invitation to dinner that very night. Thus began one of the great love stories of my life.

"Jon was a great mystery to me, and he wanted it to remain that way. The little he told me about his background is this: He was born in a lower-class neighborhood in San Fernando Valley. His mother was an Italian whose family owned Pagano's, a famous Beverly Hills beauty salon. His father, a short-order cook, was half-Cherokee.

"'My father taught me how to fight,' Jon bragged. 'I was Cochise's son.' My first thought was that my mother would have conniptions when she found out and yell, 'Not only a goy but an Indian, yet!' I had never met a Native American before, so to me he seemed exotic. Jon had grown up alone, much like me, and had suffered a similar early tragedy. His father died right in front of him when Jon was only eight years old. Like me, he never got over it, but mourned his father every day of his life.

"'My father gave me a lot of love,' Jon said. 'He taught me to be a warrior, and to defend myself as a son of Cochise should. He took me on camping trips and taught me how to use guns and knives, and how to ride horseback. He gave me enough love to last a lifetime. It's because of his love that I am able to do as well as I do. Otherwise, I'd be spending my life in jail, or get murdered on the streets.'

"He told me a very moving story about the night after his father died. His mother didn't want to stay alone in the house, so he and she went to stay with a nearby relative. Jon couldn't fall asleep, so he climbed out the window and went home. He sat there alone, waiting all night for the father who never came. When telling me about it, he said, 'When I realized that he was never coming back, I was devastated. It felt like the end of the world.' It sounded just like me waiting at the window for my dead father to return.

"Jon, too, had a working mother, and really raised himself. Again, like me, his mother remarried, and Jon hated his stepfather, who beat him mercilessly. Probably as a result, he began to get in trouble, and was called 'incorrigible.' Unable to handle him, his mother threw him out of the house. He was totally naive when she asked him to meet her for a soda. At the store, two policemen stepped in and put a pair of handcuffs on him. 'I can't control him, Officers,' his mother said, with tears running down her face. 'You'll have to take over for me.'

"He was stripped and sprayed for lice, and taken to the David Gonzales detention camp in Malibu. He considered his mother's action a betrayal, and didn't talk to her for years. Many years later, when she was dying of stomach cancer, he forgave her.

"A strong, pugnacious kid, he got into so many fights with his classmates that he also was thrown out of school.

"'Nobody messes with Jon Peters,' he said. 'The harder you hit me, the madder I get. You dare to take on Jon Peters? You and who else?' When he went to another school, he was put in a class for slow learners. Can you believe it? He is probably the smartest person I know.

"He stole a car when he was eleven and was sentenced to a year in a reform school in the San Bernardino Mountains, where he was assigned the back-breaking work of digging ditches, clearing out fallen trees, and breaking up rocks, as if he was an adult convict. At night, he was actually chained to his bed. And I thought I had it bad!

"When I sympathized with him, he said, 'Oh, it wasn't all bad. It toughened me up and taught me what society can do to you if you fight it. I learned that I could do what I wanted and, most important, how to be smart enough not to get caught.' His youthful trials and tribulations never broke his spirit, but just intensified his drive to show the world it was wrong about him. Sound familiar?

"When he was released, his mother wanted him to go back to school. He said after all he had been through, he would rather die than return to the eighth grade, stuck with all the little kids. His mother was understanding for once, and suggested he go to beauty school instead. He poked his head in the door of a fancy salon to check it out, and when he saw all the beautiful girls inside, he knew right away that it was the job for him.

"When he finished beauty school, he borrowed $120 from his mother and hitchhiked to New York. There he was hired at a 57th Street beauty parlor to dye hookers' pubic hair the color of their poodles. I need not mention that he loved his job!"

"What?" I said. "Am I hearing correctly? In my many years of practice, I've heard of all kinds of jobs, but I have to say that's a new one."

"You heard me right," she answered. "There is a lot about Jon Peters you've never heard before. Believe me, there is nobody in the world like him. When he was not yet fifteen, he got married to a girl named Marie. That's all I know about her, because he refused to talk about the marriage. I don't know whether it was because he respected her or it was still too painful to discuss. Or maybe he just wanted to talk about his successes.

Barbra and Jon Peters
in love in 1976.

"You might wonder why his folks let him get married so young. It was because they wanted to get him off their neck. Jon and Marie lived in Philadelphia, where he had two jobs, apprentice hairdresser in the daytime and a nightclub bouncer at night. Unsurprisingly, the marriage didn't last very long, and they got divorced when Jon was nineteen."

I had to stop Barbra again before she was ready. And again, she gave me a look that could set off an electric chair. She again left the office so angrily I wondered if she would ever return.

July 23, 2015

She did return, of course, and picked up as if there had been no hiatus. "Jon has a golden tongue. He returned to California, where he talked a realtor into lending him a hundred thousand dollars to open his own beauty salon in Encino. Nobody ever lent me a hundred thousand dollars when I was nineteen. His brilliance and talent made the shop an immediate success—a place where rich wives and famous movie stars competed for his professional, and often more intimate, attention. Jon is a generous man. He gave them both.

"By the early 1970s, he was the owner of three Jon Peters salons, including one in Beverly Hills. A hairdresser?" she said, turning to me and giving me a look that could stop a leaping lion. "I wouldn't call him that. By the time we met, he was already a multi-millionaire. It was nice for a change to go out with someone who had as much money as I did.

"In 1967, he got married again, this time to starlet Leslie Ann Warren, who co-starred with Elliot in *Drat! The Cat!* It's a small world, isn't it? Leslie Ann was fascinated by me and dragged Jon to hear me sing at the Hollywood Bowl. He had never heard of me. It was a big mistake. He said, 'Barbra blew my mind! She magnetized me. I couldn't take my eyes off her!' He must have decided then that he could do better than Leslie Ann.

"Although they had a five-year-old son, Christopher, they divorced shortly after. Jon knew he had to meet me, and sent me a letter saying he would go anywhere in the world to style my hair—for free. I ignored the letter.

"Then he went through a promiscuous period where he slept with every woman who would have him. The group included some pretty illustrious women, like Jacqueline Bisset, Lee Taylor-Young, and Sally Kellerman. Jon told me he had dozens of affairs, because he was afraid to commit to any one woman. He could only relax if he kept a number of women on a string at the same time.

"Then I met a woman at a party whose short boyish bob appealed to me. When I asked her who had cut her hair, she said 'Jon Peters.' Since I was looking for a new style for my next movie, I called him in London, where he was staying with some young actress or other, and said, 'I received your letter. I need a new hairstyle for my next film. When you get home, please call me.' He did. Thus it began.

"Heavily influenced by Vidal Sassoon, the great London hair stylist,

Jon specialized in slick bobs and geometric cuts. He invented the 'bad girl' look, where he made his women look like they had just been frolicking around in bed. Sounds like something only Jon Peters could think of.

"A quick, funny aside: Jon later became well known as my hair stylist. As the story goes, my short hair was being copied in beauty salons all over the country. 'Give me the Streisand look,' a client told her hairdresser. So the stylist took out a hairbrush and broke her nose."

With her deep-throated guffaw, she laughed for a few moments. I smiled but didn't laugh because I didn't think it was particularly funny. In fact, I thought it was rather nasty. But I guess as the adage goes, you can get used to anything.

"His salon was decorated in pop art," she continued, when she was finally able to stop laughing, "and soon became as famous for its unique décor as for his hair styling. Jon then borrowed another $100,000 and opened two modern salons in the San Fernando Valley. He became known as the American Sassoon, in which he cut, cut, cut, discovering a creativity in himself he had never known was there.

"Smart as he is, he soon found out where a beauty salon would make the most money, and opened The Jon Peters Salon on glamorous Rodeo Drive in famous Beverly Hills, where movie stars, rich widows, and neglected wives of producers did their shopping and willingly paid three times as much money for a product or service as it would cost anywhere else. In a short time, he became as famous for his sexual prowess as for his hair styling.

"It wasn't hard for handsome Jon to find conquests. In fact, he had to fight off volunteers. Can you believe that man? At the age of twenty-seven, he was the head of a ten-million-dollar empire employing three hundred people and had slept with the most beautiful women in Hollywood!

"Our sexual attraction was the most powerful I had ever known—so powerful that I thought about him night and day. But I was wary, and tried my best to squelch the feeling. After all, I had just come from an affair with Pierre Trudeau! Going from a prime minister to a hairdresser (there, I'm doing it, too!) is quite a downward leap!

"He paid no attention to me when I refused dates with him. He went right on pressuring me. I kept saying 'No! No! No! You are not my type.'

"He just laughed and persisted."

"Then he asked, 'How about going with me to a Mexican restaurant?'

"Since I love Mexican food, I agreed."

"'Good,' he said. 'Pick you up at five o'clock.'

"'Five o'clock? I never eat that early.'"

"'Well, you've never flown to Mexico first,' he answered.

"We flew down in a private chartered plane to a magnificent beach resort near Acapulco. It was one of those rare times that will remain a high spot in my memory forever. The sex was so great I never could have imagined such bliss. Surely Jon was the world's best lover. He was so passionate that just looking at him turned me on, and sex with him put me in ecstasy.

"I'm not a religious person, but I thank God for Jon Peters' prowess as a lover. My life would have been incomplete without the experience. I've never been happier than the time Jon and I were together.

"A reporter once asked Jon what secret hold he had over me. He answered, 'It's this thing called love.' Truer words had never been spoken.

"'I could get used to this,' I told him, in the understatement of the century.

"'Get used to it!' he answered. 'We're in this for eternity. You're the sweetest girl I've ever met.'

"What? Me, sweet? Me, the bane of everyone's existence, from my mother to my teachers to my employers to my co-workers to my lovers? I've been called lots of things, but that was a new one for me. How could I resist anyone who thought I was sweet?"

"'You'd better hold on to him, Barbra,' I mumbled to myself. 'You'll never again meet anyone who thinks you're sweet.'"

I smiled. I had often thought she had an underlying sweetness that was the biggest secret of her success.

*Jon Peters divorced
his second wife,
Leslie Ann Warren,
for Barbra.*

July 27, 2015

"With incredible speed," she began the next session, "my relationship with Jon jumped from a one-nighter to living-together lovers. I was absolutely besotted with him. We were like two teenagers madly in love. As a woman, I had never known how to have fun. We never had any fun when I was growing up. We never went anyplace. I think I fell in love with Jon because he knew what to do on Sundays.

"He expanded my sexual horizons to the ends of the universe. I told a *Playboy* interviewer that my relationship with Jon had turned me into a sexually aggressive woman. When the reporter asked how often I initiated sex, I answered, 'We're equal, buddy. We're equal.'

"'Lucky man,' said the interviewer. 'My wife hasn't initiated sex even once since we met.'

"'Poor man!' I said. 'Why don't you teach her?' He remained silent.

"Then he asked, 'How innovative are you sexually?'

"'Incredibly creative. We do whatever works,' I told him. 'I have some beautiful erotic art books which turn us both on. And we often watch pornographic movies together. But we found 'Deep Throat' terribly boring, and fell asleep watching it."

"I'm lucky that I'm uninhibited sexually," Barbra continued.

"'Not as lucky as he is,' the reporter countered.

"It was more than sex that attracted me to Jon. I loved his fearlessness. Unlike me, he was unafraid of falling down mountains, of the ocean, of sharks, and even of Hollywood-based human barracudas. He made me go horseback riding and skiing, both of which had terrified me. I loved his spontaneity and utter lack of regard for social graces.

"Also, I was sick and tired of having to hide my relationships with married men. After all, I was Barbra Streisand, movie star extraordinaire. Didn't I deserve a man of my own? Even more important, Jon was my emotional, if not intellectual, equal. I liked that I was unable to dominate him, as I had done all my other lovers. I knew that as a couple we would constantly wage power struggles, but I thought I could handle that. After all, don't I fight with everybody?"

July 29, 2015

The next session, she continued telling me about her affair with Jon. "While filming *For Pete's Sake*, we spent what little free time I had at his ten-acre Paradise Cove ranch in Malibu. The house was a strange mixture of Wild West crudeness and Rodeo Drive chic that only Jon Peters could get away with.

"His huge custom-made couches were covered in expensive fabrics from Thailand. Cowboy hats and pedigree saddles decorated the walls. He had a state-of-the art stereo system and hand-rubbed pegged floors that glistened in the sunlight. The highly creative Jon had even fashioned a Jacuzzi out of an old wine vat, so we felt warm both inside and out as its fumes wafted over us while making love.

"I, who had hated camp and outdoor life as a little girl, learned to ride horseback on a gorgeous little white horse named Cupid that Jon had given me. I was terrified that I would fall off, and held on to the horse's mane for dear life, but somehow I always remained upright. Jon was very proud of me for conquering something I was so scared of. I was, too."

"You had every right to be," I commented. "Nothing is harder to do, and nothing brings greater growth."

"You're right," Barbra said with surprise. "I know I changed a lot after that, but didn't know why. I actually became a happy person, for a while, anyhow. I was so happy at the ranch that I seldom stayed over at my Holmby Hills home, and spent most of my time in t-shirts and jeans gardening and growing orchids.

"I took walks with Jon with his pet lion, which I actually forced myself to pet. I did my own laundry–I like the way I do it better than anyone else–and even learned to bake *challah*. I made my mother some and she loved it. I'll bet my father would have, too. Jon devoured all I could make.

"But Jon had a streak of violence in him that made my friends fear for me. He was not averse to using that streak when it suited him. He was quick to lose his temper and not above using his fists to demolish anyone who bothered him, including me. He broke a wrist punching down a door in one of his fights with me. One night at Madison Square Garden, when we went to see a Muhammad Ali fight, a man heckled me. Jon let him have it, until it looked like he was about to choke the poor guy to death and the cops came and took him away.

"Except for one or two occasions, I wasn't afraid of Jon, but just considered him a very macho man. There was one time I didn't want to leave a party he was tired of. He picked me up and threw me over his shoulder kicking and screaming and carried me out the door. I loved it!

"He was like a child. In one moment, he could change from a frightening, violent man to a sweet little boy. I never knew what to expect from him. Jon denied that he ever hit me, but we had some wild tussles that included clawing and biting. He even punched a hole through a kitchen wall.

"There was also the time when we were driving to Burbank to meet with Warner executives to discuss setting up *A Star is Born*. Jon and I had a terrible argument. With his left hand on the wheel, he reached over and ripped off my blouse. *Oh yeah*, I thought, *two can play at that game*, so I swung my leg up and pressed my stiletto heel into his neck. He had to fight for control of the car. That showed him... for a while anyhow.

"Nevertheless, he was the most exciting man I had ever met, and that made me love him all the more, though not always. One night, I became terrified of his temper. It was at the end of filming *A Star is Born*. Frank Pierson, the director, saw me sneak off the set and hide behind some cars.

"Frank grabbed me by the shoulders and asked, 'What's going on, Barbra?'"

"'For God's sake, Pierson, take me home,' I pleaded. 'Jon gets so furious I don't know what to do.' Pierson suggested that I spend the night at his place, but since Jon wasn't home when I got there, I crept into the house. Pierson said later that he had watched me enter my home, looking small, tired, and terrified. What won't a woman put up with from the man she loves?"

I couldn't believe that the feisty Barbra Streisand had put up with such abuse. I didn't like the story one bit, and said so, though briefly.

"Barbra," I added, "I have to remind you that my vacation begins on August 3rd. Wouldn't you like to talk about it?"

"No!" she said, again all but slamming the door on her way out.

July 31, 2015

Barbra made no mention of my forthcoming vacation, although this was our last session before it began.

"When *For Pete's Sake* was being filmed in New York," she said, "Jon accompanied me, because we didn't want to be separated for a moment, let alone a few months. We took a suite at the Plaza Hotel, although I officially lived in my Central Park West apartment. He was engaged by the movie producers to do my wigs and hairstyles, but he took charge of a lot more in my life.

"In fact, he took charge of just about everything. He picked out my wardrobe, choosing younger, sexier, hippier clothes, so I learned to mix colors and textures of velvet and tweed, tapestry and mink with abandon and great results. He advised me on which projects and songs I should consider recording. He came on the set with me every day, watched my scenes, and told me how I was doing.

"It didn't take long for the gossip columnists to get wind of our romance. By the time we returned to Hollywood, our affair was open knowledge and we gave a press interview in which we came right out and told them we were in love. It felt great to be able to let it all hang out and not have to slink around behind the gossip columnists' backs."

"When I love a man, I like to be with him all the time, in work and at play," Barbra continued. "So I allowed Jon to take over both my private and professional lives. I very much appreciated his critiques of my work. I think he always managed to hit the nail on the head, and I never thought that what I did was good enough. Unlike Elliot, who isn't the brightest man in the world, I had great faith in Jon's judgment and business ability. Who wouldn't, when a man had made himself a multi-multi-millionaire at age twenty-seven?

"Pretty soon, he decided he would prefer working in films rather than laboring in hair salons, and said he was going to switch careers. Some people say they are going to do something and then don't do it. When Jon says he is going to do something, believe me, he does it! He soon sold his hairdressing empire for a tremendous fortune that would support most of Manhattan for a decade and established himself in the film business under my auspices. Sensing his tremendous talent, I was all for it. Not that he asked my advice...

"Jon is an odd combination of qualities. When he told the 300 employees of his salons that he was leaving, they all wept. Jon did, too.

"To give you an idea of how astute he is, he disliked *For Pete's Sake* from the word go. He thought it was a ridiculous story, and he also said there was no chemistry between the leading man, Michael Sarrazin, and me. Jon might not have thought there was any chemistry between Michael and me, but I found him very handsome. And if Jon hadn't been around, there might have been a lot more chemistry.

"In the film, young married Brooklynites Pete and Henrietta Robbins are madly in love, despite their lack of money. Pete is a taxi

Barbra and Michael Sarrazin in For Pete's Sake, a movie which reviewers criticized for the co-stars' lack of chemistry.

driver, while Henry, the household money manager–me–does whatever part-time jobs she can find. Pete learns about an investment in pork belly futures that promises to pay gigantic dividends within a week.

"The couple needs a minimum of three thousand dollars to invest, which was $2,700.38 more than they had. After trying through legal means to borrow the money, Henry, who will do anything for her husband, decides to take out a loan from a loan shark. Henry doesn't see the twenty percent weekly interest rate as a problem because she expects the investment to pay off quickly, and for much more than that.

"She runs into difficulties, however, when the futures' value doesn't escalate as Pete has predicted. When the loan shark doesn't get his money repaid on time, he threatens to kill Henry. In a panic, she resorts to working for a madam.

"A lot that is supposed to be funny happens between Henry's clients and the difficulties they get her into. For instance, bulls and cows she is supposed to be minding rush through a crystal store. I must say I never really understood their shenanigans or their so-called humor."

I thought I'd better not comment on that one.

Barbra was so involved in telling the story that she didn't seem to notice my silence. "At the end of the movie, the pork bellies go up in value," she continued, "and all's well that ends well, with passionate kisses between Michael and me that I really enjoyed. Despite Jon's assessment of our lack of chemistry, nobody can kiss like Michael. I'm sorry I never found out if his sexual talents extended into the bedroom.

"When the film was released, Jon's opinion of it was confirmed by the critics. Paul Zimmerman of *Newsweek* wrote that I looked like Jerry Lewis with cleavage, as I gallivanted through the kind of silly plot that Lewis did so well. 'But Lewis is a crazy,' Zimmerman continued, 'while Streisand comes across merely as an abrasive loudmouth.' I thought Zimmerman was unfair, because there are some very funny lines in the film. Like when I decided to work with Mrs. Cherry, the madam, to make some money for Pete. I said to her, 'I've never cheated before.' Mrs. Cherry replied, 'Cheating is when it's for fun. This is business. Like a doctor seeing a patient.'"

Barbra began to laugh.

"What's so funny?" I asked.

"I just got the pun. Mrs. *Cherry*. Haha haha!"

I laughed, too.

"Contrary to Zimmerman's comment, I had always considered myself a comic actor, and far from being 'an abrasive loudmouth.' I got my start in the theatre, after all, as Miss Marmelstein in *I Can Get it for You Wholesale*. But there I had a decent script to work with, in contrast to *For Pete's Sake*. I decided that in the future, I would always get Jon's opinion before taking on a new film, because he was too often right to ignore. Sometimes boyfriends come in very handy.

"Nevertheless, I thought Zimmerman might have had a point, and that my acting could be improved. So I joined the Actors Studio West. My first assignment was to appear in a scene from *Romeo and Juliet* with actress Sally Kirkland. I played Juliet as a spoiled brat. I guess my performance must have been OK, because Lee Strasberg, the famous director of the Studio, who I suspect had come to Los Angeles specifically to see my scene, said it was pretty good. For him, that was a rave review.

"Because of the advice of my agent, Marty Erlichman, I had actually turned down the leading roles in *Klute* and *Cabaret*, both of which won Academy awards. Jon correctly insisted I get a better agent.

"Marty was furious with Jon, and yelled at him, 'You think you're such a hot shot? I remember when Barbra was teaching you how to read!' I had to smile at that, because I had struggled for a long time to teach Jon, who is no scholar, how to use the alphabet.

"But despite Jon's lack of scholarly talents, he proved to be just as astute with my records as with my films. He sat in on my recording sessions for both my solo and my album for *The Way We Were,* selecting the best tracks and giving me suggestions, all of which I followed. The single reached number one on the charts and remained on the top ten for five months. The album also reached number one. Besides that, the solo won *Billboard's* top single of the year award, was honored with a Grammy as the song of the year, and earned Marvin Hamlisch an Academy Award for the best song of the year in a film. See why I value Jon's advice so much?

"Still, many felt that Jon was taking advantage of my status as a movie star, but I think the reverse was true: I used his wonderful instincts and judgment to benefit my career. Isn't that what an ideal relationship is all about? Each of us was given one of life's most beautiful gifts by finding the other.

"A reporter from *Playboy* came up to me one day and wanted to know all about Jon. 'There was a time you used to ask Jon questions about me,' I told him. 'Now you ask me questions about Jon. He must be makin' out very good.'"

August 2, 2015

"To celebrate Valentine's Day in 1974, Jon and I together bought an eight-acre property in Ramirez Canyon. It rises out of the Pacific Ocean at Malibu in the gorgeous Santa Monica Mountains. I couldn't help feeling gratified that at last a man was meeting his share of the bills. In fact, Jon wanted to pay for the whole thing, but I wouldn't let him. 'What am I, some penniless little waif?' I asked him. He laughed and said, 'Whatever makes you happy.' Now I ask you: Where does one find a man like that?

"From every window, the house had sumptuous views of both the ocean and the mountains. At the same time, it gave us the privacy we hadn't had on Carolwood Drive, where fans leered at us over the fences every time we set foot out the door. Those jerks followed me around everywhere. Sometimes the same ones asked for my autograph three or four times. What do you think they did with all those autographs? Use them for toilet paper? One woman grabbed onto me and chatted endlessly about how talented I was. I interrupted her with, 'You got a guy for me?' You'd think that would shut her up, but it didn't.

"She yelled, 'It's not normal to be so talented.'

"'What did you say?' I asked. 'Are *you* normal?'

"'Yeah,' the woman answered.

"'Well then, thank God I'm *ab*normal!'"

"She gave me the finger!"

After we stopped laughing, she returned to discussing the new home. "We weren't so crazy about the actual house, which was made of white stucco with sliding aluminum doors. So we had it completely remodeled. With his great creativity, Jon hired a group of professional toy makers with wood-carving talents to rebuild the outside of the house. They paneled the walls in scorched, old, oiled wood, adding stained glass panels worthy of Chartres in many of the windows. They also built in much of the furniture, like beds, cabinets, and cupboards. Before it was half-finished, I was madly in love with it, and never wanted to go anywhere outside.

"I adored the boys' rooms, which were as different from each other as Jason and Christopher, Jon's son, were. All of their furniture was built in. Each boy had a ladder to climb to his bed, one to a loft and the other to a bunk bed. Jason's room was trimmed in red velvet and Christopher's in an Aztec print. The boys got along very well, and spent many happy hours playing together. Jon even brought Jason a brother. What a man!'

"Barbra," I said, "this is your last session before I leave on my annual vacation. I can't let you leave without talking about it."

"All right, if you insist," she growled. "It's just like a shrink to take off when I need treatment the most."

I hadn't been aware she felt bad. In fact, I thought she was doing quite well.

"You're all S.O.B.'s! Do you have to leave now? Can't you wait until I feel better?"

"I'm afraid not, Barbra," I answered. "I've had plans for a long time."

To my surprise, she began to cry. "Of course *your* needs come before mine. Nobody ever puts me first. Your interruption is going to ruin my analysis. Did it ever occur to you that I am very intuitive, and know what's going to hurt me? When this analysis flops like all the others, you can blame yourself! In fact, to show you the drastic chaos you've caused in my life, I probably won't return."

"If you don't return, you'll be the one rejecting me, instead of me rejecting you."

"You're damn right. You may not come back at all."

"Like your father left you, Barbra, and never returned?"

"That's right! That's my luck in life."

"So you are holding onto my leg psychologically to keep me from leaving you, the way you held onto your mother's physically, after your father died?"

She was quiet.

"My leaving is part of your treatment, Barbra. You have to find out that I'm not your father, and that I can go away and return to you."

She grudgingly answered, "Well, we'll see *if* you return!"

September 1, 2015

Today, Barbra and I resumed her analysis. To my surprise, she ignored the fact that I had "rejected" her, and shyly handed me a package.

"I have a present for you," she said. "It is a book I have written called *My Passion for Design*." She opened the book and began to show me the exquisite photographs of her estate, which she had built totally from her own drawings. I have been in many mansions in my long lifetime and been carried away by their beauty, but never have I seen a more gorgeous construction than Barbra Streisand's home.

I was overwhelmed, among other things, by the glorious panels of wood in colors reminiscent of Rembrandt, the overflowing flower and vegetable gardens which fed Barbra and her lover all year round, the 30-foot high ceilings with elaborate two-tiered chandeliers, the windmill she had copied from an old painting and had built and installed on the property, the real silo bought from a farmer, the open passageways that framed the lovely ocean views, the screen room, the doll shop, the antique shop, and the old clothing shop she had built in the basement. Every room was different, yet all somehow blended together. She is, I realized, as much a genius as a designer as she is a singer, actress, and director.

I felt myself overcome by a feeling that was hitherto unknown to me. I'm a highly successful psychoanalyst with a wealthy Fifth Avenue practice, but high as my income is, it was paltry compared to that of the mega-millionairess in my office blithely turning the pages of her book about the mansion and gardens she had designed practically single-handedly.

To my surprise, I momentarily found myself disliking her. An unknown wave of pure jealousy rolled over me. The torment sliced its way inside of me like a surgeon's knife. Although some people consider me wealthy–I own my own condo and office on Fifth Avenue, as well as a beautiful summer house in the Hamptons–there is no way in the world that I can afford to build an eight-acre estate by the sea, where the mansion had

Barbra's first book was published in 2010.

its own windmill, surrounded by a garden to rival that of Buckingham Palace, full of every variety of rose in existence, including one called the Barbra Streisand Rose. Nor could I possibly design a palace of such beauty. To say I felt green with envy was like saying the queen's crown is a simple hat.

I envied Barbara, not only for her stunning home and gardens, but for the great talent that she brings to everything she does, including designing an estate. If I, with my wonderful career, was so jealous, I wondered, what must the poor souls who work at McDonald's feel when they hear of Barbra's extravagances? How do they live with so painful a feeling? No wonder I had repressed it for so long. Then I had a sudden insight. It is said that many people dislike Barbra Streisand. I had thought it was because of character traits that force her to take over whatever she does because she's sure she can do it better, and she can!

Now I wasn't so sure that was why people dislike her. Rather, the reason they can't bear the sight of her is not that she mistreats them, as so many have claimed, but because she reminds them of the heights only a few geniuses attain, next to which their own worldly achievements look like papier-mâché.

I felt I had to say something about my return from my vacation. "Barbra," I said, "you see that I am not your father after all, and I did return from my absence."

"Of course you did," she said. "A shrink is a shrink is a shrink."

When I thought about this incident in tranquility the following evening, I realized how good it was that I had allowed myself to experience the emotion. Now I could empathize with the envy felt by so many of my patients, which I had only understood before with my head and not my heart. Thus does a psychoanalyst grow, by allowing herself to experience the dreadful emotions we all wish would go away.

September 4, 2015

"Living with Jon was probably the closest to Paradise anyone can ever get," Barbra announced the next session. "It certainly was the most romantic. I lit the house with dozens of scented candles, the smell of which gently wafted through every room. We curled up together in front of the twelve-foot stone fireplace blazing away on the hottest of days on a mattress upholstered in heavy embroidered silk imported from Thailand. The same fabric was hung at the windows.

"After we bought the home, I didn't work for quite a while. I was having so much fun I couldn't bear to leave it. The years, of course, changed both the house and us. As you get older and become less of a hippie, you can't easily manage to get up off the floor anymore and you have to sit on a couch. So I eventually replaced the mattress with an L-shaped, light-brown sectional sofa."

"I know what you mean," I laughed. "Once I get down on the floor, I'm there for good unless someone comes and rescues me."

She laughed and continued, "To my sorrow, there came a time when I had to replace the long, lazy afternoons with working on a movie. I was running out of money because I hadn't worked much lately. I had to go out and work to pay for it, like any normal human being. I later donated the ranch to the Santa Monica Mountains Conservancy, a state agency designed to acquire land and to function as an environmental research complex. I didn't want to live with five houses and twenty-two and a half acres anymore," she explained.

"And after a while, Jon and I separated, the kids were growing up, and I didn't spend enough time there to justify the cost and the worry about keeping it up myself. It had become too much for me. But I'm lucky to have lived in the home of my dreams for almost a decade."

"You certainly are. There is no greater happiness than having your fantasies come true. But tell me more about the house, Barbra. It sounds absolutely gorgeous."

"You're right," she answered. "It was the most beautiful house I've ever seen. Every room was filled with fresh flowers from our garden, some of which I grew myself, and beautiful *tchotchkes* I had saved all my life. We made love endlessly, talked from morning til night, and sometimes all night long.

"I must admit we fought a lot, too. I usually ended up in tears and apologized the next day. Surprised that I was the one who gave in? That's because I listened to Jon's ideas–unlike Elliot's–valued his advice on every aspect of my life, trusted his opinions on just about everything, and endlessly discussed the possibilities of his producing my next record and becoming involved in 'The Main Event', the second film I was scheduled to act in for First Artists.

"On our bad days, we fought like animals. We scratched. We clawed. Once, I sat on Jon's chest and spat at him. He spat back. Eventually, our resentment turned into something else, something sexual and very sensual. It taught me that people who love each other have room for hate in the relationship. It was very freeing for me—love."

September 7, 2015

"In *The Main Event*, Ryan O'Neal, my former lover, was cast as the male lead," Barbra began. "Strange that Jon, jealous man that he is, agreed to the casting of Ryan as my lover. I guess the old maxim, 'business before pleasure,' came into effect here. But you couldn't mention Ryan's name around Jon without his going totally ballistic. He hated Ryan with a coarseness I hadn't seen in him before. But he managed to contain his rage by warning Ryan, 'You just wait until this movie is finished. We're going to get into the ring together and I will knock the crap out of you!' To jump ahead a few steps, they did. And he did.

"The film tells the story of Hillary Kramer, played by me, a successful perfume magnate and owner of a company called 'Le Nez.' I wake up one morning to find that my S.O.B. accountant has robbed me of all my money and disappeared to South America. My sole remaining asset is a washed-up boxer, Eddie 'Kid Natural' Scanlon, whom I had once purchased as a tax write-off.

"With no alternative in sight, I decide to make Scanlon, then making a living giving driving lessons, go into the ring with boxers half his age. But first I have to convince the reluctant Eddie to fight, for he thinks boxing again will get him killed. Eventually, I wear him down and get funded by friends and colleagues for his first fights, all of which go amiss because I know nothing about boxing, Eddie's out-of-shape condition, and his fear of getting hit. All the time, the two of us continue sparring on a verbal level.

Barbra stars with her ex-lover in 1979 film, The Main Event.

"Of course, the hard-driven business woman eventually falls in love with the handsome schlub. We develop an increasingly personal relationship, which ultimately leads us to find out what we really want. Nobody will be surprised to discover that it is each other.

"Ryan made me laugh when he dubbed the movie *Glove Story*. But he made my eyes water when he came to our love scenes in a smelly sweatshirt. I made the cameramen stop shooting while the wardrobe woman ran and got five clean tee-shirts. Then I squirted him with Chanel Number Five, so he wouldn't stink so much. Do you think he was getting even with me for rejecting him as a lover?"

I smiled. "I wouldn't be surprised," I said.

"Because I appeared in the film wearing tight, satin, short-shorts–and I do mean short–and a sleeveless tee-shirt without a bra," she continued, "I had to be in the best shape of a lifetime, and hired a fitness guru, Gilda Marx. I must admit she did a good job. In my opinion, I've never been in better shape.

"When I was young, I was too skinny, and then I put on a few pounds too many. Jon's eyes popped open when he saw the movie rushes. He said, 'I've always said you have a great ass, kid, but in this film, you have a great everything.' It was worth all the agonizing hours I had put in at the gym to see the look in his eyes when he said that. I thought he was going to throw me down on the viewing-room floor and make love to me right then and there.

"Unfortunately, the film received mostly negative reviews from the critics, but sometimes the box office can pick a winner better than the critics. *The Main Event* was among the top 20 highest grossing films of the year. It was also the impetus for my first foray into disco, singing the Golden Globe-nominated theme song written by Paul Jabara and Bruce Roberts."

"Were you upset about the reviews?"

"I was getting much better about that," she answered. "I was learning that I couldn't control what was said about me. If one does good work, it'll stand the test of time. Good work lasts. The rest doesn't matter.

"But I must confess to you, Doctor, that when critics write about me as 'the girl with the Fu Manchu fingernails and the nose as long as an anteater's,' it still hurts me much more than if someone wrote that I was a terrible singer, which no one ever has."

"Barbra," I began, "I thought about the awful remarks some film critics have written about you, and am so sorry you let snide comments wipe out the wonderful reviews you usually get."

"Well, maybe if I spend thirty more years in analysis, I'll get over it."

Even I had to smile at her remark.

She asked, "Did you see the movie, Doctor?"

I nodded. I had hoped she wouldn't ask me that.

"Did you like it?'"

Again I had to weigh two things: telling Barbra only the truth, versus my fear of hurting Barbra's feelings with another mean remark. Finally, the former won out, and I reluctantly said, "It isn't one of my favorite films."

"What didn't you like about it?"

"Frankly, I was bored. There was too much fighting in it. If I wanted to see boxing matches, I would have gone to Madison Square Garden."

She grinned. Then she said, being the bigger person, "Thanks for telling the truth, my friend. Nobody can fault you for that. I must say I even agree with you."

September 11, 2015

"I had wanted to make the film *Yentl* for many years," she began the next session, "but try as I might, I was unable to find a studio willing to back an ethnic movie with transvestite implications, so I put it on the back burner. But the strong desire to film the story never was very far from my mind. Then I read about a small theatre presentation of a play in Brooklyn, and it brought the desire back as fiercely as ever.

"I still was under contract to Ray Stark to do another movie for him. He sent me a sequel to *Funny Girl* called *Funny Lady*, which was written by Jay Presson Allen, the winner of an Acadamy Award for *Cabaret*. At first, I didn't like it, and shipped it back to him with a note saying, 'If you expect me to play in this piece of shit, forget it!' But Jon read and liked it, and I changed my mind. We thought the screenplay as written depicted an independent woman struggling in a man's world, which is pretty much how I see my life.

"I empathized with the older Fanny," Barbra said, "in a way I never could with the younger Fanny in *Funny Girl*. I understood her falling in love with Billy Rose, who was a lot like Fanny herself. You can only do that when you accept who you are and feel worthy of being loved. Otherwise, you are just in love with your fantasies, like she was with Nicky Arnstein. It isn't until the second part of her life that Fanny discovers who she is, and finally is able to let go of her illusions about men. In *Funny Lady*, Fanny grows up. Kind of like me with Jon.

"I took the role partly because I owed Ray Stark a picture, but more important, because I believed I would be able to play the grown-up Fanny Brice, a woman who was wiser, tougher, and more like the real Fanny than the one I had portrayed in *Funny Girl*. This time I wasn't afraid to show her glass edges. Nor did I try to be liked. Frankly, I didn't know if Fanny was so likeable. I'll always be happy I made the sequel, just as I like the older Barbra more than the smart-assed kid I once was.

"To my great regret, the movie was scheduled to begin shooting in the spring of 1974, just when we were planning to move into our newly renovated house, which we called The Barn. I wanted only to stay home and be a wife and mother, 'Sadie Sadie the married lady.' But since when do our wishes rule our lives? Not mine, anyway.

"I am a very private person, and I'm scared to death of crowds. But strangely enough, when I took the boys to the beach or shopping, nobody recognized me. They must have thought I was too small, and what would the great Barbra Streisand be doing on a public beach or grocery store anyway? That was fine with me. Sometimes—rarely—celebrity is its own reward.

"Sometimes a person would say, 'Did anyone ever tell you that you look like Barbra Streisand?' I would answer, 'Oh yes, I've been told that many times before.' Or I would lie and say, 'Of course I'm not Barbra Streisand! Would she be on a public beach? Ha ha ha. I wish I had her money!'

"April marked the end of our great seaside picnics, and the time spent hanging out with Jon and the kids in our beautiful new house. Shooting began on *Funny Lady*. With Jon at the wheel, we drove up to the shuttered gates of Columbia on April 1 for the first day of production. The film was budgeted at seven and a half million dollars on a fourteen-week production schedule. It was to be shot in New York, Philadelphia, and Atlantic City. James Caan, who had starred in *The Godfather*, played opposite me as Billy Rose, the great show business entrepreneur. Omar Sharif played my husband, Nick Arnstein, again.

"We tried to forget we had once been lovers, but it was difficult. In one scene, when we were supposed to kiss passionately, I congratulated myself on resisting the impulse to spit in his mouth.

Barbra plays a grown-up Fanny Brice in Funny Lady, 1975.

September 14, 2015

"Do you know the most wonderful thing about my relationship with Jon, Doctor?"

"No," I said, fully expecting her to talk about their sex life. "Tell me."

To my surprise, she said, "Each of us helped the other to become all we had in us to be."

"That is indeed wonderful, Barbra, and very unusual. Tell me about what qualities you helped to bring out in each other."

"He made me feel young, beautiful, and sexy—me, the girl no guy ever gave a second look at. He made me drop my agent and manager of fifteen years, Marty Erlichman, and Jon took over the job himself. He advised me to see less of my good friends, Cis Corman and songwriters Alan and Marilyn Bergman, saying they were old and stodgy, and a bad influence on me. He encouraged me to take more control of my career, and to break with convention.

"He blasted me right out of my narrow artistic rut, and helped me to think 'out of the box'. I am forever grateful to Jon. He made me a new person as well as a new artist. Without him, I might still be back in the seventies.

"I did as much for him. I made him a movie producer! I helped him break into the industry, and made him the producer of my next movie, the five-million-dollar musical *A Star is Born*. People asked, 'Isn't Peters in over his head as a producer?'

"That made me furious. So what if Jon had been a hairdresser?" she snapped, her pale blue eyes ablaze. "A lot of Hollywood producers began by selling dresses in Manhattan. People talked the same way about me. How could I act when I'm just a singer? Note the word 'just.' Nobody is just any one thing. The major purpose of living is to grow.

"I even tried to coerce Warner Brothers, who were putting up the money for First Artists, into letting Jon direct the film. He already was my manager, which earned him fifteen percent of my income. They said 'no.'

"But that isn't all he did. Jon called me up and said excitedly, 'I've got this great thing for us! It's called *A Star is Born*.'

"'Schmuck!' I answered. 'It's already been made three times!'

"'But ours will be different!' he exclaimed. He turned out to be so right!"

"It's true that ours was to be the fourth version of the film, but it had little similarity to the first three. This one was the story of two rock-star lovers, one on the way up and the other on a downward slide. The movie takes place against the background of the present-day groupie world of concerts and tours, drugs and psychedelic feelings of euphoria and despair—in no way the glamorous Hollywood portrayed in the earlier versions.

"This reimagining of the film was the work of the famous literary couple, Joan Didion and Gregory Dunne, hip rock star enthusiasts, who had just returned from a tour in which they hung out with the Uriah Heep and Jethro Tull rock groups. You'd think this experience would have given them an inside look into the rock world that no outsiders could possibly know. Whether it did or not, I don't know, but a few months later, they submitted a script to the director, Peter Bogdanovich. Surprisingly, he hated it, and passed it on to director Mark Rydell. Rydell completely disagreed with Bogdanovich and thought the script was marvelous, in that it gave a perceptive inside look at the world of rock.

"Warners refused to pay Rydell the price he was asking for his services, but instead said that he, along with Didion and Dunne, could work on the script on the cuff for three months, get two top stars committed, and put some of the famous writers' supposed insights on the drawing board. If he succeeded at all this, Warners would give him a contract to direct the movie. Unfortunately, by the time the script was finished, it was a dreadful bore, with two leading characters who were completely unsympathetic. Elvis Presley, Carly Simon, Liza Minnelli, and Cher were among the famous stars who turned down roles.

"The distraught Rydell searched frantically for a leading man he thought could bring the male character to life, and finally came up with Kris Kristofferson, a top country-and-western singer who had been popular in several sleeper movies. A tall, lean, macho man with a commanding presence, he also was able to project tenderness and vulnerability. Kristofferson very much liked the script and agreed to star in it, but Warners would not sign him without a famous female star. When his three-month trial period ended, Warners took the script away from Rydell and gave it to director Jerry Schatzberg.

"Here's where Jon Peters entered the story. He got hold of the story, read it, and thought it would make a terrific vehicle for me. Jon told a reporter, '*A Star is Born* was the beginning of Barbra recognizing her own power. It was a period of discovery for her. It was when she first realized that she could do it, that she could take control of her life and make it come out the way she wanted. I was a tool for her; the one who ran interference for her. She needed me as much as I needed her.

"'I'm the one who found the script!' he shouted. 'Yeah, me! *I* found it and talked Barbra into doing it.' In relating the story, he left out the fact that he had made damn sure I knew he wanted to be the producer. I didn't mind too much. It wasn't long before he was calling it '*my* movie.' He told one interviewer that the leading man in the film was 'a guy just like me, who is always fighting somebody.' He wasn't kidding.

"*A Star is Born* turned out to be a narcissistic, unapologetic celebration of our love affair. I think Jon's involvement in the project was preordained. The male lead was named John; he owned a red jeep; drove a red Farrari like my Jon did; and, incredibly, both were Geminis."

Barbra's and Jon's celebratory kiss after winning Best Motion Picture—Musical or Comedy—at the 1977 Golden Globe Awards for A Star Is Born.

September 21, 2015

The next session wasn't as pleasant. Barbra came in with a hostile look on her face. Her infamous mouth was turned down at the corners and her blue eyes had practically turned black. Contrary to her recent appearances, she actually looked ugly.

"You look angry." I asked. "What's the matter?"

"Brilliant you for picking that up! All that shrink school and you are able to see that I am angry. Congratulations! You're darned right I'm angry. It's your toilet. I just came from your bathroom, and it makes me furious."

I was puzzled. *My toilet?* What could possibly be wrong with my toilet? "I'm sorry, Barbra," I said, "but I really don't know what you object to about it."

"The handle is placed in an awkward position. When I finished peeing, I had to get up and turn around to flush it. Anybody with any sense would have a toilet that you could simply reach around with one hand to flush. You obviously don't care a bit about the comfort of your patients or it wouldn't be the way it is."

I couldn't help but smile. "I'm sorry," I said, "but I've never given it a thought."

"That's the trouble with you shrinks. You are so busy looking into my unconscious for castration anxiety that you wouldn't see the real problems in the world if you fell over them."

"Like the position of my toilet handle?"

"Yes. And don't be such a smart aleck! You may have had a lot more schooling than I did, but you don't know your ass from your elbow. That's the difference between you and me. I'd never have such a toilet in any of my mansions! Please have the handle changed by the next time I come here."

Ah, I thought, *she referred to the fact that I've had a lot more schooling than she has. My framed diplomas are hanging in the hall near the restroom; she must have seen them before going in. I bet she is comparing herself to me and feels inadequate, because she never went to college. She attacks me so she doesn't have to feel inferior.*

"I can't talk to such an unfeeling person!" she said. Incredibly, she got up and left my office.

What a prima donna, I thought. *I can see now why so many of her co-workers don't like her.*

I did *not* have the toilet handle changed.

September 23, 2015

Surprisingly, Barbra returned for the next session in a better mood, and didn't bring up the matter of the toilet handle. But *I* was not finished with the episode.

"Barbra," I asked her, "were you looking at my diplomas before you used the restroom yesterday?"

She lowered her head sheepishly

"I thought so. And did it make you feel jealous of all my degrees?"

She blushed, and stammered, "As a matter of fact, ye... Yes."

"Why is that?"

"You have so many degrees and I never even went to college. It makes me feel stupid."

"And does it make you feel better if you can find some way to feel superior to me, like stressing how much more you know about toilets than I do?"

"You're damn right!" she exclaimed. "Toilets and interior design. Then I can forget I'm inferior to you."

"Oh Barbra, you've got to be kidding! With your skills in acting, singing, directing, designing, and writing, I'm the one who should feel inferior! It's just that you developed your expertise from experience instead of books. You are as educated as anyone on this earth."

She looked surprised, and said, "I never thought of it that way. It's always bothered me so much that I didn't go to college." Looking at me with admiration, she continued, "Thank you, Dr. Dale. That makes me feel better. I just may be able to put it to rest now." She smiled and added, "Maybe your toilet handle isn't that important after all."

She was right. I smiled, too.

September 26, 2015

"Since I was unable to convince any studio to finance and greenlight *Yentl*," she said during the next session, "I took a little side trip and made a different kind of film, *All Night Long*. I thought it would be a fun and short project, and a simple part for me to play, even though I disliked the leading man, Gene Hackman, on sight, and never did get to like him.

"In the movie, George Dupler, played by Hackman, is a married man approaching middle age. After a temper tantrum at work in which he throws a chair out of his boss's window, he is demoted to midnight-shift manager of an all-night pharmacy-convenience store.

"I remember it," I said. "It has a nice oedipal ending."

"What do you mean?"

"The father character ends up winning the woman, and the 'boy,' his son, has to accept it, if he wants to keep his father's love."

She laughed a living-dying laugh, and said, "You mean we can't have 'the boy' taking Mama away from Daddy and win box office approval?"

"You got it," I said.

"In real life," she countered, "I'd take the boy any time."

It was my turn to laugh.

"What happened with the movie *All Night Long*?" I asked. "Was it a hit?"

"That is a matter of opinion. Some critics praised my performance as one of the best of my career, but the film received a great many negative reviews. I was nominated for a 1981 Golden Raspberry Award for my performance," she continued. "On seeing the film lately, I thought I was rather insipid. On the other hand, Stephen Holden, writing in *Rolling Stone*, said my acting reminded him of Marilyn Monroe. Not a bad actress to be compared to! Maybe I wasn't so insipid after all.

"Pauline Kael in *The New Yorker* also was full of praise for the movie. 'The director, Jean-Claude Tramont, a Belgian who worked in TV in the United States, is a sophisticated jokester.' As you know, Doctor, I always like jokesters, even if they aren't very funny."

"So do I," I confessed.

"Kael continued with, 'Hackman, who specializes in believable, realistic personalities, gives one of his most likable performances.' Maybe his performance was likeable, but he isn't."

September 30, 2015

"After that, I was determined that my next film would be *Yentl*," she began. "I didn't want the last words on my death bed to be, 'Why didn't I ever make *Yentl*?' I also made up my mind that I would direct the movie myself, even if I had to finance it with my own money. I threw myself into working on the script with even more than my usual passion.

"The story of Yentl and her father took possession of me like the demon in *The Exorcist*. I was filled with envy for the relationship Yentl had with her father, and although it brought back all the agony I felt about my father's premature death, working on the script helped me to become her and, vicariously, to get my father back. If *A Star is Born* is the tale of my love affair with Jon Peters, *Yentl* tells the story of my grief for my lost father.

"All my films change me in some fashion or another, but researching *Yentl* altered me in a very profound way. It made me feel very proud to be a Jew. I don't believe that Eve was created from Adam's rib. God is not a chauvinist. I think the sexes were created to be equal. God created Adam and then split him in two, so that each sex has both masculine and feminine characteristics.

"Why did I want to do *Yentl*? Maimonides said it better than I ever could. 'If I do not rouse my soul to higher things, who will?' There are moments you wait for and dream of all your life. Making *Yentl* was that moment for me.

"*Yentl* and I were alike in many ways. She needed to learn, just as I always desperately did. When I was sixteen, I started to study Japanese. When I was still in high school, I read deeply in Russian literature and Zen Buddhism. Like Yentl, I love acquiring knowledge—all knowledge. If sexism had kept me out of school, I would have done just as she did, and dressed up in my father's clothes to follow my passion as a boy. *The New York Times* had a good time with it. They headlined, 'Barbra to star in *Funny Boy*.'

"Incidentally, the Bible does not prohibit women from studying, but only says that we are not *obliged* to study. It is not written anywhere that women have to be subservient to men. Men have interpreted the Bible to serve themselves. I have never bought their philosophy and never will.

"An incident happened that further fueled my passion for making *Yentl*. In 1979, my brother Shelley and I went to visit our father's grave. Written on his tombstone were the words, 'Beloved Teacher and Scholar.'

Shelley took a picture of the gravesite.

"When he developed the photo, we were shocked to find the name Anshel carved on the tombstone of the grave next to my father's. Anshel is not a common name like John or William. Now, it just so happens that Anshel is the name of Yentl's dead brother, and the name she took when she disguised herself as a young man. Can you believe the coincidence? I felt as if I had received a message from my father that I had to make *Yentl*.

"I was so moved by the message from my father that I asked Shelley to go with me to visit a medium, to see if she could get me another message from him. The woman didn't look much like a medium—more like a nice Jewish lady from the Bronx. And if this were a movie, I never would have cast her in the part.

"But she knew her business. She had us sit around a table and hold hands, while she talked to the spirit of our father. Suddenly, the table began to rock and to spell out letters with its legs. The medium asked, 'Emanuel Streisand, have you any message for this lady who needs to hear from you?' The table pounded away, knocking a certain number of times on the floor for each letter. First, it spelled out 'Manny' and then 'Barbra.'

"*God, he even knows how to spell my name!* I thought with awe. With my father's encouragement, there was no way I could *not* make the movie. On the way out the front door, I looked up to the heavens and tears were rolling down my cheeks. 'Thanks, Poppa,' I said. 'I always knew you were on my side.'

"Jon and I had bought back the rights for *Yentl* from First Artists right before they sold the company. I intended to direct and star in the movie, with Jon as producer. But Jon hated the script and really didn't want to do it. He was sure it would flop at the box office, and besides, he didn't think I would be able to convincingly act the role of a boy. I decided to play a trick on him. I dressed up as a *yeshive bokher* in a European-style buttoned jacket and a hat with flaps over my ears, and rang the bell when I knew Jon was home.

"He answered the door with raised fists and said, 'Yeah? Whatcha want?' He thought I was a robber and was about to punch me in the nose when I said, 'Stop it, Jon. It's me! It's Barbra!' We both burst out laughing, but I'm afraid my impersonation wasn't enough to convince him.

"I never worked so hard in my life as I did in *Yentl,* sometimes around the clock for days on end. It scared me, for my mother had always told me it was overwork that had killed my father. So I always was afraid that if I worked too hard, I would die. I don't want to die. I have too many movies I want to make.

"So I thought I would test out my mother's hypothesis in *Yentl*. If I have to die from overwork, there is no better cause than making my dream come true. If the excessive hours didn't kill me, I would know she was wrong, as she was about most things, and I would continue to work as hard and long as I pleased. Well, it didn't. And I do."

October 2, 2015

"Jon had made it to the big time by now, and no longer needed me to help him rise into the upper echelons of Hollywood power. He had little time to devote himself to a project he wasn't interested in. We fought about *Yentl* all the time, but I was unable to get him to change his mind, and he certainly couldn't change mine.

"Finally, he reluctantly placed an ad in *Daily Variety* that I was going to direct *Yentl* for his company. He sent his assistant to Eastern Europe to photograph possible locations for the film in Austria, Hungary, Poland, Romania, and Yugoslavia. Then Jon regretted his action, and screamed at me, 'You are not going to do it! I won't let you make a fool of yourself. I insist that we work on a film together!'

"I have never been one who took orders from anyone, starting with my mother, so I answered, 'You and who else?' And I went right ahead with my plans. I was determined to make *Yentl*, with or without Jon.

"When I left the room, I began to sob. Much as I still loved Jon, I knew our affair was over. I could no longer live with a lover who did not support me one hundred percent.

"Jon said that living with me was difficult because I rarely gave in to his male prerogatives.

"'Come off it, Jon,' I answered. 'How often do you give in to my female prerogatives?' If he said, 'I'm tired. Please rub my head,' I would answer, 'I'm tired, too. How about rubbing mine?' That didn't go over very well with Mr. Macho.

"In one of Jon and my last interviews together, Barbara Walters asked if we could picture ourselves growing old together.

"'Sure,' Jon said.

"'Nobody else would have us' was my answer.

"As the seventies drew to a close, our battles grew worse and worse. After a very bad row, we sat down and said, 'Should we split? Don't we want to be together anymore?' Usually, we agreed that we wanted to stay together, but sometimes the fights got so bad we couldn't handle them on our own, so we went to see a famous couples psychiatrist, who helped us sort things out.

"But soon even he wasn't able to hold us together. When Jon didn't attend Jason's Bar Mitzvah, I knew things were finished between us. Late in 1979, he moved back into the house he owned in Encino.

"I was left alone, both in my bedroom and to make the most important film of my life. But that didn't stop me. After all, I'd been alone most of my life. To divert myself from the pain and loneliness, I threw myself into studying *Yentl* with the strongest passion I'd ever known. 'I'll show him which one of us is the fool!'

"To better understand the culture of *Yentl*, I conscientiously investigated the history of Eastern European Jews in the late nineteenth and early twentieth centuries. I went to the Hillel Foundation at USC. I sought out the great rabbis of my era to find the one who felt right to me. I picked Rabbi Daniel Lapin of the Pacific Jewish Center to serve as my guide and mentor. Not entirely coincidentally, Jason was preparing for his Bar Mitzvah at this time under the auspices of Rabbi Lapin. He suggested that I study Judaism together with my son. 'For Judaism to have any deep meaning for Jason, it will have to mean something to you as well,' he said.

"*What a brilliant idea! I thought. It will help me understand* Yentl *at the same time it brings Jason and me closer together. It also will bring me closer to my father, who had been an ardent Jew.* So I met once a week with the rabbi to talk about what I had learned and to ask him the many theological questions that my research into Judaism brought to mind. I became deeply involved with Rabbi Lapin and Judaism."

"What are your ideas about religion, Barbra?" I asked.

"Religion? Let me think a minute... In the kind of world we live in today, where a bomb can fall at any moment and end it all, people have a need to believe in something. You have to either kill yourself or work at accepting life and living it in the best way you can. You have to understand that terrors and terrorists do exist, but not let them stop you from making the best of your own life.

"I particularly like the Eastern religions because they accept death as part of life. They don't deny reality, as many Americans do. So when I need religion, I am not above using it. I don't go to a synagogue or a church. Like everything else, I do it my own way."

"Very good, Barbra," I said. "I'm impressed with how well you've thought out your feelings on the subject."

She nodded and said, "I can see that you agree with me."

Breaking all analytic rules, I answered, "I do."

October 7, 2015

"None other than Isaac Bashevis Singer, who had written the original story, was helping me with the script of *Yentl*," she began.

"You can't do any better than that," I said.

"I'm not so sure about that. He was a bossy old guy of seventy-nine, who scolded me for daring to make a movie out of his story. 'What do you know about Poland or the Talmud? Stick to what you know. You're an actress. Make a movie about acting!' he yelled.

"He didn't seem to stop you much! What made you so determined to produce *Yentl*, of all unlikely subjects?" I asked.

She answered without missing a beat, "What fascinated me the most about Yentl was her driving need to study the Talmud and become an expert in it. This, of course, was impossible at the time, because girls were not permitted to study the Talmud. When I say a driving need, I'm sure you understand, Doctor, that I knew exactly how she felt.

"In a way, *Yentl* is a modern story, for she believed, as I do, that women are as good as men, and shouldn't be denied anything because of our gender. Actually, I think it is criminal to refuse women the right to rise as high as our intelligence and talent can take us. I know how much trouble I still have in Hollywood because I am a woman. I think a man with my talents would be the number one producer and director in Hollywood by now."

She said this without a trace of vanity, but merely as a fact.

She added, "I would like to believe that my making *Yentl* will help make it easier for women who come after me.

"*Yentl* is also the story of a young girl who loses her beloved father, as I did, and who is having incredible difficulty coming to terms with her terrible loss. When I sang, "Papa, can you hear me? Papa, can you see me?' the words came from deep inside my heart," she said, clearly affected as she spoke.

I didn't tell her that, when I saw the movie, I cried along with her as she sang that song.

To my great surprise, she then asked me if I would like to hear some music from *Yentl*. "I would love it," I said without pause. She took a 2015 CD out of her large purse and the poignant tones of "Papa Can You Hear Me" soon filled the room. I listened spellbound as the air around Barbra began to vibrate to the haunting melody of a dulcimer. The room seemed to swell with her slightly nasal voice, its two-octave tessitura richly textured at both the high and low ends of her range, all the way from low, soft, and breathy, to powerful and surging.

I noted how carefully she pronounced her words, with each syllable enunciated distinctly. How different her singing and speaking pronunciations were. No Brooklynese accent to be heard in her singing! I began to cry.

"Well, what do you think of it, Teacher?" she asked.

I was too overcome with feeling to answer in words, and simply nodded my head. She understood.

"I gave up everything else in my life to do *Yentl*," she said, after a few moments. "It's a good thing Jason and I were studying Judaism together with the rabbi, or he would have forgotten what I looked like. Making the film also cost me plenty of dough. I got paid zilch for writing, and minimum Directors Guild scale for directing. I even had to pay back half of the little salary I did get when the film went over budget. But I didn't give a damn. I was making *Yentl* at last, and that was all that mattered.

"You know how I told you that singing came naturally to me, that I don't even know how to read notes? Well, I'm the same way about directing. I seem to know intuitively how to do it, without ever having been taught. It's the most wonderful feeling in the world when you have a problem and the answer comes straight to you from your unconscious. It comes from deep in your gut and passes right into your head. Do you know what I mean, Doctor?"

"I certainly do," I answered. "On a good day, it can happen to me with a patient or two, and I suddenly understand their whole problem in a flash."

Barbra was delighted to hear this. "So you're a natural, too!" she shrieked. "No wonder I like you!"

Barbra's role in Yentl resonates with her even after all these years.

October 1, 2015

"All in all, I devoted sixteen years of my life to *Yentl*," she began the next time, "and it changed my life. Although I was born a Jew, I had never really understood what it meant to be Jewish. Talking to all those rabbis expanded my thinking, and I understood for the first time how men have used Jewish law through the centuries to keep women enslaved. I've always been desperately curious to learn, and I understand how driven *Yentl* was in the same way.

"By the end of the film, she had learned that if you really care about yourself, you will not settle, but you will go to any lengths to make your dreams come true. Yentl did that by learning the Torah, and I did it by doing the story of her life. We are truly sisters under the skin.

"Directing *Yentl* was the highlight of my professional life. And what a beautiful experience it was! Every part of me, the male and the female, the mother, the loving, nurturing woman, the scholar, the portion of the film where I had to be my father, all came into play. Like *Yentl* dressed in her father's clothes, I in a sense had to become my own father. Fortunately or unfortunately, I'd had plenty of experience doing just that.

"I never got more than four hours sleep, and usually only three, during filming. For five months, I got up at five a.m., put in a full day's work in front of and behind the camera, and then watched the daily rushes until I knew them by heart. After everyone else was asleep for the night, I sat up until two a.m. preparing in my mind to shoot scenes the next day. Yet I never seemed to feel tired and people say I look wonderful on film. A mystical power supported me," Barbra said simply. "It was my father. He watched over me.

"The work itself was wonderful. All of a sudden, something is there where there was nothing before. It's like being pregnant. Every moment is creative... and frightening."

"How would you say the experience most changed you?"

"I was in a lot of pain before, and very confused about myself. There's a tremendous amount of self-hate in actors, so they need to pretend to be somebody else. I felt a lot of self-pity too. But not after *Yentl*.

"My break-up with Jon was also a positive thing for me. I used to be afraid to be alone. There was a void inside me, because of the absence of my father. Now I have myself."

"What do you credit for the change?"

"I credit my father for much of it. In some way, my father and I have merged. He has passed the essence of himself into me. I got the love I needed from him, and now I have it to give. Before, I was driven. Now I'm doing the driving. It's easier to be around me these days."

"Psychoanalysts like me would say that you created your father in the film and now you can identify with him."

"What a great way to put it! I'm sure that is exactly what happened." She paused for a moment, and then continued, "I was thrilled to win the Best Director award at the Golden Globe Awards ceremony. I was the first woman ever to win the award of Best Director. I was thrilled for me, of course, but also for other women, because I believed that my winning the award would open new opportunities for other talented women to make their dreams come true.

"*Yentl* was the most significant and fulfilling achievement of my lifetime. I had never known so much pleasure. The real joy was in the work itself. I like directing more than I like living. I like the way I am as a director, and when not directing, I wish I could live my life the way I do when I direct.

"Making the film changed me more than any other film I had ever made. Before I made *Yentl*, I *thought* I knew what I was doing. Now I *know* that I do, and never have to listen to anyone who tells me differently. Directing the film was a complete experience in itself—one that was built on everything I had ever done or learned.

"I'm in a new period of my life now because it took sixteen years to make this happen and it consumed five years of my life. I had to do it. I had reached the age of forty and it was a milestone for me.

"The process of making the film was a lot like having a baby. The pain of delivery will be forgotten and all I'll remember is the baby itself.

"There was so much I had to say in this dream of mine. It was bursting with joy, pain, and creativity. The film is about the uplifting of spirits, the affirmation of life itself, and love in a moment of doom. It is about the power of love and feeling and the strength of will. *Yentl* is a movie about caring, about the love of people and the love of learning. How wonderful to think of an idea, develop it until it is finished, and then to see your dream actually come true! It is something experienced maybe once in a lifetime, if at all. How many people are so lucky?"

I smiled and said, "I wouldn't call it luck, Barbra."

She smiled back. She knew very well what I meant.

October 12, 2015

"I wasn't so happy, however, about the results of the Academy Awards," she began. "Would you believe it? No best actress, best picture, best actor, best director, or best cinematography nominations for *Yentl*! I think we should have won them all, but I won't let myself blame anybody. Blaming people keeps you a victim, and I'm no victim. It's just the way things were.

"We got named only for best music, art direction, and best supporting actress–Amy Irving, who I trained in every word she said. And, oh yes, they snuck in an award for Best Original Film Score. It must have broken their hearts. Hollywood hated me, was sexist, and jealous of my success.

"But regardless of their discrimination against me, I'm prouder of *Yentl* than of anything I have ever done in my life. What a beautiful experience! Making the film made me a broader person. Every part of me—the maternal, the paternal, the nurturer, the intelligent, the intuitive, my head, and my heart—was brought into play. The movie was dedicated to my father. The card said: "To my father... and to all our fathers."

"The film is truly a remarkable achievement, Barbra," I said, "psychologically as well as artistically. You sublimated your grief about the loss of your father into a work of art, which is perhaps the finest manner of self-healing known to humankind."

She nodded her head, accepting the compliment with grace and dignity, knowing full well that she had earned it.

October 14, 2015

Barbra came into the next session announcing to me, "I had a strange dream, Doc, but I don't know if it was important or just gibberish. It probably didn't really mean anything at all!"

I smiled, remembering another patient who had said the same thing about a dream that led to the termination of his analysis.

"Tell me the dream, Barbra. You never know when a dream will turn out to be insightful."

"All right," she said skeptically. "But don't blame me if we waste the hour."

"I promise," I said.

"My father and I are gingerly climbing down a mountain on our stomachs, holding onto branches and grass as we slowly lower ourselves," she said. "I am not frightened because I know we are going to make it."

She was quiet.

"What comes to mind when you think of a mountain, Barbra?" I asked.

"I think the mountain at one point was rage. Rage at my beloved father that I've never wanted to admit. It was tough coming to terms with the fact that my father left my life when I was only 15 months old. I've always loved him, but have never forgiven him for leaving me. Somewhere inside, I've always felt that if he had only loved me enough, he would have managed to stay alive.

"The mountain also reminds me of a woman's breast. As you said, the nursing period was probably a good time for us both. Maybe because I really did love my mother, I could also love my father.

"In the dream," she continued, "I am crawling down the mountain, to get off of it. I am gradually trying to leave the mountain of rage behind me. I guess I also have to stop seeking my early mother, along with the image of my father. I'm rather old to still be looking for my mother's breast, don'tcha think?"

I smiled, and asked her for any associations she would make with crawling down the mountain on her stomach.

"The feeling belongs to my infancy, when I was crawling, not to the grown woman I am now. I am holding on to the grass and the trees."

"What comes to mind about the grass and the trees?"

"You and psychoanalysis. You have helped me understand that

there are some things that are not within the scope of any human being to change. The grownup in me can finally accept that staying alive was beyond the control of my father, and that he wanted to stay with me as much as I needed him to stay alive. The dream says that I know 'we are going to make it,' that I finally can forgive him."

"Very good, Barbra. You are accomplishing the hardest job in psychoanalysis. You are in the process of resolving your Oedipus Complex."

She grinned and said, "Well, whadda you know about that! Can I quit analysis now?"

October 16, 2015

"In those *Yentl* days," Barbra began, "people wondered what I was doing about men in my life. The answer is nothing. I wasn't even thinking about them. My whole life was the film." She started to laugh.

"What's so funny?" I asked.

"Like Amy, I was married to *Yentl*! A difficult moment came for me when Yentl had to kiss Amy Irving's character, my character's *bride*. Amy wanted to practice the kiss, but I put it off until the actual shooting. She told the newspapers, 'She cut off the kiss a lot quicker than I would have!'

"It wasn't as bad as I thought it would be," Barbra said. "It was like kissing an arm or a leg. Amy was very insulted.

"In Singer's original short story, the love triangle has strong homosexual undertones. Yentl finds a way to deflower the virginal Hadass on their wedding night. I toyed with the idea of including that scene," she says, twisting a strand of her long hair. "In the first draft of the script, I blew out the candle, and in the next shot the candle was missing. From that, the viewer could well imagine what Yentl had done.

"But the movies are too real for a scene like that. I can picture the audience laughing hysterically while feeling embarrassed. Even without the candle, the scene is erotic. Sexual taboos make it sexy. A fear of homosexuality can seem very sexy to some people. Being afraid of men and women touching each other before marriage can also be very sexy. Today, we've kind of destroyed the mystery of sex. We've lost the joy of wedding nights.

"I was working in Europe for eighteen months, and during that *Yentl* time, my relationship with Jon all but disappeared. Actually, we had been growing apart for years before that, but the long separation between us made it impossible to repair the emotional connection. Jon always says that I had to choose between *Yentl* and him, and I chose *Yentl*.

"But I had grown from the relationship. Before him, I was afraid to be alone. He taught me to enjoy my own company, and the wild freedom of solitude."

"Do you think that the void inside of you ever since your father died had been filled by Jon?" I asked.

"Absolutely. But unfortunately, that was not the whole story. When I was in Europe, I heard through the grapevine that Jon was bringing other women to our ranch, and was seeing model Lisa Taylor in New York.

One day, after I came home, he drove by with his arm around a local real estate agent, I was so angry that I had his Jaguar, which had been parked on my side of the property, towed away.

"I am the kind of person who likes a clean ending, and threw him out of the house. Then he sold his half of the property to me, which established once and for all that our intimate relationship was over. Jon was stunned by the breakup, and thought a 'little thing' like seeing a few 'unimportant' women was no reason to break up a deep and loving relationship. A 'little thing'? Was he kidding?

"Jon said to me, 'I can't really talk about it, because I love you, and I don't understand why you have to make such a big stink about a little hug and a bump.' Can you believe that, Doctor? Did he really believe that Barbra Streisand would be content to be 'one of the bunch'?

"At one time," she continued, "I would have stayed with him because I was afraid to be alone. But not anymore. After making *Yentl*, I felt very fulfilled from the inside. I had myself and I didn't need anyone else... except maybe you, Doctor."

I smiled. Barbra, I felt, had come a long way. She was able to accept her dependence on me. I also knew it wouldn't last forever, and that when she was ready to leave analysis, which was probably soon, she would be more independent than ever.

I couldn't help but think of Arthur Schopenhauer's remark that "Happiness belongs to those who are sufficient unto themselves. All external sources of happiness and pleasure are subject to chance." If he was right—and I am sure he was—Barbra was on her way to becoming a very happy woman.

October 19, 2015

With my tongue only partly in my cheek, I said to Barbra at the beginning of our next session, "I had a thought about you that I'd like to share with you."

"Is it good or bad?" she asked.

"It is excellent!"

"In that case, I'll listen," she said.

"I think you are going to live to a very old age."

"Oh?" she said with surprise, "Why do you say that?"

"Freud said there is a Life Instinct and a Death Instinct. When the Life Instinct is the stronger of the two, the person lives. When the Death Instinct wins out, he or she dies. From what I know of you, you are a feisty lover of life and have a particularly strong Life Instinct, which has helped you overcome obstacles that would have stopped most people in their tracks.

"You understand that terrors exist, but refuse to let them stop you from making the best of your life. Even though you were traumatized by past experiences of performing live, you've been making progress in overcoming those fears. You've been willing to repeat those incidents over and over with me, just as we decided we would do, and your determination shows your instinct to thrive. Even if this isn't an easy obstacle for you to overcome, you are unwavering in your determination to keep working on it, and that is beginning to show some progress. This is a part of your life instinct.

"It was apparent even when you were a baby. You told me you got into everything as soon as you learned to crawl, that you spent all day checking out and tasting everything around you. You loved the world so much you refused to go to sleep until you dropped over from sheer exhaustion.

"That's still true of you, the woman who worked around the clock for days at a time in *Yentl*. From what I can see, you're still in love with the world. You once said to me, 'I'd never trade my life for anybody else's. I love my life. I love what I've done. I love the things I hope to do.'

"As you said about Helen Keller, you feel more, sense more, and want more than anyone else, which leaves you open to life. Your love of food and great passion for sex is another indication of your strong Life Instinct, which, incidentally, is what makes you a great actress, singer, and director. It is the quality most characteristic of you. In fact, I would say it defines you. Therefore, in my professional opinion, you should be around for a very long time."

"Hmmmm. Interesting. I sure hope you're right. But how about you sticking around to find out?"

"I'm working on it!" I said.

We burst out laughing.

October 21, 2015

"In 2004," she began, "I appeared in the loony film, *Meet the Fockers*. Do you know the movie?"

I shook my head.

"Well, I guess I should tell you about it. Heaven forbid I should miss telling you about one of my movies, even one as lousy as that one! In the film, disaster confronts the male nurse Greg Focker, played by Ben Stiller, when his up-tight future father-in-law, Robert De Niro, asks to meet his wildly unconventional mom, Roz Focker, played of course by me, and his dad, played by Dustin Hoffman.

"Family bonding, which is difficult under the best of circumstances–like in my family, in case you didn't know–becomes even more crazy than usual. What's the matter? You're not laughing, Doc? Don't you think it sounds funny?"

I thought I'd better not answer that one.

She continued anyway. "The Jewish hippie Fockers and the tight-assed Byrneses are woefully mismatched from the word go. No matter how hard they try, Greg and his fiancée, Pam, just cannot bring their families together. I think it is a great movie, if you happen to like crude and sexual humor. 'The Fockers?' Are they kidding? How unsubtle can you get? Or maybe I should say vulgar.

"I play a sex therapist for elderly couples. That was kinda fun. In another lifetime, I wouldn't mind at all having that as my profession!"

I grinned and said, "You'd be great at that, Barbra!"

She ignored me. "Greg tells me to pretend to be a yoga instructor so we don't intimidate Jack Byrnes, but of course everything starts to fall apart. And I thought I had problems! Is everything clear so far, Doc?"

"Clear as the Nile River," I answered.

She laughed and continued, "In the meantime, Pam announces to Greg that she is pregnant, but they decide to keep it a secret from the straight-laced Jack. Dina, however, is growing envious of Bernie's and my active sex life, and consults me for sex tips on how to seduce Jack, but none of them work. I guess she has no sexual talents, because I sure gave her good advice. It really is good because I made it all up myself."

I was curious as to what advice Barbra gave them, but thought I'd better not ask.

"Greg and Pam marry that weekend. During the party, Jack asks me for some sex tips, which I really am a world expert on, and sneaks into the RV with Dina. I hope she is able to put a few of my sex tips to use."

"Do you think you are anything like Roz Focker?"

"Very little. I'm not happy with her kind of openness. I guess you can say that the only thing Roz and I have in common is that we both appreciate love and sex in our later years. Incidentally, I spent hours on top of De Niro giving him a massage."

"How did you feel about it?" I asked.

She laughed. "Well," she said, "that's one way to be on top of a great movie star! The night before we shot the scene, my own masseuse and I worked out how to choreograph it. De Niro kept yelling, 'Press harder!' I pressed until my thumbs gave out, and I got tendinitis and had to wear a brace. Anything for my art! But it was fun making the movie. And Bob is wonderful to work with. "Did you see the film?" she asked.

"No, I didn't."

"Would you like to?"

"No, thank you. If you don't mind, I think I'll pass on that one. It's not my cup of tea."

Barbra laughed. "I don't blame you," she said. "If I weren't in it, it probably wouldn't be mine either. It seems that many movie critics agree with you. I remember a few particularly harsh critiques, stuff like 'Meet the Fockers? Avoid them would be a better suggestion.'

"Do you know that I'm a pip? I've been called a lot of names in my day, but this one takes the cake. Manohla Dargis wrote in The New York Times, 'Ms. Streisand hasn't been called on here to deliver an immortal or even interesting performance, but she is a pip to watch.'

"Well, the pip is off for the day," she said, rising to leave the office.

Although she disliked the movie, Barbra played the role of Rozalin Focker in Meet the Fockers incredibly well.

October 23, 2015

"Jon and I are not lovers anymore—haven't been for the longest time—but we get along very well," she said, picking up the saga of her relationship with Jon. "He tells everyone I am his best friend. We no longer compete, and we respect each other more than we ever did. He even asked me to be the godmother of his daughter, Caleigh. I was delighted to accept, and love her like the daughter I never had. So now I don't have to adopt one!

"When Jon and his wife, Christine, were divorced, my only concern was Caleigh. I felt bad for her, since I know very well what it's like for a child to be the victim of a broken home. I vowed to do everything I could to help her have a happy life. Both he and Christine encouraged my relationship with their little girl, and I felt I was a stabilizing influence in her unsettled life.

"She called me 'Baba.' If that was short for Barbra, or she had heard the Yiddish word '*Bubbie*' somewhere and considered me her grandmother, I'll never know. Whatever it was, I found it very sweet. She was very attached to me, hugged and kissed me a lot, and never seemed happier than when we were together. I loved her dearly, as the girl child I never had.

"I adored designing a storybook bedroom for her in my Carolwood Drive home, and decorating it in pink and white, with organdy curtains. I had pink bookshelves built for her, and filled them to capacity with books and toys. It was sheer heaven for both of us—*mostly* heaven, anyway. Unfortunately, I felt a little jealous of my goddaughter. *What I wouldn't have given as a child to have had such a room*, I thought, *and to be out of my mother's bedroom and bed!*

"One night, I was rocking her to sleep while singing 'Rock-A-Bye Baby.' When I came to the line, 'When the bough breaks, the cradle will fall,' I stopped mid-sentence. 'The cradle will fall?' I said to myself. 'What kind of line is that to sing to a small child? It will scare her to death.' So I immediately dropped 'Rock-A-Bye Baby' from my list of acceptable lullabies.

"I created a fairyland for her. She had her own garden space, with a sandbox, a sliding board, and a playhouse where she and her friends and their beautiful dolls could have tea parties. I was happy to do it, but it made me a little sad when I remembered my hot water bag with a sweater that I took to bed with me every night when I was a child.

"Caleigh and I went shopping together, where she was allowed to pick out any clothes she wanted, even if some of them made me sick in the stomach. I also took her for appointments to the pediatrician, where I held her hand so she wouldn't be scared. Caleigh was the child I would have liked to have been, with an unbreakable tie to Jon, and a warm, sweet presence I could love. Also, I must admit that she filled my heart so I didn't feel lonely when she was around.

"Caleigh is now a pop rock musician, and extremely beautiful. Another reason for me to feel slight pangs of envy? Surprise! I don't. Or only a little bit. I love her and like to feel that I contributed to her success as a person and a professional too much to be consumed with jealousy. I have put so much into her that to be envious of her would be like feeling jealous of myself.

"She has sung on numerous film soundtracks, including those for *Ice Princess*, *Herbie: Fully Loaded*, and *Go Figure*. In 2005, she won the 'Ones to Watch' Award at the Young Hollywood Awards. Caleigh was then going to appear in a new reality TV show, *LA Private*, about teenage heirs/heiresses growing up in Beverly Hills, California. We know who she is the heiress to.

"Needless to say, I am very proud of her."

October 26, 2015

"Funny," Barbra mused the next session, "how it is much easier to be friends with a man than it is to be a lover."

"You're right, Barbra," I said. "There is nothing harder in the world than having an intimate relationship with a lover."

She smiled. "Thank you, Doctor," she said. "That makes me feel better about it. I'm sure you're not surprised to hear that my ban on seeing men didn't last very long. Soon after Jon and I parted, I dated Richard Gere briefly, but apparently there wasn't enough chemistry between us, so it didn't last very long. He was followed by Tina Sinatra's multi-millionaire ex-husband, Richard Cohen.

"Next on the list came the Arabian playboy, Dodi Fayed, who, as you may remember, later died in a car crash with Princess Diana.

"A renewed fling with Prime Minister Pierre Trudeau followed. Can't you just imagine the headlines, if he and I had gotten married? 'Prime Minister Trudeau Moves Up in the World and Marries Big Hollywood Star, Barbra Streisand.' Too bad it was not to be! He just couldn't take the competition.

"At a Christmas party in 1983, I met my next lover and almost husband, Richard Baskin, the millionaire owner of Baskin-Robbins ice cream. Ah, Richard Baskin! He still makes my mouth water when I think of him. Or is it his ice cream?

"It didn't hurt that he was tall, dark, and gorgeous, with an endearing smile, bedroom eyes, and a Samson-like mass of curly black hair. Oh yeah, he loved *Yentl,* and said he was very touched by its ethnic roots. I don't know whether it was that or his offer of unlimited ice cream that did the trick, but I fell for him right away, although we didn't go out steadily until the spring when I returned from a European tour promoting *Yentl.*

"I loved how protected I felt by his bearlike physique, and I enjoyed his sense of humor and taste in music, which were very much like mine. I adored how he always laughed at my quirks that most people–present company included–don't get. He also was in the business, and was a Hollywood musical director and award-winning songwriter.

"'Baskin?' I asked him when we first met. 'Any relation to *the* Baskin Robbins, which is my favorite ice cream?'

"'Yep,' he answered. 'That's my family.'

"'*Oy vey,*' I answered. 'I better not get to know you well. I eat coffee ice-cream all the time. I'd eat up all your profits.'

"'Barbra,' he answered, 'Go out with me and you can have all thirty-one flavors in my 7,552 stores.'

"'It's a deal!' I answered. 'That's the best offer I've had all day. Can we go get some now?' He took my arm and walked us to his 1931 Duesenberg Model J Long-Wheelbase Coupe Mercedes Benz. I knew enough about cars to be shocked. In its scale and power, that car surpassed all the grandest autos of the era, and perhaps any car ever built. He told me later that he had personally commissioned an exact copy of the car with no concern for expense or present day trends. He just had to have it. I can understand that well. I am exactly the same way.

"*This man shows real promise*, I thought to myself. *Who can resist that Mercedes Benz?* But more important, coffee ice cream is my best aphrodisiac. First we ate the ice cream, and then we wound up in bed. I don't know which I enjoyed more, the ice cream or Richard. At this point, I'd have say it was a toss-up. As you might expect, I loved that he would inherit a large amount of his family's riches and didn't need me to pick up the checks.

"We became so serious about each other that I pulled my usual schtick and made him a part of my next project, a pop album called *Emotion*. Perhaps because I was so carried away by Richard, or maybe because I just didn't like the songs so much, it wasn't very good. Critics agreed, saying it was uneven and lacked unity. John Milward of *USA Today* wrote that the album was my latest attempt to appear hip. The nerve of the man! I don't have to *appear* hip. I *am* hip! One reviewer even wrote, 'There are people out there who think Streisand is a genius. *Emotion* could cure them.'

I really didn't care. I decided that pop music was just not for me. We listened to the CD together, giggled until we couldn't stand up, and then went home to bed. Can you imagine a man who could make me forget I'm not perfect? That's even better than ice cream."

"That was real growth for you, Barbra," I said.

She was very pleased to hear it. "I like men I can learn from," she said, "and I have Richard to thank for that. My next musical venture, *The Broadway Album*, did better. It sold three million copies, was number one on the *Billboard* album chart, and received three Grammy nominations. I felt its success was because I had the support of a kind and loving man.

"By then, he had moved in with me. The poor guy didn't have to worry about paying the rent anymore. He was incredibly kind and accepting, and with his enormous bulk, Richard served as my bodyguard as well as my lover, though I must say that sometimes he got carried away by his wish to protect me.

"For example, when we were in London together, he tossed a pint of ale at reporters he thought were annoying me. When I told him that they weren't bothering me at all, he apologized to me and to them.

"Jon told our mutual friends that he expected Richard and me to get married. Maybe that was just to appease his conscience, for he had gotten married to his live-in girlfriend. It didn't take him very long. Couldn't he have mourned our parting at least for a decent length of time?

"My friends said that Richard was just a whim of mine, that he was 'too nice,' because I usually went for more flamboyant types. They thought I'd get bored with him and trade him in for a more combustible number. Three years later, we were still together."

October 28, 2015

"It was the subject of Richard Baskin that Barbra wanted to start off with at our next analysis. "I was well aware that he lacked Jon's spitfire personality and his vital life force. Unlike Jon and me, we had no strong conflicts of ego and will. Unfortunately, because he *was* a nice man, our relationship totally lacked roller-coaster thrills.

"I soon became so wrapped up in my new movie, *Nuts*, and in recording *The Broadway Album* that I had little time for Richard. When he said wistfully, 'Can't you quit work at seven o'clock?' I said, 'What! Stop work at seven, just when I'm getting going? You must be crazy!' He still lived at my house, but friends noted that the harmony between us had disappeared, and we began to bicker constantly. I hated to admit to myself that yet another relationship was crumbling, but in my innermost self, I had no doubt that it was.

"Richard and I lived happily together–at least I thought we were happy–for four years... until I came downstairs one morning ready to give him my usual good morning kiss, and got one of the great shocks of my life. Richard had packed his bags and was getting ready to sneak out the front door. When I asked why, he said, 'Don't know. Just need to get out of here.' Then he slammed the front door so hard on his way out that he broke my beautiful Tiffany glass window."

"That must have been terrible for you, Barbra."

"You're damn right, Doctor! And didn't I know it? I went to bed and cried for a week."

"And then what happened?"

"Then I went out and looked for somebody else.

Barbra and Richard Baskin at the 1986 Academy Awards.

"I went alone to Aspen and met my next guy, Don Johnson, at a Christmas party given by my dear friends, Marilyn and Alan Bergman. I know we talked about this before, but is something wrong with me that I keep friends for a lifetime and lovers only until the love wears out? You're a doctor. Can't you fix up that little thing for me?"

I smiled. Who could answer such a question without hurting her feelings, without agreeing that she *is* a difficult and complex person? But as usual, she was one step ahead of me.

"Don't answer that question, Doctor. I know what you're thinking—that I *am* hard to get along with."

I screwed up my courage and said, "I'm afraid I'll have to agree with you on that score, Barbra."

"Thank you for being honest," she said. I heaved a sigh of relief.

"But you didn't have to tell me," she said, after a song made famous by Kate Smith. "I knew it all the time."

I laughed. Then happy to change the subject, I said, "Tell me about Don Johnson."

"Richard still made a personable escort as he accompanied me to the Grammy Awards, where I was honored with an award for *The Broadway Album.* As I came off stage, a handsome young blond man perhaps ten years younger than me approached and patted me on the shoulder.

"'Congratulations!' he said. 'My name is Don Johnson.'

"Our eyes locked together for a long moment. Then I smiled and said, 'Yeah. Thanks.'

"'Who is Don Johnson?' I asked Richard.

"'He's just the reigning American male sex symbol and star of the top-rated 'Miami Vice' TV series.'

"'Hmm,' I said, looking over Richard's shoulder at Don as he walked out the door. Don turned around, looked at me, and winked."

October 30, 2015

The next session, as I could not have imagined, centered, surprisingly, on another of Barbra's movies. "I want to tell you about *Nuts*, a film I made around that time, which I simply love. I think I did some of the best acting of my life in it, and was terribly disappointed when the reviewers found themselves ambivalent about the film. What's the matter with those guys and gals? Janet Maslin of the New York Times didn't like it much, and her review hurt me more than anyone else's, because I usually respect her opinions. Unfortunately, most critics wouldn't recognize good acting and the truth if they fell over it... Did you happen to see the movie?"

I shook my head no.

"Since it is a film about a deranged woman, I would like your opinion as a psychiatrist on how truthful my performance is."

"I'd like to see it, Barbra. I'll try to get the DVD and watch it tonight."

She made no comment about my remark, but began to tell me about the movie. "I play a hooker named Claudia Draper, who comes from a conventional upper-middle-class family. My mother, Rose, and step-father, Arthur, are played by the great actors Maureen Stapleton and Karl Malden.

"Maureen is personally a very warm, affectionate woman, and we became close friends while making the movie. We commiserated about our sons. She was having some trouble with her son, Danny, and I told her about Jason's testing positive for HIV. I knew she would be very sympathetic." Barbra was quiet for a moment, and then said pensively, "It is sad about movie and theatre friendships. Most don't seem to last after the project is finished."

"Nothing is stopping you from calling her."

"That would be difficult," she answered. "She is now six feet under."

"Oh, I'm so sorry, Barbra. I didn't know."

She returned to her discussion of the film. "My character is charged with the murder of one of her clients, Allen Green. Her parents are overly conventional people who want to avoid a public scandal at all costs and agree with psychiatrist Dr. Herbert Morrison played by Eli Wallach, that their daughter is insane and incompetent to stand trial. Sadly, he's another great actor who's gone now. In any event, Rose and Arthur insist that their daughter be committed 'for her own good.' Claudia doesn't buy it, and senses there is something deceitful about their insistence.

"She maintains that she is innocent and killed her dangerous client in self-defense, which in the flashbacks is shown to be true. She knows that if she is found guilty, she will be given a prison sentence. On the other hand, if she's found incompetent to stand trial because she is insane, she can be put away indefinitely. And so Claudia fights desperately for the right to be tried.

"Her parents hire an expensive lawyer, but she attacks him when he insists she is insane. He walks out on the case. Who could blame him? The court then provides her with public defender Aaron Levinsky, skillfully played by Richard Dreyfuss. Claudia will have nothing to do with him until she's convinced he is on her side.

"Like a psychiatrist, the writer must have been in analysis with you, Aaron begins to look into her background to determine how this supposedly pampered child of model upper-middle-class parents could find herself in such a terrible predicament. With each piece of her past uncovered, her appointed defender gains additional insight into what had pulled Claudia into this crisis.

"There are some moving scenes between the defender and Claudia, as she gradually warms up to him. In one that particularly touched me, he comes to visit her in the institution. She says, 'Go home. That is where you should be.' He puts his hand over hers, and says, 'I'm supposed to be here.'

"The judge was played by James Whitmore, who moves the hearing into a closed courtroom, which is the scene of one enlightening revelation after another, including the pay-off, that Claudia as a child had been sexually assaulted by her stepfather—the same one who

Barbra as Claudia Draper, a deranged character, in Nuts.

claims in court to love her so much. It seems he slipped her a twenty-dollar bill after each sexual attack, which served as the prototype, of course, for her life as a prostitute.

"I felt I understood Claudia Draper very well. She is a girl who, like me, says exactly what she feels. In my search to understand Claudia's behavior, I went to see doctors, nurses, and psychologists, and visited many mental hospitals. You won't believe who taught me the most about Claudia. The schizophrenics! I felt completely comfortable with them. They are so honest and frank, and so lacking in social niceties that I found them refreshing. As you know, I, like Claudia, enjoy saying what I think, although I must say that both she and I get crucified for doing so. Do you think that means that I'm schizophrenic?"

"No, Barbra, I don't. We should all be so schizophrenic."

"Well, that's a relief. But I don't mind telling you that if being honest means you are schizophrenic, I will continue speaking the truth and risk being viewed as schizophrenic."

"Good for you, Barbra! I'm right there with you," I said.

"Well, maybe I'm not schizophrenic, but I've heard it said that I'm paranoid. I once went to a famous therapist and told him that one of my problems is that I don't trust people. He said, 'Why should you? Trust has to be earned.' I thanked him and didn't feel so bad about myself for a while. Do you think I'm paranoid, Doctor?"

"No, Barbra, you are not paranoid. Paranoia means that you imagine that you have enemies—people who hate you. You're not imagining it. You really have people who hate you, even if it's not always justified."

"Is that supposed to reassure me?" she asked.

I nodded subtly.

As she left the office, she looked at me shyly and said, "Thank you, Doctor. I appreciate very much that you are going to the trouble to see *Nuts*. It is beyond the call of duty."

"You are very welcome," I said. "I want to know your work." I didn't tell her that I make a point of looking at the creative work of all my patients.

November 4, 2015

After she came in, Barbra didn't waste a moment. "Well, did you watch it?" she said, approaching my chair instead of going over to the couch.

"Yes, I did."

"And what did you think?" she asked, leaning close and looking straight at me with her huge cornflower-blue eyes.

I was silent for a moment, trying to find the right words to adequately describe my reactions to the movie.

I swallowed, and finally said, "It was wonderful, Barbra. Absolutely wonderful! And so were you!"

Her face lit up. "You wouldn't kid me, would you, Doc? No, I take that back. I *know* you wouldn't lie to me." She smiled. "I knew those idiot critics were wrong. None of them have any insight about what goes on beneath the surface. They just can't see beyond their own heads. I should have gotten an Oscar for my performance, but those nincompoops don't know their ass from their elbow, or should I say they didn't know *Nuts* from peanuts. I'm happy I finally found someone who understands psychology and can see what I was trying to do."

She hesitated for a moment, as if she were afraid to hear my answer, and then said, "What did you like about it, Doctor?"

I decided that, like a good analyst, I would restrain myself and simply give her the information she asked for, without becoming personally involved.

"I liked just about everything about it," I said. "I thought your performance was one of your best, the story captivating, and the psychology of the film in describing what made Claudia do what she did was perfect. From what I've learned as a psychiatrist, it was completely on the mark. I also enjoyed the music, which I understand you wrote."

I said all this as if they were facts, as I'd been taught to do in my post-doctoral work at analytic school. There was no response. I looked at Barbra's face and saw that I might as well have been discussing the amount of rainfall in Texas, for all the effect my words were having on her. It was very much the same blank look as when her character listened to her parents' self-deceptive remarks in the movie.

I stopped for a moment and considered what I was doing, and saw that I was not expressing just how deeply the film had moved me. I was holding back my emotions because I had been taught that a Freudian analyst should always show neutrality, that it wasn't professional to reveal much feeling to a patient. Flinging aside that philosophy like a worn-out old shoe, I thought, *The hell with neutrality! It isn't worthy of so truthful a person as Barbra Streisand. I always learn from my patients, but never in quite so important a matter as this one. She is teaching me to be as honest as she is. If that will change the way I work as a professional, so be it!*

"Barbra," I said, "I will tell you something very important to me. I'm withholding my deep reactions to the film from you. But because you gave such an honest performance, you deserve better." My eyes welled. "I have to tell you I was so overcome with feelings that at the end of the movie I broke into sobs, and couldn't come out of an emotional cocoon for hours."

"Good to hear," she said almost immediately. "I was wondering when you were going to reveal yourself as a human being!"

November 6, 2015

For her next session, Barbra arrived looking a little perturbed.

"What's wrong, Barbra?" I asked.

"Have you ever had an earworm, Doctor?" she answered. "You know, where part of a song gets stuck in your head and you can't get rid of it?" She pulled on her earlobe as if to get water out of her ear.

I nodded.

"Well, a song has been going through my head all day and it's driving me crazy!"

"What's the song?"

"What's the difference? Any earworm will drive me nuts."

"The song itself might tell us something about you that we don't know."

"If you say so," she said skeptically. "It's 'Father, Pin a Rose On Me.' Do you know it?"

I shook my head. "Can you sing it to me?"

"Oh, now we're having a singing lesson, are we? I charge for this." Then she sang,

> "Father pin a rose on me
>
> And send me on my way
>
> For today, for today, for today
>
> I am a man."

I laughed. "Your astute unconscious is trying to tell you something, Barbra. Let's see if we can find out what it is. What comes to mind about 'Father, Pin a Rose On Me?'"

"That's easy. I was thrilled at what you said yesterday about *Nuts*, and I know my father would have felt the same way."

"Very good. As I said before, you are developing what we analysts call a good 'father transference' to me."

"A *father* transference? But you're a woman."

"To the unconscious that doesn't matter."

"You mean a patient can react to the analyst as if she were the opposite sex? That's incredible."

"You're right on the ball there, Barbra. The unconscious recognizes neither sex nor time. But do go on with your song."

She sang with more feeling than before, "'For today, today, today I am a man.' That's funny," she said with a puzzled look on her face. "I think my unconscious is out of touch with that one. I love being a woman and wouldn't want to be a man for anything."

"You're lucky, Barbra. Not every woman can say that. But remember when you told me that if you were a man, you would have gotten an award for directing *Yentl*?"

"Just at work, mind you, I wish I were a man. As a matter of fact, I work as well as or better than any man."

I nodded. She then dropped the subject and went on to other matters.

On her way out, I asked, "How's the earworm, Barbra?"

She laughed. "What earworm?" she said.

November 1, 2015

"Well, back to my experience with Don Johnson," she said at the next session, as if we'd never had the discussion about *Nuts*, or the earworm. "We met formally at a party at his rented home in Red Mountain, Aspen. The party was overflowing with famous guests, including Jack Nicholson, Michael Douglas, Oprah Winfrey, Martina Navratilova, and Bruce Willis.

"But most eyes were on Don, the host, and me. At that time, Don was the hottest person at the party. He had been voted prime time's number one star by *TV Guide*, having shot to that level as Detective Sonny Crockett in the hit TV series *Miami Vice*.

"We hit it off right away, at that very first party. It was Christmas week, and we were both in a similarly receptive mood; I had just broken up with Richard, and Johnson with his longtime live-in lover. Don was tall, handsome, and eight years younger than me. I figured that since I look so much younger than I am, the difference in years made us about the same age.

"He immediately took my hand and pulled me over to a quiet corner where we could talk. Most men are too intimidated by my fame to even approach me, so Don was off to a good start. He was a real Beau Brummel, with rolled-up jacket sleeves and a perpetual five o'clock shadow, and he was a throwback to the kind of rough men like Jon that had been my specialty before Baskin.

"I had missed that quality. Ostensibly, we had both come to Aspen for the skiing, but the immediate heat between us put the ski season on the back burner. I gave a holiday party a week later in my rented Aspen house, and of course I invited Don. That did it. Separated only by work engagements when we had to be, we were practically joined at the hip for the next few months.

"Did I ever tell you my maxim, that when you start a hot affair, it takes three months to get out of bed? Well, Don and I were no exception.

"Many of our friends poo-pooed the idea that Don and I were lovers. 'After all,' they said, 'whatever your good qualities, you and Don have two of the biggest egos in town, with the possible exception of Frank Sinatra. You are known for being as hard as your bright red fingernails, while he is reputed to be a stubborn womanizing stud.' Of course I didn't listen. Maybe I should have.

"We made our first public appearance at the Tyson-Holmes fight in

January, holding hands in front of all the HBO cameras. Soon after, I invited him to my Malibu home for a lobster dinner. Don came for the meal but stayed all night. Later, we attended a Lakers-Sonics game at the L.A. Forum, at which I fell asleep, and a movie awards ceremony at Bally's Las Vegas, where I was crowned the Female Star of the Decade. It was the first time I ever enjoyed being a celebrity.

"When Don and I held hands, I didn't have to feel apologetic for getting more attention than the man I was with, because with Don, I didn't. He was as famous as I was. We skied a lot in Aspen—at least he did. To his amusement, I struggled on the baby slopes of Buttermilk Mountain. Mostly, we just hung out together around the million-dollar home he had bought in the Woody Creek section of town."

"What was the attraction, Barbra?"

"Well, you know my penchant for falling head-over-heels in love. I'm one of those women who does everything for her man. I go completely gaga when I fall in love. Which is not to minimize Don's unique appeal. When he wants to turn on the charm, all he has to do is look at you and he can charm the fish out of the sea.

"He had everything I needed—looks, charm, worldly success, a great sense of humor, and an appealing personality. And, as you know, underneath all my glitz and glamour, in my head I'm still the *mieskeit* everyone shunned when I was a kid.

"Then, too, Don was totally in awe of me. He got gooey-eyed whenever we were together. To have this gorgeous, fascinating guy unable to take his eyes off me was very stimulating to the ego, to say nothing of the libido.

"We soon discovered that we had a lot in common. Like me, he had had a very unhappy childhood. Doesn't everybody? His parents divorced when he was five years old. 'Everything changed overnight,' he told me. 'It was as if I were alone in a rowboat in a raging sea. I had to make decisions that shouldn't be forced on a little boy.' Of course, like Jon, Don got into trouble. He was arrested for hot-wiring cars, and sentenced to a year in a juvenile detention home. When he got out, he moved in with a twenty-six-year-old waitress, to whom he lost his virginity. He must have been all of fifteen years old.

"Finally, something good happened to him. He was given the lead in his high school production of *West Side Story*, and apparently was wonderful in it. As a result, he was given a drama scholarship at the University of Kansas. True to form, he moved in with a female professor.

"His first big break came when he was featured in a nude rape scene in a play with Sal Mineo, called *Fortune and Men's Eyes*. He was terrific in it.

"I said, 'Don, weren't you embarrassed to appear bare-assed on stage when you were so young? I could never have done that. I don't think I could do it now.'"

"'Nah,' he answered unashamedly. 'A lot of women have told me how good I look naked. It's a great advertisement. The more women who see how well hung I am, the more they become available for sex.' When he said that, I gasped in admiration. Have you ever heard anything like that, Doctor?"

"No, Barbra," I answered. "I honestly can't say I have." *Perhaps it's just as well,* I silently thought. *There are some experiences you can live without.*

"I don't know about the women," she continued, "but his role in the play attracted the notice of producers, who signed him to a contract with MGM, where he was cast in a stinker, *The Magic Garden of Stanley Sweetheart.* The movie may have been lousy, but Don wasn't. He had begun to crawl his way up the slippery slope of success.

"He showed off his gorgeous full-front torso again in *The Harrad Experiment,* and then wooed and married fifteen-year-old Melanie Griffith, the daughter of film star Tippi Hedren. They were divorced the next year. When he told me about the divorce, little did I know that it was far from the end of their love story.

Barbra and Don Johnson at one of their many public appearances.

"Just like every film I make changes me in some way, so does every new relationship I start," Barbra mused at the opening of our next session. "And yet I often worry that people want to be close to me only for what they can get out of the relationship. A friend of mine who is in analysis says, 'Don't have all your paranoia analyzed away. Some of it is justified!' True, no doubt in my case. Don, unlike me, was very open and deal with people based on their own sense of worth. Gradually, this approach has rubbed off on me. In that sense, he is probably one of the best things that ever happened to me.

"It wasn't all one-sided, though. Don made some important Hollywood connections through me. With the future of his television show, *Miami Vice,* shaky, Don, who was then filming the cop thriller, *Dead Bang,* was eagerly seeking a movie career. Just as I helped Jon become a film producer, I swung professional doors open for Don Johnson. 'You want me for this picture?' I would say to a new producer, 'then cast Don in it, too.' It's a case of 'love me, but love my dog too.' A little voice inside of my head thought maybe that was something I could do for him that all his old girlfriends—or heaven forbid, his new ones—couldn't."

"You don't think that just being you is enough to hold on to a man?" I asked.

"You know me, Doctor. In my heart, deep down, I'm always the little *meiskeit* my stepfather wouldn't even buy a popsicle for.

"*Bloom County* cartoonist Berke Breathed disrespectfully called Don my 'goy boy toy.' That was very insulting to us both and was just not true. Don had a lot of depth and feeling for me. He could be very funny, too, which you know is important to me. I remember one time when we were lying in bed having an intimate conversation. I said, 'Don, you can ask me anything you want and I'll answer you.' Without losing a step, he answered, 'How much is the annual rainfall in Texas?'

"I genuinely loved him, and seriously considered marrying him. I might even have pressured him for a late-summer ceremony, but he was a little nervous about it. He had already seen three marriages fail and was afraid to risk another. As for me, why *should* I marry? I had too much money to need a man for financial support.

"Also, because of California law, I might lose half of my accumulated wealth if we ever broke up, which, considering my record, was not too far from reality. It was only my insecurity that demanded marriage. There is something exciting about *not* being married. You can never take each other for granted. At the time, I was having a ball and sang all day, happy as a lark. That was enough... for as long as it lasted.

"Hollywood was buzzing with the rumor that we were planning a September wedding when Don had to leave for Calgary to make *Dead Bang*. Unfortunately, a twenty-four-year-old girl named Penelope Ann Miller was also in it, and of course they had an affair. I didn't know it then, but she wasn't the one I should have been worried about.

"When Don failed to show up at my 46th birthday party Jon threw for me, I was devastated. I never had a worse birthday. I felt sorry for Jon, because I hardly talked to anyone there."

"It must have brought back memories of you staying at the window, waiting for your father to come home after he died," I said.

"You're right!" she said with surprise. "That's exactly how I felt, although I didn't make the connection then. Isn't the unconscious incredible?" She paused a moment, and then continued, "Don was still filming *Dead Bang* when he received a phone call from his ex-wife Melanie Griffith, with whom he had always maintained a friendly relationship, if not more. She told him she was checking herself into a rehabilitation center to combat her drug addiction. He rushed to her side. Pretty soon, they were back in the throes of a passionate relationship.

"When Melanie was nominated later in the year for an Oscar for her work in Mike Nichols' production of *Working Girl,* they announced their engagement. I was broken-hearted. I had really loved Don and thought he loved me, although I suspect now that all the time we were together, he had hidden a yen for Melanie. I curled up under my ermine bedspread for a week, and I was depressed for a long time after. That is, until they announced their divorce after Melanie ran away with Spanish lover boy, Antonio Banderas," Barbra said, with a smirk on her face.

"Up to that point, Doctor, why do you think I'd been in this revolving door of lovers? Though I guess I am fortunate that another guy has always turned up."

"I can't wait to hear about the next guy," I said. I thought I was lying, but it turned out I wasn't.

November 11, 2015

"I want to tell you about one of my all-time favorite films made by me or any other producer. It's called *The Mirror Has Two Faces*, and was one of the last I made."

"What do you like about it, Barbra?"

"Hold your horses, Doctor! I'll get to that in good time."

"Sorry. I guess I can be a tad too impatient."

"You and me both," she consoled me, and then returned to her discussion of the movie. "My character, Rose Morgan, still lives with her mother, Hannah, who is superbly played by Lauren Bacall. Hannah is a self-involved woman interested only in external beauty. I first met Lauren over thirty years ago, when she came up to me after seeing *Funny Girl*, and told me I was so damn good she thought she should slap my face. A woman after my own heart! I love Lauren Bacall, and was delighted when she won an Oscar for Best Supporting Actress in *The Mirror Has Two Faces*. It's one of the few times the Academy has rewarded a deserving actor!

"Rose is a wonderfully witty professor of Romantic Literature and, though dowdy, desperately yearns for some passion in her life. Gregory Larkin, a mathematics professor played by the great and handsome Jeff Bridges, has been burnt by a number of passionate relationships, and he longs for a sexless union based purely on friendship and respect, which he believes could bring about a painless existence. He's a man whose obsessions about sex, romance, and love cause him lasting grief and ruin his life. He spends much of his time in a brooding state of sexual obsession. It is all he can think about, and he'll do anything to get rid of such fixating thoughts.

"That's the reason it takes him fourteen years to write one book, Rose points out. Gregory has absolutely no physical attraction to Rose, so they won't constantly be tortured by passion. They will share a genuine affection, but are much too valuable as human beings to have their lives made miserable by passionate love.

"He loves her mind, her humor, her intelligence, and her interest in ideas and matters of substance. He firmly believes that such things last, while sexual passions and physical beauty fade fast. But everything becomes utterly confusing when he realizes he is attracted to Rose.

"Rose has a 'good' life. She loves teaching, baseball, and eating, though possibly in reverse order. She still lives at home under the shadow of her overpowering mother. Rose has no energy left for dating rituals, which she compares to an endless job interview.

"Rose says that in fairy tales and myths, people meet, fall in love, and marry," Barbra continued. "But we don't stick around long enough to find out what happens afterwards, how the spouses drive each other crazy. Rose has accepted the fact that she will never marry, yet inside she longs to have someone really love her.

"It was impossible to be filming '*The Mirror Has Two Faces*' without examining one's personal concepts of love, romance, and beauty, and how greatly they are influenced by slick TV and magazine ads and traditional love stories," Barbra said. "That was, of course, one of my main objectives in making the picture. As I've told you, every movie I make changes me in some way. This one opened me up to the idea that you don't have to be physically beautiful to be a beautiful person on the inside. Boy, did I need to learn that!

"Jeff Bridges is different from most men," Barbra went on, "or at least the ones I've known. He said, 'You know, I find you more appealing in casual clothes, comfortable shoes, no makeup, and fancy hair style, than when you are on stage in a spotlight as a great superstar.' I love that man!"

"Did you sleep with him, Barbra?" I mischievously asked.

"No comment," she answered, her blue eyes twinkling.

"Rose and Gregory," she continued, "are two individuals with practically nothing in common, who are brought together by a personal ad in the newspaper. Without physical attraction to complicate things, they become best friends and form an unconventional marriage, built on intellectual passion instead of sexual fire. But when Rose unfortunately breaks their bargain and is overcome by lust for Gregory, he goes off on a European lecture tour.

"Plain Jane Rose uses the time to completely renovate herself, including bleaching and perming her hair, working out at a gym, buying a sexy wardrobe, and having her mother, a cosmetician, give Rose a complete makeup job. She even has plastic surgery and becomes the beauty she never had been. Gregory comes home and begins to boil over with desire for the newly minted Rose.

"I directed the movie. I chose it purely out of love, which always makes for the best films. I believe strongly in the underlying theme about vanity and beauty, the external versus the internal. One look at me and you can understand why. And I'm always interested in films about appearances. I identify with the plain Rose Morgan, who got by in life only on her wits and intelligence. Sound familiar? *The Mirror Has Two Faces* ridicules our modern notions of sex and beauty with a brilliant combination of humor and poignancy that makes it a great rom com, if I do say so myself.

"Physical beauty, in my humble opinion, has wielded tremendous power over humanity down through the ages. It can be found in our oldest fairy tales, and today's worsening obsession with it eats up billions of dollars each year—dollars that would be better spent on books and museums. It has inspired wars as well as great art, and even toppled crowns. Think for a moment of the Duke of Windsor and Wally Warfield, who absolutely ruined his life, even while admitting to herself he was a fool to give up his throne for love.

"The illusion of surface beauty and the sexual tension it creates bring about incredible problems. We are bombarded with ads, films, and TV commercials in which impossibly perfect people hear fabulous music when they are drawn to each other. Think of Marilyn Monroe, who to my mind is the closest we can come to pure beauty. Do you think she would have looked the way she did without plastic surgery, dental implants, and phys-ed gurus? Did you see the photo of her on her deathbed? It is much more realistic.

"The theme of *The Mirror Has Two Faces* is that beauty is in the eyes of the beholder. The film illustrates that the world mirrors back to you your own perception of yourself, which is based mainly on your childhood experiences. It is a romantic comedy that has serious overtones about mother-daughter relationships, the myth of beauty, the development of self-esteem, and transformation of the self.

"My mother used to tell a funny story which is close to the truth. I have to give her credit on that one. When my father was wooing her, they were sitting at the end of a pier at Coney Island. My father said, 'Can't you smell the flowers, Diana?' My dear mother responded, 'All I can smell is the fish.'"

"I like to tell stories about positive transformations and the possibility of human development—about people who realize their potential and refuse to be ruled by the wishes of others," Barbra continued. "And I'm curious about whether love and sympathy can really heal and liberate the soul. Do you think they can, Doctor?"

"I know so. Even psychoanalysis is based on love, only we call it transference. The patient falls in love with the analyst, in the same way he or she once felt about the significant people in his or her life. But the patient sees that the analyst is different from his or her forerunners, and thus old wounds are healed."

"I guess that's why I'm getting better," she said quietly. "I love you."

Now it was my turn for my eyes to fill up.

She went on as if she hadn't noticed. But I would bet my practice that she had taken it in, because accepting the fact that I could cry after her expression of love for me was just too intense for her to bear.

Barbra and Jeff Bridges in The Mirror Has Two Faces, a story about self-acceptance and vanity—themes that would help her at this point in her life.

"Jeff Bridges said something I like very much," she went on. "'Good comedy and good drama have in common a search for the truth. And that is what our Barbra Streisand brings to her every artistic venture with inspiring intensity—her passion for the truth.' Jeff really understood what I was trying to do in that film... and perhaps every film I've ever done, not to mention my entire life. I've tried to tell the truth and nothing but the truth all my life. Jule Stein, who's known me since I was a kid, sure was right when he said, 'There is only one way to deal with Barbra Streisand: Tell her the truth. If you don't tell her the truth, then you're going to have problems.'

"Nevertheless, truth-telling can get you in a lot of trouble," she added. "Just think of Joan of Arc. In the play, she says, 'She who tells the truth shall surely be caught.' It is absolutely true. There is no place for truth in Hollywood today. When I was in *Hello, Dolly*, Walter Matthau said that nobody in the film liked me. Do you know why? Because I had the gumption to tell them when they stank.

"But I think I've mellowed a bit about truth-telling. It doesn't have to be vicious. It can be toned down or dressed up. I need to watch my tone of voice, and maybe not say every single thing I think. I used to enjoy using truth as a weapon, and consoled my conscience with, 'I'm only telling the truth.' But now I go along with what the Dalai Lama says, 'Tell the truth with compassion.' You don't say what I would have said at one time, 'Golly, you look fat today!' You say 'I've seen you look slimmer.'"

I smiled and said, "Yes, that's an improvement. But I'm glad you continue to say what you believe, however you phrase it. The quality that makes you a great artist is your constant search for the truth."

"Thank you, Doctor," she said with gratitude. "At last I found a shrink who knows what art really is."

I couldn't help smiling. I like to feel I know something about art. Having an artist like Barbra Streisand corroborate my opinion of myself was a high point for me. Such comments every now and then, when justified, are one of the satisfactions of being a psychoanalyst.

November 13, 2015

I've been thinking about Barbra Streisand a lot lately, about how extraordinarily gifted she is, and how fortunate I am that she chose me for her analyst. I've decided to write down a few more of my thoughts, bcause I feel we've reached a point in her analysis where I understand her. Creative people are always my favorite patients. Surely Barbra is at the top of the list, for she remains in the thick of current popular culture. Barbra is the last superstar on earth who is still with us. She is not only a talented actress, a wonderful singer, a revolutionary director, a passionate activist, and a generous philanthropist, but she has remained incredibly popular into her eighth decade.

While many people of her generation have retired to their rocking chairs, Barbra doesn't rest on her laurels, great as they are, but continues to come up with new and exciting material. She is the only artist in history to receive a Grammy, Oscar, Emmy, and Tony, as well as a Golden Globe, a Peabody, a National Medal of Arts, France's *Légion d'honneur*, the American Film Institute's Lifetime Achievement Award, a Kennedy Center Honors designation, and awards from the Directors Guild of America. She won an Academy Award for Best Actress for *Funny Girl* and also for the Best Original Song, *Evergreen*, from *A Star Is Born*.

With tears in her eyes, she said, "Never in my wildest dreams did I imagine that I would ever win an Academy Award for writing a song."

"Barbra," I said, "when you sing that song, what do you think about?"

"The song is about love, and love is immortal. Everybody always looks for love, so I always sing about something or somebody I love. It could be my husband, my son, or my dog Sammy. Or coffee ice cream. I love lots of things as well as many people."

I said, "Nothing about that surprises me, Barbra. But wouldn't the audience at the Academy Awards be shocked to hear that you were thinking about coffee ice cream?"

We both burst out in a loud laugh.

"I was also able to bring my feminist philosophy into *A Star is Born*, in which a woman seizes her own power," Barbra went on. "It was important to me that Esther is the one who proposes marriage to John Norman. And I refused to allow her to give up her own name at the end of the movie, as she had done in previous versions of the film. 'The Woman in the Moon,' the Paul Williams and Kenny Ascher song, was particularly significant in developing this aspect of women's lib. 'The *man* in the moon? Who knows who is actually up there? Maybe it's a woman.''

"I never thought of that," I said.

"Neither has anyone else," she said.

"*A Star is Born* expanded my life in another way, too," she continued. "Not only did I win the Academy Award for the song, but I had to learn to play the guitar for a scene in the film. I practiced morning, noon, and night, and drove everybody crazy with my playing.

"I was also very upset because my guitar teacher could write songs, but I didn't think I could. I was crying in the bathroom when Jon came in and said, 'Don't be silly, Barbra. Of course you can write a song. You can do anything you set your mind to. Go on and try to write one! Go on! Try!' Of course he turned out to be right, as usual.

"I was delighted to be learning something absolutely new to me. I have this crazy idea that learning something in a different field increases the neurons in my brain, and that it may help me live a longer and healthier life.'

"That's not so crazy a notion, Barbra." I said. "Many scientists would agree with you. As in many other aspects of your life, you are ahead of your time."

She looked delighted to hear me say so, and commented, "Good! Come and listen to me play the trombone when I am one hundred and twenty."

"I'll be there," I said, crossing my fingers behind my back in what she had to know was a joke.

November 13, 2015

As a recording artist, Barbra has won ten Grammy Awards, including a Lifetime Achievement Award and a Legends Award. She has incredible talent, as well as the deep concentration necessary to bring it all to fruition. In my opinion, the only other Hollywood person whose star has shone as brightly as Barbra's in as many ways was the great comedian, Charlie Chaplin.

When I heard she received the Legends Award, I kidded her by saying, "Barbra, I hear you're a legend now."

"Well, I don't feel like a legend," she answered in all seriousness. "I feel more like a work in progress."

"Good girl! That's why you are a legend!"

"I remember one time when I was interviewed on the *Funny Girl* set. I was exhausted and said, 'Whadda you wanna know?' In her best Brooklyn accent, the reporter answered, 'Whadda you wanna tell me?' I answered, 'Nuttin'. I just wanna go home!'

"'I really want to live a simple life,' I actually told her. 'I just want to live, to enjoy my family and beautiful home, and to be as normal as I can be.' I've been called everything else, but never 'normal.' Now that's all I want to be. I don't go to openings wearing beaded gowns. I wear blue jeans and tee shirts and just want to stay home and cook dinner. I wash the dishes and do the laundry. I really like that kind of life.

"In the mornings, I work in my garden, where I raise orchids, begonias, and the best vegetables in Malibu. Remember when we were children, when produce was delicious? I don't know what they do to ruin everything nowadays, but what you buy in the supermarkets is something else again.

"A few years ago, I went to Italy, where the tomatoes were as good as I remembered. 'Now, THOSE are tomatoes'! I shouted. Now I raise my own, and tomatoes taste like they should again. It is really the gardener who raises them. I just do the planning. I have a weak back, and if I do any digging myself, I have a backache for a week.

"I've always felt like an outcast. I'm not comfortable with success, and never was. I don't like to be recognized. I don't feel like a famous person or star. *Star* is a kind of embarrassing word for me. Maybe that's why I get so much flak from the press. I always thought it was unnecessary to expose my personal life. I want people to enjoy my work. After all, that's what they pay for. But I don't think they have any claim on my private life or time. Any feelings or thoughts I want to express can be seen in my work.

"Real stars behave in the way they do in the movies. Unlike me, they're very comfortable with reporters and photographers. In pictures in the newspaper, or in magazines, they are always smiling like ladies. In most of my photos, the look on my face says, 'Leave me alone. Get the hell outta here. How come you're taking my picture? Have you no respect for my privacy?' They click flashbulbs in my face so I can't see a thing. It's rude. It's unkind. I resent being treated like an object, a thing. I'll never get used to it.

"Sometimes people act like they own me! Well, they don't! Nobody does. To my millions of fans, I do have obligations, but they are not outweighed by my responsibilities to myself. I won't have it any other way.

"So who is Barbra Streisand, you wanna know? I'm my own person. But I really am a Brooklynite Jewish housewife at heart. I'm turning into my mother, and even she went to work."

"Why do you think being from Brooklyn forms such a large part of your identity?" I asked.

She thought a moment and said, "Brooklyn once seemed to me a city without any redeeming features, not even its ice cream. But I've changed how I think about it these days.

"Coming from Brooklyn gives me a sense of reality, a way to keep my feet on the ground. Otherwise, I'd be up in the clouds all the time. In Brooklyn, I played in the gutter. Thank God Brooklyn will always be in my blood!"

November 16, 2015

"Even though I sometimes just wish to be a Jewish housewife from Brooklyn, I continued to be a highly successful performer. *Partners*, my album from 2014, was my 33rd album to make it into the Top 10 on *Billboard*'s U.S. charts. Isn't that crazy? I'm the only female artist to achieve that honor (trailing only the Rolling Stones and even tying with Frank Sinatra!)

"But *Partners* achieved much more than that. I became the first and only recording artist to have a number one release in six consecutive decades. I'm the best-selling female recording artist who ever lived! I'm also the only woman to make the All-Time Top 10 Best Selling Artists list. I have the longest span of number one albums in history: Fifty years! I can hardly believe it."

"I should be such a Jewish housewife!" I replied, laughing.

"But what really makes me the last great superstar is that I've just outlived the others. Frank Sinatra and Elizabeth Taylor also captivated the world so completely, in such a new way. The whole world cared about the intimate details of their lives as if they were family!" She said, growing a bit more somber when remembering her late peers.

"Well, all of you certainly earned that adoration!" I said warmly, meaning every word. "You back it up with true talent and personality."

She smiled, wiping her eyes. "You're too kind to me, Doc. There are, of course, other stars who possibly might assume my level of stardom after my time is over. Madonna and Beyoncé are both remarkable divas with crazy, devoted fan bases. But they have a long way to go before they've lived a life as full as mine. Plus, they only sing; they don't hold a candle to my acting, directing, or activism. It takes more than just a pretty voice and good marketing to be me! No one, I think, will ever be quite like me," she said, with a smile.

"And no one should be, Barbra," I replied. "You're one of a kind. But do you believe that the popular music of today is more infantile than it was, say, in the Benny Goodman era, which I loved?"

"Infantile, schminfantile! You must be joking. People are people in every age. What is great will always win out. If I may be so unsophisticated as to compare it to music, it's like plumbing. Plumbing existed thousands of years ago. Then, for some reason, the secret of good plumbing was lost, but it was so good and so right that people later rediscovered it.

"If the music of the Benny Goodman era was really so good, it will come back." She gave me a dirty look, as if to say, *What? You still like Benny Goodman? You're back in the dark ages.*

I felt duly chastised.

November 18, 2015

As mentioned above, Barbra also is a great activist, partly in the political sphere. She has lent tremendous support to many politicians running for office, including former New York congresswoman Bella Abzug. Barbra knows full well that Bill Clinton was elected president in good measure because of her efforts.

She raised millions for the Democrats, and was called Bill's First FOB (Friend of Bill) by *People* Magazine. And when Hillary Clinton first ran for president in 2008, Hillary announced to the press, "Many important entertainers have put their skills and money behind me, but Barbra Streisand is worth all the rest of them put together. She is the one who brings in the major money in my campaign." Since I am a dedicated Democrat and love Hillary Clinton, I was delighted to hear it.

Barbra also dined with Clinton's Attorney General, Janet Reno, to discuss feminist issues, sat in the audience at a House Armed Services Committee hearing on homosexuals in the military, toured the headquarters of the Holocaust Museum, which broke her heart, and attended a congressional dinner at the invitation of liberal California Senator Barbara Boxer. Quite a list!

Barbra with Bill and Hillary Clinton, 2013.

Several weeks after Clinton's presidential election in 1992, Barbra was approached by Democrats wanting her to run for senator of New York against Senator Daniel Patrick Moynihan. She was flattered and considered it for a while, but then rejected the idea. "Running for the Senate is out of the question," she declared. "While the idea is intriguing, there is a big difference between having a political passion and being politically ambitious."

("Also," she added to me when I asked her about it, "I don't like the idea of standing around shaking hands and letting babies pee on me.")

The day after her Sherman-esque public declaration of non-candidacy for the Senate from New York, *Senator Yentl Flip Flops* was the inescapable headline in *The New York Post*. Former vice presidential nominee Geraldine Ferraro believed Barbra would have made a formidable candidate for Senator Moynihan's seat. But Democratic Senator Charles Schumer quipped, "It is more likely that Senator Moynihan would win a Grammy than Barbra Streisand would run against him... And I've heard Moynihan sing!"

Too bad, I thought, though I well understood that elected office is not really where Barbra lives. She would have made a great senator! But then, Barbra Streisand would be great at anything she set her mind to do.

As her analyst, I've observed an underlying theme in Streisand's many movies, as well as in her sessions with me. All her characters are pursued romantically, yet need to be constantly reminded of how beautiful they are and how much they're desired sexually. Although this characteristic could be true of any leading Hollywood lady, there is something more pronounced, more tense, and less nuanced about the reassurances that Streisand's characters require. The reason is pretty obvious. Because her mother never nurtured, coddled, or complimented the young Streisand, Barbra has always sought affirmation wherever she could find it.

But it is remarkable that, even in her need to be loved, Barbra never had the shape of her nose changed, revealing a strength of character and inner fortitude that has served her well. She wanted to be sexy, yes, but only on her terms. Barbra was and is the ultimate feminist. While she is courageous in her beliefs, she has remained a human being, albeit with insecurities we all possess.

"I am a feminist, Jewish, opinionated, liberal woman," she said proudly. "Why *should* I have my nose changed? It helps me smell a phony a mile away!"

I laughed. "That's an asset which serves you well," I said.

"Speaking of feminism, I would love to make a film where the production departments and entire film crew are all staffed by women. I imagine that Jane Fonda and many other leaders in the Women's Lib movement wish the same. Who knows? The time may be approaching when there will be as many female directors as male, maybe even more! I'm an artist and, to me, that has no gender. I hope to live to see the day!"

So what *is* the essence of Barbra Streisand? What is her core? The lucky ones among us all have a center. Mine is my writing. What makes her Barbra Streisand? I believe her center is her driving need to be great and to put her giant creativity to use—a drive which surpasses all her other needs.

Food, sleep, and even love fall by the wayside when Barbra Streisand is at work. The combination is what makes for genius. She told the author Christopher Anderson, "I always knew I'd be famous. I wanted it. I knew I had to go straight to the top or nowhere at all." She said to the *The New York Times*, "People keep asking me, 'How can you hold a note so long?' I never think about it. I just hold it as long as I want to."

She doesn't have to try to be great, but simply does what she wants to, which happens to be great. That's genius for you. That's why there will never be another Barbra Streisand, ever. And that's why Barbra Streisand is the last great superstar.

Still wondering what was at Barbra's core, I decided to ask her.

"Who are you, Barbra?" I asked. To my surprise, she didn't mention her talents.

"I'm a person of contradictions," she answered without missing a beat. "I'm scared and I'm strong. I'm supposed to be a magnificent, powerful woman, but I'm too terrified to get on a train by myself, or to travel alone in Europe. The real me, the real Barbra Streisand, is scared or overwhelmed by lots of things," she said.

"There's a part of me that lives through the fear and sits at a recording session and goes, 'No! No! No! The oboe goes here! It has to or the whole thing will be ruined!' When making music, I can't ever lose arguments. The same when I'm directing a movie. I have mental images of the film's every aspect. Every single costume, piece of furniture, and color is a part of my image. Robert Bly says the warrior has a cause that transcends himself. That is exactly what goes on in my mind. There's the me in real life.

"I'm the person who sits at a seminar and cries at the drop of a hat when everybody else is laughing. And then there's the other part of me, the warrior. When that part shows up, you would be wise to get out of the way.

"There always are contradictions in my personality. I have periods where I'm very focused and clear minded and loving. And then I go through other times where I'm absolutely dysfunctional. So who is Barbra Streisand? Don't ask me! You're the shrink!"

She burst out laughing.

I didn't think it was so funny.

November 20, 2015

To my surprise, Barbra returned to *The Mirror Has Two Faces* in our next professional get-together. "The film is often hilarious, and includes one of the funniest lines I've ever heard in a movie. A friend of Gregory's is discussing twelve girls he had recently dated, all of whom he found to be brainless compared to Rose. When he asked one of the twelve if she had read Ernest Hemingway's *A Farewell to Arms*, she replied: 'I never read diet books.'"

We both began to laugh.

"The movie also has one of my all-time favorite scenes, and one of the most poignant I believe has ever been filmed. My screen mother and I, who get along no better than I did with my own mother, have a rapprochement, and for the first time are finally ready to talk. I was deeply moved when playing the scene—so touched that it took me a full day to recover from it. It always makes me sad to remember it. Rose says, 'Mom, when I was a baby, was I pretty?' and Hannah responds, 'All babies are pretty.' The line was taken straight from my own mother's mouth."

Barbra's lovely blue eyes turned watery.

"Did you ever have such a poignant talk with your own mother?" I asked.

She closed her eyes and fervently said, "I wish..."

"Speaking of mothers, *Guilt Trip* is a movie I did about a mother and her only son," she went on. "It was filmed in 2011 in Los Angeles and Las Vegas. In it, Andy Brewster (Seth Rogen) is about to set off on a business trip from New York to San Francisco. He starts his journey with a quick goodbye visit to his mother Joyce, played by me. She makes him feel so guilty about leaving her that he invites her to come along. Across three thousand miles of constantly changing landscape, he is badgered by her nagging, until even the audience wants to shout, 'Shut up already!' But it turns out her advice is exactly what he needs to make his failing business trip a huge success.

"The writer of the screenplay, Dan Fogelman, told me that the manuscript was written about his real mother– poor guy–who was also named Joyce. Dan said with tears in his eyes that she had died a few years earlier. I thought of my own mother, who also was always a pain in the ass. When she died, I cried too.

"He said that he had taken a cross-country road trip with his mom a few years before she became terminally ill, and used it as research for the film. He added, 'We drove from New Jersey to Vegas, so I was actually locked in a car with my mother for two weeks.'

"'*Oy Gevult*,' I said, holding my face in my hands. 'I never could have survived a trip like that with *my* mother!'

"I must say, though, that I treated my own lousy mom pretty good. I paid all her bills and sent her $1,000 a month, which is pretty good money for a single old lady. My mother said her biggest problem was her lack of privacy, because I was so famous. *Her* lack of privacy? She should stand in *my* boots for a while.

"My character in *Guilt Trip* was based on Fogelman's mother, though. Like her, Joyce collects frogs almost religiously, even to the point of buying a pair of frog earrings, which you wouldn't catch me dead in. Joyce, like his mom, is obsessive about drinking six bottles of water a day and about Weight Watchers. Also like his mother, Joyce has a group of yenta friends that she heavily relies on.

"I wish I had known Fogelman's mother," Barbra said wistfully, "although I must say I know the type very well. His mother and mine must have gone to the same school in Brooklyn. When he saw the film, my son Jason said that Joyce was just like me. I think he meant it as a compliment, that I was so lifelike in the film. On the other hand, do you think he really feels I'm such a nag?" She held up her hand, and said, "No, don't answer that!"

"When he thought I couldn't hear him, Fogelman whispered to a crew member on set: 'Barbra will kill me if she ever finds this out, but she acts just like a typical Jewish mother. In fact, she resembles every Jewish mother I've known for the last thirty years.'

"Well, how could I be otherwise? I was brought up by a typical Jewish mother. I had only to think of her, and I knew just how to play the part.

"Even the road trip in the film was modeled after things that happened to the Fogelmans on the road. They didn't think it would snow in Tennessee, but it came down so hard they got stuck in a blizzard.

"The movie is really very funny at times. My favorite line comes when the traveling pair visit the Grand Canyon, a spot Joyce has always wanted to see. They stop in front of the Canyon and look at it for a few minutes. Then Joyce says, 'How long are you supposed to look at this darn thing? Ten minutes?' Andy agrees and they leave.

"It's really a story about a guy trying not to be so annoyed by his very annoying mother, a dilemma I can really understand. It also deals with a problem Jason and I have been grappling with for years—that point in every parent's life when they realize their child has grown up and they've got to let go. Jason had to run off to the east coast to get away from me."

"At that point in time," she added defensively, "he didn't realize that what I said was for his own good, or so I thought. He thought I was advising him because of my own needs, not his. I didn't understand that. How would it hurt *me* if he didn't brush his teeth, or go to the doctor when he should?

"Before *Yentl*, I felt guilty and hid things from him—chiefly my fears and my flaws. I tried to play mother. Now I'm trying to give Jason some of the love I feel my father would have given. I've stopped preaching and judging. I tell him what I think or feel, and if he doesn't accept it, so be it. It wasn't always that way. Something inside me used to cut off my feelings even to Jason when I felt misunderstood or denied. Now the love is just there. It's unconditional and it's very strong.

"I love being a mother so much that sometimes I think I'd like to adopt a little girl. Now that I'm in touch with my father and all he means to me, I'm sure I'd be a better parent than I was to Jason.

"When I was asked why I had chosen *Guilt Trip* to direct, I said, 'It's a belated love letter to my mother with all the things I wish I had said to her face.'"

Barbra got a pensive look on her face and said, "I wish I had told *my* mother I loved her while she was still alive."

"Let's do a little Gestalt psychology exercise here," I said. "Talk out loud to people, whether dead or alive. It's not too late. Tell her now."

Barbra smiled, looked up at the heavens, and shouted, "Hey, Mom up there, if you are up there. I really loved you, even if you were a rotten mother." She looked surprised and then laughed out loud.

"What's so funny?" I asked.

"She answered me," Barbra said.

"What did she say?"

She said, "I know."

November 23, 2015

"Although Don Johnson and I were no longer an item, he did something wonderful for me, which I'll always be grateful for. He read a book called *The Prince of Tides*, by Pat Conway, and couldn't stop raving about it.

"'You *have* to make a movie out of this book, Barbra,' he said emphatically. 'It will be like nothing ever seen before in Hollywood.' To humor him, I said, 'OK, send it over and I'll take a look.' *Take a look*? That's hardly an apt description of what happened. I have never been so captivated by a book. After reading the first page, I not only couldn't put the book down, but I read it through seven times in a row! I also memorized long portions of it to brand it into my soul and make it my own.

"I knew immediately that I had to make the film. Such a decision is very important to me. I'm not a woman who makes up my mind lightly, which is why, at most, I make only one movie a year. And when I decide on a film, I think it, I dream it, I brood over it twenty-four hours a day, seven days a week. I don't give of myself easily, whether to a man or a movie, but when I do, it is with all my heart.

"Making up my mind was the easy part of the job. After I had decided to make the film, I tried for years to find a studio who saw the potential of turning the book into a great movie, but try as I might, none wanted to make the film, just as with *Yentl*. I was heartbroken, and wondered for the umpteenth time why life was so hard for me.

"I thought, 'If I wanted to make some silly little comedy, the studio people would line up outside my door waving millions of dollars in their pudgy little hands. But when I ask for their help in making something worthwhile that might even change people's lives, they hide in the toilet stalls. What's with these guys, anyway? They couldn't see God if he sat right in front of them on a golden throne. They belong behind the counter of a grocery store, not serve as the heads of great studios!'

"The executives continued to kvetch about whether or not they wanted to make *The Prince of Tides,* but I made up my mind that I would stop worrying about it and leave it to the higher powers. I turned off the lights and went to sleep. Suddenly, in the middle of the night, I heard a click that woke me with a start. I sat up erect in my bed.

"Hanging over the bed was a beautiful portrait of a woman dressed in pink. A blinding light lit up the picture. The click had been the light turning on. As I sat in my bed, the phrase, 'Light up your art' kept going through my mind. It was a lot like the words of Tom Wingo to his sister in *The Prince of Tides*. He meant, 'Use your art.' I thought, 'I've had my sign from above. I certainly will make the film, even if I have to pay for it myself.' I turned over in my bed and went happily to sleep.

"A little later, there was another click, and lo and behold, the painting was lit up again.

"What?" I said to the heavens. "Didn't you believe me?"

November 25, 2015

"I tussled with every studio in Hollywood, and even some in Europe, for years, but to no avail," Barbra said, laying out the general contours of the session. "MGM-UA, who had originally signed on to distribute *The Prince of Tides*, was in the middle of a financial crisis and was forced to drop the project. Warner Brothers then turned me down. Just when I was almost ready to give up, someone up there–maybe my father–must have been looking out for me, and sent a sympathetic soul to my rescue. Guess who it was? None other than Jon Peters!

"Bright and early one morning, the telephone rang. It was Jon. It seems that Columbia Pictures, which he now headed, had agreed to take on the project, provided I accept $500,000 less than I wanted—$6,500,000— with me producing, directing, and starring in the film. Sometimes ex-boyfriends really can come in handy!

"Do you think Jon's painting lit up by itself in the night like mine did, Doctor? We always were on the same wave length."

"Who knows?" I said. "Remember Hamlet's words: 'There are more things in heaven and earth, Horatio,
Than are dreamt of in your philosophy?'

"I loved *The Prince of Tides*," I told Barbra enthusiastically. "I think maybe it is my favorite of all your films. But I saw it a long time ago. Please refresh my memory and tell me what it is about."

"Gladly. I adore the film, and love to talk about it. It is set in the South, where denial of the past and present, and the inability to mold the future, are more important than anything else. It is a place where only good manners count. In my opinion, *The Prince of Tides* is about forgiveness, and not casting blame. It is about coming to terms with things in life other than the past.

"This film means a lot to me because it's about not blaming your parents," she added. "We've all come from a childhood that is painful in one way or another. But if you continue to blame your parents for your failures, you remain a victim. The grown-up mother in me makes me a better director than I would have been as a victim. Adult women can bring a certain kind of nurturing to a film, which I would have lacked, had I not been able to forgive my mother."

She pondered a moment and then said, "In summary, *The Prince of Tides* is about forgiving my father, forgiving my mother, forgiving my son, and perhaps most of all, forgiving myself.

"It is a story about a repressed Southern man fighting for his future by coming to terms with his past." She looked up, surprised. "Isn't that what I am doing with you?"

I nodded.

"No wonder I was so involved with the film. The man's twin sister Savannah, a famous New York poet, has tried to kill herself. Tom Wingo, her twin brother, flies to New York to try to help her. There he meets Dr. Susan Lowenstein, her psychiatrist as played by me, and falls passionately in love. My character, in turn, falls deeply in love with him.

"Despite all her psychiatric skills, Dr. Lowenstein is unable to get Savannah to talk. Desperate to unlock the door to her patient's self-destructive patterns, the doctor asks Tom to act as his sister's memory. What the doctor doesn't know is that the last thing Tom wants to do is to remember his painful childhood. The doctor believes that if she can unlock the secrets of Tom's buried past, they will find the key to Savannah's recovery, as well as Tom's. Fortunately, Dr. Lowenstein is able to convince him that there are worse things than remembering.

"Tom is trapped in a world of problems. He is an unemployed football coach with a rapidly crumbling marriage and a guilt-ridden past, who finds little meaning in life. Lowenstein is not much better off. Her violinist husband is in love with another woman, and the doctor is having a lot of trouble with her unhappy teen-aged son, Bernard.

"Like Jon and me, Lowenstein and Tom help each other in many ways. Tom coaches Bernard in football and helps him to become an acceptable football player. Lowenstein enables Tom to get beneath his macho exterior and unearth the terrible memories of his childhood, when he was sodomized by an escaped convict, and forced to helplessly watch while two others raped Savannah and their mother. Tom and his brother manage to kill the convicts and bury their bodies. Sworn to secrecy by their mother, they have suppressed the memories, but the trauma had been raging on in the depths of their psyches.

"Under Dr. Lowenstein's tutelage, and with the help of Tom's recovered memories, Savannah recovers. So does Tom.

"One of the most moving scenes I ever played took place in the psychiatrist's office, where Tom falls into my lap and bursts into sobs. The scene is so moving because it was taken directly out of an experience I had in analysis. At that point, I was so repressed that I was unable to cry about anything, even my dead father. After several months of telling me it was all right to cry, the analyst came over and took me in her arms. I burst into tears.

"It seems that all the talk in the world is not equal to one good hug–hint, hint! The scene never fails to move me, no matter how many times I see it. I've had no difficulty in crying ever since."

"That was good work on the part of the analyst," I said to Barbra. "Why did you leave her?"

"I stayed with her for years, but that was the only good thing she ever did!" she said, with a mischievous look on her face.

Barbra grinned from ear to ear and returned to the story of *The Prince of Tides*. "The message the movie teaches is very important to me. Forgiveness is the great big lesson we all need to learn. It's what we all have to do to be healthy. We all need to come to terms with our past, to accept what was, and acknowledge it both to change *and* to stop living in denial. I've been working on that for years."

"You and I are trying to do the same thing in our work, Barbra. We just have different ways of going about it."

"You're right!" she said, her face lighting up. "I never thought of that!"

"Of course Lowenstein and Tom become passionate lovers and desperately want to stay together for life. But the conscientious Tom rises above his love for the doctor and returns to his wife and children to work on his marriage. Dr. Lowenstein has cured her patient with her love, but she is left alone and grieving. Using my history of loss, I did that scene very well!

"In writing the script with screenwriter Becky Johnston, who moved into my house for three weeks to collaborate with me, I consulted with psychiatrists and therapists for half a year to help me understand mental illness. I may have problems, Doc, but I'm not sick. Agree?"

"Indeed I do, Barbra. You may be different from most of us because of your extraordinary talents, but you are not sick. I wish all my patients had your energy and ability. Freud said that to be healthy, people need to be able to love and to work. I believe you are quite capable of both."

She smiled and said, "So I wasn't so far off base when I told that obnoxious fan that I was glad I was abnormal!"

I nodded.

"I knew it!" she said, and returned to her saga. "I was captivated by the concept of the wounded healer I play in the film. I have encountered many in the medical field who spend their lives helping other people but are unable to cope with their own problems."

I looked at her skeptically, and could imagine her someday saying something similar about me to another analyst.

But Barbra Streisand is nothing if not perceptive. "Don't worry, Doctor," she said. "I would never say such a thing about you."

I wanted to believe her.

And I almost did.

November 25, 2015

"For my leading man in *Prince of Tides*," she informed me, "I picked Nick Nolte over other actors like Warren Beatty and Kevin Costner, whose names had been tossed around by the media, but they weren't how I envisioned Tom. When I heard Paul Mazursky, who directed Nick in *Down and Out in Beverly Hills*, say that he had a whole lot going on inside of him that he was not going to tell you about, I suspected that Nick was *the man*.

"I saw the agony in his eyes and face, and felt that he was a vulnerable man who would not be averse to exploring his own sexual and romantic feelings, and those dark emotions we all have buried inside us that we think we hide from each another. Tom Wingo is trying to come to terms with his repressed femininity, and eventually learns to appreciate it. I wanted Nick in the part because he is so completely masculine on the outside. When I learned about his years of hard living and drinking, and his agonizing childhood, I saw that he and Tom were very much alike in their hidden sensitivity.

"Early in his career, Nolte caused a sensation in the bad boy role of Tom Jordache in the wonderful television miniseries, *Rich Man Poor Man*. The media called Nick the new Robert Redford, but he was not happy about it, and spent the rest of his career trying to prove that they were wrong by moving from one character role to another and disguising his handsome features. 'I'm not one of those pretty boys who can't act,' he announced in a television interview.

"'Why do you want *me* for the slender, blond Tom?' he asked me. 'For my current role, I weigh two hundred and fifty pounds, and have black hair and a mustache coming down over both lips.'

"'That's OK, Nick,' I said. 'We can fix all that.'

"'And indeed she did,' he told a reporter. 'She made me go on a diet on which I lost over thirty pounds, sent me to work out regularly in a gym, and had me shave off the mustache and have my hair dyed to a golden blond. One day I looked in a mirror and saw Tom Wingo looking out at me. *Damn*, I thought, *that woman can fix anything*.'

"Nick and I had a lot in common, but nothing so important as the fact that we both grew up fatherless. Frank Nolte was stationed in the Philippines during World War II, and father and son never met until Nick was three years old. As it did with me, the early lack of a father and their inability to get close in later years left scars on Nick that lasted all his life.

"Nick had another disaster happen to him when he was ten years old that also marked him for life. During a terrible fall, he impaled himself on a neighbor's white picket fence, and mangled his groin. You are a Freudian, Doctor. I don't have to tell you what that does to a man. In this case, Nick developed what looked like a third testicle, a deformity that brought ridicule from his peers and provoked in him the need to flaunt his masculinity. I wondered if I, a woman, would be able to crack his masculine bravado. I soon realized that I could, and the characteristic became very useful to Nick as the character of Tom Wingo.

"As if he didn't have enough problems, Nick took to drinking as a teen-ager and was thrown off the football team. You can imagine what that did to an already depressed young man. To shore up his self-esteem, he joined a regional theatre. It took, and he spent years with them learning his craft. At last, Nick had found something he could do well!

"He then was hired to perform in several fine television mini-series, followed by an excellent film, *The Deep*, with Jacqueline Bisset. He soon earned a reputation as a fine actor. His handsome appearance (when he didn't ruin it playing old men and character roles) didn't hurt, either.

"Fortunately, he had given up drinking a few months before we began filming the movie. Like Wingo, he had reached an emotional crossroads and had begun the long road to self-discovery. Like me, he was also an artist consumed by pain—someone who needed a canvas to express himself. As his director, I wanted to capture and capitalize on his pain.

"He admired and understood me as much as I did him. He said, 'Barbra was the perfect person to bring this story to the screen. The reasons are quite obvious. All her life, both public and personal, her motto was 'Live and Yearn.' Such a successful person could easily live in the world of have, but she isn't able to. She lives in the world of want.'

"He was so right. I think it goes back to not having a father, and to having a mean stepfather who never talked to me," she said. "As you know, I always wanted to get his approval and love, but couldn't do it no matter how hard I tried. My father was an elegant scholar, but also a phantom father.

"In contrast, my stepfather liked watching boxing matches. So one day I decided I'd call him Dad and crawl on my stomach underneath the TV so I wouldn't interfere with his boxing when I passed by. I groveled at his feet and brought him his slippers for two days! It didn't help. Nothing made him treat me any better.

"He never asked me how I was. He never said a word to me. He didn't recognize me, and he looked right through me. He disliked me. What stays with a child for life is the want, the yearning. The seeking-approval aspect permeates one's adult life. That's the reason I could sing love songs at eighteen. It was why I imagined love to perhaps be more powerful than it really is."

On the way out the door, Barbra Streisand, the non-small talker, surprised me by turning around and saying, "A Happy Thanksgiving to you, Dr. Dale."

Will miracles never cease?

November 27, 2015

"Chris O'Donnell, who would soon become a star in *Scent of a Woman*, originally won the role of my teenage son, Bernard, in *Prince of Tides*, but Pat Conroy thought Chris wasn't right for the part. He said Chris was too handsome and blond to play the maladjusted Bernard. I agreed, but was sorry to see him go, thinking wistfully that he would have made a nice goy toy. Oh well, you win some, you lose some.

"When my son Jason read the script, he very much wanted to play the role of Bernard, an angry, rebellious teenager who plays the violin to please his virtuoso violinist father, although what he wanted more than anything else was to play football. But I thought that at twenty-four years of age, he was too old to play the seventeen-year-old Bernard. I also didn't want to be accused of nepotism. I was wary of repeating Francis Ford Coppola's fatal mistake of casting his daughter in *The Godfather Part III*, for which he was blasted by critics and the public alike.

"So I turned down my disappointed son, and asked Pat to find someone more appropriate for the role. Looking through enormous piles of photos of unnamed young actors, Pat picked one out, saying, 'This guy looks like my image of Bernard.' I was surprised to discover that the actor he chose was my own son, Jason Gould.

"Production had to be halted briefly when my mother, eighty-two years old at the time, was hospitalized with heart surgery, which made me rethink my philosophy of life. For the first time in my long film career, a movie lost much of its importance and took its proper place in my world. I found out what I had refused to face before, despite thirty years of analysis," she said, giving me a dirty look. "I discovered that despite all those years of being mistreated by her when I was growing up, I desperately loved my mother, and I couldn't bear the idea of losing her. Too bad she had to almost die for me to learn that. In a way, that's what *The Prince of Tides* is about—learning to appreciate your mother.

"When it opened on Christmas Day in 1991, the critics loved it—and me! The great reviews and the huge media blitz paid off handsomely. The film earned nearly $32,000,000 in only twelve days. Can you believe it? Shortly after, it received seven Academy Award nominations, including Best Picture, Actor, Supporting Actress, Art Direction, Cinematography, Screenplay Adaptation, and Musical Score. Even with the Best Picture nomination, would you believe that once again I was not nominated for Best Director? That finally led to accusations of sexism within the

Academy, and I later became the third woman nominated for Best Director by the Director's Guild.

"Surprisingly, when the Oscars were handed out, *The Prince of Tides* didn't win a single award. That stung, but I knew in my heart of hearts that I had made a great movie."

November 30, 2015

The next session, I said, "Barbra, I marvel at your incredible talents, both as an actress and a director, and have been wondering which you prefer doing."

She thought for a moment and then said, "That's a hard question to answer. At times, I love and hate things about both. But when I look back, I would say that I'm more comfortable directing. I find it hard to bare my soul, to do personal things in front of a camera. I'd rather do them in private, which is probably why I'm not as good an actress as I could be. I'm a very reclusive person who has been forced to live her life under a public glare.

"For example, Nick Nolte said to me that I cut the love scenes too short in *The Prince of Tides*. I looked at the rushes and had to agree with him. I cut them prematurely because it really embarrassed me to make love in public. In my opinion, it's something that should be done only for and with the person you love. Try telling that to the studios or the audiences! To my credit, however, I went back and, embarrassment be damned, re-shot the love scenes to Nick's and my satisfaction.

"I have to add, though, that despite acting's drawbacks, I have played scenes, like the one when I sang 'Papa, can you hear me?' to my father in *Yentl*, that have left me on a high for weeks on end. Maybe even for life!

"On the other hand, when I direct, I am very patient and compromising, despite being a perfectionist. As a director, I find I have the ability to accept things I cannot change, a quality I wish I had in real life. When I'm directing, I live my life the way I would like to live it all the time. But I'm afraid I haven't gotten to that point yet."

"Very interesting, Barbra. In my opinion, you're a genius at both. To see you act, no one would ever guess that you were uncomfortable."

"I'm relieved to hear that," she said. "I'm always sure my terror shines out of all my pores."

December 2, 2015

Barbra changed the subject in her next session. "Interesting about sexism in movie-making," she said, observing that there was a meeting on the subject by the Women in Film organization, which happened shortly after an Oscar fiasco. "Where a man is *commanding*, a woman is *demanding*. A man is *uncompromising*, a woman is a *ball buster*. He's *assertive*, she is *aggressive*. He *strategizes*, she *manipulates*. He is a *leader*, she is *controlling*. He is *committed*, she is *obsessed*. He *sticks to his guns*, she is *stubborn*. If a man wants to get it right, he is looked up to and respected. If a woman wants to get it right, she is difficult and impossible. If he acts, produces, and directs, he is called multi-talented. If she does the same, she is called vain and egotistical.

"The only thing to do is what I have always done: try to ignore the so-called authorities and just go about my business.

"I know in my heart that, in the end, the truth will always come out. Whatever is said about me is said. I have no control over it. You can't control life. But I have to admit it sometimes upsets me when things are written about me that aren't true," she added.

"Why can't someone as successful as you just let it roll off your back?" I asked Barbra.

"Because I believe performers worth their salt know that their work, if it's to be properly communicated to an audience, has to be based on the truth. If I'm truthful at the moment when I'm acting or singing, my work is good. If not, the audience knows it. I'm well aware of how easily a lie can become the truth in people's eyes if repeated often enough. Things I never said repeatedly show up in articles and unauthorized books. For example, I read everywhere that I said, 'Brooklyn to me is baseball, boredom, and bad breath.' It's a great line, but I never said it."

"Along the same lines, I've read reports that you won't allow employees at the MGM Grand to make eye contact with you. What do you think of that bit of 'information'?"

"Do you believe that crap? We started a 'truth alert' on my website because of silly rumors like that one, which is so stupid it's not even worth discussing. People say that if I walk into a room and hear a guy playing a wrong note, I have him fired. They're making me into some monstrous diva, and I'm really just a normal person who goes about my business and doesn't bother anybody. Do you think I'm some kind of crazy diva, Doctor?"

I shook my head emphatically.

"Good! I do my own makeup. And my hairdresser's been with me for twenty years now. Does that sound like a diva? I don't know why we need to denigrate people. It's so sick."

"That must be hard to live with, Barbra. You'd think they would know you by now. But the people who love you *do* know you, and they are the ones who are important."

"Still, I am defined by such falsehoods. It drives me crazy. Suffering is resisting what is. I've learned that if you want to suffer less, you have to come to grips with what is."

I left my office that day thinking what a wonderful woman Barbra Streisand is, and how the world would be a much better place if more people followed her philosophy of life.

December 4, 2015

"Today I want to tell you about one of the most important people in my life," she began.

"What, another man? I thought you and Jim..."

She laughed. "No. Surprise! This one happens to be a woman."

"A woman?" My ears perked up, and I leaned forward in my armchair.

"Don't get all excited, Doc. I'm sorry to have to tell you this, but we didn't have a lesbian affair. Women can love each other," she said with a devilish grin, "without jumping into bed with each other."

"I am well aware of that," I said weakly.

"Even if she wasn't a man, you can add her to the list of people I loved and lost."

"Who is she?" I asked, tactfully, I hope.

"Sue Mengers, my long time agent and friend."

"Oh? You haven't mentioned her to me before. Tell me about her."

"I first became interested in Sue when I heard a story about her. In January 1979, Sue, the first enormously successful female agent in the movie business, was taking a Saturday afternoon flight from Los Angeles to New York when a woman on the plane attempted a hijacking. Her demands were unusual: She wanted Charlton Heston to read a message on television. At JFK Airport, police boarded the plane and the hijacker was subdued, with no fatalities among the passengers or crew.

"Sue announced to everyone on the plane that the worst part of the hijacking had not been the panic it caused or the fear that she was going to die. The worst part had been the hijacker's demand to have Charlton Heston deliver a message. 'I could easily have gotten Barbra Streisand,' Sue said. I guffawed when I heard the story."

I did, too.

"Sue had first encountered me seventeen years before," Barbra said, after we stopped laughing. "In October 1961, she was a twenty-nine-year-old secretary at the William Morris Agency. She went to the Gramercy Arts Theater in Manhattan to see a performance of *Another Evening with Harry Stoones*, featuring Dom DeLuise. Also in the cast was a young singer who had been taking acting classes around town: me. I was only nineteen years old, but I had several sketches in the show.

She thought I was a nothing—a veritable 'snowball in the sunshine,' she told me fifty-three years after the fact. Believe me, I never let her forget it and teased her about it every time she wanted a larger percentage of my salary. 'Who me?' I would say. 'How can I pay you so much money? I'm just a little singer who has no talent.'

"*Another Evening with Harry Stoones* should have been called *Another Misfortune for Barbra Streisand*. But for me and a rapidly advancing agent, it marked the start of a fifty-year relationship that would place us in the center of one of the most exciting eras in the history of motion pictures. It soon became clear to every successful producer and director, and every important studio CEO in town that, to get to me, they first had to do business with Sue Mengers. We became known as a Hollywood package deal.

"Sue had always possessed a shrewd instinct for recognizing talent, and it wasn't long before she forgot her initial impression of me. She soon began to believe that I possessed the great voice of my generation. When the ballsy, tough, sure-footed Sue, who had long since showed a gift for speaking her mind with actors and directors, heard me sing in New York nightclubs and on recordings, it marked the birth of her lifelong obsession with the woman who eventually became her number one client and best friend—me.

Sue Mengers, Fred Glaser, and Barbra celebrating On A Clear Day You Can See Forever.

"Sue always saw me as a kindred soul, and I felt the same way about her. We both were sharp, witty, Jewish New Yorkers with a clearly defined personal style, me favoring the eclectic Greenwich Village thrift-shop look, while the bleached blonde, zaftig Sue had classic showbiz taste, with fur coats and flowing caftans. At a time when most women had red dishwasher hands, neither of us would be caught dead without being elegantly manicured."

"They are still beautiful," I said, hiding my own unpolished fingernails behind my back.

"We had both grown up close to poverty, Sue in the Bronx, and me in Brooklyn. We each had lost our fathers early in our lives. Sue's had killed himself with an overdose of barbiturates in a Times Square hotel when she was fourteen years old. I think no pain must be worse than that for a child. We spoke frequently about the grief, rage, and anxiety our fathers' deaths had instilled in us. After all, who would better understand how we felt?

"But our anger, justified or not, mostly was directed at our mothers. Ruth Mengers, whom Sue often referred to as 'The Gorgon,' was no more supportive of her daughter than Diana Kind had been to me. Both mothers were critical, scornful, and skeptical that their daughters could ever make their dreams come true.

"Sue and I also had the same kind of sense of humor. She once was quoted as saying, 'I used to be flattered when Barbra would ask my advice about some artistic problem she was having, until I found her also asking the gardener the same thing.' Come to think of it, maybe it isn't so funny!

"The greatest connection Sue and I shared was a positive one: We each possessed an overpowering urge to do something significant and distinctive. We often talked late into the night about how we would move up in Hollywood together and make history. One of the greatest delights of my stardom was that I could say to my mother, 'Admit it, Mom, you were wrong!' Of course she didn't, but nobody could deny that I had the last word.

"If you haven't forgotten," she said, giving me a look that could kill (I'll have to remind her one of these days that I am *not* her mother and do not forget important matters she tells me about), "I was cast as Fanny Brice in *Funny Girl* in July 1963. After the show went into rehearsal at the Winter Garden Theater, Sue was always hanging around backstage, hoping to see me. By then, I was known as the biggest female recording star in the United States. Sue sat for hours in the back rows of the Winter Garden, watching in amazement. She told an interviewer that I filled every moment of every single song with a fire and presence that seemed magical. Who knows why she was so obsessed with me? Producer Jerry Weintraub may have hit the nail on the head when he said, 'Sue thinks she is Barbra.'"

I didn't say anything, but thought I wouldn't mind being Barbra Streisand either!

"When *Funny Girl* opened on Broadway on March 26, 1964," she continued, "I was praised as the greatest theater performer in years—the top star of the era. Sue continued to turn up at the Winter Garden, night after night, solidifying our friendship even further. We were so close that some people thought we were lovers."

Barbra looked straight at me.

I was getting more than a little annoyed. "Oh come off it, Barbra," I said. "You know I know better. Stop provoking me and get back to work!"

She grinned her Cheshire cat grin and continued. "With *Funny Girl*, I had achieved authentic stardom, and Sue was not far behind me. In late 1966, she left Korman and moved to CMA, where she began to work for my agents, Freddie Fields and David Begelman. At that point, they'd had plenty of opportunity to be impressed by the forceful young agent, to say nothing of her top client.

"In the biggest motion-picture event at CMA that year, Columbia Studios was preparing the screen version of *Funny Girl*, with me reprising my stage role. Following the huge success of *The Sound of Music*, movie musicals were big business. As a personality, *Sound of Music* star Julie Andrews was white bread, while I was pumpernickel raisin. Don't you love that analogy? I do.

"Sue was sure that my enormous success as a stage actress and recording artist would lead to stardom in the movies, which would more than justify my two hundred thousand dollar salary for *Funny Girl*. I hoped so. Me, the poor little mieskeit girl from Brooklyn, once was thrilled to be making sixteen dollars a week!

"By 1968, Fields and Begelman surmised that the future of CMA was in Los Angeles and not in New York. They moved most of their operations to company headquarters at 9255 Sunset Boulevard and sent Sue to Los Angeles as well. Her job was to carry out the hostess functions that the actress Polly Bergen, Fields's wife, had formerly handled for the agency.

"With Sue's gift for charming everybody and making anywhere she went seem like a party, she was the perfect person to take over this role for CMA. I usually hate parties, and don't go to many, but I always went to Sue's. If you haven't been to a party given by Sue Mengers, you haven't been to a real Hollywood party.

"A lover of everything about the film industry, Sue was thrilled to be in L.A. She found an ideal house for giving parties in Beverly Hills, and, of course, it was close to mine in Holmby Hills. Her house was a rental, a small, pink guesthouse with an elaborate flower garden behind it. Green and gold tapestries were casually thrown around, and the place was filled with pot smoke whenever there were parties. Sue herself rarely was seen without a joint. Ali MacGraw, who was one of Sue's clients and best friends, said the place reminded her of a harem.

"Sue often told friends that she understood me better than anyone else did. Inasmuch as people rarely understood me, that wasn't too hard to believe. She already imagined the day when her bosses at CMA would be out of the picture and she would be my only representative. I kind of liked that idea, too.

"In January 1969, Sue and I traveled to London for the royal premiere of *Funny Girl.* Columbia Pictures was going all out for the occasion, putting on various events, including an enormous party at Claridge's. When the plane landed, Sue and I emerged, both clad in enormous mink coats, with a jumble of shopping bags and expensive luggage.

"By the early seventies, Sue's legend, like her, had unfortunately ballooned. She was constantly profiled by important magazines and newspapers. She turned up as a slightly disguised character in various books and films. She was at least partly the inspiration for the character of Ethel Evans, the plump, ambitious, star-fucking PR agent in Jacqueline Susann's *The Love Machine.*

Her friend Gore Vidal used her as the model for his cunning Hollywood agent, Letitia Van Allen, in *Myra Breckinridge.* In 1973, Dyan Cannon hilariously burlesqued Sue in the murder mystery *The Last of Sheila.* Cannon's performance was so close to the real person that Sue demanded to know why the director, Herbert Ross, hadn't simply cast her in the role.

Still later, in 1981, the talented Shelley Winters did a hilarious take-off on Sue as a stout, pushy agent in Blake Edwards' spoof of Hollywood, *S.O.B.* Sue's readiness to make surprising remarks, her cutting wit, her ability to alleviate tension in a room by coming out with what everyone else was thinking but was too scared to say, endeared her to many. After the Manson murders, I confessed to her that I was frightened for my life. 'Don't worry, honey,' she told me. 'Stars aren't being murdered. Only featured players.'

"Perhaps the strongest evidence of her flourishing reputation came in early 1975, when she was the subject of a long segment on CBS's '60 Minutes' in which she explained her talent for signing clients: 'In the beginning, it was through aggression. Now it's through reputation, with a little aggression thrown in.'

"It did CMA lots of good to have so colorful a star on its payroll and, as Sue herself pointed out, her fame never overshadowed the stars or kept them from signing with her. And the likes of Ann-Margret, Peter Bogdanovich, Tuesday Weld, Cybill Shepherd, Burt Reynolds, Diana Ross, and Jacqueline Bisset kept signing. Sometimes I wondered if I was so successful because of my talent or because Sue Mengers was my agent."

Barbra speaking with director Peter Sellars and Lord Snowdon at the Claridge's Party for the Royal Premiere of Funny Girl.

I cast a dubious look at her. She smiled and cheerfully went on. "With 1972's highly successful *What's Up, Doc?*, Sue became famous as the most successful packager in the film business. She had put me and Ryan O'Neal together with director Peter Bogdanovich, and now her phone was constantly ringing with calls from actors, directors, and screenwriters. At long last, I was her official property.

Fields and Begelman felt the time had come for Sue to handle the entire representation of CMA's biggest star—yeah, me. The film industry's biggest female agent was now representing the biggest female star in Hollywood. What a great pair we made!

"I was soon occupying most of Sue's time. Even though she did not handle the musical end of my career, there were numerous decisions to be made about the heaps of scripts submitted to me, including the hundreds of details that needed to be worried about. (It's nice to be rich: I pay someone to do the worrying for me.) I was honored that Sue chose me to be maid of honor at her wedding to Belgian director Jean-Claude Tramont in 1973, although I must say I had a sneaking suspicion that I would not have been selected for the honor if I were not the famous Barbra Streisand.

"I was always very careful about which projects to accept and took a lot of time to make up my mind. Sue and I often bickered like sisters, usually when she wanted me to accept an offer I was see-sawing back and forth on. She was totally obsessed with her work and career. Unlike in my early years, I was not. In fact, at times, she couldn't get me to work. I had turned down *They Shoot Horses, Don't They?* and *Klute,* because there was no director attached when the pictures were offered to me. Both roles went to Jane Fonda and won her Academy Awards. I must say I have had second thoughts since then about those decisions.

"When Sue pressured me to accept a script that she thought would make us a whole lot of money, she could be as manipulative with me as with her other clients. She very cleverly knew just how to push my buttons. She knew intuitively that underneath all the glitter of stardom, I still felt insecure about myself, and she understood how to make me feel unworthy about my talent or my age. 'You're getting on, Barbra,' she would say. 'You'd better do this movie. You may not get many more offers.' So of course I would make the movie, often to my regret."

"Barbra, does it still bother you when you feel misunderstood?"

"I must say it disturbs me less and less all the time. I've learned not to take things personally. People have their own meshugas—things they wish they had done with their own lives and didn't. I realize it isn't my problem. It really makes me happier when I can let go of such feelings."

"Good for you, Barbra. Would you go so far as to say you feel at peace with yourself?"

"Yes," she answered without missing a step. "The most wonderful thing about aging is that you finally see life as it really is, and have learned how to be your authentic self. There are other advantages to growing older," she added. "You get away from yourself more, from always thinking Me Me Me. And you realize there are parts of you that are too ingrained to change, so you stop trying. You are able to say to yourself and others, 'Like it or not, this is who I am.'

"I've come a long way from my Las Vegas days, when I had to take Lomotil, lost weight, and couldn't sleep. I was scared I would disappoint people because I wasn't good enough. But in the process of growing up, I've come to understand that I'm pretty good. I don't know why I'm good, but I know I'm good. And now that I have that inner knowledge, it's alright for me to have imperfections. Whoever I am is good enough for me."

"I know what you mean, Barbra. I feel the same way. Age does have its rewards. Where do you think you got the confidence to believe in yourself today at such a deep level?"

"I think it is genetic. I got it from my father. He was an extraordinary person, who became a highly educated man, even though he came from parents who didn't even speak English. When I miss him, I read his books. I read about him over and over in the book *Leaders of Great Education*. I also read and reread the thesis he wrote in 1933 about examining behavior. I think it is brilliant. Even though I never knew him, I find myself becoming more and more like him."

"That's the best way to handle grief, by identifying with the one you have loved and lost. I'm sure your father would be very proud of you, Barbra, for carrying on his legacy."

She looked at me. "From your mouth to God's ears," she said.

December 4, 2015

I went home that night and felt a little sad.

Barbra, I thought, *is doing so well that she'll be ready to leave analysis very soon. I'll never see her like in my office again.*

On the other hand, I consoled myself, *it's nice to really know such a star.*

And if I miss her, I can always watch one of her movies or listen to her albums.

December 7, 2015

Returning to her long relationship with Sue Mengers at the next session, Barbra said, "I would find myself in the CMA offices listening to Sue talking to one of her other clients on the phone. 'Yes, darling,' she would say. 'Of course, darling.' Then she would hang up the phone and say, 'What a cunt!' I asked Sue if she spoke that way about me behind my back, but she always seemed horrified that I would even think her capable of such a thing. Now I'm not so horrified.

"The year 1973 saw the release of *The Way We Were*. I had grabbed the role of Katie—I thought it was the strongest acting opportunity I'd ever been given—and received my second Academy Award nomination for it. Unfortunately, I lost the Oscar to Glenda Jackson for *A Touch of Class*, something Sue took as a personal affront. So did I. I thought Jackson did not begin to compare with me as an actress.

"In 1974 and 1975, I had two more box-office hits, with the manic comedy *For Pete's Sake* and the musical *Funny Lady*.

"Unfortunately, my next project caused a problem in my relationship with Sue. It was *A Star Is Born*, the remake set in the world of rock and roll. As I mentioned, the film was largely a Jon Peters affair.

"I was at a crisis in my personal life. With the failure of my marriage to Elliott Gould and the love affairs with Ryan O'Neal and Pierre Trudeau over, I was vulnerable to Jon Peters's overwhelming campaign for my attention. As I've told you before, Jon obsessively advised me about every aspect of my life, including what hairstyle to wear and how to dress. Soon, despite his absolute lack of experience in the business, he was telling me which films to make, including *A Star Is Born*.

"At first, Sue dismissed Jon as a social-climbing hairdresser and did not consider him a real threat. But she did not allow for what takes place in the bedroom with a lover. Jon's influence over me only escalated in the coming years, and Sue, more often than not, found herself openly clashing with him. She hated Jon Peters like a second Hitler, and wished him a similar ending.

"But her loyalty to me never faltered. Andy Warhol wrote that at the premiere of *A Star is Born* in New York on December 23, 1976, Sue rushed around the lobby pressuring everybody to tell me that the movie was magnificent or I would be upset. Three months later, on Oscar night, after her former client, Faye Dunaway, received the Academy Award for best actress in *Network*, Sue went to a victory party director Sidney

Lumet was throwing. Sue said to Dunaway's agent, 'Don't let this little trophy make Faye think she's a movie star. She's not. The only movie star in the whole town is Barbra Streisand.' I loved Sue Mengers!

"The year 1979 was not a good one for American films, but that didn't bother Sue. As always, her major concern was finding the right script for me. It was a tough task, because I was always fussy about material. Sue had turned down a number of scripts for me out of hand because she thought them unsuitable for me, including *Julia*, a World War II–era weeper that became a big hit for Twentieth Century Fox, with Jane Fonda and Vanessa Redgrave. For this, I had to pay her fifteen percent of my income?

"More important, Sue was absolutely against the most important project of my life, *Yentl*, which as you well know, I had long pictured as my entry into screenwriting and directing. Sue could not imagine an audience which would want to see me playing a woman disguised as a boy, who winds up falling in love with a fellow student of Talmudic law.

"How wrong could you be? Sue remained against *Yentl* to the bitter end. She yelled, 'How *can* you play this? You're gonna play a *boy*?' Sometimes, she was downright disrespectful about it in front of other people, not noticing, or not caring, that she was hurting my feelings.

"But Sue put all her ingenious deal-making talents behind *The Main Event*, the script I told you about by Gail Parent and Andrew Smith, about a woman who loses all her money and tries to put her financial life together again by promoting a has-been prizefighter. Sue knew the script was only second-rate, but she thought it would turn out to be a hit for me and Ryan O'Neal. The role of the prizefighter appealed to Ryan, who was a boxer himself with a twice-broken nose as proof.

"She was right this time, because the movie came out during the summer of 1979 and earned more than forty million dollars on an eight-million dollar budget. I didn't care for the end result, however, but Jon, who loved to box and was heavily involved in the production, was crazy about it.

"I resumed work on my *Yentl* screenplay and continued to look for backers, even though Sue never stopped making contemptuous remarks about my beloved project. Just as I refrained from listening to my mother's advice, I paid no attention to Sue's discouraging words. Thank goodness for my mother! She taught me that I would be wise to ignore any advice but that of my own inner child.

"It later became clear to me that Sue's lack of support for *Yentl* was the beginning of the end for us. The crisis in our friendship arrived with a seemingly harmless, off-center little film, which Sue's professional and personal lives locked horns over, with catastrophic and long-lasting results.

"In 1980, Jean-Claude Tramont, Sue's husband, had an idea that looked like it might bring him the Hollywood success he had been ardently pursuing for a long time. The idea was a comedy with half-serious overtones about people in Los Angeles who work at night. Since the idea for *Night People*, as it was originally called, had started with Jean-Claude, Sue was able to get him the job as director.

"Sue set about getting her people into *All Night Long*, as the film was eventually called. Her client, Gene Hackman, was perfect for the role of George. She felt the part of Cheryl would make a great change of pace for me, but deeply concerned with *Yentl* as I was, I passed.

"By this time, I had been holed up in my house with *Yentl*'s script for ages and I was getting an intense case of claustrophobia. I needed something that would take me out of myself for a while so I could return to *Yentl* a new woman. One night, while I was a guest at Sue's new house on Bel Air Road, she asked if I might reconsider playing Cheryl in *All Night Long*. Sue was doing quite well herself, having recently re-signed with ICM for a salary of six hundred thousand dollars a year. That woman sure had a way with the almighty buck!

Barbra and Hackman gave great performances in All Night Long, a film whose box office suffered from poor marketing.

"I was feeling very alone, frustrated, and tired. She said her husband's movie, which would involve only six weeks' work, would give me a nice, relaxing pause from my writing. That intrigued me. Then she added that she would get me more salary for *All Night Long* than any actor or actress had ever made—four million dollars. That kind of salary was unheard of at the time. Naturally, that intrigued me, too. So, after looking at the script again, I agreed.

"It is amazing that Sue, with all her professional expertise, had no idea that she was throwing her husband into a potentially volatile situation. Not a single person in her elite professional circle believed that casting her best friend in her husband's movie was a workable situation. But Sue, who was stubborn as a mule, would not be dissuaded. Sound like anyone you know? No wonder we were friends.

"With my name above the title, she was sure that *All Night Long* would be a big hit and Jean-Claude would finally enter the golden circle of Hollywood's top directors. She also believed the film would forever cement her reputation as the most powerful woman in Hollywood, who had the *chutzpah* to take a tremendous gamble in pairing her top star client with her unknown husband and win.

"But unfortunately for all of us, except my banker, *All Night Long* turned out to be the Hope Diamond of Hollywood, which, like the original, was a curse to everyone concerned. The glorious experiment came to an inglorious end.

"*All Night Long* was something genuinely unusual; a gentle, subtle comedy that couldn't be put into any kind of descriptive box. It was Robert Altman-esque in that it dealt with the run-of-the-mill problems of yearning Los Angeles suburbanites, with their cookie-cutter houses, low-paying jobs that led nowhere, forgettable dinners at lousy restaurants, and unfulfilled dreams. Hackman's performance was excellent—his best in years. As the confused Cheryl, I gave a thoughtful performance in a new kind of role for me.

"But when I saw advance copies of the ads for the film, I was horrified. It showed me sliding down a fire pole with my skirt hiked practically up to my tush, which gave a completely distorted impression of what the movie was about. It was really a homey little European kind of film, which would have been great for art houses. Instead, as a pseudo-sexual film, it flopped miserably. I felt terribly betrayed.

"Despite my whopping paycheck, I was hurting over the fact that my suggested *All Night Long* rewrites had been ignored, as well as the fact that the print ads undermined the tone of the film. I felt that Sue had not gone to bat for me. That, along with her hostility toward *Yentl*, upset me very much.

"You know me, Doctor. When I don't like something, I do something about it. So I invited Sue to my home on Carolwood Drive, sat her down in my gorgeous garden with a glass of champagne in one hand and her customary joint in the other, and said, 'We just don't have the same taste in material anymore, Sue. I think I need a different agent. We'll still be close friends.'

"After a stunned silence, Sue responded, 'Absolutely not. If I'm not your agent, then I won't be your friend.'

"I felt shocked and violated by Sue's reaction. Although I have to admit to my own tendency to cut off people who hurt me, I immediately decided to drop Sue from my personal life. My career was the only thing that really mattered to her, anyway, so I shut that off from her, too.

"For years, Sue had told her friends that it was a mistake to think of clients as friends, although she had constantly broken that rule herself. Ali MacGraw and Candice Bergen were her close friends, but no client was more important to her than me. My leaving her was especially traumatic because she had considered us soul mates. I think I broke her heart.

"I had always been at the top of Sue's client list, her biggest star and the greatest proof of her own exalted position in Hollywood. My abandoning her, which she always blamed on Jon Peters, was like a little death for Sue, who saw it as a gigantic and crushing failure, and the beginning of a downward slide she never recovered from. Her world came crashing down around her, and nothing could ever replace it, even if ten major stars walked into her office and said, 'We're all here to sign with you and we'll never leave you.'

"Sometimes I wake up in the middle of the night with the thought, 'I think I killed her.' But what else could I do? I can't be close friends with someone who doesn't stand behind me."

She wiped away a lone tear, and asked, "Do you think I did the wrong thing by dropping Sue, Doctor?"

I didn't know what to say, and finally came up with, "A wise friend of mine once said, 'We do what we do.' You did what you had to do to live the way you want to."

She looked relieved, and went on with her story

"Without me as her most important client," Barbra continued, "Sue's empire slowly began to crumble. MacGraw, Hackman, Bergen, and Bogdanovich, among other top stars, left her, and her old enthusiasm all but vanished. 'I *hate* actors' became her new slogan, which she chanted everywhere. A low-grade depression set in as Sue gradually realized that her glory years were over and done with.

"The movie business was changing in ways she neither liked nor understood. Creative Artists Agency had become a serious competitor with ICM. Sue and the top agents who worked with her believed in a one-to-one approach, in which a single agent handled each client. But the CAA executives, whose philosophy I of course disagreed with, believed that a star's career required continuous supervision by many agents who simultaneously nurtured their clients around the clock.

"Despite my feelings that grown-ups shouldn't need or want hand holding, their technique worked very well. Sue's personality and her skills in doing business as a hostess were growing increasingly unimportant in an industry dominated by M.B.A. graduates with no interest in the movies, but a great desire to make tons of money. They could just as happily have sold garments on Seventh Avenue in New York.

"Sue left ICM in March of 1986, but later returned to the profession a few years later, when she attempted to revive the dying motion-picture department at the William Morris Agency. But she was able to steal away only one of her former clients, the loyal Christopher Walken. One day, after failing to lure back Richard Pryor and Mickey Rourke, Sue quipped, 'These days I couldn't get Mickey Rooney as a client if he crawled his way back to Hollywood.'

"As for Sue and me, after *Yentl* came out in 1983 and became both a critical and commercial success, we gradually reconciled. But Sue had never really forgiven me for our earlier break. Instead of hanging onto my every word, little hostile remarks would slip out of her mouth. Ali MacGraw remembered a time when she, Candice Bergen, and I were meeting at Sue's house. I began a lengthy monologue about my career. I guess it was boring, because after about twenty minutes, Sue said, 'Can we just skip to *Yentl?*' I felt like punching her in the nose.

"Nevertheless, Sue continued to be useful in giving me career advice. In 2004, Universal was casting the part of the uninhibited mother of the bridegroom-to-be, Greg Focker, in *Meet the Fockers*, and Sue kept nagging me to play the role. Although it never was one of my favorites, I took her advice–I also needed the money–and signed my John Hancock to the contract. To my surprise, the film became a huge box-office hit when it opened in December 2004. Who can account for the poor taste of the public? Sue complained to all her friends that I should have paid her a commission. 'Who asked you?' I responded.

"As the years passed, Sue fell victim to major health problems; heart disease, throat cancer, and type 2 diabetes, to mention a few. It didn't help her health or her psychological state when Jean-Claude, whom she really loved, died in 1996. But even in her last years, Sue remained involved in a few Hollywood deals. In 2011, her old friend Lorne Michaels, together with Evan Goldberg and John Goldwyn, was producing *The Guilt Trip*. Everyone was sure that the role of the mother would give me the opportunity to do some wonderful acting. Goldwyn contacted Sue and asked her to try to persuade me to take the part.

"She called me and told me about the script. I said, 'Sue, I'm not sure if I like how it sounds.'

"She answered in her usual style, 'Barbra, you're never sure about anything! But it's not 1975 anymore. You may never have as good an offer.'

"Never sure about *anything*? Is she kidding? Has she forgotten *Yentl*? Nevertheless, she twisted my arm enough that I said yes and did the film.

"*The Guilt Trip* didn't make out so hot at the box office, but to my surprise, I gave one of the most insightful performances of my career. How could it be otherwise, given my experience with my own Jewish mother? Despite our personal break-up, I'm grateful that Sue never wavered in her belief in my talent. She had good taste!

Barbra and Seth Rogen star in The Guilt Trip, 2013.

"In the fall of 2011, shortly after her 79th birthday, Sue developed a severe case of pneumonia. On October 12, she lapsed into a state of semi-consciousness. Ali MacGraw hurried in from Santa Fe, and Sue's longtime friend, the agent Boaty Boatwright, immediately flew in from New York to stay at Sue's bedside. Word had gotten around that Sue was approaching the end, and the telephone began to ring constantly, with calls coming in from the likes of Michael Caine and Julia Roberts.

"Almost 50 years to the day after Sue had first seen me on the New York stage, I got a phone call from her friend, Boaty, to tell me that Sue was dying and that if I wanted to see her alive one last time, I had better come immediately. 'She wants you to sing to her,' Boaty added.

"I dropped whatever I was doing and rushed to her bedside. Sue looked ghostly pale, as if she weighed about a third of her former self. Wrinkled skin like that of a giant elephant was hanging down in flaps from her neck and face so that she was barely recognizable. Although she was unable to talk, she smiled when she saw me and took my hand.

"I love you, Sue," I whispered into her ear. "Forgive me for breaking off our friendship. I've always regretted it."

"Sing to me," she whispered, so softly I could hardly hear her.

"I began to sing, 'How much do I love you?/ I'll tell you no lie/ How deep is the ocean? How high is the sky?'

"It was hard to continue. The tears flooded my throat.

"She squeezed my hand. I left sobbing, as though I had lost my best friend, as indeed I had.

"A few hours later, Sue Mengers, the master agent whose final years were a slow detachment from the Hollywood life she loved so much, was dead. Every major newspaper in the world ran an obituary. Her reputation had outlived those of some of the great stars whose careers she helped form. 'Brilliant, schmoozy, and often devastatingly funny,' the obituary in *The New York Times* read. 'Ms. Mengers broke through a glass ceiling to become one of the first women to wield true power in the agency business.'

"I was broken hearted, and knew I would never find a better friend. Remember the first line of *The Ballad of Reading Gaol*, by Oscar Wilde? It goes, 'Yet each man kills the thing he loves.' I helped kill Sue Mengers."

"No, Barbra, you didn't kill Sue Mengers. What killed her was her bad health. If there was a psychosomatic cause, it was her inability to live with loss. What you did do was to be instrumental in building her wonderful career, thus greatly enriching her life."

She burst into tears. "You may just have put to rest my torturing guilt about Sue Mengers," she sobbed.

December 8, 2015

Perhaps because she was still upset about Sue Mengers, Barbra surprised me by calling and requesting an extra session. I agreed, but when she came in, she found herself unable to talk. Finally, she said, "Sorry, Doc. I can't think of anything to say today."

"Hmmm," I said. "That's not like you. Is there something you don't want to talk about?"

"If there was, do you think I would *tell* you?"

I thought a moment, and decided I didn't want to sit there all session looking at my nails. So I said, "Okay. Let's try something different. Let's play a little game called Truth or Consequences, which I played when I was a child. You should like that: You love the truth."

"What are the consequences?"

"I double your fee."

"Ha! Fat chance. OK. Sounds like fun. Fire away."

"Good. If you were a car, which car would you be?"

She laughed. "Well, sometimes I'm a Mercedes Benz, and at other times a 1925 Rolls Royce. My idea of stardom is owning a Rolls-Royce and driving it in sneakers. Then there are the times I'm just a broken-down Ford."

"Not today, I hope."

She laughed. "No, not today."

"What car are you today?"

"Maybe just a plug-in hybrid that runs on gas and electricity."

"What animal would you be?"

"My husband says I'm a hamster."

"Cute and cuddly?"

"You got it. Although some of my fellow directors wouldn't agree."

"And if you were a color, what color would you be?"

"I think... red wine."

"Why wine?"

"It is so beautiful when you hold it up to the light."

"I agree, and I like to do that, too. What bird?"

She laughed. "I'm a tweety bird. I tweet all the time. No, skip that. I'm some exotic jungle bird. And sometimes just an ordinary little sparrow, which surprises my fans."

"What century are you?"

"I think the 19th, and the 15th, or no, maybe the 14th... Oh, Christ!

Oh yeah! B.C. I can't answer that one because I think I'm all of them, depending on my mood."

"What composer?"

"Bartok. We're both a little strange and dissonant."

"What article of clothing?"

"A crepe black satin slip."

"Hmmm sexy, huh?"

"You got it."

"What painting by a famous painter?"

"This really is a great game. I like it. And I like that you're occasionally an out-of-the-box shrink!"

"Glad you like it. What painting by a famous painter?"

"*A Woman Bathing* by Rembrandt."

"Do you mean the painting in which the model is raising her chemise?"

"You caught on to that one, Doc!"

"What famous historical character would you be?"

She pauses. "I don't really identify with anybody. I just want to be me."

"Good for you! What drink?"

"Diet Coke. Good taste, no calories. It just lets you be. That's me."

"What furniture?"

"It depends on when you ask me. Right now, Louis XV, XVI, Victorian, and Art Nouveau."

"What flower?"

"Gardenia. It's sweet and smells like holy heaven."

"What singers do you love?"

"Ray Charles and Florence Foster Jenkins."

"Who is Florence Foster Jenkins?"

"She was an American socialite and amateur operatic soprano who was known and ridiculed for her lack of rhythm, pitch, and tone; her aberrant pronunciation; and her generally poor singing ability."

We both laugh. I say, "That doesn't sound much like you, Barbra!"

"Maybe you don't know me as well as you think you do."

"Could be. What item that can be bought at a soda fountain?"

"Seltzer."

"No taste. That's not you."

"It's how I feel now."

I wondered again what she was not talking about, but knew better than to press her for an answer. "Let's talk about the press now."

"Must we?"

"Why not? How do you feel about some of the terrible press you get?"

"Captured." She laughed. "Slaughtered, barbecued, and pickled!"

"I can imagine. I don't know how you stand it."

"I guess I've had to grow a thick hide. Also, I got plenty of practice listening to my mother's criticisms over the years. I guess I should be glad. She really toughened me up."

"How do you think the public feels about what has been written about you?"

"As a matter of fact, I think most people, because of the power of print, believe what they read. I only wish they would stop and think about the personality of the person doing the interview. Maybe he is tired. Maybe he has gas. Maybe the laundry put too much starch in his shirt. Maybe he just had a fight with his wife. Interview subjects have an awful lot to put up with.

"I wonder if readers realize that each personality is being seen through the writer's eyes, neuroses, intelligence, and perception, or the lack of each of them.

"Critics?"

"What critics?"

"Some of the gossip columnists—"

"Oh, you mean the yentas," I said. She laughed.

"Forget that question. Let's move on. Compared to you now, what were you like when you were eight?"

"Smaller."

I giggled. "Ha ha! I mean what kind of kid were you in school?"

"Don't you remember anything? I told you I got A's in all my subjects and a D for conduct."

"Sorry about that. Please go ahead."

"I really haven't changed at all!" She laughed again. "I make great movies, and I'm a pain in the ass to the studios."

"Were there any movies you especially liked as a child?"

"It didn't matter what the movie was as long as it was in Technicolor."

"Now that you are making Technicolor films yourself, would you say that your dream has come true?"

She paused. "That's hard to answer. I never really wanted to be a movie star who signed autographs. I only wish people would stop and think about the feelings of the person they are annoying. We're human beings, too. We, like they, want to eat an uninterrupted meal and not have autograph books stuck in our faces between bites of steak. As a child, I really wanted to be the character in the movies I saw; I didn't want to be the actress. I wanted to be Scarlett O'Hara, not Vivien Leigh."

"Do you ever worry about losing your voice?"

"Of course not. I think worry makes you lose your voice! I don't believe in indulging my vocal chords. What makes me sing is my inner self. If I want to hold a note because I think it's right at the moment, I hold the note, and if I don't want to, I don't. I never sing in the shower. In fact, I never sing by myself because my voice sounds awful to me. When I had a sore throat as a kid, my mother used to put a woolen sock around my neck. I still do that, fastened with a safety pin. One day the safety pin is gonna open in bed and puncture my vocal chords! *Oy vey*! That I worry about!"

"I know you love to eat, yet you have to discipline yourself as an artist. How do you handle the struggle between the two?"

"How do I handle it? With difficulty! I'm eight pounds overweight, that's how I handle it! I'm a complete hypocrite about food. What I do is have chocolate cake for dessert, and put Sucaryl in my tea!"

"Have you ever encountered prejudice?"

"I don't know. I never applied to a country club." She laughed.

"Do you always love to laugh?"

"Well, a lot of things strike me as funny. It's a good thing, or I'd jump off a bridge."

"Have you any hobbies? What do you do for fun?"

"I go to dance classes, I'm learning Italian and, among other things, I read about Zen Buddhism. It's not hard. In fact, it's simple. There's nothing to understand. That's the secret. It makes me think that in the United States, we have a terrible way of living. I hardly have time to read. So when I do, I like simple books. Sometimes I think, '*Everything* is important.' And then there are other times when I think, 'That isn't important at all.'"

"Besides the two you earlier mentioned, who are your favorite singers?"

"They all died, sadly enough. People like Bessie Smith."

"What would you do if the bottom dropped out of the Barbra Streisand market tomorrow?"

"I wouldn't be surprised. Everything is momentary. You do a good picture, great. You do a lousy one, nobody wants you. That's why you have to have a life outside of a career; a husband, children, and maybe antique furniture."

"What is it like way down there, inside Barbra, where the singing comes from?"

"Well, as somebody once said to me, 'There's a whole area inside you that has never been touched.' I guess it keeps people interested because I have secrets. I won't tell. Not even to you, Doctor!"

"Not even in free association?"

"No. With what I pay you, nothing is free."

"This was a great session," she said on leaving. "I feel better. Can we do this every time?"

December 9, 2015

Barbra came in wearing a sad expression, with drooping eyelids and downturned lips. She said, "Sue Menger's death gave me a lot to think about. It made me realize how old I was, and that I'd better face the fact that my days are numbered. It's not easy."

"You are a strong and healthy woman," I said to Barbra. "It is highly unlikely that you will die soon. Still, this seems an opportune time to discuss the big question: How do you feel about death and dying?"

"Are you kidding? How does anybody feel about dying? How do you feel about it? I absolutely detest the idea. Remember in *Dreamgirls*, when the wonderful Jennifer Hudson sang, 'And I Am Telling You I'm Not Goin'?' She meant she wasn't going to leave the group. Well, I have only one thing to say to you about death: I'm not goin'!"

"Ever? Why not? Are you afraid to die?"

She thought for a moment. "It isn't so much dying I'm afraid of," she said. "It's more that I can't bear to stop living. I was the kind of kid who hated to go to bed at night; there was so much more I wanted to do. That's exactly the way I feel about dying. I can't die yet; there is too much left undone."

"Like what?"

"There are a lot more films I need to make. I need to find out what Jason does with his life. I want to hold hands with my husband Jim for eternity. Dying now would be like reading a book and stopping in the middle. I have to know how the book and my life will end.

"When I was a little kid, my mother gave me a chocolate bud. After I gobbled it up, I asked her for another. She said, 'I knew you'd ask me for another one. I happened to save two for you, but I knew you'd ask for another no matter how many I gave you, so I only gave you one. Here's the second one now.' That's the way I feel about life. No matter how many days I have, I'll always want more."

"What about aging? Does getting older bother you as well?"

"I really don't mind aging. I came to terms with my looks a long time ago. If you have to be seventy-two, I'm not a bad looking seventy-two."

I nodded in full accord.

"I've never been happier in my life," she continued. "I refuse to give all this up. I can't bear the idea that every hour brings me that much closer to death. You're a doctor. Can you say anything that will help me live with it?"

I thought for a while. "Yes," I said. "I think so. I believe I told you before that I think you are going to live for a very long time. People die of a broken heart. Your loving father died when you were only fifteen months old. You didn't die. Your mother was constantly nasty to you and unsupportive when she should have been loving, but you didn't die.

"Louis Kind abused you, but again you didn't die. Nor did you die when you weren't accepted into the glee club in high school, even though it was the most important thing in the world to you at the time. You left Elliot and were broken-hearted, yet even then you didn't die. Weaker people might have died on each of those occasions. You didn't.

"You somehow managed to cope and live through all that. In the same way, you will be able to survive... whatever life brings you for a long, long time. I hope it is good, but you know the old adage, 'Into every life some rain must fall.' You are a determined woman who has survived the most dreadful storms all your life. There is every reason to believe you will continue to do so for a very long time."

She didn't answer. She was too busy thinking.

Barbra and Jim Brolin
cutting their wedding cake

December 10, 2015

"I promised you that I'd get around to telling you about my greatest love, my husband. Today, I am finally going to," she said.

"Good," I said. "I thought you'd never get to him."

She ignored my quip. "I met this wonderful guy, Jim Brolin, at a dinner party," she began. "And then I married him." A slow smile lit up her face.

"Tell me about it, Barbra."

"Don't get me started, or I'll go on all hour."

"Is there anything better to talk about?"

"Truer words have never been spoken. Okay, but don't say I didn't warn you." She took a deep breath and, as she had indicated, spoke about her latest and last love for the rest of the hour.

"He energizes me," she said. "When I'm with him, my creativity and emotions are recharged. I've never been so happy in my life."

"How wonderful, Barbra! That's the most fantastic thing I've ever heard you say! Tell me what makes you happy."

"My family, my friends, my dog, my home, my gorgeous view of the ocean, my garden, the constantly changing conditions of nature. I don't have to have big things. I like to donate to charity, to provide help for what I believe in. For instance, I support the Barbra Streisand Women's Heart Center. Do you know that heart disease kills more women than all cancers combined? And yet very little is being done about it."

"Barbra," I said, in a chastising tone, "I read something important in the newspapers about you donating to charity that you never told me."

"Yeah? What's that?"

"I read that in 1986, you founded *The Streisand Foundation* that has donated over sixteen million dollars to noteworthy causes like nuclear disarmament, civil rights, voter education, and women's issues. Sixteen million dollars! Very few of us even see that much money in a lifetime, let alone donate it to charity. It is really wonderful of you. But how come you never told me about it?"

Looking shyly at the floor, she said, "I was afraid you would raise my fee."

December 11, 2015

"At the last session, you asked me what makes me happy," she began. "That's an easy one to answer with certainty. Most of all, Jim makes me happy. He's all I've ever wanted in a man."

"It delights me to hear that, Barbra. Please tell me more."

"I'll tell you about his life before we met, so you'll understand him better. He wasn't originally named James Brolin, but was born Craig Kenneth Bruderlin. He became interested in acting while he was still in school and, like me, changed his name when he was twenty years old because he thought Brolin sounded more like an actor. It does, don't you think? I suspect fewer people would be interested in watching an actor named Bruderlin. It sounds like some kind of cheese.

"This is his third marriage. *Oy vey*! His first wife was Jane Cameron Agee, whom he married in 1966, just twelve days after they met. Talk about a rush job! I was determined not to duplicate that. In 1984, eighteen years and two children later, the couple divorced. Sadly, Jane was killed in a car accident on February 13, 1995. I think that, in the still of the night, Jim still mourns her. I guess you don't forget eighteen years so easily."

"Is that alright with you?"

"Sure," she answered. "I wouldn't want him to forget me ever, should I be so unfortunate as to die before him."

"I doubt if anyone ever could forget you, Barbra!" I said.

She smiled and continued with the saga of Jim's life. "In 1985, he met the actress Jan Smithers on the set of *Hotel*. He took a little longer this time, and they didn't marry for a whole year, at which time they had their daughter Molly. Smithers filed for divorce in 1995. I never did find out why. When I ask Jim, he just shrugs and says, 'Who knows?' I can make a guess, but I'd rather not. I might not like what I guess. From his marital history, Jim didn't sound like a very good bet. But then, neither did I.

"I love this story. Did you ever hear the old adage, 'Turn a corner and meet your fate?' Well, it was like that with me and Jim. We met at a dinner party at John Travolta's house, which neither of us had wanted to attend, but decided at the last minute to drop in on. There I saw this guy with the most beautiful face I've ever seen on a man, and I had to go over and meet him. But you know me! I never would have told him so at that point. Instead, I informed Jim that I didn't like his hair because it was spiked. He knew at that moment that I was *the one*.

"It seems that my direct nature captured the guy's attention, because I told him the truth. Most people don't tell the truth because they are afraid of it, but I love the truth, and I would never say anything that isn't true. For one thing, it makes life simpler. You don't have to worry about what you said before, because what you say is simply the truth. On the other hand, it makes a lot of people hate you because they can't continue fooling themselves."

"That's one of the best things about you, Barbra, among the many nice things I could mention. When you say something, I always believe you. I wish I could say that about all my patients. Some are very foolish. They supposedly come for help, but how can I help them if they don't tell me the truth, and I don't know what is going on in their lives?"

"Thanks, but you cost too much money for me to lie to you!"

December 14, 2015

"As I said during the last session," Barbra continued, "Jim knew the moment he laid eyes on me that I was *the one*."

I laughed. "Did you, like Jim, know right away that he was *the one* for you?" I asked.

"No," she answered. "It took me a few months to come to that conclusion. It happened gradually and naturally. I don't remember a particular moment when I said, 'Aha! I'm in love.' We got married on July 1, 1998, and have been married ever since. The Mormons have a nice tradition: People who get married in their temples can get married for eternity. It almost makes me want to become a Mormon!

"Over the two years of our courtship, I really changed. Friends said I was no longer on a roller coaster of highs and lows. My laid-back lover–and boy, is he laid back–was just what I needed to make me feel serene.

"In 2013, the tabloids had a wonderful time reporting that our marriage was on the rocks because of my obsessions with my work and son Jason. Is it so strange to be obsessed by them? I didn't get where I am by sitting and examining my toenails. And who wouldn't be obsessed if their son was HIV positive? I laughed when I read about our 'separation' in *The National Inquirer*. Jim and I are the best thing that ever happened to each of us, and there is no way I'll ever let him go, even if he wanted to leave me, which he doesn't. He says he didn't know what happiness was until he married me.

"A funny thing happened in a supermarket, where Jim and I were standing at the checkout line holding hands. The man behind us said, 'I'm happy to see that you two are back together again.' I said, 'Yeah? When were we apart?'"

December 16, 2015

"Tell me about the wedding, Barbra. Did you elope, or was it a large affair?" I asked.

"Was it a large affair? Are you kidding? Is the Pope Catholic? I've never been to one like it, before or after. On June 14, John Travolta and his wife, Kelly Preston, gave an intimate dinner at their Brentwood mansion for a few hundred friends, including Tom Hanks, his wife, Rita Wilson, and the usually reclusive Marlon Brando. Only one person was late—noticeably late. Guess who? Me.

"The phyllo duck appetizer sat untouched, along with the Tagliolini Alfredo and the 1975 Château Lafite Rothschild. But when I finally arrived, I managed to upstage even the Godfather himself when I told my hosts for the first time that I had just met with the rabbi who was going to perform my wedding to Jim Brolin. Travolta was thrilled and got misty-eyed when he realized that he and Kelly were the first ones to be let in on the secret.

"Before dawn of the wedding day, four vans had dropped fifty pink water lilies and a hundred candles into the swimming pool and adorned the tables with pink miniature rosebushes. Two days before the wedding, when a 2,800-square-foot ivory voile tent was put up on the ocean-view lawn, the ever watchful paparazzi began to get suspicious, but much as they prodded, I didn't inform anyone what was going on. It was nobody's business but ours.

"On July 1, the second anniversary of our first date, I walked down the aisle in my formal Malibu living room, escorted by my darling son Jason. I wore a shimmering crystal-beaded gown designed by Donna, with a fifteen-foot diaphanous veil. It cost almost as much as the house. I felt like a real bride for the first time, with a gorgeous bouquet and the whole *schemer*. The one hundred and five guests included my eighty-nine-year-old mother, Donna, Travolta and Kelly, Tom and Rita Hanks, record producer Quincy Jones, and one of the best directors in Hollywood, my dear friend Sydney Pollack.

December 18, 2015

The next session, she continued describing her wedding. "After a dinner of soft-shell crabs, rotisserie-cooked baby chickens, and porcini ravioli, which I gulped down with great fervor, we danced to 'I Finally Found Someone.' I couldn't have said it better myself.

"The dancing was followed by a half dozen toasts. My incredibly efficient assistant, Renata Buser, gave me a tribute that brought tears to my eyes. She said, 'Jim, you have the rarest flower.' Isn't that a lovely compliment from an employee of twenty-four years? And the folks in the business say I'm hard to get along with!

"Then Josh Brolin, Jim's son, read an original poem Jim and I will treasure forever, 'My father and his bride/Look at how they watch each other…'

But the highlight for me came when I, who suffer from terrible stage fright, sang two love songs to Jim, without feeling even a tinge of fear or panic. I knew I was among friends who loved me. How could I be scared?

"When Jim was called upon to make a toast, he said, 'What? You expect me to follow that? I don't think so. Knowing me, I would only screw it up.' But of course he didn't. The dearest man in the world said, 'I can't tell you how lucky I am that this has happened to me so late in life. It is a miracle. Every night is a new adventure. Sleeping is a waste of time. I can't wait to wake up in the morning to see her again.' Isn't that the loveliest toast you ever heard?

"We really enjoyed the toast made by the late, great Marvin Hamlisch, who wrote my big hit, 'The Way We Were,' and we were thrilled when he sang a new song he composed just for the occasion. The song included the wonderful line, 'Don't know where you leave off and I begin,' which exactly expresses my feeling about me and Jim.

"Of course being me, I had to quip, 'After all of Marv's Oscars, Grammys, and Emmys, here he is, back to playing at weddings!' I'm the luckiest woman alive to have such wonderful friends, and to have had them all there to celebrate our wedding.

"After the ceremony, the guests were served Crystal champagne by the pool. Travolta said it was the most beautiful wedding he had ever attended. He and Kelly both cried. He said, 'It is a rare honor to be at such a magical wedding. Barbra was always my favorite movie star and Jim the TV star I liked best. This is an unusual event in that it really cares about its guests.'

"'I'm the happiest person in the world,' Jim said, jumping up and, in one fell swoop, hugging his eighty-three year-old mother Helen, his eighty-seven year-old father Henry, his son Josh, his daughter Molly, and his two grandchildren, Trevor, aged nine, and Eden, who was four. I'm happy he feels that way, but I think that of the two of us, I am the luckier one. He is so gorgeous he could have had any girl in the world.

"My longtime friend, songwriter Marilyn Bergman, said, 'In all the years I've known Barbra, I've seen her looking happy many times, but there was always a dark cloud lurking underneath. At her wedding, there was only a clear blue sky,' filled, in this case, with the delicate aroma of five-hundred gardenias, two-hundred lilies of the valley, two thousand, five hundred blooming stephanotis, and four-hundred roses. A team of ten florists attached seven hundred and fifty roses to the staircase I would descend. I needn't add they were Barbra Streisand roses, named of course, after me. In case you don't know it, I love flowers. This was one time I had enough to satisfy even me. When we left for our honeymoon, I ordered the staff to keep them alive as long as possible. On coming home, I pressed some, because I wanted to keep them with me for life.

"What a night! It was completely different from my first wedding to Elliot, which was performed by a Nevada justice of the peace, with me wearing a tee-shirt and jeans. I hadn't had a real wedding before. But then, my whole first marriage was so different from this one that you'd never know it was supposed to be the same thing. Elliot and I were children playing at being married. Jim and I are mature lovers. He calls me 'Beezer.' Nobody else could get away with it. I let him say it because he says it with love.

"After the fifteen-minute traditional ceremony was over, the guests gathered around our oceanfront pool and lounged beneath the big top. When we came into the tent, we were announced as 'Mr. and Mrs. James Brolin.' I was thrilled to hear it, because it was the first time anybody had ever called me Mrs. Brolin. We entered the tent to our favorite song, Gershwin's 'Isn't It a Pity?'"

"Why is it your favorite, Barbra?"

"Because it describes so well the way I feel."

"And how is that?"

"I'll sing you some of the lyrics, and you can judge for yourself."

"Isn't it a pity
We never met before?
Here we are at last.
It's like a dream.
The two of us
A perfect team.

Imagine all the lonely years we've wasted.
Me with the neighbors.
You at silly labors.
What joys untasted.
My nights were sour,
Spent with Schopenhauer.

Let's forget the past.
Let's both agree
That I'm for you
And you're for me.
And it's such a pity
We never, never met before.

"It's true," she went on. "Look at all the years we spent fumbling around looking for a mate, when all the time we were only a few blocks apart and didn't know it was each other we were pining for."

I smiled and said, "You remind me of a thought I had years ago while riding the New York subway: I looked at all the people who were sitting near me and thought: *It is possible that the man sitting next to me could have been the love of my life, and the woman across the aisle my best friend, and we'll never know it*."

"How right you were," she said, and added just like any patient, "I love it when you tell me what you're thinking.

"Jim and I must have been at many of the same parties or concerts over the years," she added, "and never gave each other a passing glance. We wasted so many years! It really is a pity..."

It was time for Barbra to leave, and I stood up.

"What!" Barbra shouted. "Time to leave? When I'm right in the middle of telling you about my wedding?"

"I'm afraid so," I answered.

The great Barbra Streisand mock-glared at me and pseudo-stomped out of my office.

December 21, 2015

Apparently, she had not yet finished describing her wedding day, so on she continued at our next session. "Shortly before 1 a.m., after the celebrators had thinned out, we went inside to pack for a brief honeymoon in the Channel Islands off Santa Barbara. We couldn't take any more time because Jim was scheduled to return to his syndicated TV series *Pensacola: Wings of Gold* on July 8. But the few days there were magical. Sweet Jim said, 'Never mind, dearest. We have the rest of our lives to honeymoon.'

"The whole marriage thing kinda hit me by surprise," Barbra said. "I had just begun to enjoy being alone. I believe in order to be happy with another person, you have to learn first how to be alone."

"You are a wise woman, Barbra."

"I've mentioned before that Jason is HIV positive. But now I'm not alone in my concern about my child. Jim's son has medical problems that may be even worse than Jason's, but at least he's leading a decent life now.

"Forty-one- year-old Jess Brolin was reported to be homeless by *The Daily Mail.* According to them, Jess ran out of money in 2011 and lived in a truck for a while before turning to life on the streets. According to the *Daily Mail*, he was sleeping in empty lots not eighty miles from our home in Malibu. I don't know whether it's that bad, but it's very painful to have the whole world advised that your stepson is sleeping on the streets. But then, if I believed everything the papers write about me and my family, I'd jump off the Golden Gate Bridge.

"When Jess's mother, Jane Cameron Agee, died in the car accident, Jess received a six-figure inheritance, which, if one believes *The Daily Mail*, he must have frittered away. Jim has repeatedly offered him help and support, and we will continue to do so, but for some unknown reason, Jess will not accept it. I suppose even a homeless man has his pride. We love him dearly and only want what is best for him, and we hope that if he really is destitute, he will accept our help.

"On the other hand, James' younger son, Josh Brolin, takes after his father and is a wonderful, award-winning actor. He, too, has his troubles, although they are more normal to his generation. He recently checked into a drug rehabilitation center, where the psychiatrist told us that Josh suffers from a sociological illness, and is not neurotic. Is that supposed to make us feel better? If so, it has failed miserably. Josh also has personal difficulties. His divorce from actress Diane Lane was finalized in 2013. I was sorry about that, because I really love Diane."

"That's too bad, Barbra. But some people need two or three marriages before they find the right one."

"Yeah, people like me. Josh first ran into trouble as a teenager, when he admitted that he stole cars to pay for drugs. But I'm happy he is strong enough now to seek help when he needs it, and we are very proud of his accomplishments.

"Jim is going to direct another film called *Ruby McCollum*. When a reporter asked him if he'd ever consider directing anyone in his family, he answered that he could direct his son Josh, and Josh could direct him. Then he added, 'But I'm not so sure about my wife. She's so much of a director herself. But I would be blessed if she directed me. I'm putty in her hands anyway.'

"When I asked Jim if he could ever give up acting for directing, he answered, 'Sure, in a minute. I started out with a dream of being a director and doing cinematography. I actually bought my first film camera at fifteen. I've been a big film fan all my life but never believed I was good enough to direct. I thought it was only for people whose families were in the business. I've always wanted to belong to a movie family. In marrying you, Barbra, that big dream of mine has come true.' Nice man!

"In an interview, TV's Meredith Vieira asked Jim, 'Your marriage to Barbra Streisand seems to be a very happy one. What is the secret of your wedded bliss?'

"I was thrilled when he answered, 'It's being with someone you can negotiate with. If we need a referee, we don't hesitate to bring in someone to talk it over with. I'm in my third marriage, yet I don't believe in divorce. I hope I've learned from my mistakes, and that Barbra's and my marriage will go on as long as we live. Maybe even beyond. Who am I to say?

'In my first two marriages, I can guarantee that I was more than half the problem. I was unable to negotiate with my wives. Barbra and I are different. When we disagree, we negotiate very easily. Before we got married, we went to a marriage counselor for guidance, which helped us learn how to do it. I believe everybody who gets married should go to a counselor for a few months before their wedding. It will save the couple reams of money and prevent a lot of heartbreak.' Nice he believes that, isn't it? I picked a good man this time, don'tcha think?"

"As a psychiatrist, I think it is wonderful that you went for counseling together and found it so helpful. But–and I do have a but–no relationship can be that good all the time. As admirable a man as Jim is, nobody is perfect. Isn't there anything about him that gets on your nerves?"

"Anything? Are *you* married? Is your marriage perfect? Come off it. Of course there is! And I'm sure I get on his nerves too.

"I have a little story to tell you that'll get your goat," she continued. "Jim charmed me when he was wooing me. He said he could cook and, since I can't boil water without burning the pot, I thought, oh boy, this guy is a real catch! He understands that the way to my heart is through my stomach.

"So he came over with a sushi roller—you know, that wooden thing used to beat spouses over the head with, and made sushi. I love sushi. So, I thought, 'This is great. I'm really picking a good one this time. I hope he makes sushi for me every night.' Well, wouldn't you know, he never made it again. Sometimes when I'm hungry and there is nothing to eat in the house, I fume, 'Where the hell are your cooking skills when I need them, Jimmy boy? I'm hungry enough to eat a cow!'

"I also think he is a little bit lazy, and that laziness, I'm sorry to say, gets on my nerves sometimes. I was delighted when he was cast in the sitcom, *Life in Pieces.*

"'That's great! Go to work!' I said. 'For God's sake, get out of the house, get up out of that hammock for a change!'

"'Nah,' he answered. 'I may never get out of this hammock again!'

"*Life in Pieces* tells the story of an extended family through the significant events of their lives. The show includes the staging of a mock funeral to mark the seventieth birthday of the family patriarch John, played by Jim.

"'If you don't get up off that hammock, the funeral may turn out to be a real one!' I said.

"'Really?' he joked. 'I am considering not taking the job.'

"'Over my dead body,' I answered.

"'Too bad,' he answered. 'Malibu in the summer, in the hammock. What a waste! I'm surprised I'm working.'"

She laughed and said to me, "Well, nobody's perfect, except for you and me, of course, and I'm not sure about you."

December 23, 2015

I began the session by asking her to tell me some of the things she and Jim like to do together.

"Well, Doctor, we stay in bed a lot," she answered laughingly. "On Saturdays, we never get out of bed at all. And we stay in whatever we were sleeping–or not sleeping–in, even when we go down to the kitchen. Nobody is there except our little dog Sadie, unless Jim's daughter or Jason is visiting. Then we put on some loose clothes.

"Those are good times, too. We watch films, or I write or paint. I bought a little easel recently and started to draw, and find it very soothing, even if my 'works of art' will never hang in the Metropolitan Museum of Art.

"Jim and I don't have to be doing anything. We just hang out a lot. Once in a while, I feel guilty because I'm not working. So I say to myself, 'Just a minute, Barbra! You've been working since you were eleven years old, so what is there to feel guilty about? It's really all right to do nothing but rest and play.' I used to be much more ambitious, but now I like to relax and have fun. Kind of making up for lost time.

"We go to a lot of films, and we also travel a lot. We both love boats, so we often go on boat trips. I love antiquing, and I daydream of hiring a U-Haul truck and driving down the East Coast looking for bargains in American antiques. And as I told you, I'm building a house. It's hectic, but I love it. I'm escaping from one chaotic world to another. I design all the time—my clothes, furniture, house. I could spend all day designing, painting, and coloring."

"You have a very rich and full life, Barbra. If anyone deserves it, you do."

"You're right," she said with surprise. "I've always thought of myself as a hard worker and nothing else, but now I'm enjoying the other side of me."

"So Barbra," I said, "we won't meet this Friday, because it's Christmas Day."

"What?" she shouted "You mean I'm going to miss my session because it's CHRISTMAS! What kind of Jew are you? At least with all her faults, my mother didn't celebrate Christmas!"

She slammed the door so hard I thought it would fall off its hinges.

December 30, 2015

She didn't mention Christmas again, so I hoped she had forgiven me for my flaw and didn't bring it up. I asked her, "What was it like meeting your in-laws for the first time, Barbra?"

"It was nice," she answered. "I used to have the fantasy that someday, when I got married, I would have a wonderful mother-in-law, who I could go to lunch with and tell all about myself. A real mother who was exactly the opposite of mine. I lucked out there, too. Helen is all of that. It is nice to have one's fantasy come true.

"They were really surprised when they met me, and I doubt if they have gotten over it yet. People expect a celebrity to be up on a high horse, wearing a crown on her head and an ermine coat. I guess because my in-laws know that I am in the movies, they expected me to be all dolled up in some glamorous gown. When I met them, I was, to their astonishment, wearing a shaggy sweater and jeans, and put my feet up on the table.

"They found out that despite my stardom, I'm really just like them. We are all private people and enjoy small things like staying at home. I'm really just a home body, and have no idea about what's going on in the Hollywood community... I guess we all lucked out.

"When Jim left for Ireland three months later to direct *My Brother's War*, we burnt up the phone lines," she said. "One time, I fell asleep on the bathroom floor with the phone pressed against my ear.

"You've seen Jim, haven't you?" I nodded. "Then you know how handsome he is. That face! I just love it! I love to hold his face between my two hands and look at him as long as he'll let me. I can't get over how beautiful he is! He's perfect. He has the most beautiful bone structure, teeth, nose, eyes, forehead, jaw. It makes up a million times for my own lack of beauty. We meet people, and they are sure to say, 'Jim, you look so great.' And he does, too. He even looks like that sleeping."

Jim Brolin could keep up his relationship with Barbra despite his own busy career, including his TV show, Pensacola: Wings of Gold.

Barbra never missed an opportunity to let people like me know how great her sex life was, and to offer advice about how to keep their own going. "Keep it hot!" she advised without any prompting. "Never let it lapse for a day, if you can help it. Don't let sex die, because it is the life force that makes the world go round. It's more fun than anything else on earth! As Mae West said a long time ago, 'Too much of a good thing is wonderful!'"

Barbra sounded like Wilhelm Reich, an unconventional psychiatrist of the last century, who above all else believed in the power of the sexual instinct. I wish all my patients felt the way Barbra does about sex. But then I might have a lot fewer patients.

"Well, I guess you know the whole story now," she continued. "In a nutshell, we fell in love, got married, have great sex, and are living happily ever after."

"To what do you most attribute the happiness of your marriage?"

"We are always very honest with each other."

"Thank you, Barbra," I said, looking at her with admiration. "I'm not surprised to hear you say that. It is so much you. How wonderful that you've found a mate who feels the same way!"

"I can't believe that we've been together for eighteen years," she said, shaking her head. "It all flew by so quickly. Whatever happened to all those years? It's one of the great mysteries of life. All of a sudden, you wake up and find that twenty-five years have passed," she said, looking off into the distance. "How can they have gone by so fast? It's incredible!"

"Yes," I said. "I often wonder the same thing. I turn around and it's tomorrow. By the way, tomorrow is New Year's Eve, and we won't meet on New Year's Day. Have a happy, healthy New Year, Barbra," I said.

"Hmmm. Yeah," she answered. "I don't take stock in such things. But I can see that you'll use any excuse you can to skip one of my sessions!"

January 4, 2016

I greeted her with, "Welcome back in the New Year." She scowled. Barbra Streisand is no chit-chatterer. "By the way, Barbra," I said, "I enjoyed hearing you describe your wedding. It was as good as having been there. You're a lucky woman, and nobody deserves it more. You remember the adage, 'All things come to he who waits?' Jim was certainly well worth waiting for."

"I'm happy you're that interested. Most people are bored stiff and begin to yawn when I want to talk about my wedding. But then, you're not like most people. And of course, let's not forget that you get paid to be interested."

"Isn't it possible that I might be interested even if I weren't being paid?"

She smiled. "I'd like to believe that," she said, "but it is too good to be true."

"Trust me, it's true," I answered. "Things still going well with Jim?"

"Couldn't be better. I'll give you an example of the way Jim treats me. On August 27, 1998, he was honored with the 2,115th star on the Hollywood Walk of Fame in an official unveiling ceremony. We were announced as 'Mr. and Mrs. James Brolin.' Jim's family sat there smiling throughout the 11:30 a.m. ceremony, which took place in front of the Johnny Grant Building, next to the historic Hollywood Roosevelt Hotel, and across the street from the landmark Grauman's Chinese Theater, where my own Walk of Fame star has been sitting since 1976. Our stars can practically look across the street and wave to each other.

"The ceremony marked our first public appearance since our wedding. Before close to one thousand delighted fans, photographers, and television cameras, we spoke about what the special occasion meant to us. I said, 'Jimmy dear,'–I love to call him Jimmy–'I'm delighted to be here as your wife. I think this is an honor you really deserve, both as an actor and a director. I'm very proud of you, sweetheart.' Then I turned to the audience and said, 'I thank you all for sharing this incredible moment in my husband's career and both our lives.'

"Jim then said, 'When I was a teenager in L.A., I always wanted to be part of Hollywood, but I never dared to dream that I would be implanted in this sidewalk, beside my incredible wife.' Then he looked at me and said, 'Can you believe that I told my wife not to show up here today? But she didn't listen to me. I don't think she ever will. Since when does Barbra Streisand Brolin–everybody cheered–listen to anybody?

"Wiping away a tear, he said, 'I just want to thank you, my loving and gorgeous wife. Just being with you makes me swoon and feel dizzy and get the vapors many times every day. I'm sure that will always be true. My beloved wife, I can never say I love you enough.'"

Barbra and I were both moved and remained quiet for a moment. Then she said, "Well, Doc, what do you think?"

"I think you are a lucky woman and he is a lucky man."

She leapt up from the couch, bounded over to my chair, and planted a kiss on my forehead. Since my childhood, I've been a lover of the silver screen. I immediately made a mental note to keep my forehead out of the water when I took a shower that night.

As soon as Barbra left, I raced to the phone and called my son, Jonny. "You know how much I've always been in love with films and film stars," I began. "Well, a patient of mine who is a famous movie star came over to my chair today and kissed me!"

"Who is she?" he asked. "I presume it was a she, or you might have had a very different reaction."

I laughed. "You might have something there," I said. "But you know I can't tell you who she is. It would be a breach of confidentiality."

"Okay. But Mom, would you give her a message from me, please? Tell her she can come over and kiss me anytime."

I love that kid, and I'm delighted that he has such a great sense of humor. I'll bet Barbra would like him, too.

Barbra with husband Jim Brolin's Star on the Hollywood Walk of Fame.

January 8, 2016

It was with a relaxed and pleasant expression on her face that Barbra came into my office this early January morning.

"You look happy today, Barbra," I said. "What's going on in your life that makes you smile so sweetly?"

"I mustn't look happy very often," she responded glumly, "if my shrink has to make a point of my not looking miserable!"

I was sorry I had opened my mouth, and hoped I hadn't ruined for her whatever had been pleasing her. But the happy look soon returned to her face. "Sometimes," she said, "although I must say rarely, I'm delighted with what the media has to say about my marriage. Last night, I opened *The New York Post* and read in Cindy Adams' column, 'Barbra Streisand and James Brolin are the greatest couple in the world! Although they are completely different from each other, they seem a perfect fit.'"

She beamed, and so did I. Then I said, "Speaking of newspapers, Barbra, I see in the supermarket that *The National Enquirer* has you and Jim divorcing again. What do you think of that bit of news?"

"It's not worth answering," she said disdainfully.

What's with me today? I thought. *I'm really putting my foot in my mouth! Could it be I'm jealous of her happy marriage to her handsome husband?* I shuddered. *I better do a lot of self-analysis tonight!*

"Me? Divorcing Jim?" she said, in answer to my previous remark. "That gorgeous, sweet, most loving and gentle of husbands? I'd have to be nuts. But I'll quote you what Jim has to say about the idea. 'Ha, ha. If my sweet wife and I can ever get out of bed, I have long planned to paper our vintage barn's outhouse walls with these excremental articles from the tabloids that are devoid of even a sniff of truth. Of course, she has held me back with her gift for perfect decor. But I still say my idea is more authentic. Ha, ha. Right?' See what I mean, Doc?"

"Again I say: You are a lucky woman, Barbra. Tell me more about what it is like for you to be together with Jim," I began. "Maybe I'll learn something."

She smiled and said, "The first time Jim and I got into a conversation at the party, we just sort of locked spirits and I forgot that anyone else was in the room.

"Jim felt exactly the same way. He told me later, 'After twenty minutes, I was a goner, and after two hours, I knew we would get married, that we belonged together.' He offered to take me home and

I coyly refused. I told him thank you, but no thank you, that someone was coming to pick me. But when he insisted, we went to my house and talked till three in the morning.

"Our next get-together was much bumpier. We met at my goddaughter Caleigh's birthday party. It seemed terribly awkward, for some reason," she continued. "A whole lot of people came between us, and we had no chance to speak to each other. At the end of the party, he said, 'I'll call you.' I expected him to call me that night, but he didn't. I thought, 'That's probably the end of it.'

"At the time, I was in a state where I just wanted to be alone, to stay in bed and read political journals and eat coffee ice cream. I thought, 'If he's not the kind of man who keeps his word, I'm not interested. Relationships are not for me; they are too difficult. I'm better off in my bed with my books and my ice cream.'

"But a few days later, I received a fax from him. It said, 'Answer this or I'll start faxing smut,'" she said laughingly. "He left his phone number and added, 'Tonight, yes?' I thought that was adorable. In fact, I keep the note framed on my desk.

"So we went out again. We saw a movie and discussed how unnatural it was to go out on a date. Then Jim had to fly to the Philippines for two weeks to work on a film. He and I faxed and called each other all the time he was away. Sometimes we spoke for hours," she added. "I spent enough money on the phone bill for an ordinary family of four to live for a year.

"It didn't take long for him to broach the subject of marriage," she continued. "In fact, he *kept* broaching it. But I thought he was joking and I always laughed it off. Then one day I realized the man was dead serious and the relationship was no laughing matter. For me, true love comes when the infatuation period wears off and the couple is ready to commit themselves to each other's personal growth. So, after making him sweat it out for a few months, I finally said yes.

"Then I rejected his choice of ring. 'This is way too much. I don't know how I could wear this thing during the day,' I said of the original nine-carat stone he bought me. I wanted something much more modest, a 1.16-carat Tiffany ring.'"

"Weren't you worried about hurting his feelings by turning down his choice of ring?" I asked.

"No way," she answered. "I say what I mean and I mean what I say. That's who I am."

I looked at her with admiration. "Under the circumstances, I don't know whether I could have done that," I admitted.

January 13, 2016

"I love the lyrics of 'If I Never Met You,' which I sang to Jim at our wedding," she began, "because the idea is one we often marvel about. It brings out the gratitude you feel when you meet someone unexpectedly, and that someone changes the course of your entire life. What if we had bumped into each other ages ago? What if we had been able to spend more of our lives together? If only...

"There were so many times over the years when we almost met. Both of us, for instance, were once interested in buying the same apartment in Manhattan. I turned it down and Jim bought it only a few minutes later. It is entirely possible that we passed each other unnoticed in the lobby. "We were also on the same movie studio lot thirty years ago. I was filming *Hello, Dolly!* and Jim was under contract to Fox. One morning in bed recently, he said, 'I can just imagine what might have happened. You walked by my dressing room, and I could have grabbed you and pulled you in. It would have been wonderful. You would have helped me to grow up much faster, and I could have taught you a lot about life that you were too naive to have experienced.'

"We also could have started a family together," she said with a sad look on her face. "I would love to have had Jim's babies. But it wasn't to be. Still, I shouldn't complain. He has the children he should have, and I have the child I should have."

"Have you thought about adopting a child?" I asked.

"Thought about it, yes, but done it, no. A child shouldn't have *alter kockers* like us for parents! We always just missed meeting each other at the time when we could have had children, but it wasn't *bershart*. We met when we were grown up enough to handle our relationship.

"We're both unshakeable believers in the philosophy that life takes its own course, if only you allow it to. I believe very strongly in fate, in the theory of a *bashert*, but I also think you make your own fate. I think there is a destiny, but human beings have to give it a little shove. As the old maxim goes, 'God helps those who help themselves.' I might not have gone to the dinner party and never met Jim. I had to push myself that night, and he had to push himself, too, and thank God we did.

"You'd think a couple of show-biz veterans would whoop it up in the limelight. But not us. We don't like to get all dolled up and go out in public. We never go to movie premieres. We never go any place where there are cameras to hound us. We are absolute homebodies. We stayed in bed practically all last weekend. We rarely get dressed. We like to spend time exploring nature. We read our favorite books or poetry out loud to each other. We love to have nothing scheduled to do.

"Directors have noticed a decided difference in me during rehearsals. Marvin Hamlich once observed, 'She'll be very intense, then Jim will walk into the room and she lights up. Frankly, it's wonderful to see the change.'

"I used to be all work," she said. "It's where my perfectionism showed up the most. When I'm cutting an album, I play it in different rooms, standing on ladders, kneeling on one knee, on good and bad stereo systems. I say, 'We have to lower the introduction of this one, raise the volume on that one, bring in the violin over here, blah, blah, blah...' I do that because I care very much about producing a work of art that will last forever. But work is no longer everything. I now turn down films, television offers, awards, and interviews," she said. "Finding love changes one's priorities. I don't care about work nearly as much as I did. I think a lot of my work was a sublimation for love and relationships. When I was bored or lonely, work was my cure. Now that I'm content, I don't need to work so much or so often."

I reminded her, "But in spite of your change of heart, your plate still seems pretty full this year of 2016."

"Well, yeah," she answered. "It's a lot of work and plenty scary. I really resent the amount of time it takes me away from Jim. He is so good for me. Last night, it was absolutely wonderful. He came home and dragged me away from a business meeting of eight people and took me to the movies. Can you imagine me taking off from work to go to the movies? I should have known him years ago. When I have to tour, I only go places we'd like to go as a couple, like Australia.

"We're so good for each other! I'm teaching him stronger work habits, and he is teaching me how to give it all up and just have a nice day. It's hard to let go of old habits," she added. "I believe that history repeats itself and we involuntarily fall into the same old patterns. But the great thing about aging is that we grow more and more conscious of who we are. When you love someone, you learn to accept his or her flaws as well as good qualities.

"Whenever we argue–all couples do, and we're a normal couple–I'm learning to take a gentler, kinder approach. I have to remember to argue from my vulnerable side and not scream out my rage, in order to express the deepest truth. That way, the other person is able to hear me. It's a lesson that has taken me many years to learn. I'm also teaching Jim to speak his mind and his heart, and not to say what he thinks people want to hear. He says the first thing that hit him about me was my directness and honesty—that with me, you don't have to interpret my meaning because it's right there. Because he comes from a family that beats around the bush, he had to get used to it.

"But he always knows where he's at with me, and that puts us on really solid ground. If I say 'I love you,' he knows I mean it. I'm thrilled he understands this about me and loves me anyway. My frankness turns a lot of people off. Jim also has learned to give me a taste of my own medicine, and lets me have it when he feels the need. I may not like what he says, but I love that he says it."

January 15, 2016

"What is the private Jim Brolin really like that his public doesn't know?"

Barbra beamed. "What I like most about him is that his eyes shimmer like sparklers every time he looks at me. He always says that his greatest regret is that we didn't meet thirty years ago. He might say, 'Maybe it wouldn't have worked out way back then. You were very busy and I was who I was.' But then Jim being Jim, he always adds, 'But I think it would have.'"

"Is he ever scared of you? You are very formidable, you know."

"No," she answered. "He loves women, and has a deep respect and regard for them, yet he is the kind of man who is not threatened by women in the least. Nor is he threatened by being in the public eye, even if he's there more because of his relationship with me than his TV series. He said he filmed an episode late last night in San Diego and then drove three hours up to Malibu just to spend time with me. He looks forward to us getting out in the sun together, or taking a long walk together. One of the wonderful things about him is that his attention never wanders when he is talking to me, or to anyone else, for that matter. I think his unwavering interest is the key to his sex appeal. He is what people used to call a ladies' man, not one with a line but a person who would rather have a deep heart-to-heart talk with a woman than hang out at a bar or gym.

"He is philosophical about a career that could have been better had he not been a bit lazy. He says, 'The only things I need out of life are a cup of coffee, the paper, the ocean, and you. Even if I never make another dollar, I'll be fine.' Should his TV series fail, I think he could have a successful future behind the camera. As I may have mentioned, he bought a movie camera as a teenager and began to shoot film on his own. But he didn't know where to go or what to do. He didn't know anyone in the business, and it was a lot more difficult for young directors then. Jim, like me, was a very shy kid. He surfed, but he wasn't a joiner. He says, 'The only club I ever joined was the car club. You didn't have to talk.' He was terrified in high school when he had to read a book report in front of the class."

"How then did he get to be an actor?" I asked.

"Funny you ask that," she answered. "It really was a stroke of luck. When he was eighteen years old, a studio representative stopped him on the street and asked if he wanted to be an actor. He answered, 'I've never thought about it. How much does it pay?'

"His mother, unlike mine, was very supportive of him, but his father thought that chasing after an acting career was a waste of time. He changed his mind, however, when his son became a paid contract actor at Fox and went to Europe to make *Ryan's Express* with top Hollywood actors like Frank Sinatra.

"He worked harder than anyone I've ever known, except me, of course. When he was asked five years later to audition for the *Marcus Welby, M.D.* series, he was ready. His performances in the co-leading role made him a household name. But he regretted that the deeper he got into acting, the further he got from directing. His series *Hotel* followed in 1983. He thought he was in love with the leading lady.

"These days he *knows* he's in love. Everybody else knows it, too. Although we are considered the most glamorous couple in Hollywood, we spend our time together in low-key ways. We love to go for long rides in beautiful San Bernardino County. Jim drives, and I make sandwiches on my lap in the car. We stop at truck stops and check out trucker *tchotchkes* and kitschy souvenirs, which I love. I've never really done any of that sort of thing before, because I've always been a workaholic.

"We're great for each other. He has an incredible ability to relax, to just accept whatever is. I've always been a perfectionist. He brings peace and calmness to my intensity and energy. He'll drive for hours and pull in at a hotel where we don't even have a reservation. It's beyond belief. It's so un-Barbra-like, but I just love it.

"Jim's laziness may not be good for his career, but it's wonderful for me. He gives me permission to laze around with him, and he shows me a side of America I've never seen before, and in return I hype him up so that he works a little harder than he wants to.

"Another one of the great things he's done for me is to teach me to celebrate my mistakes, and not worry about them. You'd be surprised at how that bit of advice has changed my life. Well, maybe not you, but anybody else would.

"We'd both given up on love before we met. We speculate sometimes, 'Is this what happens when you give up? Does it mean you won't find that special person if you go out looking for him or her, but only when you give up?' We both swoon every single day of our lives together. We're always saying, 'How did this happen? How did we get to be so lucky?' It's a whole different way of life. You thought you knew what loving was, and then suddenly you realize that you'd had no idea."

"One of the things I admire most about Jim is how much effort he put into becoming a sensitive man. Ten years ago, a friend recommended that Jim enroll in a love and communication seminar. While there, he learned to hug people for the first time. Before that, he had always just extended his hand. He told me, 'One day, I went up to my dad and embraced him. I thought he was going to pass out.' Now he grabs people, which he never was able to do before."

January 18, 2016

"What is the most important discovery you've made in analysis, Barbra?" I asked.

"You know those corny things they sing in love songs?" she answered. "Well, I've found out the hard way they're true. Money isn't important. It's love that gives meaning to life."

"Erich Fromm said it very well," I said. "'If I am what I have, and if I lose what I have, who then am I? It is love that gives meaning to life.'"

"That is exactly how I feel," Barbra said. "If I lost everything I own, I would still be me, Barbra Streisand, lover and beloved of Jim Brolin.

"Jim and I are set to celebrate our 19th wedding anniversary on July 1, 2017," she said, smiling contentedly.

"Barbra," I said, "on February 6th, it will be a year that you began your analysis with me. You have done very well. You seem much happier, and enjoy a wonderful intimacy with your husband. You've stopped driving yourself so desperately, and you have a great relationship with Jason and Caleigh. In general, you enjoy life much more than you did a year ago. I don't think you need me anymore, and it's getting to be time for you to leave."

"Yeah, sure," she grumbled, her face dropping. "I was wondering when you were going to throw me out. You're just like everybody else. Just when I get to love somebody, they kick me out."

"Oh, come on, Barbra, you know better than that. Just the fact that you can say you love me is wonderful progress. You know I enjoy working with you very much, and I will miss you terribly. In fact, I'll mourn your leaving."

"You'll *mourn* my leaving?"

"Yes, very much."

We both were in tears. "Okay, Darcy," she said, "you're the doctor. What's say we mourn each other together? Why don't we talk on the phone every February 6th, so I can see if you survived the year without me?"

"Good idea. I'll look forward to the sixth of February every year. That's my birthday, you know. Your call will be a birthday present to me."

February 6, 2016

On February 6, three huge bouquets of Barbra Streisand Roses were delivered to my office door. I unwrapped the beautiful box and gasped. I had never seen such gorgeous flowers.

The note inside said:

> "From someone who loves you and is happy you were born. Happy, happy birthday to my beloved, splendiferous analyst! May you have at least fifty more, so you can wish me a happy one hundred and thirtieth.
>
> Much love,
> Barbra"

BIBLIOGRAPHY

BOOKS

Andersen, Christopher. *Barbra: The Way She Is*. London: Aurum Press, 2007.

Considine, Shaun. *Barbra Streisand, the Woman, the Myth, the Music*. New York: Delacorte Press, 1985.

Edwards, Anne. *Streisand*. London: Weidenfeld and Nicolson, 1997.

Nickens, Christopher and Swenson, Karen. *The Films of Barbra Streisand*. New York: Citadel Press, 2000.

Santopietro, Tom. *The Importance of Being Barbra*. New York: Saint Martin's Press, 2006.

Spada, James. *Streisand, Her Life*. New York: Crown Publishers, 1995.

Waldemann, Allison J. *The Barbra Streisand Scrapbook*. New York: Citadel Press, 2001.

Wright, William. *Pavarotti: My Own Story*. New York: Doubleday, 1981.

ARTICLES

A Born Loser's Success and Precarious Love by Shana Alexander, *Life Magazine*, May 22, 1964.

A Hurricane Named Barbra Streisand by Alan Ebert, *Ingenue Magazine*, November 1963.

A Matured Barbra Does 3rd Special by Frank Judge, *TV Magazine*, October 8-October 14, 1967.

A Passion for Truth by Jerry Roberts, *The Hollywood Reporter: Streisand Special Issue,* October 20, 1996.

America's First Voice, Interview, April 1993.

Architectural Digest Visits: Barbra Streisand by Pilar Viladas,

Architectural Digest, December 1993.

Architectural Digest Visits: Barbra Streisand by Peter Carlsen,

Architectural Digest, May 1978.

Barbra by Linda Ellerbee, *Live!*, December 1996.

Barbra! by John Hallowell, *West,* September 1, 1968.

Barbra: A Personal Scrapbook by Claudia Glenn Dowling, *InStyle*, November 1996.

Barbra and Jon: The Main Event by Robert Gutwillig, *Look Magazine,* June 11, 1979.

Barbra and Rozie's Mother Used to Hope for Her Own Name Up in Lights by Judy Klemesrud, 1970.

Barbra and Ryan in Bogdanovich's Salute to the Zany Comedies of the '30s What's Up, Doc? by Jacoba Atlas and Steve Jaffe, *Show Magazine*, April 1972.

Barbra's Fight against Fear by Susan Price, *Ladies Home Journal*, July 1994.

Barbra's Gay Son: I Think She Knew by Deborah Mitchell, *New York Daily News*, December 25, 2000.

Barbra's New Direction by Paul Rosenfield, *Ladies Home Journal,* February 1992.

Barbra Puts Her Career on the Line with 'Yentl'—and Learns Lessons About Her Power and Her Femininity by Anne Fadiman, *Life Magazine,* December 1983.

Barbra Streisand and Her Two Lovers Chase a $10million Dream, Woman's Day, May 10, 1976.

Barbra Streisand at Home, House Beautiful, August 1974.

Barbra Streisand: Chutzpah Power, Funny Girl... Cover Girl... Gall into Glamour, Harper's Bazaar, November 1972.

Barbra Streisand: Finding the Father She Never Knew by Wayne Warga, *McCall's*, January 1984.

Barbra Streisand: For the First Time, She Talks About Her Lover, Her Power, Her Future, People Magazine, April 26, 1976.

Barbra Streisand Hits the Top: Success is a Baked Potato, Life Magazine, September 20, 1963.

Barbra Streisand Makes Mark as Singer by Frank Langley, July 11, 1963.

Barbra Streisand Moans: I Was Happier as a Beatnik by Jack Collins, *National Enquirer*, July 4, 1965.

Barbra Streisand: New Singing Sensation, by Chandler Brossard and David Drew Zingg, *Look Magazine*, November 19, 1963.

Barbra Streisand Shares the Album of the House She Called Home for 20 Years by Marilyn Bethany, *InStyle*, June 1994.

Barbra Streisand: Singing, Swinging Show-Stopper! by Edwin Miller, *Seventeen Magazine*, October 1963.

Barbra Streisand Stages a Hit by Rod McKuen, *Digital Audio & Compact Disc Review*, February 1986.

Barbra Streisand Talks about her 'Million-Dollar Baby' by Gloria Steinem, *Ladies Home Journal*, August 1966.

Barbra Streisand: The People-Need-People Girl by Liz Smith, *Cosmopolitan*, May 1965.

Barbra Streisand: The Secret Sadnesses of a Second-Hand Rose by Justin Roberts, *Women's World*, May 1966.

Barbra Streisand: The Way She Is by Michael Shnayerson, *Vanity Fair*, November 1994.

Barbra Talks: A Streisand with Style by Frank Judge, *American TV Magazine*, April 25-May 1, 1965.

Barbra: The Superstar who wants to be a Woman by Elizabeth Kaye, *McCall's*, April 1975.

Barbra: The Whole Incredible Story of how a 'Misfit' from Brooklyn Turned Herself into a Superstar by James Spada, *McCall's*, September 1981.

Barbra's Quest for the Best by Shaun Considine, *TV Guide*, August 20-26, 1994.

Bea, Billie, and Barbra, Newsweek, June 3, 1963.

Behind the Scenes at a New TV Special with Barbara, Monsanto Magazine, October 1967.

Body of Work: Barbra Streisand's Films, The Hollywood Reporter: Barbra Streisand Special Issue, October 18-20, 1996.

Broadway: The Girl, Time Magazine, April 10, 1964.

Celebration of a Father by Brad Darrach, *People Magazine,* December 12, 1983.

Collision on Rainbow Road by Marie Brenner, *New Times Magazine,* January 24, 1975.

Conversation with a Superstar by J. Curtis Sanburn, *Harper's Bazaar,* November 1983.

Dancer, Choreographer, Show Doctor, Now Film Director Herb Ross Talks Shop by Lydia Joel,

Dance Magazine, December 1967.

Diva Democracy by Jack Newfield, *George Magazine,* November 1996.

Dolly's Dilemma—her $20 Million Movie is Stuck on the Shelf While Producers Argue by John Gregory Dunne, *Life Magazine,* February 14, 1969.

Funny Girl, This Week Magazine, February 5, 1966.

Funny Girl Goes West, Life Magazine, September 20, 1967.

Good-Bye Brooklyn, Hello Fame by Pete Hamill, *Saturday Evening Post,* July 27-August 3, 1963.

Hello, Barbra! by Jerry Roberts, *The Hollywood Reporter: Barbra Streisand Special Issue,* October 18-20, 1996.

Hello, Barbra! by Liz Smith, *Sunday News Magazine,* November 11, 1983.

I Remember Barbra by Jerome Weidman, *Holiday,* November 1963.

Instant Barbra by Polly Devlin, *Vogue,* March 1966.

Johnny Arrives at the Garden by Robert Wahls, *New York News,* September 19, 1965.

Movies by David Denby, *New York Magazine,* December 16, 1991.

Night Club Singer Is Chosen for 'Funny Girl' Lead, by Louis Calta, July 26, 1963.

Only Two A's in Barbra by Norman M. Lobsenz, *Pageant Magazine,* November 1963.

Prince of Tides Sidesteps Book's Pitfalls by Janet Maslin, *The New York Times,* December 25, 1991.

Queen of Tides by Kevin Sessums, *Vanity Fair,* September 1991.

Returning to her Childhood with a Fairytale Party, Barbra Streisand Celebrates her 50th Birthday by A. Berliner, *Hello!,* May 9, 1992.

She Doesn't Want to Talk, So She Tells a Story, Times Magazine, December 8, 1991.

Singer Presents... Barbra Streisand and Other Musical Instruments by Venia Ellis, *Singer Light Magazine,* November 1973.

Singer's Success Story: A Near-Legend at Twenty-One by Rona Barrett, September 16, 1963.

Singing Valentines, by Kotlowitz and Rosenthal, *Show Magazine,* February 1963.

Streisand: A Star is Reborn... with the Help, She Says, of the Man She Loves by Jan Ardmore, *Ladies Home Journal,* November 1976.

Streisand, Gernreich: The This Minute Kids by William Claxton, *Show Magazine,* September 1964.

Streisand: Her First Long-Playing Interview by Lawrence Grobel, *Playboy,* October 1977.

Streisand's New Direction by Jeannette Kupfermann, *The Sunday Times,* March 4, 1984.

Styles for a Super Star, Milo Beauty and Barber Supply, March 11, 1984.

SuperBarbra by Thomas B. Morgan, *Look Magazine,* April 5, 1966.

Superstar Barbra Says this is Her Last Film Musical by Robert Feldman, *The*

Australian Women's Weekly, April 16, 1975.

Superstar: The Streisand Story by Joseph Morgenstern, *Newsweek,* January 5, 1970.

The Barbra Streisand Nobody Knows by Chaim Potok, *Esquire,* October 1982.

The Cachet Look: All Summer-Long, by Geri Trotta, *Playbill Magazine,* June 18, 1962.

The Complete Detroit Streisand: Portrait of Miss Somebody as a Nobody by Bettelou Peterson, *Detroit Magazine,* March 27, 1966.

The Kosher Kid from Brooklyn by George Perry, *The Sun Times,* January 12, 1969.

The Lady is a Champ, Cue Magazine, July 6, 1979.

The Legend of Barbra Streisand: 'Nothing's Impossible' by James Spada, *Billboard,* December 10, 1983.

The Luckiest People in the World by Sheryl Berk, *McCall's,* December 1999.

The Mouse That Wails, Rogue Magazine, November 1963.

The Streisand Look by Joseph Adcock, *The Sunday Bulletin Magazine,* July 31, 1966.

The Way They Are: James Brolin and Barbra Streisand by Holly Sorensen, *McCall's,* March 1998.

'They All Come Thinking I Can't be That Great' by Diana Lurie, *Life Magazine,* March 18, 1966.

What's Next for Barbra? by Cliff Jahr, *Ladies' Home Journal,* August 1984.

BRIEF YIDDISH GLOSSARY

A bissel meshuga: a little crazy

Alter kockers: old codgers

Bachaded: mixed up

Bershart: meant to be

Bubbala: little one

Bubkes: nothing

Chutzpah: nerve

Farbisener: grouch

Goy/goyische/goyim: Gentile/Gentiles

Grubber yung: a coarse young man

Hazuri: junk

Kvelled: beamed with pride

Kvetched: complained

Latke: fried potato pancake

Maidele: little girl

Meshugas: craziness

Meshugena: crazy person

Mieskeit—ugly person

Naches: joy

Plotz: burst

Potch: smack

Schemer: mess

Schmattas: clothing, rags

Schnozz: nose

Shabbos: Sabbath

Shadkhn: matchmaker

Shiksa: non-Jewish woman

Shul: synagogue

Tchotchkes: assorted little items

Tush: rear end

Ver gehardget: drop dead

Yeshiva: a Jewish school

Yeshive bokher: student in a Jewish school

Zaftig: busty

ACKNOWLEDGEMENTS

I enjoy writing all my books, but *Barbra Streisand: On the Couch* is my favorite. I love this book. Writing it was the most fun I've ever experienced while working on a book, and this is my twenty-fourth. Barbara is such a witty person, with the grandest sense of humor I've ever come across, in person or in books. At times, her humor seemed to crawl inside my head, so I began to become funny (I hope) like her. When I reread the book, sometimes I can't remember whether a quip was made by Barbra or by me. So I'd like to thank Barbra Streisand for the many clever and humorous comments she has made, many of which I have "stolen" from her interviews.

Secondly, my warm thanks go to Bruce Bortz, my fabulous publisher and editor, who has published all my *On the Couch* books. Thank you, Bruce, for being thoughtful, encouraging, and knowledgeable at all times. I am very fortunate to have found you. Because you so generously publish all my books, I don't have to waste time looking for agents and publishers, and thus am able to write a book a year. At my age, that is a great gift. Thanks, too, for all the books you send me.

I would like to thank my dear cousin, Sylvia Williamson, for her early editing of this and many of my other books. Thank you, Sylvia. You have been a wonderful editor and friend.

Thanks, too, to Sylvia's son, my second cousin Mark Flicker, for allowing me to use and (greatly!) expand upon his meeting with Barbra Streisand when he was a young man.

I also would like to thank my readers, Virginia Mueller and Phyllis Orenyo, who made valuable corrections to the manuscript.

I thank my cousin Beatrice Wies for many years of encouragement, particularly at a time when I wasn't receiving too much support.

I would also like to thank my late husband, Rudy Bond, who was always proud of my work. Too bad he isn't around to read *Barbra Streisand: On the Couch*. Rudy had a wonderful sense of humor (I wouldn't have married anyone who didn't) and would have particularly enjoyed this book.

Thanks to my dear friends, Pat LaMarche, Lois Zells, Helen Dennis, and Drs. Arlene and Arnold Richards for the wonderful book signing parties they've hosted for my books. I'm lucky to have such wonderful friends, whom I hope will be around for many, many years, unlike the majority of my other old friends who have "shuffled off this mortal coil."

Special thanks to my friend and assistant, Afton Monahan, without whose unending help this book would never have been written.

I would like to thank my children, Janet Bond Brill, Ph.D. and Jonathan Halbert Bond for being the wonderfully warm, loving, brilliant, successful, highly gifted individuals they are. (All right, all right already. So I'm a little prejudiced. Even Barbra is, about her son.).

I also cannot thank my dear departed son Zane, my best friend, who died all too early, for his wisdom. When I was considering changing careers in late mid-life, I said to Zane, "Do you think I'd be crazy to give up a high paying job for a low paying job?" He answered, "I think you'd be crazy not to."

And extensive thanks to my darling grandchildren, Rachel, Mia, Jason, Matthew, Alex, Remy, Olivia, and Damian, for lighting up my life: Your proud Nana is delighted with your collective beauty, intelligence, and talent. Special thanks go to my dear Mia, who kindly agreed to be the first reader of this book.

I want to thank my exceptional daughters-in-law, Rebecca Bond and Judy Bond, who greatly enrich my life, and have a gift for keeping their husbands happy. I will always be grateful to you both for that.

ABOUT THE AUTHOR

Barbra Streisand: On the Couch is the fourth of Alma Bond's *On the Couch* series, and is Dr. Bond's twenty first published book. She received her Ph.D. in Developmental Psychology from Columbia University, graduated from the post-doctoral program in psychoanalysis at the Freudian Society, and was a psychoanalyst in private practice for thirty-seven years in New York City. She "retired" to become a full-time writer, but now maintains a small practice in addition to writing. Her last book, *Margaret Mahler, a Biography of the Psychoanalyst*, received two awards: Best Books Award Finalist, USA Book News; and *Foreword Magazine*'s Book of the Year Finalist.

Her Maria Callas book, *The Autobiography of Maria Callas: A Novel*, was first runner-up in the Hemingway Days novel contest.

Her sixteen other published books include: *Camille Claude: A Novel*; *Old Age is a Terminal Illness*; *Who Killed Virginia Woolf?: A Psychobiography*; *Tales of Psychology: Short Stories to Make You Wise*; *I Married Dr. Jekyll and Woke Up Mrs. Hyde*; *Is There Life After Analysis?*; *On Becoming a Grandparent*; *America's First Woman Warrior: The Story of Deborah Sampson* (with Lucy Freeman); and a children's book, *The Tree That Could Fly*.

She presently has another book in production, *Michelle Obama: A Biography*.

Dr. Bond also wrote the play, *Maria*, about the life and loves of Maria Callas, which was produced off-off Broadway and is currently touring Florida.

Dr. Bond is a member of the American Society of Journalists and Authors, the Dramatists Guild, and the Authors Guild, as well as a fellow and faculty member of the Institute for Psychoanalytic Training and Research, the International Psychoanalytic Association, and the American Psychological Association.

Dr. Bond is the widow of Rudy Bond, the acclaimed stage, screen, and television actor, and author of *I Rode a Streetcar Named Desire*. She is the mother of three children, Zane P. Bond, Jonathan H. Bond, and Janet Bond Brill, all of whom are published authors, and she is the proud grandmother of eight, none of whom has published a book . . . yet. But as a wise friend of Alma's put it, "In her family, it's pretty much publish or perish."